TRISKELION

Book Two of the Spirit Level Series

BY
ALEX MARTIN

Many years ago, when my children were very young, we went on holiday to North Wales. On the dockside at Caernarfon with the Menai Straits streaking out to the distance in front of me, I had a strange vision. I saw and heard a dreadful scene. Along the bar of sand on the other side of the swirling waters, I clearly saw many women, dressed in long black tunics, their hair streaking out behind them, and their mouths open in fury, hurling curses. I felt cold as I watched, although it was a hot summer's day. This flashback to nearly two thousand years ago was fleeting but it has inspired this story.

ACKNOWLEDGEMENTS

Many thanks to Jane Dixon-Smith of http://www.jdsmith-design.com/ for the inspirational cover and her complete and immediate understanding of the concept

Thanks to Jo for her intuitive prompts, to Phil for his constant technical support and infinite patience and to Tom for his brilliant insights

This book is a work of fiction. All the characters and places therein are a product of the author's imagination. Any resemblance to people or places is entirely coincidental, although the only written account of the Roman's invasion of Anglesey is taken from an eyewitness, the Roman historian, Tacitus.

(Anglesey was called Mona by the Romans but legend has its name as Ynys Afallach, or Apple Island, sometimes known as Avalon)

TRISKELION

Chapter One, Present Day

"Someone's hammering at your door, Fay." Percy drew back an inch of curtain to peek outside at the narrow street of red-brick terraced houses. "Oh no, it looks like Paul! How did he find me? What can I do?" Percy looked so distressed, for a second, I panicked too.

I took a deep breath. "Go into my bedroom. Hide under the bed, in the wardrobe, anywhere."

Percy went white. "You're not going to let him in, are you? For God's sake, don't even open the door!"

"Look, he'll just keep pestering us if he thinks you are here. If I tell him you're not, hopefully he'll leave you alone." This didn't sound convincing, even to me, but what else was I to do?

"Fay, you know he's violent. You've seen him hit me. Please, don't open the door!"

I hesitated in the sudden silence. Then the thumping on the door started up again. "I can't let him get away with this. The neighbours will be wondering what the hell is going on." I was angry. Why should Percy's husband terrorise me too?

I sought spiritual reinforcement from my long-lost boyfriend, who had died far too many years ago. Robin, my love, I need you now. Please, tell me what to do?

At once my heart calmed, and I felt in control again. I hadn't heard Robin's beloved voice, but I felt stronger, equal to that idiot at the door, anyway.

I pointed to the only other room in my tiny flat. "Go into the bedroom, Percy. I'll deal with the rat."

I went to the front door, closing the inner door of my flat behind me. The hallway was communal, papered in anaglypta paper painted over in an ugly olive green. My personal flat door had a Yale lock that no-one could open

1

without a key. The key was in my jeans pocket, but Paul Wade wouldn't know that.

I yanked the old Victorian front door open. Percy's husband stood there; his fist raised like a battering ram ready to bash it again.

It was as much as I could do not to jump backwards in case his arm followed through. "What's the meaning of all this noise? Oh, it's you, Paul. What are you doing here?"

"Don't give me that. I know she's here." He was so angry his words came out like a snarl.

"Who?"

"Listen, Dumpy, don't play games with me. We both know who I'm talking about."

"Not only are you disturbing the peace, Mr Wade, you are insulting me. Not the best way to get information out of anyone."

"Ah, so you do know where she is." He folded his arms in triumph.

At least that meant I wasn't going to be on the receiving end of his knuckles. I took courage from his new posture. "If you mean your wife, no, I don't."

"Of course, I mean Persephone. Who else?"

"Then you must look elsewhere. I have no idea of her whereabouts."

"Don't talk bollocks. She's in your grotty-looking flat. Bit of a comedown from Meadowsweet Manor," he wagged his finger in my face, "which is where she belongs."

"More insults. Really, you are the rudest man I have ever met." I started to shut the door. The damn thing always stuck in the middle where it had scraped an arc in the wooden floor.

Before I could push it shut, Paul Wade shoved his stout-looking walking boot in the gap. "Not so fast. I'm coming in to search the place."

I pushed the door harder, and it suddenly freed itself, squashing his foot.

"Ouch! You…" Paul's already ruddy face darkened, and his scowl deepened.

2

"You'd better take your foot away, then, hadn't you?"

Instead of obliging, he leaned his bulk into the door, making it impossible for me to shut it. It was no contest. He put all his weight into a shove against the wood and I fell backwards on to the tiled floor.

Paul loomed over me. "Which flat is yours, Miss Armstrong? Hah, seems your arm isn't so strong, after all. Come on, which door is it?"

Just then, Mr Singh from the corner shop turned up, laden with a box of groceries for Mrs Sykes upstairs who had become too frail to walk up the road. I felt a pang of guilt that she must be terrified at the goings on in her hallway.

"Miss Armstrong! Is everything alright?" Mr Singh, ignoring Paul entirely, put down his cardboard box of groceries and stepped into the hall, extending his hand and helping me to get upright again.

"Thank you, Mr Singh."

Mr Singh turned around and stared at Paul. "Who is this gentleman? Is he molesting you?"

"He's just leaving." I got out my mobile phone. "And if he doesn't, I'm calling the police."

"Very good, miss. I think you should." Mr Singh was nodding his head vigorously, bless him. He was a very slight man, in fact he probably weighed less than I did. Mr Singh was always helpful, saving me from many a domestic emergency in the past, but I had never expected him to have to act as my bodyguard. Paul Wade, tall, well-built and hardened from his treks in wild country as a photographer, could have flattened us both if he'd wanted to. Neither of us was a match for him but the threat about the police seemed to have had the desired effect.

"I'm going, but I'll be back. I know where you live now. Don't think you'll get away with this." Paul stepped outside then looked back at the front of my house as if making a note of the number.

3

"How did you find me, as a matter of interest, Paul?" I stood, shoulder to shoulder with Mr Singh. His quiet composure strengthened me.

Paul pointed down the street to where my little hatchback was parked. "I knew you lived somewhere around the dodgy part of Swindon, and I know your car, don't I? Not that difficult to pick out such an old banger."

"I think you should go now, sir." Mr Singh looked incensed, and I could feel his body trembling ever so slightly where our shoulders touched.

"Alright, Curryface. I'm off." Paul looked at me again and pointed his stubby finger at my face. "I'll be watching you."

"If you don't go now, sir, it is I who will telephone for the police to come after that racist remark." Mr Singh stepped forward in an attempt to look menacing, which, to my surprise, appeared to work. All bullies are cowards.

Paul Wade turned on his heel and crossed the road to his huge SUV 4x4 and pinged its automatic key. We watched him drive off until the big car turned the street corner and was out of sight.

"Oh, Mr Singh! I can't thank you enough. You really saved my bacon there!"

"Bacon? Isn't that from the pig?" Mr Singh showed his beautifully white, even teeth in a broad smile.

"Excuse me, but I have to do this!" I reached out and squeezed the breath out of the poor man in a great big bear hug.

"Oh, Miss Armstrong, no need for that! Believe me, I've seen much worse in my native Delhi!"

A door opened at the top of the stairs and Mrs Sykes peered down at us. "Mr Singh? Is that you? Have you got my groceries?"

Mr Singh rolled his eyes at me and winked before picking up the box laden with goods from his corner shop and mounting the stairs.

I could hear Mrs Sykes's querulous voice demanding explanations until I unlocked my inner front door and shut out the noise. Then the shaking started in earnest.

"Has he gone? It *was* Paul, wasn't it?" Percy's lovely face was quite white.

I nodded. "Yes, he's gone. For now."

Chapter Two, The Isle of Anglesey (previously known as Ynys Afallach), around 2000 years ago

Unusually for Imbolc on Ynys Afallach it hadn't rained for days. Any early frost had melted away, leaving the ground dry and hard. Three Celtic children squatted on the dusty earth in the bare patch in the middle of their settlement, playing in the fitful sunshine.

Gaine spread her little hand wide and picked up three runestones together. "I did it! I get another go."

"Go on then, but you've got to pick up four now." Plump Rhiannon chewed on her thumb nail while she watched Gaine throw her carved pebbles on to the ground.

The pebbles flew high in the air and the children watched where they fell.

"You'll never pick up four when they're so spread out!" Emrys, who was two years older than Gaine, laughed.

"Oh, won't I?" Somehow, not quite understanding how she did it, Gaine's hand swooped across the dirt and scooped up four scattered pebbles all at once.

"You used magic!"

"Did not!"

"Your mother gave you a spell!" Rhiannon looked indignant.

"No, she didn't, she's too ill." Gaine curled her fingers over her special stones. One day soon, her mother would show her how to read the future with them and what all the symbols meant. She liked the one with the three swirly circles best. It had a complicated name she couldn't yet pronounce, triskelion, she thought it was. Her mother said its meaning wasn't simple either. Something to do with energy and time but she hadn't really understood it.

Rhiannon juggled her own runestones between her fat little fingers. "Could have given it to you before she was sick."

Gaine shook her head so hard her long plait of red hair whipped around her shoulder to land on her front. She flicked it back angrily. "She's been sick for ages. Mother says it's because I'm to have a baby brother."

Rhiannon tossed back her dark, unbound curls in response. "My mother has had four babies and she never got sick."

Emrys frowned at Rhiannon. "Everyone is different, Rhiannon. Gaine's mother has never been strong. You know that and you should be kinder."

Gaine never heard Rhiannon's reply as it died on her lips when she stood up and bowed her head. Gaine and Emrys turned around to see why and saw their chief Druid priestess, Gaine's grandmother Bryonia, standing in front of them, looking grave. All three children fell silent, as most people did in her commanding presence. Bryonia was tall and her black hair flowed freely down her slender back. At the base of her long neck there lay a golden torc, embossed with the same triskelion symbol Gaine favoured. The weight and beauty of the necklace emphasised Bryonia's high status within the commune of Druids who lived slightly apart from the Celtic tribe.

"Gaine, you must come to your mother. It is time." Bryonia held out her long slim arm and held out an open palm in invitation.

"What about the baby?"

Bryonia shook her head. "The babe did not survive, child."

Gaine put her small hand inside the grown woman's. She felt funny inside. No-one ever took Bryonia's hand, except in the most important of circumstances. Gaine had a creepy-crawly feeling in her stomach as she walked across the dusty space between the stone huts her Celtic tribe inhabited and walked down the narrow track, almost hidden by sloe trees and blackberry bushes, that had previously been forbidden territory. Gaine's little mouth dropped open as she entered the sacred grove of oaks encircling the rustic shelters which housed the Druids.

A tall stone stood on the grassy sward inside the circle, its surface cut deep with the three circles of the

7

triskelion and she fingered her favourite runestone in her pocket. As always, it reassured her, but she still gripped her grandmother's hand more tightly.

"Be not afraid child. While I am by your side, I will always protect you."

Gaine didn't answer. She was too busy taking in the surroundings everyone talked about but never saw. The Celtic children often spoke in whispers about the ritual sacrifices conducted by the Druid priests to placate the Gods, that they'd overheard their parents speak of in awed, hushed voices.

She vaguely knew this was the hallowed ground that visitors from other tribes stood upon when they came to engage in trade for wheat and gold but also where the less fortunate were taken to learn what judgements would be passed upon them by the Druid elders and receive their harsh punishments. No-one from her village was ever allowed to witness those. Gaine didn't understand it all, but she knew the elders ruled over this island and the mainland beyond and all the other tribes respected but also feared them for their connection to the Gods.

Gaine's family, like others, served the everyday needs of the elders but only the Druid priestesses and priests and their apprentices were allowed beyond the confines of the village to where their quarters lay. Today was the first time she had crossed that bridge into the inner world of the all-powerful Druids.

Bryonia lead her away from the other stone buildings to a larger one, set apart and alone with many plants in neat beds surrounding it.

"Come inside, Gaine. This is the healing temple, and your mother lies within."

Gaine forgot about everything else the moment she was inside the big, round space. Herbs smoked in the entrance, making Gaine's eyes sting and tear up even though their smell was cleansing and soothing. Her mother, Ereni, lay on a pallet of straw. Her face was the colour of stone, ashen white and grey, and her body was as still as the dawn.

Ereni was covered by a flax sheet, except for her face, and Gaine could barely make out the rise and fall of her chest. A little bundle lay at her feet, swathed in linen.

"Mother, oh, Mother!"

Bryonia squeezed the hand she still held within her own strong one. "Go to her, little one. She has something she needs to say."

Gaine needed no prompting but ran to her mother's side and knelt down next to her. Ereni turned her slender neck towards her only child and smiled tenderly. "Dear Gaine. So young. So beautiful you are, daughter. I am sorry I could not give you a little brother."

Gaine reached out and took her mother's hand in hers. It was cold to the touch, as if the lifeblood had already left it. "I'm here, Mother mine."

"I am dying, Gaine. Soon, I shall be gone to be with our forebears."

The tears formed from the smoke now ran down Gaine's cheeks. She kissed her mother's lifeless hand.

"Listen, to me, Gaine. I have not long. I want you to go to your grandmother as her apprentice. She wishes it too."

Gaine glanced over to Bryonia, who stood, tall and erect, at the foot of the bed. Bryonia inclined her dark head in assent.

"She will train you as a Druid priestess like she is. You must follow her wishes in every respect, Gaine. She has much wisdom to teach you, but I can teach you nothing more. When I breathe my last, go to your grandmother to the sacred spaces, and I will watch from above with all the love in my heart. Death is but a parting, little one. I will always be with you."

Ereni shut her eyes, exhausted with the effort of speaking. She never opened them again.

Gaine, although she was only seven years of age, kept vigil that long night by her mother's bedside and Bryonia watched over them both. By dawn, Ereni's spirit had left her body. Gaine sensed its passing as a bird escaping its cage. She felt joy, not sorrow. Her mother would know no more pain; she would never suffer again. She was free.

Gaine laid her head over her mother's cooling corpse and slept.

Chapter Three, Present Day

"I'm not safe here. I must go. This isn't fair on you."
I'd never seen Percy bite her immaculate fingernails before.

"Go where exactly?" I filled the kettle and switched it on.

"I don't know." Percy started to pace my small sitting-room.

"What about your parents?"

"They live in Spain now."

"You could get a flight. Might be an ideal solution." I put a teabag in each of two mugs.

Percy ran her fingers through her long auburn hair. "Paul knows where they live. We holidayed with them once."

I saw Percy's tall, slim frame shiver.

"Not a good experience?"

She looked at me with her big, hazel-green eyes. "The worst. And anyway, my Mum suffers with anxiety these days because of Dad's dementia, and they have a live-in carer in the spare bedroom. I couldn't risk Paul coming to find me at their place when they've got enough on their plates."

I poured boiling water over the teabags. "Fair enough. Anyone else?"

Percy sat down on the bed settee where she had slept. "Not really. I have friends in London I knew from my modelling days, but we've lost touch since I got married."

"Not keen on Paul, by any chance?" I handed her a mug of tea.

Percy gave a wan smile. "You could say that."

I sat down on my office chair in the corner near my tiny makeshift desk. "Blimey, I need this cuppa."

"Oh, Fay, I'm so sorry I have brought all this trouble into your life."

I waved my hand in dismissal. "My life was way too dull."

"You are very kind, but who needs all this drama? It's not your problem. You're still recovering from the damage that poltergeist Rose Charlton did to you at Meadowsweet Manor, and that was all my fault as well. And I almost broke your nose playing squash."

I gave a shaky laugh. "Now you come to mention it, you are responsible for a long list of injuries, especially when you were channelling the ghostly Rose. I confess I was completely terrified when I heard you talking in her strange, high voice, seeking vengeance for the death of her favourite man."

Percy shivered. "I don't remember those times very well, only the horrible wounds I inflicted on you through her when I came out of my trance. How can I ever repay you?"

I sipped my tea. "You can't, can you? With money, I mean?"

Percy put down her mug. "I'm totally skint. Paul was the breadwinner and he's probably already blocked our joint account. I can't just leap straight back into modelling. It's years since I did a professional job and it would take time to rebuild all my contacts, plus I'm that bit older. I doubt I'd get any work these days. I look a wreck."

I gazed at my old school rival. Her beauty was luminous, her figure flawless and her bone structure quite perfect. I couldn't see a reason why she couldn't go back to her original career as a photographic model and said so.

"You must be joking! It's so competitive. You have to be virtually anorexic to be considered thin enough for the catwalk, or even fashion shoots. No, I think my modelling days are over."

"Well, I can't say I'm relishing the prospect of going back to being an accountant. My holidays are all used up ridding Meadowsweet Manor of its resident ghost."

"And I won't even get the benefit of it not being haunted now I'm not living there with Paul anymore." Percy drained her mug of tea and sighed.

"Are you really never going to go back to him?" I picked up her mug and took it, and mine, to the sink.

12

Percy shrugged. "I couldn't, Fay. I almost hate him now. The way he treated you – and again today…"

"What about the way he treated *you*?" I swished water into the mugs and stacked them to dry.

"I know. I suppose I'll have to start divorce proceedings. What a mess." Percy stared out of the window at the rows of parked cars along the residential road.

I had no idea how to console her after her momentous decision to leave her husband and it wouldn't help if I owned up to being perplexed at what she had found attractive in him in the first place.

I went back to my little desk and switched on my computer. I took a quick look at the news, startled the headlines were all about climate change instead of the normal scandals about corrupt politicians and murderers on the loose. Judging by the scale of disasters across the entire world, if somewhere wasn't flooded, it was on fire. The list of calamities overwhelmed me. I shuddered at the horrific images before I opened my inbox and remembered the email I'd received. To distract Percy, and to help me forget about my own fears for our doomed planet, I said, "I didn't tell you about the response we had to our new website that we launched last night, did I?"

"Hmm? No." Percy didn't really seem to be listening.

"Oh, come on! You must remember? We were high on success and beer and set it up as a joke. We called it '*Spirit Level*'?"

"Um, it's all a bit of a blur. I was so upset and tired." Percy rubbed her eyes.

I tried not to lose my patience. "We set up a business as psychic detectives and opened a website. You know, where we said, '*Do you want to reach out to a loved one who has passed over?'*

Percy blinked, as if waking up. "Of course, I do! I think we must have been mad."

"You could be right, in fact I'm sure you are, but unbelievably someone's seen it and is interested. Listen to

13

this response we've had. I read it this morning when you were still out for the count.

'Can you help me? I gotta real problem up here in Anglesey. Got a studio on the island to record me music and got some weird prowlers hawnting the place. If you guys can make them piss off, I'd be greatful. No expense spared.' Hear that?" I looked across at Percy who was definitely listening now.

"Who is it from?"

"It says - email me at rickoshea@email.com."

"As in ricochet?"

I laughed. "Yes, I suppose so. He sounds like a right joker, but he did say no expense spared."

"Doesn't mean he'll pay up." Percy came over and read the screen over my shoulder. "Goodness, he can't spell for toffee. He can't be genuine."

"Let's google him." I put the name into the search engine and read the results out loud. "Rock star Rick O'Shea is lead guitarist with the amazing Dreamers band; married to super-model and lifestyle guru Sherry Smith. He lives in sunny California and is reported to be a very rich man. The outrageous parties the couple throw are legendary in the glamorous world of the rich and famous."

Percy raised her perfectly curved eyebrows. "Then what's he doing in - where was it?"

"Anglesey."

"Where's that?"

"North Wales, I think." I stared at the image of the musician and his wife posing on a red carpet at an award ceremony.

"Bit of a step from California."

"And very wet by comparison."

Percy fetched her reading glasses and put them on. "Gosh, look at those diamonds. She's more out of that dress than inside it."

"Yes, it doesn't leave much to the imagination but she's very beautiful."

Percy snorted. "Anyone can look that good if they have enough plastic surgery."

"Ooh, feeling jealous?"

Percy whipped her glasses off. "No way. I bet she lives on shakes and water. I know what misery that entails." She flopped back on the sofa. "You know, I really don't think I can go back to that way of life."

I helped myself to a chocolate digestive from the ever-present stash in my desk drawer. They never filled the vacuum my late boyfriend, Robin, had left behind, but I lived in hope. "Don't blame you. I wouldn't have the discipline."

Percy roared with laughter. "That, I believe!"

I took another biscuit. "Want one?"

"Why not? I'll make the tea this time."

As the kettle sang into boiling point a second time, I re-read the email. A strange sensation of recklessness stole over me. "You know, Percy, why don't we go for it? I know we only set up that website as a joke last night when we were tipsy, but we've already got a client and a well-off one at that. Maybe we really could make a living out of ghostbusting. What do you think?"

"You must be mad! After all the danger we've only just survived during our last experience?"

Percy looked genuinely aghast. The more familiar worm of doubt crept back in and squashed my wild yearning for more adrenaline-soaked excitement.

Percy straightened up and looked down at me as I sat at my desk. "And what about your job? Aren't you due back at work tomorrow?"

"I am, it's true. I suppose I could take sick leave, but I don't really want to go back to that dreary existence any more than you want to starve for your art. I'd be happy to give them my notice and never go back." The reckless daredevil that had seized me moments ago seemed to be regaining its strength.

Percy resumed chewing her nails. "But wouldn't that be risky? What about this flat? Your security?"

It was my turn to shrug my much broader shoulders. "I've got savings. I wouldn't have to give up this flat for a while. I've got good references from other jobs and let's face it - everyone needs an accountant. We never go out of fashion or get too fat and ugly, which is just as well in my case."

"Oh, Fay, you are so hard on yourself." She went to the kitchen corner of my living room and made two fresh mugs of tea in brooding silence. When she passed mine to me, her eyes were shining.

"Alright then, let's do it! It's mad after what we've been through, but I haven't got a better idea and, like I said last night, what's the worst that can happen?"

With shaking, trepidatious fingers, I typed our acceptance into my laptop and sat back to drink my tea. Five minutes later my inbox pinged.

"He's replied straightaway! Says we can start as soon as we like. He claims he'll pay us a handsome fee and provide free accommodation." I looked up at Percy, who came and stood behind me to read the screen again.

"Really? He must be worried."

"Sounds too good to be true to me. I mean, he doesn't know us from Adam and, for all we know, he could be a pervert or something."

Percy shook her head. "No, we've checked him out on Google. We know he really is a musician."

"I suppose. He does sound pretty desperate about his ghosts."

She chewed her lip. "But then, so am I, Fay. Desperate, I mean. To be quite honest, I'm more terrified of Paul turning up again than dealing with another phantom. Look, I know this sounds crazy, but can we go today? At least we'd get away from here."

"What, now?"

Percy nodded. "Yes, I've only got a small suitcase of stuff. I barely unpacked last night. I can't relax here now I know Paul's guessed where I am."

"But don't you have to contact a solicitor or something?" I was startled at the prospect of such a sudden departure.

"I can do that from my phone from anywhere. Please, say yes?" She looked so worried.

I ran my hand through my short, mousy hair. "I need to decide about my job. It's a big decision."

Percy spread her hands wide. "Of course, you do. I'm being selfish wanting to escape on a whim like this."

"No, you're not. It's a great opportunity. It could change our lives, though I must say, I never expected any response from our larking about last night. But you know what? I've been sensible all my life, especially since Robin died, and where has it got me? Absolutely nowhere. I'm depressed, bored, confined, and friendless. This might not make me happy but at least I could stop pretending I'm not weird."

"We could always turn round and come back if it's dodgy."

I nodded, and my unusual desire for a wild adventure sparked down my spine again. "Look, let me ring work and see if I can get another week off."

"Alright. I'll get on to a legal firm in the meantime." She went into the bedroom to use her mobile and left me to it.

I re-read Rick O'Shea's reply to my email. I could barely make out the Welsh address. It was unfathomable. I copied and pasted it into Google Maps, surprised to see how far north it was. Anglesey was right at the tip of Wales and an island to boot. I never knew that. Butterflies took flight in the pit of my stomach, chasing the euphoric sparks away. Did I really believe my own words that it wouldn't matter if I lost my job? Never mind that I hated it, it paid the mortgage. I remembered the glossy picture of Rick and his wife, dripping diamonds on the red carpet. There was no denying it would be fun to enter that world and get paid doing what I was really good at; what I'd denied and lied about all my life. It would provide some compensation for all those sneers and sarcastic comments I'd endured at school and later at work, except when Robin had been alive. He had believed and protected me. And then he'd paid the ultimate price for it. Ghosts could be vindictive. Rose Charlton had proved that.

I felt a frisson across my back and a sensation of someone stroking the back of my neck. It didn't frighten me as it was so tender.

"Robin, is that you?"

I touched my hand to my cheek where a featherlight caress lay. I closed my eyes and Robin's face appeared in my mind's eye. He was smiling and nodding.

"Should I do it, Robin? Will you still protect me?"

He nodded again and then was gone. I opened my eyes and a tear trickled down my cheek where I'd sensed his fingers had been. It dawned on me that if I changed jobs from safe accountancy to communicating between the living and the dead, Robin might always be at my side. Then, without giving myself time to change my mind, I typed my notice in an email to my office and signed off my contract, forfeiting my wages and all dues owed to me.

It was done and I was free.

Another surreal wave of euphoria swept over me, so much stronger than the little hint of it I'd had before. It wasn't just the sense of being footloose and fancy free for the first time ever. Oh no. It was the memory of Robin's smiling, loving face. Knowing the love of my life was around me again. The long-dead Rose Charlton had caused his fatal accident on Roundway Down, of that I was sure, but she had also helped me to reconnect with him again after years of desolation in an abyss of loneliness.

If I couldn't have him alive, it would be some consolation to know his spirit was travelling alongside me while I contacted the dead.

Chapter Four, Present Day

I hadn't expected the journey to take so long. It took us almost two hours just to reach the jumbled junctions around Birmingham before we finally turned off into Wales. And what a different world it was.

I was relieved to turn off onto a smaller road. The scenery quickly changed from city sprawl to raw open countryside, pretty farms, and market towns, but once we entered the national park of Snowdonia the view through my rain-spattered windscreen became dramatically different. Mountains, some dusted with the first snow of the coming winter, soared around us, their tops shrouded in low cloud.

I glanced across at Percy. "Wow, I didn't expect it to be quite so impressive. I hope we don't have a breakdown; it's deserted round here. It's getting hard to see through this slashing rain. My feeble wipers weren't designed to cope with this wild weather."

"I'll put the blower on. Which button is it?"

I didn't dare take my eyes from the road and waved vaguely at the central island on the dashboard. Percy fiddled about until a blast of hot air shot out of the vents beneath the windscreen.

I peered through the misty glass, ignoring the ache in my neck from straining to see where the next bend would appear. "Well done, the condensation is beginning to clear, but I can still hardly see the white lines in the middle of the road."

Percy nodded. "Just look at those gushing gullies streaming out at the side of the road. They're like little rivers."

I looked and shivered. "Waterfalls, more like. Good job there are deep ditches. Look at the map on your phone, would you? How much further is it?"

"It's a while yet but if we turn on to a smaller road just before this town called Capel Curig, we can cut across the mountains and reach Caernarfon more directly. The other

19

way is a bigger road but miles further. How do you feel about driving through a more remote area?

I didn't want to tell her how scared I really felt. "Alright, as long as you're sure you can map read us through it. Is your Satnav working?"

"Don't need it, it's a simple route along a lake. We can't go wrong."

"If you say so. I don't fancy getting stranded in these mountains."

"Look, there's the turning." Percy pointed at the big road sign.

I took a deep breath. "Okay, here goes." I flicked on the indicator. "On your head be it."

Percy didn't reply, just held on to the handle in the door as I turned the car sharply to the left. Immediately, the road narrowed, and the mountains reared up on either side, appearing much bigger than before and a lot more threatening.

"Spectacular, isn't it? Oh, I feel so much better with every extra mile between me and Paul." Percy wiped her passenger window.

Percy looked a lot calmer than I was feeling, but then Percy wasn't behind the wheel. My eyes ached with strain. I didn't reply but put the headlights on full as the skies had now darkened with clouds so dense, they looked almost navy-blue. Their cumulus shapes bulged and lowered in the gaps between the mist covered mountain tops.

"Are you sure we shouldn't put the Satnav on?" I switched the windscreen wipers up to the next speed as the clouds looming towards us released their load and hail bounced off the car, mixed with the rain.

Percy stabbed a digit at her phone. "No signal. Can't even check the map now."

"Can't you switch it to a mobile network or find a hotspot?"

Percy fiddled with her phone and then shook her head. "Nothing. I suppose the mountains get in the way of any signal."

"I'm not sure this cross-country route was such a good idea. Look at the hailstones on the bottom of the windscreen."

A drift of little balls of ice had mounted up against the vent on the bonnet of my ageing car, making the windscreen steam up again on the inside.

"Can't that heater go any higher?" I felt as cold as the icy hailstones condensing against the glass.

Percy turned the heater up to full. "We'll just have to accept having cold knees while the condensation clears."

I navigated another chicane in the winding road. "Yes, I'd rather sacrifice warmth than not be able to see where I was going with these confounded bends."

"I'm sure it's not much longer." Despite her words, Percy's voice had lost its confident, reassuring tone.

I remembered the news headlines that morning shouting about the changing climate. "I wonder if the weather has always been this dramatic?"

Percy nodded. "I was thinking exactly the same thing. The weather forecasters keep banging on about records being broken for heatwaves or rain falling so fast it causes floods everywhere lately. Oh, look at that lake! It's huge and if you look at its banks, they are really high, almost topping them in places. That can't be normal."

I shivered. "Wow! It is beautiful but a bit too remote for my liking."

As if in answer, we came to a small town. Percy looked out of the window. "We could stop here for the night, if you'd like?"

I was so tempted to stop but instead I took a deep breath. "No, let's press on. It can't be much further."

"Okay, looks like all the shops are shutting up for the day anyway."

We were soon through the little town and driving along its tree-lined outskirts. The wind blew the first of the autumn leaves on to the car which then stuck to the busy wiper blades, still batting away the rain hurling against them. Limestone boulders replaced the trees on one side and a stone wall girded the other. On the other side, an even bigger lake stretched its ruffled surface for miles, the heavy rain making pockmarks in the little waves. I couldn't see too far ahead, as a lumbering lorry in front of us was spraying dirty water behind it and I hung back to avoid the gritty spray.

"Can't you overtake him?" Percy glanced across at me.

Irritated, I retorted, "No, I can't. These bends are lethal. I can't see further than the bonnet what with the leaves, the spray and the rain. I swear the rain is different here. It's like being in a washing machine."

Percy seemed to accept this and sat back in the passenger seat. "Fair enough."

Eventually, the heavy lorry turned off into an enterprise zone and the road levelled out. I could finally relax as the rain eased and we drove through pretty countryside with a string of small villages lining the route.

By the time we arrived in Caernarfon it was beginning to get dark. I drove under the lit streetlights, grateful for some illumination. "What time is it?"

Percy glanced at her pretty wristwatch. "It's nearly seven o'clock."

"Seven o'clock? That's wine o'clock in my book." I peered through the streaming rain looking for signs to the Town Centre.

Percy grinned. "Definitely! Listen, I think we should rest up here for the night. I'm tired, aren't you? I don't think I can face searching for a remote farmhouse tonight."

"I agree. Anglesey is the other side of a stretch of water, isn't it? Can't remember the name."

"Yes, this is Caernarfon, but as Anglesey is an island, you have to go over a big bridge to reach it." Percy took her phone out of her fashionable bag. "Ah, I have signal again. I'll see if there is a suitable hotel around here."

"Alright. We should be able to charge expenses on top of our fee, so why not? And anyway, that feeble lunch at the motorway services didn't stick with me and I could do with a good feed."

Percy laughed. "I think that's a given, Fay."

Miffed, I defended myself. "It's a medical fact that releasing adrenaline makes you hungry, you know."

I drove through roundabouts and underpasses until we came to the old harbour amongst winding, medieval streets, heading for the ancient castle whose tower I had glimpsed looming over the other buildings.

Percy looked up from the little screen in her hands. "Ah, here's one, right next to the castle, it's called The Anglesey Arms."

"Sounds appropriate, but doesn't that mean it's over the water?"

Percy shook her head. "No, it says it overlooks it."

"Perfect. I'm sold." I drove under a stone archway and parked next to the castle. "Wow, that's an impressive pile. Must be ancient."

The stone edifice of Caernarfon Castle towered above us, casting a massive shadow across the wet road from the streetlights. I knew a moment of foreboding but then the more mundane pangs of hunger took over.

Chapter Five, The Isle of Anglesey, around two thousand years ago

Gaine never forgot her gentle mother but over the years, she had learned to accept her loss and obediently surrender to her learning. Every day began with silent rituals before the 'seeing' women met to pray and intuit any messages from the Gods.

It had taken Gaine many years to be able to 'see' but increasingly her visions were clearer than those of the other Druid women, even though she was not yet fully grown.

Today, behind the skin of her eyelids, Gaine could see foreign soldiers, their swords raised in battle, rushing towards her. Although deep under the spell of meditation, aided by the ritual herbal tea, her heart began to beat fast with fear and her breath quickened.

There was one soldier, riding a huge white horse and leading the others, yelling in a language strange to her Welsh ears. His helmet could not hide his saturnine face, lined in deep gouges either side of his open mouth; his nose was straight and his blue eyes, dark with dilated pupils, were evenly spaced under his black eyebrows. His cuffed forearm, the one holding his sharp sword above his head, had muscles standing out like strong cords. The red feather from his headgear streamed out behind him, like his steed's plumed tail. The soldier stood high in his stirrups and his leather skirt revealed legs as lean and toned as his arms.

Gaine's tribe had fighters like this but none possessed armour ingeniously made of metal so no arrow could strike the wearer's heart.

Gaine gasped, drawing in her breath sharply when the horseman turned his murderous face towards her own and stared down at her with ruthless eyes, as if he could see into her very soul.

Her conscious mind kicked in, interrupting her dream state. She wasn't there. How could he see her? She had never been on that battlefield, and may the gods ensure she would never go there. The foreign soldier brandished his weapon at her, he was coming towards her at a gallop! Instinctively, Gaine recoiled, her body trembling in anticipation of that gleaming sword cleaving her in two.

She cried out and fell back on to the packed earth floor. The vision had gone and, for once, she was glad. Someone shook her shoulder, lifted her to sit up again. Gaine opened her eyes to find Bryonia bent over her, the other women in the seeing circle staring at them both.

"What did you see, child?"

"I…I"

"Tell me! Tell me now, before the image fades. I command you, Gaine!"

"A soldier, foreign. White horse. He had a sword. He looked into my eyes. His were dark from evil intent and so were his features. He wanted to kill me!"

"Anything else? I must know all."

Gaine shook her head. "It's disappearing. I can't remember much. Except…"

"Yes?"

"Armour. He wore metal armour."

"Any headgear?"

"Yes, a metal helmet with red feathers. They streamed behind him his horse galloped so fast."

Bryonia stood up. "As I thought. You have seen the Roman soldiers of which we've heard tell. This does indeed bode evil. I must consult with the elders. You have done well, Gaine. Go to the healing temple and rest."

Bryonia turned to the other adult women. "Take her and give her a healing spell. Anoint her with oils. Burn sage in the room to cleanse her spirit. Take your time. The child has gone deep."

"Very well, Priestess."

Gentle hands gathered Gaine into a standing position and guided her to the next hut. She entered the hallowed space and made no protest when the women laid her tenderly on to the pallet bed on the dais in the shadowed corner where two tallow torches always flickered.

The women removed her clothing and smoothed her skin with fragrant oil. Gaine could smell mint and camomile as the unguent seeped into her receptive body. Then, when every one of her muscles had relaxed, they covered her first with linen and then wool and lit the sage brush at the foot of the bed. Gaine fell asleep quickly and slept dreamlessly.

Dawn crept through the opening above the central fire and woke her, hours later. Gaine rubbed her eyes and looked around her at the beautiful room. Other women lay curled asleep on the other side of the round space. Woollen rugs adorned the walls of the special hut where the priestesses healed their sick, making it look warm and friendly. A peat fire glowed with red embers and smoke spiralled up to the sky through the hole in the circular roof. Her bed was comfortable, the sacking packed with dry lady's bedstraw. She could have lain there, undisturbed, as long as she wanted - no-one else was awake - but her sleep had refreshed her utterly and the energy of the new day coursed through her youthful body.

Gaine sat up and reached for her tunic. She slipped it over her head and tied her girdle around her slim waist. She looked across at the other women, who all slept soundly. Thirsty for fresh water, Gaine stepped outside into the early morning, breathing the misty air deep into her young lungs, displacing the sage smoke.

Yesterday's dream no longer had any power over her. Her visions were always like that. Though always so vivid and real at the time she could let them go into the past or the future, wherever they belonged and where they no longer concerned her. While she was still a girl and she had recalled them for Bryonia, as far as Gaine was concerned, it was up to her leader to do what she would with the information. Somewhere in her wise woman's foreknowledge, Gaine sensed she might one day be the priestess who made all the decisions, took on all the responsibility for the community around her; the old and the weak; the young and the vulnerable. But not today, not on this delicious May morning with the year so near

26

midsummer and all the excitement that would bring. Let her age protect her – for now – and the future, with all the foreboding she sensed about it, could wait.

So, just now, her only problem was her thirst. She ran lightly to the glistening lake whose waters always yielded the most delicious drink and quenched the driest thirst. Sometimes the women would do their seeing in its reflection, but Gaine had no desire to return to her last vision; she wanted no reminders of any burdens she might have to carry or invading armies she might have to fight.

Kneeling on its banks, Gaine dipped her hands into the water, breaking the skein of its meniscus so little waves rippled out on its glassy surface in concentric circles. She scooped up the cool liquid in her cupped hands and drank deeply, exulting in its cool hydration as it soothed her throat and cleared her head. Wanting more, she drew off her tunic and slid into the water, diving down into its reedy depths, letting the silky smoothness caress her naked body.

Needing oxygen, she glided back up and broke the surface with larger circular waves, splashing her hands to keep afloat, heedlessly breaking up the circles into chaos. She shook out her long red hair and watched a rainbow form in a sunbeam from the spray that arced from her head.

A laugh welled up from deep within her and its happy noise dissipated into the strands of white mist hovering above the lake. Again, a little voice from the future whispered, "You will never be this carefree again."

Out loud Gaine whispered back, "But I am now in this moment! So let me be!"

Only the birds heard her, but they sang out their joy and understanding to her, making her laugh all over again.

Chapter Six, Present Day

Percy flicked open umbrella. "Come on Fay, get underneath with me or you'll be soaked."

I needed no prompting and huddled under the flimsy rain cover with her. Together, we splashed through puddles until we reached the black and white rectangular building hunkering down under the stone castle walls. The pub, with its whitewashed cheery façade and square Victorian shape, looked out of place tucked under the massive wall of ancient stone above it. It clamped to the castle walls on one side, like mistletoe clinging to its host tree in a parasitic stranglehold.

As Percy collapsed her brolly and shook out a shower of water, I knew another moment of unease as I looked up at the tall hexagonal tower dominating the building a few yards away.

Percy gave me a quizzical look. "What's up, Fay?"

I found it hard to articulate the gloomy sensation. "Don't know exactly - that tower dwarfing the place. Feels overpowering."

"Never mind," Percy put her hand on the door handle. "Let's go in and get warm."

Inside, the pub welcomed us with an open fire and the familiar waft of stale beer. My shoulders dropped with relief. "What do you fancy to drink, Percy?"

Percy gave one of her ravishing smiles to the bar girl. "White wine spritzer, please."

The girl behind the bar was dressed as a Goth with black lipstick and her face had been pierced in various strategic places by silver ornaments.

I nodded at the beer taps. "Half a draught Guinness as well, please."

The girl stopped chewing her gum. "Coming up." She turned towards the wine glasses hanging by their stems against the mirrored back wall.

I propped my wide bottom on the red leather barstool by the wooden hexagonal bar, presumably designed to match the castle tower nearby. I licked my lips in pleasurable anticipation, while Percy settled herself on an old settle near the roaring fire. It had been a long and arduous drive. A residual raindrop slithered down inside the back of my neck, reminding me of the cold, inclement weather I'd driven through to reach this old Welsh town. I stared absentmindedly at the empty beer glasses. I loved dimpled mugs; they were much more satisfying to drink from than straight glasses.

Then, out of the corner of my eye, I saw one of the mugs move towards me as if getting itself ready to be filled with my favourite black stout. In disbelief, I blinked and focussed my eyes on the marbled counter. It was all I could do not to shriek out loud when the empty beer mug moved again.

I darted a quick look at Percy to see if she'd noticed, but she just looked as nonchalantly elegant and beautiful as ever, gracefully lounging on her wooden pew and gazing at the flames roaring up the chimney.

When the mug actually left the worktop and hung suspended in mid-air, a strangled sound did escape me.

The bar girl swung around and laughed. "Oh, he's at it again."

"Who is?" I shut my mouth belatedly when I realised it still hung open.

The dark-haired young woman plopped an ice cube in the wine glass destined for Percy. "Happens all the time." She hung the tongs back on their hook.

I swallowed. "Does it? How? Is it some sort of trick?"

The girl shook her ponytail. "Nah, it's the ghost, isn't it?"

My shoulders rose up and scrunched into tension once more. "Ghost?"

The bar girl stared at me as if I was being thick and raised her eyes to the smoke-stained ceiling. "Yeah, the resident ghost. Must have been a bartender like me, I reckon." Unphased, the girl took the mug that still hung suspended in the air and plonked it down on the drainer under the Guinness tap.

I held up my hand in protest. "Um, if you don't mind, could I have a different glass?"

The younger woman pouted. "I've started pouring it now."

"All the same, I'd rather have another one."

The bar girl gave me a filthy look and ostentatiously poured the unwanted beer away. Sighing heavily, she put the dirty glass in the none-too-clean bar sink and reached for another. "This do you?" Once she had poured the beer into the glass mug, she placed it in front of me next to Percy's glass of wine and water.

Feeling dazed as well as dog-tired, I flashed my debit card across the payment machine. It pinged its acceptance and I bundled the rectangle of plastic back into my bag, still trying to compute what I had just witnessed. I slipped off the bar stool and took the drinks over to Percy by the fireside.

"Did you see that?" I put the drinks down on the sticky tabletop.

"See what?"

"That mug move on its own?"

"What, your beer mug? Don't be daft." Percy picked up her wine glass and sipped it delicately.

I watched my Guinness settle in its dimpled mug. The creamy soft froth floated effortlessly to the top of the glass where it lay in a thick unctuous layer that I knew from experience would taste delicious, and yet I didn't pick it up. Somehow the prospect was no longer so appealing.

Percy noticed my abstinence immediately. "Are you alright, Fay? Aren't you thirsty? That's not like you."

I looked at her, then at the bar with the glasses standing still and to attention in serried rows, before turning back to my friend. "No. It isn't. Thing is, that's the second beer our friendly Goth served me."

"You didn't slug one back before this one, did you? That would be going some, even for you." Percy set her glass back down on the table.

"No, I haven't touched my beer. You're not going to believe this, but apparently this place is haunted."

"What?"

"I know, here we are ghostbusting and they've greeted us at the first fence."

"You mean a ghost moved the beer glass?"

"That's right."

"Oh, come off it, Fay. You're just tired after that long drive through the mountains."

"I am tired, it's true but the girl behind the bar confirmed it."

Percy looked across at the young Goth, who was now serving an older man in a leather jacket with three white skulls on its back.

"I tell you, Percy, the empty beer glass moved towards me on the counter, then hung suspended in mid-air and that girl just picked it up as if it was the most ordinary thing in the world." I picked up my glass at last and sipped the bitter brew. The taste was reassuringly normal.

Percy smiled at her. "It's hard to take you seriously when you've got a white moustache."

I wiped my mouth with the back of my hand. "Scoff all you like, missy. It was real."

"Hmm, maybe you're right." Percy put on her reading glasses and read out the menu. "No main course salads."

"Goodness, Percy. Even you couldn't want a salad tonight!" I snatched the menu from her. "I'll have steak and chips and another Guinness. I have a feeling we'll need to build up our strength for tomorrow."

Percy looked worried. "What sort of a feeling?"

"Just a hunch. What are you having?"

"Mussels, as we're so near the sea, and do you know what? I'll have chips too, like the French do."

"Chips, eh? Okay. Another wine?"

31

"Nah, just some water. I have a bit of a headache."

I got up, scraping my chair on the wooden floorboard. "Okay, I expect you're hungry. Must be a permanent state when you eat like a bird."

Not bothering to listen to Percy's sharp reply, I went to the bar and ordered the food, keeping a wary eye on the beer glasses. Nothing moved on the shelf behind the bar, so I re-joined Percy to wait. To my delight, the food arrived swiftly and was both hot and tasty.

"I vote we stay here overnight, ghosts or no ghosts." Percy stretched her legs out to the blaze.

I noticed Percy's plate was completely empty. "See, I said you were hungry."

The bar girl came over to collect our plates and put another log on the fire.

Percy tucked her legs back under her. "That was great. We were wondering if you have any rooms free for tonight?"

"There's only a family room left, I think." The girl clattered the plates together.

"Do you mind sharing?" Percy raised her eyebrows at me.

I was so dog-tired I would have slept on the floor and shrugged. "If it's separate beds it's alright."

The girl shook her ponytail so much her nose-ring wobbled. "One's a sofa bed, mind."

Percy nodded at the girl. "That's alright, could you reserve it for us?"

"Okay. Consider it yours. Pay at the bar before you go up." She took the plates and went through a swing door behind the unusual hexagonal bar.

I looked at Percy. "So, who gets the short straw then?"

"Do you mean the sofa bed? Oh, I don't mind."

"Noble of you."

We sat by the fire for another half an hour until Percy's yawns prompted me to gather up my things. "Come on, sleepyhead. Time for bed."

I paid for the room and got the key.

"It's on the top floor. We have no lift I'm afraid, you'll have to use the stairs but it's en-suite, so you won't need to leave your room and the double bed is a large one." Our friendly Goth smirked at us.

Irritated, I didn't smile back. "And breakfast?"

"Oh, yes, in the dining room. You can give your orders in the morning. Full Welsh or vegan, whatever you want."

"Thanks." Percy took up the key and led the way to the staircase.

"She obviously thinks we're gay." It annoyed me how I kept getting labelled this way.

"Oh, who cares? Let's just get some kip."

The room had two windows, one overlooking the street and the other over the sea. I peered out before drawing the curtains. "Should be a good view in the morning, the sea is so close you could almost touch it."

Percy took no notice. She was staring at the sofa bed. "Oh, good, it's one of those flop-out Futons. Great for my back, no notchy springs."

I turned back towards her. "If you say so. We could toss for it."

Percy smiled brightly. "No, I mean it. I would prefer this."

"As you like." I threw my bag on to the large double bed and headed for the bathroom. I climbed straight into bed on my return and was asleep before Percy had finished her ablutions.

My dreams were littered with flying beer mugs, black lips pierced by silver rings and wet roads gleaming around hairpin bends. When the glasses shattered on the wet tarmac, puncturing a tyre making my car skid off the road, I saw a yawning chasm below me with a lake pitted with hailstones. It was when the car started to slither down the slope that I actually woke up.

"Wha...What's that noise?" I sat up in bed, blinking in the dark. I could hear something rattling and looked at the outline of streetlight escaping around the curtains. Was it the wind coming off the sea? I heard the sound again. No, it wasn't the window frame, it was a door handle. Was Percy stuck in the bathroom after a nocturnal flit to the loo? I looked across at my friend, whose slender form was still definitely under the covers on the other side of the room. I rubbed my eyes, forcing them to focus in the half-light. I tried to remember where the bathroom was in the unfamiliar space. Ah yes, in the other corner but the bathroom door stood ajar, and the bleak light issuing from its opaque window revealed it couldn't be the culprit.

A crawling sensation broke out on my skin. Slowly, I turned to look at the main bedroom door and realised the noise was emanating from that direction. I sat higher up in bed to get a better view and to my horror saw the handle turn. Who was trying to get in? The Goth from the bar? The manager? Was there a fire? I sniffed but could detect no smoke.

The door handle shook again, more vigorously. I had no idea what to do. Surely the hotel staff would ring the room service phone if there was an emergency? And they had my mobile number too. Percy had been reluctant to give hers. She still thought Paul might find her.

The handle, old, rickety and made of brass, moved up and down, more slowly this time, bringing back into my present predicament.

Careful not to disturb Percy, I gingerly climbed out of bed and tiptoed towards the door, but as I approached it, I heard footsteps moving away on the other side of it. Must be a prankster. I turned the key in the lock. The old metal felt unusually cold in my hand. I peered out into the corridor. No-one was there.

Then, from inside our room, someone clapped. I whirled round but all I saw was Percy's sleeping form.

I looked up and down the corridor again, but it was deserted. Not only did my hand feel unusually cold now, so did the rest of me. I turned back to seek the warm refuge of my bed.

"Agh!" On the way I bumped into something in the darkness, frantically brushing off the hand that touched my arm.

Percy's familiar voice soothed my fears. "Fay! It's only me. What's happening? Why aren't you in bed?"

I rubbed my arms to get warm. "Some odd goings on. Didn't you hear the door handle turning?"

"No. You're imagining things again."

"I'm bloody not."

"Now come on, Fay. Go back to bed. I think you're suffering from pre-performance nerves."

Percy flopped back onto her mattress on the floor. "Goodnight again."

"Let's hope so." I lay in my comfortable bed, every nerve straining to hear more eerie sounds, but none came. Eventually I slept but my dreams were just as disturbing as before.

Chapter Seven, Isle of Anglesey, around two thousand years ago

Gaine submitted to the female hands fluttering around her. They combed out her long red hair and tied two braids from her forehead to join the cascade rippling down her back, thereby giving symmetry to the whole. Her crown they garlanded with May flowers – blossom from the apple trees woven with young oak leaves and interwoven with fragrant woodruff. Over her head they threw her white tunic. It was newly woven from linen harvested in their flax field and lay slippery and smooth against her freshly washed skin. She felt clean all over. Even on her bare feet, where no speck of dirt dared to nestle between her toes. Her ankles and wrists bore circlets of flowers made from blue forget-me-nots and daisies, knotted together with the green reeds that bordered the lake of fresh water.

Bryonia came in when the women had finished. They hung back as their priestess inspected her granddaughter with raised eyebrows and a soft smile.

"You are beautiful, Gaine. This Beltaine night, you will become a woman. Are you ready?"

Gaine nodded.

"I must hear you say it, Gaine."

"I am ready, my lady."

"Yes, I truly believe you are. Come, let us go to the feast and you will set the flame to the Beltaine fire."

Bryonia took Gaine's hand in hers. The elder woman's fingers were cool and relaxed, but Gaine's were hot and damp with perspiration. Gaine felt a reassuring pressure from her grandmother's hand and answered it with a squeeze.

In a low voice only Gaine could hear, Bryonia said, "It is normal to be nervous. You should be excited. Your initiation into the Beltaine ritual as a grown woman is an important moment in any girl's life, for tomorrow you will no longer be a maiden, unless you wish it so."

"Yes, grandmother."

Bryonia paused on the threshold of the healing chamber and signalled the other women to leave. When they were alone, she turned to face her granddaughter and placed her hands lightly on Gaine's shoulders. "Have you chosen your Jack-in-the-Green?"

"I have." Gaine's stomach lurched uncomfortably as she made her admission.

"Good. I have an idea of who he might be, but keep it as your secret, Gaine. You are in control of this night, no-one else, not even the man you choose for your Pan. Hold on to your womanpower through your whole life, however long or short it may be. Your feminine force must be used wisely and for good, never evil. Every action we take has an effect in this world and, I believe, in others. Never abuse that power or wield it for your own selfish gains. If you love another, love openly in your heart. Give of yourself but retain your sense of self. Self-love is essential to master, as I have taught you, and the beginning of all other loves. Do not love possessively, however, but give yourself freely and set your lovers free when the time is right. Do this with compassion and respect. Do *everything* with compassion and respect, Gaine. Now, *I* set *you* free. You are no longer my student but another priestess in our community, but you will always be my granddaughter. Come, let us celebrate with the others."

Bryonia kissed Gaine on her forehead and looked deeply into her eyes. Bryonia's blue ones were full of love, serious but twinkling at the same time, as only hers could.

"Know you are loved, as was your mother, who will be with us in spirit this night, watching over you as you leave your childhood behind."

"Thank you, Grandmother, for all you have done."

"It has been the greatest pleasure of my life." Bryonia turned to face the doorway and squared her shoulders.

Gaine, moved by her words, went to stand by her grandmother's side and together they left the sanctuary of the healing chamber and stepped out into the May evening.

The air wafted warm with a slight breeze in the lingering daylight. Side by side, Gaine and her grandmother walked down the well-trodden leafy path to the sacred oak grove. Gaine could hear the distant swish of the waves upon the shore far below them. The sea was in a gentle mood tonight even though the tide would be high from the full moon later. The waves were whispering on their way inland up the straits, rather than roaring and spitting as they so often did.

Honeysuckle scented the path on either side and the lush spring green grass, studded with fragrant bluebells and the pure white stars of ramson garlic, brushed against their skirts as they fell into step. Both tall and slender, the two women resembled each other with their long limbs, angular, high cheekbones, and piercing blue eyes, except Gaine's hair flamed red while her grandmother's was jet black. Ereni, Gaine's mother, had been quite different. Small and delicate with light brown hair and kind hazel eyes, she had always been quiet and gentle and content to be near the fireside, tending to domestic tasks, unlike her mother and her child, who hunted with the menfolk and fought as fiercely alongside them when occasion demanded.

A feast had been laid out on the stone table at the back of the oak circle. Men, women and children clustered around it, chatting and laughing, but fell into respectful silence as Bryonia and Gaine approached.

Bryonia led her granddaughter to the Maypole in the centre of the circle. A big dead branch had been placed there, as it was every May, lancing its point up towards the moon in a manly stance. A triskelion had been carved into its bark. Its three joined-up circles symbolising the continuation of life through the generations, powered by the sun. Gaine remembered her favourite runestone bore the same symbol, even more loved now she understood its meaning. Smaller sticks surrounded its base ready to be lit by the maidens of Beltaine. This year, Rhiannon and Gaine were the only two. Rhiannon, as plump and dark as ever, stood between her mother and her eldest sister, looking as self-conscious, nervous and proud as Gaine felt.

Bryonia let fall Gaine's hand and raised both her arms up to embrace the sky. "Tonight is Beltaine, my beloved people. The Earth has renewed herself once again in the miracle of the seasons. Winter is finally behind us and none of our community has perished in its icy grip, thank the Gods. The seeds of the new crops have been sown and a lamb sacrificed to the Gods for our feasting this evening.

"Come one and all and celebrate the coming of summer!"

A cheer went up and horned cups were searched for and clasped in eager hands.

"A toast!" Bryonia lifted her cup high. May the Gods give us fertile land and good crops."

She drank from her vessel before raising it again. "May the Gods give our women full bellies of children that shall be born healthy and whole."

More swigs of cider followed the first, accompanied by guffaws and chuckles.

"Let this coming year provide us with food enough to store for the following winter. May we also be free of invaders seeking to conquer our lands." Bryonia's more sober last wish, drew murmurs from the crowd and some headshaking.

Then she smiled at them all. "But tonight, it is enough to drink and be merry! Let our maidens come forward with our Jacks-in-the-Green!"

Gaine and Rhiannon came forward tentatively, joined by two young lads wearing face masks resembling goats, with horns growing from them above their heads. They looked grotesque but none looking on them were frightened by the familiar sight of Pan in all his glory.

"Rhiannon, Gaine? Get a taper each and light the Beltaine fire!"

The two girls were handed lit tapers which they touched to the kindling underneath the pyre. Up went the flames into torches of gold and white and up went the roar of the people gathered around it.

Gaine was dreading the next part of the ritual, but someone thrust a wooden cup containing a special elixir in her hand and gave the same special brew to the other three initiates. "Drink that, me dears, and you'll have no fear of the flames."

"Drink, drink! You must drink it all in one go or you'll be burned alive!" Came the shouts from her tribesmen and women.

Gaine tipped her drink down her throat. It was bitter and aromatic but as it went down, it warmed her until her body felt as inflamed as the fire itself, so when the women stripped her of her clothes, she found she no longer minded. The four youngsters started to giggle uncontrollably. True to tradition they joined hands around the fire and danced in a circle of abandoned nakedness, laughing and shrieking without any shame, egged on by the willing onlookers who clapped and sang as they watched and laughed with them.

"Jump! Jump!" They chorused and the four dancers dropped their clasp of each other and duly leapt over the bonfire, yelling their heads off.

One of the boys grabbed Gaine's hand once they had landed safely on the other side of the burning wood. "Come, come with your Pan, Gaine!"

She knew his voice so well and felt no fear, only exhilaration and joy. Together, they ran away from the adults, who would now feast the night away before indulging in their own carefree Beltaine couplings.

Emrys didn't stop running until they reached the other side of the oak grove. Panting, he threw off his Pan mask and enfolded her in his strong, young arms. He didn't kiss her straight away but released her instead, tipping his head to one side, eyebrows raised in query. Gaine was a Druid Priestess and now she knew her power. It was for her to give consent, not her man.

Delirious with the drugged wine, warm from running and leaping over the flames of Beltaine, Gaine threw her head back in a deep-throated laugh, "I consent, Pan, with all my heart and body and soul!"

Emrys laughed back and kissed her as thoroughly and deeply as she desired.

"I scouted out the perfect spot for us, Gaine. Come, my love, and lay with me here in this mossy hollow. See, Mother Earth has provided us with the perfect love nest."

Together, arms entwined, they sought the refuge of their green, velvety mattress. Gaine's fevered state and Emrys's hungry hands soon had her moaning in delight, and she lost her maidenhood in ecstatic gratitude, enveloped in a passion she had never known before and amazed at the thrilling pleasure she experienced.

They lay undisturbed together all that night but slept little for they were young and eager and in love.

Gaine never forgot that blissful night for the rest of her life.

Chapter Eight, Present Day

Breakfast was as good as the bar girl had predicted. Of course, I had a full Welsh fry-up and Percy had a green smoothie she made up herself in the liquidiser provided on the buffet counter, next to all the fresh fruit I had ignored.

Afterwards we asked the plump young waitress for directions to Rick's house, whose name was unpronounceable to our English tongues, so we showed her the address on a scrap of paper.

She replied in an attractive, soft Welsh lilt. "I don't know where that farm might be, never heard of it, but Anglesey is an island, you know. It can only be reached by crossing the Menai Straits. You'd best take the Britannia Bridge, it's the first one this side of Caernarfon on the A55. More coffee?" She held up the stainless-steel pot.

I tried to picture the route in my head. "So, straight along the seafront, is it?"

"Oh, no, you'll have to double back to get to the main road or you'll end up in the water!" The girl giggled.

Percy smiled back. "Um, hope you don't think we're mad, but we had some strange goings on last night."

The girl nodded, looking unsurprised. "That'll be our resident ghost. I blame the hangings."

I scalded my throat gulping my fresh coffee too fast. "Hangings?

The waitress pointed at the castle looming through the window. "See up there? See that old door high up in the castle wall?"

We obediently looked and nodded.

"Pushed them out, they did."

"Who? Prisoners?"

"Oh, yes, noose around their necks, like and," the girl waved her hands outwards, splashing some coffee on to the pristine white tablecloth, "whoosh, gone." She mopped ineffectually at the dark stains. "Can I get you anything else?"

42

Percy shook her auburn head. "No, thanks. So nice to be somewhere you can get a smoothie. It made a lovely breakfast."

I couldn't let that go. "What little you ate of it."

Percy gave me a withering look. "Well, Miss Armstrong, you certainly made up for it."

"One does one's best." I grinned at my friend, wiped the bacon fat from my mouth and put down my napkin without remorse.

Percy put her pristine napkin neatly on her unused plate and stood up. "Incorrigible. Right, let's settle up and get going."

Once we had gathered our things and checked out of the hotel, we stood a moment beside the wall between the sea and the land, gazing at the spectacular view. The island of Anglesey beckoned to us from the other side of the watery stretch of the Menai Straits, whose strong currents swirled below us.

The landscape on the island looked surprisingly flat and ordinary, in contrast to our drive through the Snowdonian mountains. I had been standing there for a few minutes absorbing the scene when I became aware that the hubbub of people around me had hushed and I had the horribly familiar sensation of cold creeping up my body that usually preceded one of my intuitive sightings. My eyes were drawn to the distant shore. The modern view disappeared into a vague mist but through it I could see tall figures, clad in long black robes, holding flaming torches alight above their heads. They stood standing together in a line on the island's shoreline, a sandy beach in front of them and tall trees behind. I screwed up my eyes and focussed on the distant detail.

All the people I could see appeared to be women and their hair streamed behind them in the wind. From their mouths issued the most eerie and desperate keening sounds. One of them, who had long, white hair, turned to look at me directly and her piercing stare chilled me even more. The women were wailing loudly, calling for help. The woman

43

looked at me with disconcerting directness. Her blue eyes seemed to burn into my very soul with their fierce anger.

The woman pointed to the big stretch of water churning between us. I looked down and was shocked to see men wading across to the island. They wore helmets, a few with bedraggled plumes of red feathers on their heads, and in their hands, they brandished lethal looking spears. Horses plunged beside them, their eyes white and wide with fear, their nostrils flared as they struggled against the current. I could see their uniforms clearly - metal breastplates and strips of leather ended at their knees in a masculine skirt, revealing their muscular bare legs. Deep in the recesses of my mind, I recognised them as Roman soldiers.

The female chief turned back to look at me, commanding my gaze with her magnetic charisma. Such was her power I could not tear my eyes away. The middle-aged woman had a strong, lean face with a beaky, arrogant nose, high cheekbones and her blue eyes were ablaze and dark with fury. She wore a golden torque around her neck and flourished a highly carved ornamental staff in one hand, while the other still held a fire torch, whose flickering flames alternately cast shadows then bright light across her stern, enraged, screaming face. A younger woman stood next to her, surrounded by a clutch of distressed children.

I now felt as numb with the cold as if I too was in the freezing waters of the Menai Straits. The woman's compelling eyes drilled into me and though the language was alien to me I understood her plea. "Help us! Come to our aid! They will kill us all! Save us!"

Someone shook my arm, jolting me out of the scene and abruptly back into the present day.

"Fay! Fay! What's happening? Are you alright?" I looked down to see Percy's hand on my sleeve.

I shook it off impatiently. "What? Yes, I'm alright. Why did you interrupt me?" I was angry at losing the vision. The mundane everyday sounds of people passing by, chattering bland nothings to each other, once again intruded on my thoughts, wrenching me away from the turbulent scene I had witnessed. I blinked and saw Percy staring anxiously me.

I gave an involuntary shiver. "God, it's cold."

"Have you had an episode?"

I told Percy what I had seen. "They were making a sort of wailing sound, very emotional and scared. Desperate, in fact."

"Poor things." Percy looked out over the water as if trying to picture what I had described.

I felt a rush of affection for her and squeezed her arm. "Thanks for not doubting me."

"Why on earth should I, after all we've been through? I have complete faith in your second sight."

I shrugged my big shoulders. "I'm not used to having a fellow conspirator."

"We're not conspiring!" Percy gave a wobbly laugh.

"No, well, you know what I mean."

"Sadly, I do. We must do some research on the history of this place. Maybe what you just saw is connected to Rick's problems? Perhaps it was those terrified women warning us off all along? You know, all those nocturnal shenanigins last night at the hotel?"

I shivered and hitched my bag higher on my shoulder and started to walk to the car. "I doubt it. The Romans were in Britain about two thousand years ago." Denial was easier than believing the ghastly scene I'd just witnessed had been real. I was determined to shake off the image.

Once we reached the car, Percy went to the driver's door. "Shall I drive?"

I handed Percy the keys. "Good idea, I do feel a bit wonky after that blast from the past."

Soon we were driving along the busy main road towards the bridge with the Menai Straits glinting alongside. Progress was slow due to the surprisingly heavy traffic.

I looked out of the passenger window. "It's a big expanse of river, isn't it? Or maybe it's the sea?"

"Huge. I wonder what they did before the bridge was built?"

"Ferries I suppose." I still hadn't warmed up and leant down to turn up the heater.

"Ah, here we are. It's quite a way from Caernarfon, isn't it?" Percy indicated to turn onto the bridge spanning the water.

"I'd better check the map on my phone." I tapped in Rick's address, but it said no Satnav information was available there. "Not on the map. Seems he's in the depths of the countryside."

"Is there a village in his address?"

"Ah yes, okay. Just keep going on this road for a while and then I'll tell you where to turn off and then I guess we just ask around."

"In the unlikely event there will be anyone to ask."

"Good point."

Percy smiled. She looked more relaxed with every mile we put between us and her husband. "Well, it's one way to meet the natives."

"Hah! If we can find any."

We drove on for a quite a while after crossing the Menai Straits, passing through lots of agricultural land which rose above the water far below us, glinting through the trees.

"Seems a peaceful sort of place, however violent it's history." I too felt more relaxed now, as the dramatic scene along the shoreline faded from my mind.

"Show me somewhere that doesn't have violence in its past." Percy changed gear to navigate a bend.

"Hmm. I think we take a right here." I pointed at the junction ahead.

Percy turned the steering wheel. "Oh, this is a tiny track."

I held on to the door handle to steady myself. "Bumpy too."

"More trees here, makes it a bit dark to see."

A soft rain had descended on the gentle landscape with a creeping mist shrouding the distant view, coming off the sea.

We passed a farm track and I saw a board, partly obscured by nettles. "Let's stop and look at that sign, see if it's Rick's place."

Percy brought the car to a halt, and I clambered out.

"What does it say?" Percy spoke through her open car window.

I swiped at the nettles. "Ouch! Didn't think they'd still have a sting at this time of year. I can't make head nor tail of it. It's in Welsh."

A human form emerged through the mist from the farm track, with a dog running alongside.

"Oh, hello." I hoped my smile looked friendly.

"Bore da."

"Sorry?" I squinted at the approaching figure, trying to decide if it was male or female, it was hard to tell.

"Oh, English, are you?"

"That's right. Um, we're looking for a house." I read out the name of our destination phonetically. "Gorf why so far?"

"Never heard of that."

"Oh, we thought we were close." I peered into the mist that was rapidly intensifying into a fog. "Lovely spot."

"Humph."

"Can I show you the name on my phone? I probably haven't pronounced it correctly."

As the figure came closer, I could see she was a woman. She took a pair of glasses out of one of the many pockets in her colourful patchwork coat and put them on. Her white, unbound hair fell forward across her weather-beaten face as she leaned forward to peer at the little screen.

"Oh, Gorphwhysfa!"

She made it sound like '*Gaw-voice-far*'. "You know it?"

"Of course, you're already here."

47

"So…could you give us directions to Rick O'Shea's house?"

The woman slowly took off her glasses and placed them back in the pocket they'd come from. She stared at me intently, obviously weighing me up. "What are you going there for? There's enough going on there already, if you ask me."

I wasn't sure how to answer that. Her eyes were shrewd and intelligent. I decided to tell the truth. "Mr O'Shea has offered us a job."

"Are you in the music business too? Infernal racket."

"Not musicians, no."

The woman tucked her hair behind her ear and pointed westwards, towards the sea. "Just follow the track. If you go too far, you'll end up in the water."

"Thank you, Mrs, um?"

"Howell."

"Thank you. I'm very grateful to you."

"Can't say as I return the compliment." Mrs Howell muttered as she turned back and walked away in her muddy Wellington boots, her collie dog trotting obediently by her side.

I stood a moment watching her disappear into the fog, wondering why her face had seemed oddly familiar.

"Psst! Fay! What did she say?" Percy leaned out of the car window.

"It's just along this track. Not far, by the sound of it. It's hidden by trees, but she said we'll find it eventually - unless we go too far and do a 'Thelma and Louise act' over the cliff's edge!"

"Charming. Hop in then." Percy started up the car engine again.

The further along the track we drove, the thicker the mist became.

"I can barely see at all!" Percy sat hunched over the steering wheel with her nose almost pressed to the windscreen.

We were making little progress, so I made a suggestion. "Perhaps we should get out and walk?"

"I think *you* should."

"Thanks a bunch."

Percy didn't laugh back. "No, I mean it. I really can't see but you could feel your way with your feet, and I'd be able to see you."

"Suicide mission?"

"You'll be fine."

I unclipped my seat belt. "It is a far, far better thing I do…"

Percy flapped one hand at me. "Get on with it before we plunge into the ocean."

"I feel completely expendable." I got out of the car and slammed the door shut.

I walked carefully in front of the car, now crawling noisily along in first gear, and peered through the fog. I could barely make out my feet, let alone the tussocks of grass down the centre of the narrow lane. I could hear their uncut tops brushing against the exhaust pipe under the car, so I kept to the left-hand side, hoping Percy could see me as well as the track ahead and praying nothing broke the chassis of my old hatchback.

The fog only got thicker as we crept along until I despaired of being able to see anything at all. Then, through the muffled air, I heard a voice - a deep voice shouting something.

A man's figure loomed into view, craning his neck forward to see.

"Who's there?" The man was tall, he towered over me.

"My name's Fay Armstrong. We're looking for Rick O'Shea."

"Hey, man! I've been expecting you. You're the ghostbuster, ain't ya?"

"Mr O'Shea? I'm glad we've found you."

"That's me but you can call me Rick, yeah?"

49

"Thanks. This fog is so dense, we couldn't see a thing from the car."

"Yeah, it's a bastard alright. Good job I saw you, 'cos if you went that way you'd be in the briny, like."

"So Mrs Howell said."

"Oh, her. Crazy hippie woman."

I didn't respond to that. I wasn't about to referee a neighbourly war. "So, where can we park the car, Rick?"

"Follow me."

I beckoned to Percy, who was staring anxiously through the car windscreen. I walked alongside Rick for only a few yards when he pointed to his right. There was an open-sided barn, half-full of haybales. Percy pulled over in front of it and silenced the engine. The air was deathly quiet without its thrum in the swirling damp mist.

Percy climbed out of the driver's seat and walked around to join us.

Rick had gone ahead of us and was now standing in front of a substantial old building, made of local limestone. Three floors high, with a slate roof presiding over two wide gables, it made an impressive pile. From the steps in front of the dark blue door, Rick yelled across the yard. "Grab yer stuff and come on in!"

We got our suitcases and handbags out of the boot and walked over the cobblestones, slick with the dewdrops condensing all around them, before stepping inside the grand old house.

Chapter Nine, Present Day

Once inside the hall, Rick flicked a switch on the wall which illuminated the large room and then lead us into an even bigger kitchen. I found it hard to adjust to the brightness after the gloom of the thick fog outside and blinked before taking in my surroundings. The room was fitted with old-fashioned units from the 1970s, all made of pine and battered with age and the whole space was cluttered with dirty washing-up, scrumpled-up, damp-looking tea towels and a half empty box of old, cold pizza.

"Yeah, sorry about the mess. The domestic help seems to have given up on us, like, since we got haunted." Rick smelled of tobacco smoke. Under the red bandana, his dark hair grew down to the collar of his black T-shirt and was streaked with grey. He looked underweight but wiry and kept his torn jeans up by means of a big brown leather belt, the same colour as his worn cowboy boots. His skin had a dry, parchment look to it. His stained teeth gave away his smoking habit. Aware of me staring at him, Rick returned my gaze with eyes of a surprisingly piercing blue above his aquiline nose and an apologetic smile on his once-handsome face. He certainly didn't give off the same vibe as he had on the red carpet, wearing a sharp suit, in the photo we'd studied.

Rick fished in his pocket and drew out a pouch of tobacco and a packet of Rizla's. "Fancy a fag? Or perhaps you'd like a joint? I've got some really mellow stuff from Marrakesh. Black and strong, just the way I like it."

I had to suppress a smile when health-conscious Percy recoiled at his invitation. "No thanks. I never smoke anything."

"Oh yeah? What about you?"

I shook my head. "No, thanks."

Rick took his time rolling his cigarette and then put it, unlit, behind his ear, tucked under his cotton bandana. "So, this ghost malarkey. Reckon you can sort it?"

I had no idea if we could so I just said, "We can try."

Rick looked at us appraisingly. "Thought you'd be a couple – you know – man and woman – from yer names, like."

I heard Percy's sharp intake of breath and answered for us both. "No, just a mix up with nicknames. I'm Fay Armstrong and my friend's full name is Persephone Godstock."

"Blimey, that's a mouthful, but very feminine. Suits you." Rick looked Percy up and down. "Nice, very nice." He mumbled under his breath.

Percy frowned and backed away even further. "We are business partners. Nothing else."

"But you got to be mates, ain't ya? I mean, ghostbusting must get scary. You'd need a good pal at yer side, I should fink."

I put my bag down. We obviously weren't going anywhere soon. "Yes, of course we're good friends. Now, do you think we could see our quarters, or do you want to discuss terms?"

"Whoa! Hoity bloody toity, missus. My manager will sort that. You'll meet him in a bit. His name is Eddie. You don't mess wiv' Eddie, gettit?"

Rick wandered over to the big sofa in the corner of the room and cleared a space on its littered surface. He plonked himself down next to the debris of unopened letters, crunched-up beer cans and plastic food wrappers. "Tell you what, I'll get Eddie over to show you around. Then maybe we could have a takeaway, girls, and chat things over. What do you say?" His lined face broke into a charming grin, and I realised how attractive he must once have been; maybe still was to some.

He took his phone out of his jeans pocket before they answered and spoke into it. "Eddie? Come on over will yer, mate? Got them ghostbusters here, like."

Rick clicked his phone off and lit his rolled cigarette. "Sure you don't want one? A cuppa perhaps?"

I was dying for a cup of tea, but after I looked at the sink, piled high with dirty mugs, I decided to decline. "Think I'll pass. Are we staying here in your house?"

Percy looked at me beseechingly.

"Nah, we've got little cottages all around the estate."

"The estate?"

"Yeah, that's right."

Percy looked out of the big windows at the foggy scene. "We couldn't see any other buildings; the fog is so dense now."

"Yeah, comes off the sea. Another joy of being here." Rick blew out some blue, fragrant smoke.

Percy turned towards him. "So, is it foggy often then?"

"Nah, just sometimes, though more often lately. Weather's all over the place." Rick was beginning to look bored.

I thought it time to turn the subject. "So, Rick, these hauntings, as you call them, do you want to talk about what's been happening?

Rick waved a vague hand in assent and lit his rolled cigarette from a flip-open silver lighter.

"Would you rather we wait for your friend?"

"Do you mean Eddie?" Rick laughed. "He's a lot more than a friend. We been together for thirty years now. Used to be my roadie. Handled the security – know what I mean? Turns out he's a wizard at the accounts malarkey too. All-round good bloke."

I grabbed one of the wooden dining chairs scattered around the large refectory table and parked myself on its grubby surface. Percy swiftly joined me, and we exchanged a brief, exasperated smile.

Just as I opened my mouth to reintroduce the subject of ghosts and the reason we were here, the door from the yard opened and a burly bald man with tattoos on his turkey neck entered the kitchen.

Rick looked relieved to see him. "Eddie, mate! Here's them ghostbusters I told yer about. Can you show them the ropes, like, only I want to go and write down some music that's rattling around my head?"

Eddie strode up to the table and extended a meaty hand. He welcomed us in a gruff voice without a smile. "Pleased to meet you."

"Hi Eddie," we chorused together, making me feel like an embarrassed schoolchild, so I stood up, annoyed to find I was a foot shorter than Eddie too.

Eddie shook hands briskly and asked us our names. "Right then, let's take you to your accommodation, shall we?" He had a London accent, the same as Rick's but without the dropped consonants.

We obediently picked up our bags and trotted after Eddie, giving Rick a wave goodbye. Rick's wave back was swiftly followed by the full-throated cough of a chronic smoker as he took a drag of his joint.

Back out in the yard the fog had intensified. We never would have found the cottage without Eddie's bulk in front of us, guiding the way.

"Here you are, this one's yours." Eddie put a yale key in the lock of the front door and we entered the cottage together. "Let me shut the door behind you. Bloody awful weather, isn't it? It's a wonder you found us."

I gave him the benefit of my grateful smile. "We met your neighbour on the way here, Mrs Howell. Just as well we did, because Rick's house isn't listed on Google maps, and we'd never have found it without her directions."

"Ah, yes, that's Bryony. She's a tenant on the estate. Grows veg and stuff with some other ecofreaks. It's been so long since Rick's been here, he'd forgotten she lived here. Now we've found out she's got a lot of cronies installed here too which we hadn't reckoned on." Eddie let out a long sigh, replaced by a polite smile. "Anyway. Let me show you around." He swept his arm to encompass the open-plan space. "It's only a small place but it's done-up nice."

"It's lovely." Percy looked very relieved.

A woodburning stove sat in the centre of a limestone fireplace with a couple of sofas set around it under the beamed ceiling. To the other side of the central open-tread staircase there was a well-fitted kitchen and a small set of table and chairs.

"Glad you like it. There's two bedrooms upstairs, either side of a bathroom. It's not huge but it should fit the bill. Think it used to be an old barn and it's been done up for holiday makers. The cleaners gave it the once over and made up the beds before they scarpered. If the sun comes out tomorrow, you'll see the view. That's really magic, I have to admit."

I wandered into the kitchen. "It looks perfect, Eddie. Shall we get ourselves settled in and then come back to the house?"

"Yeah, then we can talk business and get some grub."

"Okay." I held my hand out for the key to the front door.

Eddie gave me the key and let himself out. I let out my breath. "Phew! Thank goodness we're not staying with Rick and his mate."

Percy was investigating the kitchen. "God, yes. Lucky escape. This all looks lovely and clean."

"Let's bag a bedroom each and check out upstairs. Seems we'll have to wait until morning to get the lie of the land outside."

We climbed the straight stairs and inspected the bedrooms.

"Not much to choose between them. They're both nice, aren't they?" Percy called across the landing.

I sat down and bounced on the divan bed. "Good enough."

After we'd unpacked, we scavenged the kitchen, delighted to find tea bags and a pint of milk, still surprisingly in date, in the fridge amongst some other basic foods.

"Why do you think Rick is so reticent about talking about the hauntings he's brought us here for?" I stirred my regular two spoons of sugar into my tea.

Percy sipped mint tea from her mug. "Hmm. So refreshing. Yes, I'm not sure. Seemed a bit odd, sort of coy about it?"

The sweet tea was very welcome, and I smacked my lips with satisfaction. "Probably just scared. Doesn't want to stir the energy up."

Percy nodded. "Yes, we were the same at Meadowsweet Manor, remember?"

"I shall never forget it. Lord, what have we got ourselves into?"

Chapter Ten, Present Day

That evening, after a pizza takeaway supper, Rick and Eddie asked us to join them in the recording studio which was housed some way from the main house down a long, tree-lined path near some woods. The two men brought large torches with them because of the lingering mist, and shone their bright beams into the brushwood on either side, startling rabbits and owls as well as me.

Eventually, we came to a ramshackle stone building, scarred by the remains of ivy roots on its limestone walls. The soil around it looked churned up and muddy, as if recently cleared of trees and shrubs but before I could take in anymore, Eddie put a yale key in the lock and the door creaked open.

"Shut the door tight, girls, will ya?" Rick almost blinded me with his fierce torch as he pointed it at my face.

I dutifully obeyed and the heavy door shut with a firm click. Eddie flicked on the electric lights and the shadows retreated from the corners in the big space, but the distinct tang of mice droppings remained.

"Where should we sit?" Percy shivered.

"You cold, luv? 'Ere, have my jacket. I soon warm up when I'm playing." Rick slipped his leather jacket around Percy's slim shoulders and squeezed them.

Percy rewarded him with one of her ravishing smiles.

Rick blinked a couple of times in response and pointed to a scruffy sofa in the opposite corner. "Park yerselves over there. I'll light the log burner."

"I'll do it," Eddie spoke gruffly, sounding annoyed.

Rick seemed impervious. "Cheers, mate. I never can get it going, can I?"

"Nah, you never can." Eddie went over to the stove and started to scrunch up some old newspapers lying in a pile next to it.

I loved lighting fires. It reminded me of my old Dad. "I'll give you a hand."

Eddie looked a little mollified. "Loads of work, if you ask me, I'd rather have an electric radiator, but your friend looks like she needs a warm-up, and we don't have the capacity for more electrical equipment."

"Has this place always been a studio, Eddie?"

"Nah, It was an old barn and Rick got some guys to renovate it, but the circuit is quite limited. No central heating either, I'm afraid but it's so remote it's nice and quiet, so it was a quick fix."

Percy who had put her slender arms into Rick's leather jacket and sat, feet up, looking very relaxed on the sofa. Her auburn hair was loose and streamed out behind her against the blue chenille fabric. She looked like Shakespeare's tragic Ophelia, but then I remembered she had drowned, not a good role model. I shook off the image and concentrated on screwing the rolled-up newspaper into knots.

"That's plenty, girl. If you put all of them on, we'll have a chimney fire." Eddie took out some of the knobby paper bundles and replaced them with sticks of kindling.

"I hope that's not a premonition." I handed Eddie some of the smaller logs.

"Bloody hell, don't curse the place. I've had the chimney swept, you know. First thing I did when we had the woodburner installed." He put a match to the paper and shut the glass door. There was a roaring sound as the flames leapt up the metal flue and disappeared. Instantly, the enormous room seemed more cheerful, less functional and fusty-smelling.

I remembered Mrs Howell complaining about the noise of Rick's music and looked at the walls, which seemed to be unclad stone. "I thought music studios were always soundproofed, Eddie?"

Eddie closed the log burner door but as it was glass, the flames could still be seen. "Yeah, we thought about doing it but there didn't seem much point. It's as silent as the grave in here and no one can hear us."

"Mrs Howell can."

"Well, she'll just have to lump it, won't she? It's a big expense, soundproofing a great big barn like this one."

"Doesn't Rick have a proper recording studio in California?"

"Yeah, that's right and quite frankly, we'd be better working there for this album, if you ask me, but he doesn't want to, so that's that. I dunno why he wanted to come to this Godforsaken spot in the first place, but I can't budge him now." He got to his feet with a sigh and wandered off.

I sat enjoying the fire catch alight until it settled into an amber and red heart with just the odd spark lazily careering up the flue. I looked across at Eddie, but he had already gone over to the mixing desk and was flicking on various switches and plugging in his tablet to the machine. Rick, who'd been lounging on the settee next to Percy, smoking a joint, heaved his wiry frame into an upright position and took up an electric guitar.

He plugged a pedal into the guitar and pressed it with his foot with the ease of long practice. "Right, Ed. Let's see if we can recapture the magic, shall we?"

I went over and joined Percy on the sofa. I was looking forward to hearing Rick's brand of music, not really knowing that much about him before, but nothing could have prepared me for the blast of sound that assaulted my ears as Rick strummed his first chord. Percy had also instinctively covered her ears for protection. It was only then that I noticed both the men had headphones on. I waved at Eddie frantically, but his attention was on the mixing desk, as he added a synthesised – and deafening – drumbeat to the guitar solo.

"I can't stand this!" I yelled at Percy. We both got up and went over to Eddie.

Percy grabbed his arm and pointed to her ears with the other hand.

"What?" Eddie lifted one earpiece from his ear.

"Have you got any more headphones?" Percy shouted over the din.

Eddie grinned. It made him look almost handsome. He fished under the desk and drew out two pairs of earmuff headphones. I grabbed one set and passed the other to Percy and we quickly clamped them to our heads.

The relief was profound. I could still hear the music, but it didn't hurt anymore because I could control the volume with the little switch on the headband. "I'm sure my ears have been permanently damaged."

Percy nodded back. We made our way back to the comfy seat and sat down.

More rhythmic noises issued forth from the synthesiser as Eddie laid other tracks over the drumbeat. I noticed Percy's trainers tapping out the beat and tried to resist the impulse with my own shoes, but it was surprisingly hard. The tune the men were belting out was really compulsive; in fact, it was downright irresistible. I didn't know what I had expected, really. Rick O'Shea was a world-famous rock artist, so why had I thought he wouldn't be any good?

The notes from Rick's guitar soared over the rhythms emanating from the synthesiser, making it sound like a human voice singing with full-throated ease. Soon, my trainers were keeping time alongside Percy's, and I forgot I was on professional duty in a barn in a remote corner of Wales.

I shut my eyes and let the music float over me. Memories of a concert I'd been to with Robin, my very first one, came flooding back. I could feel his hand in mine, sticky with sweat and spilt beer. I'd been as slim as Percy then, and Robin's arm around my waist, pulling me against him so our hip bones banged together, made me feel sexy and vibrantly alive. I laughed up at his face when the band took a break and the music quieted for a minute.

He leaned in and kissed me, bringing me closer, holding me tighter. When the music started back up, I was in heaven, my lips pulsating with life, my heart pounding with all the love I felt for Robin. I opened my eyes to see him laughing, throwing his head back in that abandoned way he had, his curly brown hair all over the place as usual, adding to his carefree charisma.

"I love you, Robin." I hadn't realised I'd spoken out loud.

"I love you more." His voice was clear above the music, the northern accent unmistakably Robin's. I leaned back into him and turned to face the stage.

Then something made me blink my eyes and the image receded. There was only one musician playing the guitar and no crowd of teenagers jostled around me. Robin's hip bone hadn't really been bumping against mine. My side was actually pressed into the buttoned round arm of the battered Chesterfield sofa, and no-one was holding my hand. I put my fingers to my lips and found them cold, untouched by anyone else's. I darted a furtive look at Percy to see if she'd noticed, but Percy was looking at Rick and smiling, nodding her head as well as her feet to the beat pumping out into the big room.

Had I imagined it? Was it just a vivid memory, triggered by the song Rick was playing? I didn't recognise it. Was Robin's spirit here now? And if so, was it because we were about to encounter danger from that other world again and he knew we'd need protecting?

None of the others seemed to have noticed. Maybe I hadn't spoken out loud? I thought I had. And I was sure I had heard Robin's rich voice, his broad Yorkshire accent. Then I remembered everyone was wearing headphones. No-one could have heard me talking gently to my lover over the tumultuous noise filling the room as the piece reached its finale.

The chords of Rick's guitar rose higher and higher. The beat of the synthesiser drove the rhythm on into a relentless crescendo of enveloping sound, tearing at my churned-up, confused emotions. Tears pricked my eyes. And then, just as the song peaked, roaring to its conclusion, all went abruptly silent and dark. Suddenly, the only faint noise was the crackle of the logs through the fire-glass of the wood-burner and the only light was the soft glow from their flames.

I pulled my phone out from my jacket pocket and switched on its bright torch. I looked straight at Rick standing in front of me, revealed in its single beam.

"What the hell?" Rick looked comically frozen, the veins on his scrawny, muscular arms, standing out from the effort of playing; his arm held wide in mid-air, the plectrum pinched between thumb and forefinger, poised to strike the guitar string for one last explosive chord. His mouth was wide open in shock.

I swung the torchlight towards Eddie standing at the synthesiser in the corner.

He looked equally dumbstruck. "Not again! Shit!"

Rick slowly, carefully, took his guitar strap over his head and leaned it on its stand with impressive control. He looked like he could barely contain his anger. His mouth, no longer open, curved downwards in a grim curve. His eyes, so recently glazed over in some sort of musical ecstasy, were pinpoints of fury.

"Why then, hey? Why bloody then, just at that point? Why couldn't the power have gone after we'd finished? We only needed one more minute, seconds even, and that song could have been laid down. I've never played that track better. Tell me you got it, Ed? For Gawd's sake!"

I could just make out Eddie's bulky silhouette in the semi-darkness. He'd gone over to the light switch by the door and was futilely flicking it back and forth.

"I dunno, Rick, do I? I can't bloody see nothing."

"But you hooked up that tablet thing of yours, didn't ya?" Rick had joined him now, so I pointed my torch-beam at the pair of them, standing glaring at each other like two fighting stags.

"I, I, dunno, I said. I thought I had but I can't find it now."

"Tell me it's not true. Tell me you've got it!" Rick was losing his control now. Even in the narrow shaft of torchlight, I could see him beginning to shake. His hands had balled into fists.

A punch-up would not be helpful. I got up and marched over to the two men, shining the light straight at them so their faces blanched white. "Look, it's no-one's fault."

Rick turned his blazing eyes full on to my face. I took a step back; I'd never seen anyone so angry, not even Paul Wade at my flat door. Was that only yesterday?

"Now listen 'ere, lady. You're being paid to sort this out. Well, aren't you?" Rick shoved his face close up to mine and a waft of stale tobacco washed over me.

"Then bloody get on and sort it!" Rick turned on his booted heel, wrenched open the door and walked outside, letting it bang shut behind him.

Chapter Eleven, The Isle of Anglesey, around two thousand years ago

Emrys and Gaine did not return to their tribal village for some days, and no one came searching for them. Emrys had let it be known to the elders that he had squirrelled away enough caches of food to last them at least a week.

Gaine, tearing at some dried rabbit meat with her sharp white teeth, grinned at her lover. "I had not thought you devious, Emrys. How long have you been plotting and preparing for this time?"

Emrys laughed. "Since you were born!"

Gaine threw an apple core at him. "I don't believe you!"

Emrys batted it away. "Well, maybe not that far back. Perhaps since your mother died, remember? We were playing 'pick-up-stones' and Bryonia called you away. My heart was so sad when you realised your mother was gravely ill, I knew I loved you then."

"It's impossible to have known that then! You could only have been nine years old."

"I knew."

"And it never changed?" Gaine had not expected his reply.

Emrys shook his tawny head. "Never." He took her hand in his. "And it never will."

Gaine leaned forward and kissed him thoroughly. "I love you, Emrys."

"You are my love forever."

"Emrys, can we not live together after Beltaine? Many couples come together on this night but then live singly again, but I do not want to."

"It is our choice. I never knew my father. My mother would never tell me his name, only that he came from the south, from across the Straits, and visited our village at the time of the Beltaine fires. Sometimes I wonder if she knew it herself."

"Do you mind?"

"I do. I would like to know from whence I came. Whose blood runs through my veins."

"And yet, are we all not of one blood, under the stars?"

"I would have it so, yes. But men seek territory. It is in their warring nature."

"Not in our tribe."

Emrys spat out an apple pip. "No, because they serve the Druids who do not seek to own the land, but they control those who do. There is much talk of invasion in the south."

"You are talking of the Romans, are you not?"

Emrys nodded silently.

"Did you hear about my old vision of the Roman soldier trying to kill me?"

He took her in his arms, with her back to him so his legs wrapped around hers. Gaine felt no one could hurt her while she stayed within the shelter of his shielding body.

"I heard rumours."

"It was true. I was only a girl and often I forgot my vision dreams then, but not this one. It has always stayed with me. Ugh, the image of his face! The bloodlust written clear upon it. His poor horse beneath him, foamed with sweat, splattered in blood and mud..." Gaine shuddered and Emrys clamped his legs fast about her thighs.

He kissed the nape of her neck, parting her long red hair to do so. "I will always guard you with my life, Gaine."

"I don't want you to sacrifice yourself for me, but to live with me always, as my husband. Will you, Emrys?"

"I will be glad to have that honour, my lady love."

Five glorious days later, they returned to their village. They went immediately to Bryonia's separate hut, asking for permission to enter at the doorway.

"Welcome in, young lovers!"

Hand-in-hand, they went inside and Bryonia enfolded each of them in her strong arms. She looked at Gaine. "No child yet, but there will be."

Gaine bowed her head in acknowledgement that her maidenhood had passed.

Emrys stood tall. "We wish to live together."

Bryonia frowned. "You may, of course, do as you wish but you are young yet and I have much to teach Gaine. I do not want her time compromised. It is important that she learns Druidic craft while I am still here to teach her. I would prefer it if Gaine lived with me still, as a priestess, and you go to the Holy Island to learn your destiny."

"But Grandmother!" Gaine started forward. The thought of not sleeping with Emrys every night was a terrible one after the last few days of togetherness.

Bryonia held up an imperious hand. "Trouble is coming, and sooner than I expected. Your time together will come, but I ask you to wait to set up home. You have free will, of course, but I ask this of you on behalf of our people. They will need your skills.

"But can we not live together and learn in the daytime?"

Bryonia shook her head. "In normal times, yes. I would love to grant your wish, child, but I have a special task for you. I ask you to wait until your training is complete and to stay apart. If you are with child, you will not be able to accomplish all that is necessary. I know what I ask of you, but your love will be a true one and I intuit you will have a long life together. But first, you must apply discipline. Can you do that?"

Emrys looked at Gaine, his dark brown eyes brimming over with love, but his eyebrows raised in query. "I will abide by your decision, my love."

So, this is what being an adult entails, Gaine thought. Every fibre in her young body craved more lovemaking with the beautiful young man before her. She knew now what passion lay under his quiet demeanour, the ecstasy of consummated love, and Bryonia wanted her to sacrifice this pleasure just as she had discovered it? To give up being together just as they had fallen in love?

She looked at her grandmother, startled to see the compassion written across her stern face. Bryonia looked as if she knew exactly what she was asking her to renounce, but Gaine wasn't going to agree without a fight.

Boldly, Gaine threw her grandmother a question so personal, she would never have asked it in any other circumstance.

"Have you never been in love, Grandmother? Or has it always been leadership you wanted? Have you never loved someone so much, you would willingly die for them? Or is it only power you seek?"

She heard Emrys gasp out loud at her angry words.

Bryonia inhaled deeply. "I know what I ask. You show spirit in your questions and have a right to an answer. Yes, I have loved. I loved someone very much, but he could not stay by my side, even after your mother was born. He had to journey far away, and I have never seen him since. I do not even know if he lives."

Gaine spread her hands wide. "Why did you not travel with him, if you loved him so much? I would go anywhere with Emrys."

She clutched Emrys's hand, and he gripped hers firmly, intertwining their fingers, just as they had in the passionate moments they had so recently shared.

"I wanted to, oh, how I wanted to, dearest Gaine. That is why I know what I ask of you. Our destinies lay apart. I to lead the Druids and to deepen my spiritual understanding as their priestess. He to fight battles in distant lands. Time has granted me peace and the sure knowledge that I followed the right calling." Bryonia looked at Gaine, her blue eyes flinty with an inner fire. "I do not say it has been easy or that what I shall ask of you will be so. I ask only that you trust my wisdom and foreknowledge. You too have a destiny to fulfil."

"And Emrys? Is he also to be shackled?"

Bryonia looked shocked. "I am not asking either of you to become slaves!"

Gaine's blood ran hot in her veins. She trembled from its heat. "What then?"

Bryonia took one of their hands in each of hers. "I only ask you to wait. Your love is true. It will last. I repeat, I have seen it. Trust me."

Gaine let out her breath. The touch of Bryonia's hand had cooled her blood and calmed the fast beat of her heart. She looked again at her lover, who had never taken his eyes from her face.

"I will wait, Emrys. Will you?"

"Always, Gaine. I will always wait for you."

Bryonia lifted their hands to her mouth and kissed them together before letting their three-way clasp fall apart.

"Go now. Be private together once more before you must part. Come back to me separately tonight, after you have broken your fast and I will give each of you your predestined tasks."

Gaine and Emrys bowed their heads in submission before leaving.

Outside, Emrys kissed her. "Let us go back to our secret nest, my love, and make the most of our last tryst."

She followed him silently.

They lay down on the moss, already crushed and bruised from their bodies, and came together tenderly, slowly, until the waves of passion overtook them once more.

Later, they lay together, heads touching, tears mingling, lips pressed together until the twilight bade them leave.

They parted before the village. Emrys went ahead and Gaine watched his lithe young frame disappear. She was proud of him for honouring Bryonia's agonising request and respecting her decision, but her future looked very lonely without him.

Chapter Twelve, Present Day

In stark contrast to the fog shrouding the Gorphwhysfa Estate when we had arrived, I woke the next morning to find the sun throwing a rectangular frame of brilliant yellow light around the drawn curtains. Unable to sleep any more, I got up and crossed over to the window, gasping out loud involuntarily as I drew the tartan curtains back to reveal the stunning view.

To my left were the satellites of limestone farm buildings clustered in a huddle behind the rear of the main house, with the flagstone yard between them. In the other direction, lay a patchwork of fields already harvested except for one full of tall stalks of ripe corn, standing in exhausted straight lines. The coastline etched a rugged line beyond the agricultural land in the distance, but a hill topped by a hump obscured the sea. I screwed up my eyes to see better and a sharper focus revealed a stone mound, edged with rough grass. An ancient burial site perhaps? That might be worth investigating.

Beneath me, a little track wove between the nearest field and the farm buildings, looking newly bruised by feet and machinery. I wondered if it was the one we'd trodden last night in the heavy mist. It led to a nearby grove of oak trees extending away towards the beach in a triangular shape. The footpath disappeared into the widest group of trees which then narrowed as the land descended abruptly towards the ocean. I could see the water clearly here, over the tops of the leaves, twinkling under the cloudless blue sky above it. I marvelled at the countless tiny waves rippling across its azure surface to the horizon, lending a sense of infinite perspective.

Nestled amongst the first rounded group of oaks, I glimpsed another slated roof and noticed it had a newly repointed stone chimney poking up through the ridge and guessed it was the music studio.

I rested my elbows on the wide, welcoming windowsill and drank in the beautiful panorama laid out before me like an oil painting. How I wished Robin was by my side sharing in the magnificent scenery. I tried to call his spirit to me. He'd come when I'd made my decision to take up this work so why couldn't he reassure me he was here now? I longed to see, hear, or sense his presence with every fibre of my body, but only silence and sunshine surrounded me, one more welcome than the other.

For once, it took a long while for me to realise I was hungry. I dressed quickly in response to the familiar demand and went downstairs to find Percy doing her daily stretches on the rug between the sofas and the log burner.

"Hallo, partner-in-crime!"

Percy looked startled and dropped her elegant pose. "Oh, good morning, Fay. Thought you were never going to wake up."

"Oh, dear. What time is it?"

"Almost ten o'clock."

"No wonder I'm famished."

"There's bread in that stone crock on the counter and butter in the fridge." Percy touched her toes. "And some bacon, I think."

"Perfect. I suppose you've had a disgusting green shake or something." I filled the kettle and switched it on.

"No, actually. Couldn't find anything green so I had an omelette."

"Blimey, that sounds like real food."

"Hah. I couldn't eat much of that pizza covered in all that congealed fat last night. It was virtually cold. So, I admit, I was starving this morning."

"Fair enough, you don't have to convince me, duckie. Fancy a cuppa?" I took a mug from the cupboard.

"Yes, please."

I took down another mug and put a teabag in each. "I tell you what, that view is amazing. Can you see the sea from your bedroom?"

Percy gave up on her exercise, walked over to the table and sat down. "Gosh, yes, it really is something. I adore being near the sea."

"Yeah, I know. I got spooked in the night…"

Percy interrupted her. "What?"

I waved my hand in denial. "Don't get excited. Nothing ethereal, just normal anxiety stuff. Mostly wondering what the hell we were doing here and why we thought we could do this job at all."

"God, I know. I was thinking much the same at three o'clock this morning. And remembering the terrors we experienced last time."

I passed Percy her mug of tea, and leant against the worktop, sipping mine. "Ah, that's better. But then I looked out of the window this morning and saw that glorious vista and thought, well, this has to be better than working in my dreary office counting numbers ad infinitum." No need to mention my sore need of Robin. That was a burden I must bear alone.

Percy laughed. "Yes, it's all rather interesting. I just hope we get paid. We still haven't agreed a fee with anyone."

I turned to the fridge and took out the ingredients for a bacon sandwich. Whenever my longing for Robin threatened to overwhelm me, and it was often, I knew I could turn to food for more earthly comforts. I tried to keep my voice light and positive, scared that if I didn't, I might just break down. "If we can make a go of Spirit Level, life will never be dull."

"No, not dull, just terrifying. I think I'm still suffering from post-traumatic stress from our last encounter. Will our adrenal glands stand up to it on a long-term basis?"

I turned the bacon over in the sizzling frying pan. "Which glands?"

Percy laughed again. "Oh, never mind. Now, once you've stuffed your face, what shall we tackle first?"

I lifted the fried bacon on to the thickly buttered bread and slapped them together, so the butter oozed out, liquified by the hot meat. I brought my plate to the table and bit into the savoury sandwich with abandoned relish. "Just perfect." I swallowed my first tasty morsel and mumbled through the next. "Walk?"

Percy averted her eyes and got up to look out of the kitchen window. "Lovely idea. Let's see if we can have a stroll through those woods and reach the sea. It doesn't look too far."

I just nodded and focussed on my delicious sandwich.

A quarter of an hour later we set out for our exploration. Percy, as organised as ever, brought out a rucksack and packed it with our cagoules, a thermos of tea and, with a smile, some biscuits, no doubt intended for me rather than her.

"Very good work. Always said you'd have made a good Girl Scout. I'll bring this umbrella." I drew out a brolly from its metal stand by the front door. "Very thoughtful of the owners to provide one."

Percy raised her eyebrows. "This is Wales, don't forget."

I opened the door wide. "Dr Livingstone, I presume?"

Percy inclined her head and went through into the sunshine.

I shut the door. "Shall we explore the jungle?"

Percy pointed to the big house. "Don't you think we should pop our heads around the door and see if anyone's there first?"

"Nah, they will be in the land of Nod, I'm sure. They've got our mobile numbers if they really want to find us. Come on, let's head for those woods I saw from my bedroom window." To myself, I added, maybe Robin will be waiting amongst those lovely trees. He always preferred to be outdoors.

Percy inhaled energetically. "Do you know, this is my favourite time of year? The Chinese call it the fifth season - late summer. And this is my absolute favourite weather, too. Crisp, sunny, clear. You feel you can really think straight when it's like this."

I fidgeted with the straps of my rucksack. "Yeah, I know what you mean but I prefer proper summer when it's so warm you can sleep out under the stars." Triggered by an unexpected memory, I caught my breath as a lump formed in my throat. I remembered Robin walking on ahead of me on Roundway Hill that fateful midsummer night so many lonely years ago. Ah, if only he hadn't, he would be here now. He would have loved this new, mad enterprise, being a psychic detective alongside us. But then, that was what had killed him. Fear once again gripped my insides and turned them to mush, making me regret my fatty breakfast.

"Fay? Are you alright?" Percy paused in her stride.

"Yes, of course. Something in my eye." I pointed ahead to something I'd glimpsed through the trees. "Oh, look. A stile. Seems to be calling to us, don't you think?"

Percy frowned but, to my relief, didn't pursue her enquiry further. I shivered under my jacket, wondering why all these memories of Robin kept surfacing in this lovely place without any comforting connection to keep the balance.

Once over the stile, the path descended into the thick patch of woodland. Oaks predominated, and, with their leaves not yet fallen they blotted out the sun, so its beams fell in dappled patterns on the well-trodden path through their tall branches.

Percy kicked a large stone to one side. "My good deed for the day. That could easily trip someone up. In fact, this path looks very well used for such an isolated spot. I think maybe we came this way last night to the music studio, but it was so dark, I can't remember clearly."

I was still feeling unsettled by these constant, too-tender flashbacks to that other walk with Robin and didn't answer.

The woods thickened until I could no longer hear the sound of a distant tractor that had accompanied our walk so far. The birds fell strangely quiet too, as if they were holding their breath, leaving only the rustle of the leaves as they swished against each other in the light breeze, their shadows

73

making the pebbles on the path look like they were dancing under our feet. The composting leaves under the trees lent a damp, fecund aroma to the air. I began to feel a little dizzy. Then, after narrowing, the path split abruptly to either side, forming a T-junction. Ahead of it, the trees parted to reveal a very large, perfectly circular clearing. In the dead centre there stood three giant stones in the shape of an enormous table; two acting as supports with the biggest one laid horizontally across them as a capstone, like a miniature version of the ones at Stonehenge.

Goosepimples broke out along my arms, and I came to an abrupt halt. Feeling shaky, I used the tall umbrella to support me like a walking stick.

Percy's mouth hung open as she gazed at the stone pile. "What is it?" Percy's voice was no more than a whisper, as if she didn't want to disturb the uncanny silence within the giant circle of trees.

I looked around at the massive oaks surrounding the stone edifice, marvelling at their perfectly spaced distance from each other, noticing how exactly they formed their spherical boundary.

I had the fanciful idea that the trees were weighing us up. "I think this could be an altar."

Percy nodded and started to walk towards the structure. "Oh, look, Fay. There's something on it." She went up to the stone table and picked up a bunch of flowers and branches.

"I'm not sure you should touch them." As I spoke, the trees around us gave a sort of collective quaking movement, brushing their leaves and branches together, breaking the profound silence, stirring up the humus-rich air.

Percy quickly placed the bouquet back on to the flat stone above the other two. She dusted her hands from the pollen the flowers had shed and sniffed her fingers. "Smells like normal flowers but they had a sort of energy I could really feel."

I didn't like the sound of that notion, but it confirmed the oppressive sensation I'd felt the minute we had stepped into the clearing. I joined her by the stones and noticed a faint carving on the capstone. Three conjoined inner circles, almost imperceptible with age, danced along its lichened surface. I traced my index finger along their curves, noticing the faintest outline of a circle around the carving.

Percy sneezed loudly. "It's only the pollen making me sneeze, isn't it?"

I looked at her alarmed face. "Of course, it's only the pollen. Don't be daft." I cast my eye over the flowers. "I'm no expert but I think those are herbs, aren't they?"

Percy nodded. "Yes, there is sage, rosemary and thyme and some others I don't recognise. I think this orange flower with the reed-like leaves is montbretia, which is more of a roadside weed. Do you think they symbolise something?"

I walked around the assembly of stones, looking at it from every angle. I wasn't sure what I was looking for. Ancient blood, perhaps? "Yes, I think they probably are. A sort of sacrifice."

Percy went pale. "Sacrifice? Goodness, Fay, do you think that this was a sacrificial table years ago? You know, where people were murdered?"

Another quiver through the trees stopped my answer. Then, out of the corner of my eye, I saw the flash of movement amongst the trees beyond the immediate ones forming the circle. Yes, something colourful and bright amongst the universal greens and browns of the forest. It lasted no more than a second.

I laid my hand on Percy's arm. "I think there's someone here other than us." I whispered the words.

"What? Did you see someone?" Percy kept her voice low.

"Maybe. I have a sense we are being watched, don't you?"

"Yes. It sounds silly but I thought it was the trees."

I dropped my hand. "So did I, but I think it was more mundane. Another person. I can't be sure, though."

"They can't have gone far - they must still be nearby…unless?" Percy's voice trailed off, leaving the question hanging in the air.

I spun around slowly, raking the circle with my eyes. "Unless it was a spirit, you mean? If so, I can't see anything now, living or dead. Maybe I just imagined it. This place has quite an atmosphere."

"Doesn't it just? I sense that this used to be a sort of green cathedral – a place of worship where people have gathered for hundreds of years."

"If not thousands." I hunched the rucksack higher on my shoulders. "Let's walk on towards the sea and get the lie of the land."

Percy pulled her coat tighter around her slim frame. "And get into the sunlight to dispel this strange atmosphere."

"Look, there's a narrow path heading that way on the other side of the stones. Come on, let's go." I started to walk along the stony track.

The woods abruptly ended where the sand dunes began. The sudden blast of sunlight made me blink after the shade of the dense foliage of the oak trees.

Percy gave a gasp. "Wow! That is fantastic! Look at those waves!"

The ocean stretched out before us looking wonderfully blue and benign from the reflected clear sky.

I let out my breath, suddenly aware of how tightly I had been holding it back. "It's idyllic, like a holiday brochure. I'm glad to be free of the woods, aren't you?"

Percy nodded. "Let's go to the beach, I think we can scramble down these dunes."

I followed her down the steep incline and soon we reached the sandy stretch bordering the water. I wriggled off my backpack, which had begun to chafe. "I'm in need of fortification."

Percy laughed. "Go on then, I could do with a cuppa myself." She folded her long legs neatly under her and sat like a svelte pixie, crossed legged on the beach, with the tufted grass of the rising dune behind her.

I poured out two plastic cups of hot tea. "That was a very strange experience back there."

"Wasn't it just? We need to do some research about the ancient history of this area."

"Yes, but it isn't just ancient stuff we need to find out about. Those flowers you found were fresh."

"A cult, do you think?"

I shrugged. "Maybe. Someone must still revere that altar. That bunch of herbs was obviously an offering."

"Could be simply that someone scattered a loved one's ashes there perhaps. Or do you think it could be connected to Rick's issues?"

"Well, if he keeps avoiding the subject how the hell will we ever find out?"

Percy put down her empty cup, unfolded her legs and leant back against the warm sandbank behind her.

We sat in pensive silence for a while, then Percy got up. "Let's go for a paddle!"

She ran down to the sea's edge and pulled off her socks and shoes before rolling her posh walking trousers up above her knees and plunging into the waves. "Oh my God! It's freezing!"

I watched from the shore. "Well, if it wasn't, this place would be crawling with tourists."

"Come on in, Fay! It's wonderful! You don't feel the cold after a couple of minutes."

I stood up, undecided, but temptation won. "Oh, well, why not?" I pulled off my footwear and yanked my jeans higher. When the white foam cascaded over my legs, I couldn't help but laugh. "You're not kidding about the temperature! God, I haven't done this since I was a kid, and even then, not very often."

"Oh, I know!" Percy pranced in the shallow water. "It's so primeval and liberating!"

We splashed about, shrieking our heads off but when my jeans got soaked way above my knees by one particularly huge breaker, I cravenly quit. "Hell's teeth! Right, that's enough. I'm off."

Percy looked reluctant but followed me out of the sea.

After another sip of hot tea, I hoiked the rucksack on to my back. "I don't think there's much point putting my shoes and socks back on, my feet are so wet. Let's walk along the beach till we've dried off a bit, shall we?"

"Good idea." Percy stuffed her socks into her walking boots and then stopped. "Oh look! Isn't that Mrs Howell and her dog?"

Sure enough, a distant female figure, clad in colourful clothes, was walking towards us.

Mrs Howell's long, swift stride soon brought her close. Her dog greeted us by cavorting around us as if he'd known us all his life.

"Down, Derwen! Behave yourself!" Mrs Howell was frowning furiously. The sheep dog gave us a look of utter empathy before returning to her owner's side where she sat, obediently looking up at her with adoring eyes.

"That's better, girl." Mrs Howell stroked the dog's sleek head. The way she looked at us standing shoeless, the edge of the waves trickling over our bare feet, made me feel ridiculously vulnerable.

Mrs Howell nodded towards us. "Still here then?"

I tried to give what I hoped was a polite smile. "As you see."

Percy's smile looked much more sincere. "Lovely morning, Mrs Howell."

Mrs Howell's piercing blue eyes surveyed them both. "Been for a walk, have you?"

I stared her out. "Yes, we've just come from the woods up there. Interesting spot."

Mrs Howell's eyes narrowed, before flicking up towards the grove of oak trees. "Ah, I see."

Percy moved to where the sand was dry and began pulling on her socks. "We were wondering about the history around here, Mrs Howell. We saw an interesting arrangement of stones, laid together like a sort of table – in the woods back there."

I saw the hackles rise slightly on Derwen's shaggy back as Mrs Howell visibly stiffened.

Mrs Howell tucked one of the long strands of her white hair back behind her ear. "Oh that. It's just a cromlech."

"A what?" I took my cue from Percy and started pulling on my damp socks. I didn't want to be left behind if we had to beat a sudden retreat.

Mrs Howell flicked her gaze up to the trees beyond the sand dunes. "A cromlech is an old heap of stones that meant something donkey's years ago. That one is so ancient everyone's forgotten about it."

Percy finished tying her shoelaces and looked up. "Really? Someone had laid fresh flowers on it."

Mrs Howell shifted from one foot to another. "I wouldn't go there again, if I were you. Never know who you might meet. There are some strange people about these days."

I stood up in my newly shod feet and tried to ignore the abrasive crunch of the sand between my toes. "Oh yeah? Like who?"

"Day trippers. You know the sort. There was a murder there once. It's not safe for two women alone."

"When was that?"

"Can't remember. You do ask a lot of questions. I must get going. If you want to get back to the house, there's an easier path over there through the dunes. It's marked and you can't miss it - there's a signpost showing the way. Just don't stop till you get there. The path runs through the cottages, you see." Mrs Howell started to walk in the opposite direction to the one she had indicated with her carved wooden staff. "Come on, Derwen."

I gave her a wave goodbye, but my heart wasn't really in it. "Goodbye, Mrs Howell."

The older woman waved her free hand in response without looking back at us. Her dog did though, as if confused by her owner's abrupt departure, but she was soon dutifully trotting by her side.

I watched them go as the distance shrank their size. "Hmm. She obviously doesn't want us prowling around those woods."

"No, exactly. I wonder what she's hiding."

"Maybe we won't be dealing with ghosts at all but a resentful living woman who simply wants her peace back."

Percy scanned the panorama before them. "Well, who could blame her?"

We walked back to our cottage along the easy path Mrs Howell had indicated and were soon back in its cosy embrace.

"Let's dump our stuff and see if we can raise some life next door." I took off the rucksack and slung it on the kitchen floor.

"Yes, I think we need to really find out why we're here." Percy took a brush from her bag and combed her long hair in the mirror.

"You don't have to worry about your hair, you know. It looks fabulous whether windswept or brushed."

Percy returned my smile with her brilliant one. "Thanks, Fay."

"Come on, enough of the preening. Let's go and see our boss."

Eddie answered the estate house door to our knock. He had a mug of aromatic coffee in his hand and dark shadows under his eyes. "Morning ladies."

"It's almost afternoon." I glanced at my watch, surprised to see it was nearly midday.

Eddie ran his hands across his eyes. "Didn't sleep too well."

Percy shut the door behind them. "Oh dear."

Eddie made himself busy grinding beans and filling a canister with water. Various jets started whooshing steam. "Rick will be down in a minute. He's got an uncanny knack of sniffing out coffee."

As if summoned, Rick appeared in the doorway. He looked surprised to see them. "Oh, I'd forgotten about you lot. Have a good night, did you?"

Percy smiled at him. "Yes, thanks."

Rick gave a crooked grin, exposing his tobacco-stained teeth. "Oh yeah? Can't say I did."

I settled myself on the low sofa. "We saw Mrs Howell on the beach just now. You know, Rick, we need to hear exactly what you've been experiencing because it occurred to us that it could just be your neighbour trying to frighten you because she's fed up with the noise. Isn't the music studio right by the circle of oak trees with the cromlech?"

Rick shrugged. "Can't see why that matters."

Eddie put three other cups of coffee on the table with a carton of milk and a soggy packet of white sugar. "Help yourselves. Have to say, that's a nice theory, but it doesn't check out. There's no way she could have engineered what we've been through."

Rick picked up a mug and stirred in three spoons of sugar. "Nah, Eddie's right."

"So, what normally goes on then?" Percy sipped her black coffee.

"Bloody hell, where do I start?" Rick scratched the tattoo on his left arm. "Last night was no exception and it's the electric going off that really pisses me off. I mean, I love my acoustic guitar, but you can't record nuffink, can't see nuffink without light. It's game over."

"How often has the electric gone, then?" Fay sipped her coffee.

Rick looked at Eddie, who answered for him. "It's got worse lately. Gone off every time we've been working."

"And how long is it off for?" Percy came and sat on the sofa next to me.

"Depends. It varies. Sometimes we can flick on the trip switch and it's okay again. Sometimes, it won't come back on till the morning when we've got up and tested it again."

"That must be very frustrating. But it still begs the question that it could be someone who is very much alive.

Are you on a local electrical circuit? Have you contacted the local electricity board?" I put my empty mug on the table.

"First thing Eddie did, wasn't it, mate?"

"Yeah, we thought the same as you at first, but the Leccy guys said it all worked perfectly. They couldn't understand it neither. Said, sometimes it cuts out in bad weather, but we've had power cuts when there's been no wind or rain or anything that might set it off."

"Anything else happened?"

"Stuff's moved on its own." Rick looked at me and I suddenly remembered the beer glasses in the Anglesey Arms.

"Stuff like what?"

"Guitars, sheet music, microphones." Eddie stirred milk into his second mug of coffee.

Rick lit a rolled cigarette and spoke through a blue haze. "Thing is, it's so disruptive. It's like someone's stopping me trying to record every time I play."

Eddie set down his empty mug. "Look, Rick, we can record it again."

"It'll never be the same. I never took notes nor nuffink."

Eddie stood up straight. "I'll remember it, I'm dead certain."

"But I won't get that *feeling* again, see? It's all about the feeling and I haven't had that since Sherry ditched me. Don't you get it?" Rick stood up again and went to the front door. He wrenched it open and let it bang shut behind him.

"He's very upset, isn't he?" Percy sat down in the chair Rick had just vacated.

Eddie scowled. "You don't say. I'd better go after him." Eddie followed Rick outside.

I looked at Percy. "Are you feeling as out of your depth as I am?"

Chapter Thirteen, The Isle of Anglesey, around two thousand years ago

In the months that followed Beltaine, Bryonia ensured Gaine had little time to reflect on the delightful way she had lost her maidenhood. The chief priestess kept her granddaughter so busy Gaine did not miss Emrys half as much as she'd expected. The day after the May fires Emrys had left their village, escorted by an elder to the Holy Island off the west coast and Gaine did not see him all summer long.

She wanted to miss him, think about him and remember his caresses, but by the time she collapsed into her bed each night in the healing chamber with the other priestesses, she was too exhausted to think about anything but her rest.

She rose daily with the other women when they spent the next hour in silent contemplation of the dawn. Then they broke their fast with flatbreads cooked on hot stones spread with honey from their bees. The other priestesses took it in turns to give Gaine apprenticeship in their skills, which were many and various.

Every morning during that long summer, she and Fion, the herbalist, walked for miles on the wild lands surrounding their settlement. "You must always choose a dry morning to pick our plant sisters when the sun is at its height, cariad."

At first, Gaine simply watched Fion as she knelt beside a particular plant and read its energy. Always Fion would whisper to the plant, stroking its leaves with the tenderness of a lover. Sometimes she would sing a song dedicated to its healing powers. Only when Fion nodded she could join her, would she allow Gaine to pluck its bounty and lay the leaves, roots or fruit in her woven willow basket.

"If you don't respect the herbs, Gaine, their energy will not heal as well."

Gradually, Fion taught her the right words to say to each bush, weed or shrub, which parts to pick and when and, most difficult of all, to merge her energy with that of the plant so as not to disturb it.

Fion watched her carefully, only letting her pick when she was satisfied her sensitivity was right. "Always you must ask the herb if you can take from it before you pick, my child."

Impatient with these rituals at first, Gaine soon learned to revere the character of each herb. Some were generous and gave gladly, like hawthorn and elderberry who each gave of their fruit and flowers eagerly. Others needed to be persuaded, like lily of the valley or broom and Gaine learned this was because their dose must be carefully titrated as too much could harm. It was the plant's warning to healers.

"That's right, cariad. Listen to the wisdom of each herb. It takes time and discipline to hear them."

They would return with their laden baskets to the still room next to the healing temple. Within its quiet sanctuary she learned how to dry or preserve them in honey or vinegar, shading them from the sunlight which would degrade them.

Fion explained, "Sun and rain make them grow, but once harvested, these must be denied to them, lest they fade too quickly and lose their potency."

Gaine loved to see the drying bunches of the herbs, or friends as she now viewed them, hanging in the darkest corner of the chamber, conserving their energies, drawing them inwards and concentrating their properties, ready for when they would be needed by the sick or wounded.

She learned surprising things about those she had always taken for granted as being part of the scenery. Dandelion's flowers ensured the flow of urine, its roots cooled the liver but always its brown resin stained her hands for weeks after she gathered it.

Fion chuckled softly when Gaine tried to wash off the brown dye. "It will not harm you, cariad. It is the mark of a healer's hands, and you should be proud they are stained.

Wait until it is the season for the elderberries. Then your fingers will be purple!"

Fion's favourite plant was the elder, whose rich dark berries made excellent wine to fortify them through the winter and stave off the cold but whose summer flowers, when dried, provided the means to break a fever through sweat. Fion also recommended the white plate shaped yarrow heads and the refreshing aroma of mint from the riverside to bring forth healing perspiration when an infection had taken hold. Gaine loved to mix the dried herbs into blends for infusions and store them neatly on shelves in the healing chamber in their hessian bags once they had finished their drying on the hanging racks.

All summer she learned her craft, making salves from comfrey leaves for bruises or calendula petals for cuts, sealing the clay pots with beeswax from their hives. Gaine learned how to pick the nettle without suffering its sting and to preserve its mineral rich green juices that made bones grow strong and true.

"It is good you learn so quickly, cariad." Fion would say as she recounted the recipes gleaned from past wise women. "And even better you can remember them, for then we can add our own remedies to the lore of our foremothers and teach the herbalists who will come after us."

Gaine had always been interested in plants but now she respected them for their wonderful healing properties, seeing their shapes through new eyes. Fion believed their appearance gave clues to their use.

"See this spring leaf, Gaine? See how prickly the skin is and the white patches on its lung shaped leaves?"

Gaine plucked one, smarting at its bristles.

Fion smiled, "Yes, lungwort resembles the lungs and will heal the grippe. As will this one, that resembles a colt's foot."

Gaine looked down at the cluster of hoof-shaped leaves nearby, hugging the ground in a shady spot.

"This is good for a cough, along with comfrey, a sister of the lungwort."

"There is so much to learn!"

She did not just work with Fion but also with gentle Bronwen who showed her how to make unguents for massage from the aromatic herbs like lavender, camomile and rosemary. As Fion had done, Bronwen always asked permission from the oils she used, and this ritual always preceded any treatment given to those who needed it. Gaine found she worked at a different pace now, taking time to prepare and savour the healing plants she used and the kind women around her gave her daily examples of stilling her mind, disciplining her body, and living in a way that made her feel wide awake in every moment. Now she took nothing for granted but looked upon the rain with gratitude, the sun with more pleasure and appreciated walking amongst the wilderness with a deeper awareness of the valuable pharmacy it sheltered.

When she had learned how to restore tired muscles and bones with soothing, deft movements of her hands, Bronwen and Fion took her to see Bryonia for the first time in many months.

Inside Bryonia's private chamber, the two wise woman bowed their heads in obeisance. "Your granddaughter is ready, my lady." Fion spoke for them both. "Gaine has learned her craft with plants and shown great discipline, patience and skill."

They turned to Gaine, who stood a little behind them and each took one of her hands and extended them to their chief Priestess.

Bryonia took Gaine's fingers, and the two other women dropped their hands and left the chamber. Gaine felt the strength in Bryonia's grasp and her hands began to tingle.

"So, my child, it is time for the final part of your training as a healer."

"What am I to do, Grandmother?"

"Now you must learn to harness the energy from the Gods."

This puzzled Gaine. "How can the Gods come through us, Grandmother?"

Bryonia smiled, though Gaine thought she looked weary. There had been many visitors coming to their settlement lately and whispers of great unrest beyond its confines.

"I will show you, my child. Come, let us sit a while in contemplation, just as you do every morning and for your visions. Now, empty your mind of any earthly cares and let your breath guide your thoughts. Quiet your heart and listen to the silence."

Gaine sat for a full half hour like this and was startled when Bryonia softly broke it.

"Good, that is good. I can see your aura is at peace. Now focus your breath on the middle of your forehead, Gaine. Imagine all the energy of the stars on a clear summer's night pouring their light into that mid-point in your brow. Keep your eyes closed and your mind still, as you have been taught in the seeing circles."

Gaine let all sensations fall away from her and became aware only of the white light behind her eyelids and the tingling feeling on her forehead. She expected to see one of her visions but before any image appeared Bryonia spoke again.

"Now you have the energy pouring into your brow take your mind down your arms and let it focus on the palms of your hands. Let it flow and pool there."

Gaine did as she was bid.

"Can you feel the energy between your hands?"

"Yes, Grandmother."

"Gently open your eyes and hold your palms so they face each other in front of your heart."

Gaine reluctantly opened her eyes. Usually that meant any vision was lost, but the zinging in her hands increased, if anything.

"Now, keep your palms facing each other, but stretch your hands wide to either side. When you can no longer feel the energy between them, hold them still."

87

Bryonia watched her as she let her arms open out sideways to their fullest extent.

"I can still feel it, Grandmother, but my arms won't go any further."

Bryonia gave a tiny nod. "It is as I hoped. The healing force is strong in you. Bring your hands closer together and tell me what you feel."

As Gaine drew her hands in, she sensed an invisible force field resisting the movement, although she could see nothing.

Bryonia looked pleased. "I can see the resistance. Do not make them touch. It is enough. You may relax."

Gaine didn't want to stop. This was exciting. She felt she could do anything with this thrilling energy, if Bryonia would only show her.

"Do you remember what I said to you on the night of Beltaine about your feminine power?"

"Of course."

"It is the same with healing power. It must never be used for evil, only for good. Never forget that or use it in vainglory. Abuse it at your peril for it will turn in on you and make you bitter and full of hate because of its immense power and your ability to gather it unto you. Using it lovingly to help others. You may also use it to heal yourself, should that become necessary. That is one way to apply the self-love we discussed back then. You remember that, too?"

"Yes, Grandmother."

"Next time we shall harness the energy in a more disciplined and organised way, and you will give me hands-on healing using unguents. Then we shall know."

"Know what?"

"Your calling. Now go, I need to be alone."

Gaine got up silently, in the graceful way the other women had taught her and retreated outside. The leaves on the trees were beginning to brown and summer was on the wane. The herb gatherings would be of roots, seeds and nuts from now on and the many apple orchards bore heavy boughs of red fruit.

Gaine wandered to the lake, as she so often did when she had new learning to absorb and drank deeply of its waters. She sat until the circlets of the disturbed water settled again into a calm mirror on this still, early autumn afternoon. She looked at her reflection on its surface and once again focussed on harnessing this new, remarkable energy as Bryonia had taught her. Her red hair was tamed by one single plait, so long she could sit on its tail and her face had lost its early plump youthful contours, and now her cheekbones and jaw defined it.

Then, behind her mirrored image, Gaine saw Emrys. He was kneeling as if keeping vigil. He looked older and had grown a beard. His face looked grave, with new lines creasing his brow. Purple shadows bruised the skin under his eyes. He bore a scar along his jawline that was old and had healed but would never fade. There were grey hairs amongst the tawny red ones and his body sagged with fatigue.

Gaine longed to comfort him and held out her hand to touch his dear, worn face, but the water parted under her fingertips and the image broke into a thousand fragments, leaving her wondering at its message.

All that winter Gaine continued her apprenticeship into the healing arts, learning to discipline her body by fasting and meditation and deepening her knowledge in the process. Bryonia continued to teach her how to harness the invisible energy all around them and finally, taught her to read the runes and learn their symbols. The triskelion remained her favourite and she carved another stone with its three joined circles and pierced a hole in the top so she could thread it on a leather thong and tie it around her neck.

"I am glad you favour the triskelion, my child." Bryonia stroked the pebble around Gaine's neck. "It is the most complex of the signs and, as you can see, I have chosen it for my torc."

"What does it mean, grandmother?"

"It has several meanings, and much of the skill in reading the runes is deciphering what each means in the context of the others."

Bryonia fingered the three spirals carved into her golden torc. "The spirals could be seen as three legs, indicating everlasting motion, going forward, if it fits with the stones next to it. Or it can mean the continuity of life everlasting, that energy continues on and on through the generations, through time. Or it can simply mean the three aspects of life – the earthly world in the present moment, the spiritual world where our souls exchange energy, and the celestial world of the Gods themselves."

Bryonia went to the wooden table. "Come, my dear, let us read the stones for you."

Gaine eagerly joined her and picked up the little pebbles, each carved with a different symbol. She juggled them within her palm, just as she had as a little girl playing pick-up-stones, before casting them across the wooden expanse.

Bryonia drew a deep inward breath and closed her eyes. Then she sat down at the table and gazed at the pattern created by the stones for what seemed a very long time to Gaine, who was brimming with questions about her destiny.

Eventually Bryonia nodded slowly and smiled. "All is well, my child. Your life will be long and for the most part happy, but you will bear many burdens. You will meet your challenges like the brave Druid you have become, and on this earth you will succeed."

"What do you mean by 'on this earth', Grandmother?"

"You are drawn to the triskelion because you will travel in time. Your work will continue long after your spirit has left this earth. Your destiny stretches over many years, my dear, and you will reach many souls."

Gaine, young and longing for Emrys, initially dismissed this forecast, though she recalled it many times afterwards. She wanted to know about the here and now. "But will Emrys be with me? Will we be together again?"

Bryony smiled again. "All will be well, my child. Trust in the future. Have no fear."

With that Gaine had to be content, for she was dismissed to join the Celtic warriors for the next stage of her apprenticeship. These men and women lived alongside the priestesses on the other side of the villagers and kept the tribe fed by hunting for deer, boar and rabbits.

Bryonia's parting words stayed with her a long time. "Prepare yourself with the skills of the hunter. These also you will need. Before the healing come the battles."

Hunting with the warriors of the tribe was as demanding as the more intellectual pursuit of herblore. Her young body toughened with the long days stalking deer and boar and her limbs grew muscular and strong using her new bow and her lethally sharp knife on the trails through woods and over grassland. She learned how to listen for sounds in the undergrowth and trained her eyes to seek movement in the far distance. After a few weeks of shadowing the seasoned hunters, they allowed her to join in the kill and gutting of their prey. Gaine learned not only the anatomy of the game but also the ritual of gratitude for a life given to sustain others, treating the fallen animal with the same respect she had learned to give to healing plants.

So passed the cold months in a never-ceasing round of acquiring new skills, mastering hardships, and overcoming the increasingly demanding challenges set by Bryonia and her priests and priestesses, but of Emrys there was no sign or word.

Gaine was relieved to learn that she would not have to be initiated into the rituals of the elders. Bryonia, when asked about it, said Gaine's work need not encompass the darker arts practiced by them and she need not get involved in the gold or wheat trades they presided over or passing judgements on miscreants. Her skills as a healer would serve.

Spring came late that year, and the harvest was barely sown before Beltaine. Still Emrys had not returned and watching other young people leap over its fires made Gaine long for him and begin to despair she would see him again.

The next morning, she decided to broach the subject with her grandmother.

"Come in, Gaine." Bryonia looked up from her work. Her worktable was littered with rune stones and other seeing tools, and she looked grateful to set them aside.

"Good morning, my lady. Forgive me, but I wanted to ask about Emrys. Will he ever return to us?"

"Ah, Beltaine has made you miss him."

"Yes, Grandmother."

"You have learned well this last year as he will have done on the Holy Island, where the great and good lay buried."

"Will he stay there forever?" Gaine's voice dropped in her anxiety.

Bryonia stood up to her full height and looked at her granddaughter levelly.

"No. We shall need him soon. We shall call a seeing circle tomorrow morning. I sense the time approaches that I have been dreading."

"What do you fear, Grandmother?"

"Your vision of the Roman soldier invading our island of Afallach."

"But this foreknowledge allows us to defend ourselves, doesn't it?"

Bryonia nodded. "Yes, I will call all the tribal warriors home." She smiled. "And that includes Emrys."

Gaine wasn't as pleased as she had hoped. That old vision of the Roman soldier was still vivid in her memory, and she feared for Emrys. She feared for them all.

Chapter Fourteen, Present Day

Coming back from a long walk the next morning, we found Eddie outside the big house, standing alone on a rise in the ground that afforded a panoramic view of the coast. He was smoking a cigarette, a filtered one. I watched as he lit a new fag from the stub he had only just finished.

He seemed to be muttering to himself.

I decided to intrude; after all, we were here to investigate, weren't we? "Wait here, Percy."

Percy took the rucksack from me. "I'll head back to the cottage, I think."

I walked over to where Eddie stood, leaning on the post and rail fence, staring into the distance. "You alright, Eddie?"

Eddie swirled round, looking startled. "What?"

"Just wondered if you were okay?"

He turned back to look at the view. "Leave me alone."

"I'm sorry, just trying to be friendly."

"Don't want a friend. Need someone to sort this mess out. I can't understand why the power went last night. If only it had lasted five more minutes. It's all back on this morning, as if nothing had happened." Eddie sucked his cheeks in as he drew on his cigarette. He shut his mouth and the smoke exited through his nostrils, grey against the blue sky.

"It does seem odd you didn't use back up the power. Have you considered a generator?"

"Tried that – too noisy."

"Ah, yes, I suppose it would be. I thought these days people recorded on computers and they have their own battery, don't they?"

"Yeah, well, I always mean to back it up on my tablet but for some reason something always happens – I leave the charger in the house or find its battery has run down when I didn't expect it to. I tell you it messes with my head."

"Oh, I see."

"Yeah, I expect you can see what a numbskull I've been."

I joined him at the fence and gazed across to the sea. A haze had misted the horizon so I couldn't tell where the sea ended and the sky began. "All I see is a very loyal mate to Rick. Everyone forgets things sometimes."

"Hmm, maybe, but it's happening more and more. Sometimes I think I'm going mad. It's this place. It spooks the hell out of me."

"What a shame. It's so beautiful."

"Oh, yeah, bloody gorgeous, if you like being stranded without any decent shops, pubs, or any sort of normal modern life and sodding rain most days."

I smiled. "I take it you don't."

Eddie ground his cigarette stub into the earth beneath our feet. "You could say that. I liked it in Florida. Lovely climate, at least it used to be. Lots to do. Plenty of babes." He glanced at me sideways. "Sorry, that didn't come out right."

"It's alright, I get the picture." Embarrassed, I turned my face towards the sun, relishing the warm rays.

Eddie shoved his meaty hands in his pockets. "So, you and your friend seem close?"

"Yes, we went to school together."

"Really?"

"Yes, we drifted apart for many years, but we ran into each other a little while ago." I rubbed the bridge of my nose where the recent scar from my squash injury still showed a line of vivid red.

"What got you into this line of business then?" Eddie turned to face me.

I was aware of his shrewd eyes weighing me up. "Couldn't escape it really. I tried. Trained to be an accountant, egged on by my sensible mother."

"That doesn't sound very exciting."

"Believe me, it wasn't! You must know, Rick says you're a wizard at cooking the books."

Eddie grimaced. "He says that because he's too lazy to do it himself."

"That's a bit harsh."

With a shrug of his broad shoulders, Eddie turned back to stare at the view. "You obviously don't know him that well yet."

"But he is talented, isn't he? Everyone's heard of him."

"Hmm, not for a long while. He's just rehashing the old stuff and the band are getting old. Didn't want to come over here until he's written the main part of the tracks. Lazy sods don't want to hit the road like they used to when they were young rockers. That's where the money is these days - live concerts - now vinyl and cds have had their day. People will still pay a lot for seeing their favourite band play again. Mostly, Rick's fans are comfortable middle-aged people trying to relive their wild youth, you see."

I nodded. "I can understand that."

"Yeah, but he needs a new hit. He really needs to reach the young ones – a new digital audience - if he's going to make enough dough. It's digging a deep financial hole, this divorce from Sherry and, um, there's other debts."

"Any kids?"

"He's got two he acknowledges from his first marriage. Probably loads he doesn't even know about – life on the road when he was young – like I said, lots of babes."

"And Sherry is their mother?"

"God, no. She wouldn't let her body get out of shape even for that. She's gone off with her personal trainer. She's obsessed with her looks. He's well out of it."

"Sounds like it."

Eddie winked at me. "Your friend, what's her name again?"

"Persephone, Percy for short."

"Yeah, well, she's a real looker. Just Rick's type, you know."

95

"I don't think she's interested in Rick. She's just come out of a very bruising relationship and it didn't end well. She's still recovering."

"A short fling might be just what she needs." Eddie raised his eyebrows in enquiry.

"Honestly, Eddie, I really don't think so."

Eddie shrugged. "How about you?"

I was shocked, no-one ever fancied me. "*Me*? You must be kidding."

"I wasn't thinking of Rick."

I felt my face go hot and frowned. "I'm not interested either. We're here on a job, remember?"

Eddie grinned. "Thought it was worth a shot. No offence?"

I shook my head, partly in disbelief at the way the conversation had turned. "None taken, but we really need to talk about this assignment. Tell me more about what's been happening. Getting information out of Rick is like drawing blood from a stone."

"Yeah, tell me about it. He just wants to focus on his music."

"So, what was the first thing that happened?"

"It started quite subtly, really."

"Oh, yes?"

"Things weren't where we left them. Windows opening after you'd shut them and doors banging in the night. Didn't think much of it at first."

"And then?"

Eddie screwed his eyes against the strong sunlight. "These power cuts started happening. Every time we tried to record something, and weirdly, just like last night, when we'd really got going. Boom! Power would go off."

"And what about your computer battery?"

Eddie shrugged. "Never seemed to work. At first, I thought the battery was flat or it wasn't charging but then it would be perfectly fine. We'd just had the studio converted from an old barn and installed new electrics so, like I said before, I got some sparkies in to recheck the wiring in the studio but they found nothing wrong."

I studied his lined face. "And this must have affected Rick?"

Eddie nodded. "Bit of an understatement. Listen, I'll come clean. The pressure's really on for him to make some serious dosh. It's not just the divorce. I've, well, let's say, been creative with our tax returns and, Rick doesn't know this, but they've caught up with us here in the UK. Big bill, very big. That's why I persuaded him to come over here. Lay low for a bit."

"So, who owns this land then, Eddie?"

He raised his eyebrows in surprise. "Didn't you know? It's all Rick's."

"Rick's? What, the whole estate?"

Eddie nodded.

"Wow! Then surely, he could sell it?"

Eddie pulled yet another cigarette from its packet. "I've asked him. He won't hear of it."

"Why is that?"

"Look, lady, just take my word for it, will you? He inherited it. Been in his family for hundreds of years. It means something to him. Won't even borrow against it. It's a taboo subject."

"Oh, how mysterious."

"Yeah, well. We all have our secrets, don't we?"

I found myself staring at his double chin. When Eddie turned and looked at me as if aware of it, I quickly looked away and muttered something about lunch.

"See you later then." He looked relieved when I turned and walked back to the cottage.

I found Percy exercising for the second time that day. Her posture looked gravity-defying as she was upside down with her legs over her torso and her feet, amazingly, touching the floor.

"How do you *do* that?"

Percy unwound her body into a prone position and then sat up, cross-legged. "It's not as hard as it looks. You should try it. Does wonders for your core."

"My core? I'm not an apple."

"Yes, you know, your tummy muscles."

"Ugh, my stomach will never retreat. Want a cuppa?"

Percy joined me in the kitchen area. "You know, we need to go shopping."

"Missing your green yuck shake of a morning?"

Percy laughed. "Yes, actually. There has to be a supermarket somewhere around here."

I took my phone out of my jeans pocket to look at a map online. "There's a reasonable sized village not too far away, or we could simply go back to Caernarfon, but I wanted to visit Mrs Howell this afternoon."

"There's no law says we can't do both."

I switched off my mobile. "True enough. Let's go to Mrs Howell's first and then shop."

"Okay. I'll make a list." Percy found a pen, put on her reading glasses, and started writing on the back of an old envelope.

"You seem more concerned with the domestic agenda than helping Rick."

Percy looked up, frowning. "Not at all. He was genuinely upset last night, and I completely understand why. That track they were playing was incredible."

"Yes, yes, it was. I hadn't realised how good he is. I'm more of an easy listener sort of music fan."

"Oh, I like a bit of hard rock myself."

"I'd be careful how you phrase that if you are speaking to Rick, if I were you."

Percy laughed. "Naughty. He's a bit past it anyway."

"Never say never. Had any thoughts about the power cut?"

Percy shook her auburn locks. "Not really, have you?"

"Yes, that's why I want to visit the lady next-door."

We decided to drive the short distance to Mrs Howell's house.

"A quick getaway might be needed." I got behind the wheel.

"Don't exaggerate, Fay. She looks pretty harmless to me, but it would be good to get straight off to the supermarket afterwards."

"Hmm, I don't suppose our visit will last long. She's never been very welcoming." I started the engine.

"How about I do the talking, for once?" Percy clipped on her seatbelt. "I rather like her. I'm a frustrated hippy at heart, you know."

"All that yoga. Can't be good for you." I put the car into first gear, and we bumped along the lane.

"At least it isn't foggy today."

"Yeah, cracking view, isn't it?"

"And this time we can see her house instead of just mist."

"And there it is. Rather eccentric." I put on the handbrake and cut off the motor next to a little white cottage.

Percy peered through the windscreen. "Do you think so? It's very organic looking, shall we say. I got interested in how houses are built when I lived at Meadowsweet Manor, and I'd say this was made of cob."

"Oh yeah? What's that?"

"Shit."

"I beg your pardon?"

Percy laughed. "I'm not swearing! It's usually a mixture of local mud and straw with a bit of manure to glue it all together."

"Charming."

"I think it is. I love the way there's no corners. Look, all the edges are rounded. It's very feminine and I adore the thatched roof. It fits seamlessly into the landscape."

I got out of the car. "If you say so, duckie. Let's go and knock on the ever-so-cute front door, shall we?"

"Sarcasm is the lowest form of wit, you know."

My vigorous knocks on the thick wooden door yielded no reply. "Looks like the hobbits aren't at home."

"Oh, stop it, Fay!" Percy looked quite cross. "Let's go around the back. She's probably in the garden on a lovely day like this."

I obediently followed Percy's willowy form around the side of the house and into a haphazard garden teeming with very healthy-looking plants and vegetables of all sorts.

"There she is!" Percy pointed to a white head of hair amongst the green vegetation. "Hallo there, Mrs Howell."

The white head and beaky nose rose above the artichokes revealing the colourful dress beneath it. "What do you want? Most people knock."

Percy gave Mrs Howell the benefit of her beautiful smile. "We did knock at the little cottage over there but got no reply. It's such a gorgeous day we wondered if you might be in your garden. Gosh, what a lot of fabulous vegetables you grow here, Mrs Howell. You must have really green fingers - it all looks *so* good."

Mrs Howell straightened her back and threw her trowel to the ground. The metal pierced the fertile soil like a spear. "The cottage is let to tenants. My house is over there but the two gardens connect." She nodded her head in the other direction. "I'm rather busy, as you can see."

Percy widened her smile. "And to good effect. I'm longing for some vegetables and fruit. In fact, we're just about to go shopping. You don't happen to sell your produce, do you?"

Mrs Howell's scowl lessened. "I do, as a matter of fact."

Percy stepped a little closer to the older woman, but I hung back, knowing I couldn't handle the abrasive gardener nearly as well as Percy.

Percy looked genuinely delighted. "Fantastic! I would much rather buy from you than a supermarket, Mrs Howell."

"Would a vegbox do you?"

"Oh, that would be perfect!"

Mrs Howell dusted the soil from her hands. "Come with me."

They both ignored me and walked off towards a polytunnel. I didn't mind, I now had the perfect opportunity to explore.

Chapter Fifteen, Present Day

When Percy and Mrs Howell disappeared into the polytunnel, Derwen the border collie trotting after them, I wandered off in the other direction. On the other side of the vegetable garden from the little cob house there was a larger building, a sort of miniature version of Rick's impressive domain, made of big chunks of the local limestone. A neat path led up to the front door, which stood open in welcome. I looked about but could see no-one else, so I accepted the tacit invitation and went inside.

The hall was floored with big slate flagstones and my trainers made no sound upon their irregular surface. On the hall table were leaflets about the area and information about classes to attend. I glanced through them. Mostly they were banging on about Tai Chi, yoga, meditation. I'd dabbled in Tai Chi myself and found it useful to ground myself when the spirits had been pestering me beyond bearing a little while back. It had helped so I had some respect for Mrs Howell's lifestyle.

I wondered if there was a Mr Howell. I hadn't noticed a wedding ring and it had been us who had used the title of Mrs, not the lady in question. There was a noticeboard above the hall table bedecked with posters, most of which advertised various courses run from the house and listing their organic produce for sale. It looked like we could do most of our shopping here as they sold eggs, goat's milk and, surprisingly, pork and bacon, as well as every vegetable known to man.

There was still no-one about, so I wandered into the room on my right. It was a big room, with plants in the corners and plenty of books on shelves, mostly about self-help and written by gurus. A large old-fashioned tapestry rug covered the flagstones in the centre and dotted about on its colourful Indian patterns were yoga blocks. There was a pile of rolled up yoga mats leaning haphazardly in the recess to the side of the impressive fireplace. In the other recess stood a Victorian gateleg table, hosting a kettle and some clean, cheap mugs with boxes of herbal teabags next to it. No biscuits I noticed but a there was a tall Kilner jar of nuts and seeds. No hint of a sugar bowl.

The sash window stood slightly open and shed abundant light into the pleasant room which smelled, predictably, of spent incense, leaving a hint of foreign spice in the air.

No prizes for guessing where the classes were held then. I went back out into the wide hall and into the room opposite. Here, a long dining table, covered in a flowery oil cloth, dominated the well-proportioned space with rows of chairs along its length. Set into the interior wall was a serving hatch, with a trolley laden with plates and cutlery underneath it.

I heard the sound of chopping coming from the other side of the hatch and went along the hall to find the door to what I assumed must be a kitchen. I pushed the door open and found a young man sitting at a small table assiduously chopping cabbage into very thin slices. More Kilner jars littered the table and there was a big bag of salt next to them.

"Um, hello?" He looked at me with big, brown eyes and spoke with a strong foreign accent.

"Hi. I'm Fay. I'm staying on the estate for a bit."

"Cool. I'm George, well really my name is Georg, but I've adopted the British way of saying it. I live here all the time."

"Can I come in?" He looked such a sensitive soul, I didn't like to just barge in.

George half stood up. "Of course, you can. Everyone welcome here. I would shake your hand but is bit cabbagey."

"That's alright, George. What are you making?"

He sat back down and took up his knife again. "Sauerkraut. Is excellent probiotic."

"Is it? Great." The green mounds already compressed into some of the jars looked utterly revolting to me. Percy would have loved them. I sat down opposite him.

"Yeah, is brilliant for microbiome."

"I'll bet. So, are you the cook around here?"

George shook his dark head. "Oh, no. We take it in turns and today is my day in kitchen."

"So, you're having sauerkraut for dinner?"

"No, this will take weeks to mature in the jars before is ready."

"Ah, I see. So, what's on the menu?"

I wasn't the least surprised with his answer. "Lentil bake and roasted root vegetables."

"Oh, nice." I was definitely getting better at lying. "Sounds yummy. Do you have another job? Looks like you make a lot of your own food here?"

"Oh, yes, my job is the pigs. I love them."

"Don't you find it hard to eat them?"

"No, because I know they have great life. I make sure of it."

"I'm sure you do. How many people are here?"

"Well, I live with my wife and baby in cob house by vegetable garden. We have lots of people staying in the farmhouse when teaching courses are on. Then there's Bryony, who runs the place. She is amazing." The brown eyes lost their sad look.

"But you don't come from round here, do you, George?"

His face resumed its sad demeanour. "I come from Russia. Big difference here. I not well when I arrived, and Bryony healed me. Was mountain off my shoulders."

"She does healing, too?"

"Yes, she understands about energy at deep level. She uses herbs too, of course."

"Of course." I cleared my throat. "And you decided to stay?"

George picked up a big handful of shredded cabbage and began to stuff it into one of the jars, layering it up with heaped spoonfuls of salt. I refrained from saying I'd heard too much salt was bad for you.

"I stayed while I was ill and then I not want to leave. Is beautiful here. I feel like fish in water and I can sculpt. Bryony said is part of my healing journey. And then I met my wife, Gwen, and now we have our daughter, Carys. Her name means 'much loved', you know."

"That's lovely, and I'm sure she is, George. You sound very happy."

"Happy, yes, but not so much now that rock star has come back."

I sat up straighter. "Why is that?"

"We can hear his rock music all the time from here. Bryony says it affects the energy grid."

"Ah, I see." I didn't, of course.

George seemed to guess as much. He put down his sharp knife and looked at me earnestly. "You know about vibration affecting auras, yes?"

I just nodded. I couldn't lie *that* much.

George shrugged his shoulders. "Well, then." He picked up the next batch of cabbage leaves and compressed them into the glass jar.

He seemed to think that explained it all and I was now reluctant to show my ignorance. Pride comes before a fall, but everyone has their limit. "It's been great meeting you, George. I'm going to find my friend now. She was with Bryony buying a vegbox."

"Okay. Maybe see you at one of the classes, then?"

"Hmm, maybe. Bye for now." I shuffled off back out into the sunshine, now a little hazy. I ambled around the back of the farmhouse and discovered some chickens happily picking over the lawn and flowerbeds and beyond them a small field, churned into wet mud with a couple of equally contented-looking pigs rootling around it in the brown sludge. A path wound back towards the vegetable patch, so I followed it and found Percy chatting animatedly with Bryony who was washing a bunch of carrots in an old Belfast sink.

Percy turned to me with one of her amazing smiles. It was almost as if the corners of her mouth reached her ears. It was ridiculous she thought she wasn't still photogenic.

"Hi, Fay! Look at all these wonderful vegetables Bryony has got for us!"

"Super." They did look good.

"And there are eggs as well – free range of course."

"Naturally."

"And - I think you will be pleased about this - I've bought sausages and bacon too."

I perked up at this news. "We shall have a feast."

Percy nodded, brimming with enthusiasm. "An organic feast." She smiled at Bryony who, to my surprise, actually smiled back.

Bryony lifted the carrots up from the sink and shook off the excess water before deftly using one of the stalks to tie around the others to create a bunch. "There you are, I think that's the lot."

Percy fished in her Gucci handbag, which was slung across her chest. "I insist on paying, Bryony. It will be too awkward if you don't let me."

Bryony regained her stern look. "Very well, that will be twenty pounds altogether with the meat and eggs."

Percy looked genuinely shocked. "That can't be enough!"

Bryony lifted the box up. "It's what we charge."

I came forward and handed over a twenty-pound note. I had no idea if Percy had any money whatsoever in that chic bag, having just abandoned her marital home and spouse.

Bryony took it in a very matter-of-fact way, for which I was grateful. "Thank you. You can come back for more when you are ready. We usually box up on a Wednesday, which is our delivery day, but I can find enough for you two anytime," she shot me a sharp look, "depending how long you stay."

"I can't thank you enough, Bryony." Percy took the box from her. "Bye for now!" We walked back towards the car and Percy put the food in the boot and we climbed in.

"Well, isn't that marvellous?" Percy clipped on her seatbelt.

"I shall be glad not to be hungry, that's for sure. Did you find out anything about the power cuts?"

Percy put her hand over her mouth. "Oh God, I completely forgot about why we were there! I'm so sorry, Fay. I got so excited about all the organic produce I got a bit carried away."

"Bloody hell, Percy! Your health obsession is not as important as solving this problem. We're here on a professional job – our first one – not on retreat at a spa!" I turned the ignition key.

"Sorry."

"No thanks to you, I did get some info. There's a tender soul living here – a sculptor called George – who looks after the pigs. He's got a wife called Gwen and a baby daughter called, um Carys, I think it is. He came here from Russia in a bit of a state and Bryony put him back together again."

Percy giggled. "Like Humpty Dumpty?"

I frowned. "You just aren't taking this seriously, are you?"

Percy folded her lips and looked away out of the car window as we began to bump back up the lane.

I gripped the steering wheel. "The important bit is George's resentment of Rick's loud music. Said it ruined the vibe and the, what did he call it? Energy grid, or something."

"That makes sense to me, I think."

"Oh yeah? How?"

"Well, if they are all sensitive, they'd want peace and tranquillity, wouldn't they? Especially if they run yoga and meditation classes."

"Yes, but I got the impression there was more to it than that, but I haven't a clue what it is."

"Did you find out anything else?"

"No, and with your sleuthing abilities absent, we haven't really got very far, have we?"

Chapter Sixteen, Present Day

We drove off to the nearest village and stocked up on ordinary items, such as loo roll and washing up liquid and essential ones such as bread – and wine. Then we returned to the cottage to put it all away.

"I'll make some supper." Percy shut the fridge door.

"Please, can it contain sausages?" I couldn't restrain the pleading tone in my voice.

Percy laughed. "Yes, of course. I don't mind eating meat if it's organic."

"I couldn't care less." I uncorked a bottle of red wine and took out a couple of glasses from the cupboard.

We chinked glasses and sipped. Percy made a face. "Ugh, not the best I've tasted."

"It'll do." I took mine over to the sofa and set about lighting a fire. "I don't know about you, but I need to relax this evening. Do some thinking."

Over the welcome sizzle of sausages in the frying pan, Percy answered. "Yes, we do need to mull it all over."

With the fire lit and our delicious meal consumed, we sat down together. I was feeling mellow and replete for the first time since the wonderful feast Percy had cooked me after we'd sent Rose Charlton back to the afterlife where she belonged, but that time Paul Wade had ruined it.

I stretched out my legs and held my stockinged feet to the blaze. "The one person who hasn't said much is Rick and he commissioned us. Don't you find that strange?"

Percy set down her wine glass. "Yes, very."

"You seemed to bond with him. Do you think you could ask him a bit more tomorrow?"

She nodded. "I could try."

"Do you find him attractive?"

Percy stared at the fire. "Sort of, but he's way too old for me."

"Well, he certainly fancies you, so I nominate you to extract info from that source."

"And what are you going to do?"

"I think I might sniff around the farmhouse again. See if I can bump into George, or his wife."

"Not Bryony?"

I shrugged. "Yes, her too. Everyone is so cagey, aren't they? But I can just sense the undercurrent, can you?"

"Not really. Seems like a storm in a teacup to me. It could just be faulty wiring."

I took another sip of wine. "Hmm, possibly – or it could be sabotage. If Bryony and her cronies feel Rick's activities are interfering with theirs, they might be messing with the electrical circuit, despite what Rick's electrician guys said. For all we know, they could be secret hippies in league with Bryony's lot."

Percy put another log on the dying fire. "Unlikely, but unless we see more ghostly evidence, it all comes down to just the power cuts and a few things out of place."

"And yet, Eddie was saying this place spooked him and hinted that Rick has a mountain of debts but although he owns this place, he would never sell it."

"What? He owns the whole estate? I hadn't realised that."

"Yes, but he refuses to even countenance a sale. Strange, he doesn't seem the sentimental type or very Welsh to me. If anything, he has an Italian look about him, don't you think?"

Percy nodded. "Yes, he does with those blue eyes and straight nose. I suppose his hair must have been totally black when he was young."

"Probably. So, the only way he can make some serious money is to make a hit album and do some concerts on the back of it."

"Well, that would put the pressure on, what with his divorce and everything."

I stifled a yawn. "Exactly and you are the girl to find out more about all of that."

We clinked glasses again. "Here's to a successful day's sleuthing tomorrow."

We didn't stay up much longer. The combination of the warm fire and wine had made us both realise how tired we were.

After a perfunctory trip to the bathroom, I fell asleep as soon as my head touched the pillow but later that night, something woke me.

I'd been deep in a dream that I instantly forgot when the sensation of being shaken roused me from my slumber. I sat up in bed and looked at my phone, which I'd left charging on the bedside table. It was one o'clock in the morning. I put on the lamp and saw that the glass of water next to it was trembling slightly and rattling against the base of the lamp. No wonder it had woken me up. I rubbed my eyes and tried to concentrate. Was this infernal noise the vibration George had been on about? Or was there some agricultural machinery thumping away in a barn somewhere? A tractor doing some mad nocturnal ploughing? Then the unmistakable riff Rick had played last night sailed over the thump-thump beat. Nothing ethereal about that. It was just the nocturnal musician trying to lay down that elusive track again.

I opened the bedside drawer and pulled out the small headphones that came with my mobile and shoved them into my ears to try and stop some of the noise. It wasn't enough. I tried pillows over my ears, then cotton wool instead of the headphones but nothing worked. After a couple of hours of torture, as the bass beat on and the riff was repeated over and over again, I resorted to listening to white noise from an app on my phone but that was too uncomfortable. I finally managed to drown out the auditory assault by inserting some soft waxy earplugs I'd used for music festivals.

A few hours later something else woke me. I sat up in bed feeling disorientated, unsure of where I was. I pulled out my earplugs and realised that the place had fallen utterly silent at last, and it was the sudden quiet that had woken me. Had Rick and Eddie managed to record that song this time and called it a night?

110

The darkness this deep in the countryside was almost complete. I leant my tired head against the pillow and lay listening to the blissful peace.

Although I longed for sleep, my brain had perversely decided to wake up. Why were we here? Why on earth had we set up this crazy business in the first place? Who were these alleged spirits Rick wanted us to eradicate? Or should I say exorcise? We were both beginning to seriously doubt their existence. I stretched out in the comfortable bed and closed my eyes in a bid to beckon slumber.

My thoughts turned, as they so often did in moments of solitude, to my beloved, long-dead lover, Robin. The nights were always the worst. If only I could turn to him in a shared bed, hear the reassuring rhythm of his breathing, feel the warmth from his living body close to mine. Tears pricked my closed eyelids. He had come to me so very briefly to rescue me when the ghostly Rose Charlton had attacked me. That vengeful harpy had stayed visible longer than Robin before they had both evaporated that dramatic night at Meadowsweet Manor. I had thought it unfair then and still did. Why could I never summon him? The only man, just a boy really, whom I had loved, heart and soul, and who remained the only spirit I could never see properly, except for that one time. Sometimes I heard his voice with its broad Yorkshire accent and saw rare, brief glimpses but it was always fleeting and frustrating, although more frequent here on Anglesey than any other time since he'd died. Had opening that Spirit Level website unblocked our connection? If so, it was well worth it.

I turned onto my side and drew my legs up into a foetal curve so tight I could hug my knees. Why had Robin been snatched away so soon? I would never love anyone else, however I long I lived. In the depths of my grief, shortly after his death, I had tried to take my own life to join him, but my nerve had always failed. I knew that was why I ate too much. It was a consolation, my sole comfort; the only thing that momentarily took away the pain, and besides, being chubby protected me from the unwanted attentions

111

from any other man, although it hadn't put Eddie off, but his attempt had been half-hearted at best. A sign of a desperate man who was also lonely.

But I wanted no other man, not ever. I wanted Robin.

I gave up on the pursuit of sleep and, feeling my way in the dark, went downstairs to make myself a drink. There were still embers in the fire grate, so I opened the glass door of the log burner and added some kindling. The red glow soon caught, and I put on a proper log. I made a cup of tea and sat looking at the flames. Just as I was beginning to feel sleepy again the wood in the fire shifted, and I debated whether to put another log on and sleep on the sofa in front of it rather than return upstairs.

As I gazed at the flames, trying to make up my mind, sparks flew up the chimney and the wood reconfigured its shape as it settled again. Now, the flames resembled a human face. A trick of the light, perhaps? But no, without adding fuel the flames were climbing higher and the image clarified into the face of a young woman. She looked petrified and was shouting something. I sat up, all thought of sleep banished. I focussed my eyes on the burning apparition. I couldn't make out what she was saying, it was in some ancient language I couldn't begin to understand, but her fear was tangible. She had long red hair and it streamed out behind her, flickering in the firelight as if it too were a flaming torch. Where had I seen that before? Suddenly I recalled the vision I had seen on the wharf at Caernarfon when I had stared at the distant shore. Yes! She had been there too! The chief of the clan had turned and shouted some instruction to the young woman who had yelled back in response. I concentrated fiercely, trying to remember the details, but then, there was a crack, as if sap had exploded inside the log and the fire dissipated into a sullen, almost black heap of ash, taking all its flames with it.

I instantly got up and put another kindling stick on, in an attempt to recapture the girl's face, but it never caught, despite seeming bone-dry, and the fire quietly died as if all the oxygen had been sucked out of it. I slumped back on the sofa, more confused than ever, trying to make sense of what I'd seen. Then I had an idea. I tip-toed back up the stairs to my bedroom, grabbed my phone and switched it on.

Hurriedly, I googled the history of the Menai Straits and discovered that a massacre had indeed taken place there in AD61 when the Romans had invaded Anglesey and slaughtered the Druids living on the island. The atrocity had been committed on the very spot where I had seen the women wailing and screeching at the fighting men in the water. So, it was true. I hadn't made it up. But how did that fit in with us being here? Why had that young woman appeared in the fire? Perhaps the hauntings Rick employed us to erase actually were real? Perhaps they were connected to this ancient tragedy and not just faulty wiring?

I felt a blast of very cold air surround me and jumped into bed, pulling the duvet right up to my neck. A wind whipped up outside and rain hit the window with a vengeance, breaking the uncanny silence. I slid down under the covers and listened to the elements wreaking havoc outside. A faint whiff of smoke assaulted my nostrils before the rain quenched it and finally let me relax into sleep.

Chapter Seventeen, The Isle of Anglesey, around two thousand years ago

The day broke bright, as only a May morning can. Gaine sensed tension in the air the moment she awoke. The moon still gave a white pearly glow over the landscape and the sun had not yet risen by the time she reached the lakeside. Even the Druid elders had not yet risen for their first meditation.

A mist hovered above the still water, hanging suspended in the air as if also waiting for what this day might bring. Gaine felt a thrill of expectation run through her as she slipped off her shift and slid into the cool water, parting the mist with the warmth of her naked body.

Gaine dived down amongst the silken weeds, stroking the silvery fishes that swam past her, brushing against her legs. She broke the water with barely a ripple as she surfaced. She had not long before the others stirred. She waded out of the lake reluctantly, wanting, needing more solitude, more time to absorb the strange expectant mood of the beautiful morning and intuit its meaning.

The moon and the stars had barely faded before she returned to the healing chamber for their collective quiet time. Already fire spiralled smoke from the village bakery, signalling the day had begun.

Sitting cross-legged on the earthen floor, Gaine closed her eyes, again reluctantly. Her intuitive mind longed to keep them open and check for new arrivals. Bryonia had said she would send for the warriors, that Emrys would be amongst them. Somehow, she just knew it would be today.

Normally Gaine loved the start of her long day when all the Druids gathered, young and old, trainees and teachers, with only the dawn chorus breaking their silence. Her energy mingled with theirs and all were strengthened by it. Today, she could barely keep still, or apply the discipline she'd learned this past year so painstakingly and ignore the little itches or pains that could so easily distract her focus.

114

Finally, Bryonia signalled the end of the ritual by softly banging her leather bodhran with the long, carved bone she kept for the purpose. Gaine tried to get up gracefully but in truth, she leapt up and ran outside, grabbing a flatbread hot from the baking stone, not waiting for honey to sweeten it. She kept running beyond the lake to where the ground rose, overlooking the sea to the west, towards Holy Island, towards Emrys. The track to the Druid settlement lay far below her, giving her a bird's eye view of any who might walk along it.

She sat on a tussock of grass, taller than any of the others, facing west, all day. She ignored the insistent pleas from her stomach to be fed, running swiftly to the lake to slake her thirst before returning to the same spot, willing Emrys to return to her.

The heat grew intense after midday and despite all her hard lessons, hunger and fatigue from suppressed excitement overcame her and she lay back on the warm grass and drifted into a doze.

"So, this is how you spend your time as an apprentice priestess, is it? Training as a warrior is a lot stricter, I can tell you!"

Gaine sat bolt upright and blinked at the sun shining directly into her eyes. A dark shape loomed against the brilliant sun, then bent down on one knee, a broad grin across his young face.

"Emrys! You're back at last! Oh, I knew it would be today. I've been waiting all morning."

"All morning? It's many hours since noon. Come, get up and let me feast my eyes upon you."

Gaine took his arm, feeling how much stronger it had become during his absence, and scrambled to her feet. Emrys kept her at arm's length for a few moments, looking her up and down hungrily, like a starving man with his favourite food in front of him. Then he gathered her in his arms and kissed her long and hard.

Gaine, dizzy from sleep and fasting, surrendered willingly into his embrace, kissing him back with equal fervour.

Eventually, they fell apart, gasping for air.

"How I've missed you, Emrys!"

"And I, dearest, beloved Gaine, and I."

"Did you come alone?" She couldn't stop touching him, running her hands along the new beard that covered his jawline.

He kissed her shoulder, already sunburnt from her vigil, making it hot all over again. "No, a dozen other warriors came alongside me. I greeted Bryonia with them but left as soon as I could. I knew you would be here, waiting for me but I didn't expect you to be asleep on watch!" Emrys roared with laughter and kissed her again.

"Must we go straight back?" She longed to revisit their love nest from last year's Beltaine glories.

Emrys frowned, looking suddenly older. "I am on strict instructions to return within the hour. There is to be a meeting of all the people."

"I've heard rumours of Romans on the mainland. Is it true?" She didn't really want to talk about it. She just wanted to be in his arms and forget everything else.

He nodded, taking her hand in a firm grip. They started their descent down to the track below. "Yes, they've invaded the mainland, raiding many villages. Some traitors have traded with them though. Bryonia will tell you all. We must not be late."

Emrys broke into a run down the steep incline, preventing further talk. Soon, they were amongst the other villagers, all gathering in the circle in the centre of the settlement. The Druid elders formed a solemn line behind Bryonia who stood alone in the middle of the murmuring crowd.

It seemed Gaine and Emrys were the last to arrive because as soon as she spotted them, Bryonia began to speak in clear, ringing tones.

"We must prepare for battle, my beloveds. The invaders we have foreseen are at our borders across the water. The warriors must sharpen their spears and make many arrows. The women must hoard their stores, make extra bread, and harvest what crops they can. Dry those that can be dried against a famine that might follow. We do not yet know how long we have before they reach us, so do all you can."

A ripple of horror ran through the group.

Bryonia threw back her long now-white hair in a defiant gesture. "We shall not be conquered. You are Celts and a proud people and we Druids will protect you. Together, we shall not submit to these foreign soldiers but fight them and defend our land."

A huge roar went up and Gaine felt its vibration course through her bones. Emrys squeezed her hand, still held fast in his hardened palm.

Bryonia called Emrys and Gaine to her chamber straight after the meeting. "I have not much time to talk with you, but it is good to see you again, Emrys. I have heard good things about you from your teachers. I know you two long to be together as man and woman, but I cannot allow it."

Gaine stole a glance at Emrys and saw a muscle twitch in his cheek.

"The Romans will be here very soon, sooner than anyone expected. I have a scout who has come this moment with this news, but unfortunately not in time for the gathering just now. Maybe that's as well. We shall see. We must gather our resources while we can, and you each have tasks to do. You will together be responsible for the children of the tribe, should they become separated from their elders. You must take them to the west, where the sun sets, and the elders are buried. Keep them secret and safe from the Romans so that they can preserve our line. Maintain our way of life but do not boast of your Druid knowledge to anyone outside your group. This will be the most important thing

117

anyone will do. I have seen it. Go now. Prepare as best you can. Rest and eat too, you will need all your strength."

The very next morning, Gaine stood behind the Druid elders and the Celtic warriors on the shoreline of the straits, a child's hand in each of hers, aghast at the prospect so suddenly before her. The invasion had begun already, taking them all by surprise before anyone had had time to begin their preparations.

Both the children clinging to her were sobbing, their whimpers barely audible above the keening of the priestesses standing at the shore's edge. Flaming torches revealed the women's haggard, angry faces and the men piling in behind them, holding swords, spears and axes snatched up in a moment's haste.

"Shush, now little ones." But the other children around her clutched at her robes and hands. She could feel their trembling bodies through her long cloak. Gaine inched forward, using the trees along the sandy strand as cover. She could see the soldiers now, getting glimpses of their war-like faces as they approached. Some waded through the swirling channel between Ynys Afallach and the mainland. Some tugged reluctant horses alongside them while others paddled furiously in small coracles in the choppy water.

Then the priestesses parted in the centre of their line and Bryonia marched into the gap created. Their chief priestess was older and taller than the rest. Her hair, streaming out behind her like the other women's, was long and white and the robes reaching to her feet were deepest black. Her tunic clung to her legs in the wind, revealing their slender length. The other women quieted in her presence, looking imploringly to her for the leadership she had always given them. Gaine looked too, hoping Bryonia would have some way of stopping the encroaching Roman army.

Bryonia lifted her fire stick and brandished it about her head and addressed the throng around her. "Do not be silent in the face of this evil enemy, my fellow Druids and my brave Celts. They shall not enter this land, for we shall curse them. Join me in condemning them all to die!"

Bryonia lifted up both arms wide. One still held the burning flame and the other an elaborately carved staff. From her mouth she uttered unearthly sounds. The volume of her curses was so loud, it sounded inhuman. Gaine heard words she'd never encountered in all her years of learning coming from the depths of Bryonia's lungs. Their spell seemed to cast right over the channel of water between Ynys Afallach and the mainland, enveloping the soldiers in its power.

The children stopped their whining and pointed their small fingers at the menacing men. "Look, Gaine! Look!"

The soldiers had ceased their wading and rowing, arrested by Bryonia's curse.

"It's working, Gaine!"

"They're not coming anymore!"

And it was true.

Gaine strained her eyes, keeping them trained on the soldier out in front, standing stock still in the churning waters. Gaine tried to read his horrified expression, tried to understand what it meant. He still held his sword high, but his arm was stationary. In his other hand he held the bridle of his terrified white horse, who was panting like a dragon with long strands of hot air billowing above the ruffled waters from his flared nostrils.

"She's frozen them, Gaine! They are statues, unable to move!" Emrys had come up beside her. He too had young children with him.

Gaine nodded at him without taking her gaze from the Straits. "Are you not fighting, Emrys?"

"The warriors wouldn't let me. My orders are to stay with you and the children, even through the battle."

"The Druids said the same to me. Why have we been given this task and not allowed to join in the fight?"

"I know not. I'd rather be chopping the neck off one of those Roman shoulders."

Gaine snatched a glance at him. "I also."

Bryonia's voice rose to a screaming pitch, and she brandished her staff towards the waters between them and the soldiers. Suddenly a great mist stole up, dividing them and obscuring them from the Roman invaders. The Druids glanced triumphantly at each other and the warriors behind them loaded their bows with arrows, ready to release them at Bryonia's command, but Bryonia's voice never faltered in her incantation and her eyes did not waver from the banks of the water.

"She's brought up the water Gods to shield us!" Gaine knew a desperate moment of hope.

Emrys touched her hand. "Look, the mists have parted. Oh no! They are moving again. Bastards!"

Gaine's stomach contracted. The soldiers rallied as the mists failed. The Roman leader had mounted his steed and now stood tall in his stirrups next to a boat that rocked perilously from side to side, shouting encouragement at his men, stabbing his sword into the air towards the island. His face looked familiar, and with a pang of recognition, she knew it was the ruthless Roman soldier she had seen in her vision all those years ago.

"Seems he's convinced them not to be afraid." Gaine held the children closer to her side as the soldiers, roaring defiance of the Druid's curses, gained ground. Too quickly, the first of them reached the beach and were now running up full pelt to the line of screaming, defiant women who stood first in line.

Gaine turned the faces of the children into her skirts.

Emrys said. "No, let them look, Gaine. Let them see the slaughter of our kin. Let them never forget."

Gaine could barely look herself as the Roman soldiers clashed together with her beloved teachers, the gentle women who had shown her how to heal with flowers and herbs and flowing powerful energy. Why couldn't they use that against this aggression? But nothing could stop these murderers now. In horror, they watched the warriors fight the invaders pouring on to the beach, launching arrow after arrow but none could pierce the metal helmets and breast plates of the advancing army.

These men were seasoned warriors, she could see that now. Yelling back at the Druids, slicing off heads, spearing chests, effortlessly fending off blows from sticks, stones and knives, they set about the people she loved, cutting them down like wheat in the field. The Celtic warriors behind the Druids fought bravely with arrows and swords but the Roman metal breastplates and helmets meant their attempts were futile.

Emrys, tears running down his cheeks, cried out. "I'm going to join the fight! I can't stay and watch like a coward!"

Gaine grabbed his arm. "No! Emrys. Bryonia herself instructed us to guard these children with our very lives. You must come with me. These children have to escape! They are the future. We must take them to safety." Even as she spoke, she heard Bryonia's deep powerful voice above the fray, speaking in their native Welsh. As usual, Bryonia had sensed her need. She had never failed her.

"Gaine! Emrys! Leave! Take the children west into the land of sunset. Go now! Do not waste a moment in delay."

Gaine looked across at her grandmother, the woman she revered and loved and trusted above all others, even her own gentle mother. Their eyes met in a brief moment and Gaine nodded her assent. Bryonia gestured inland then pointed to the children. Even as she turned back towards the sea, the Roman leader took advantage of her momentary distraction and plunged his bloody sword into Bryonia's neck above her golden torc. Red blood spurted in a gush from her artery into his face. The Roman general looked angrier than ever and dashed his hand across his eyes, blinded by the blood of his foe. Bryonia slashed at him with her burning torch, setting the red plumes of his helmet on fire and scorching his face. He fell to the ground but not before slashing his sword upwards into Bryonia's unprotected belly.

She fell on top of him and for a few seconds, Gaine watched transfixed, wondering if Bryonia had, even at the hour of her death, killed the Roman leader and known triumph, but the big man wriggled free from under her. To her utter revulsion, he sliced off Bryonia's head and lifted it up by its white mane, blood still pumping from its sawn-off neck, her golden torc wrenched from it and lying on the ground next to her body. A roar went up amongst his men and they set upon those who remained with even more ruthless vigour.

Gaine screamed out her agony, her revenge, her curses, but the words were lost in the wind off the sea. The little hands clutching at her pulled at her dress.

She looked at Emrys who stood looking just as horrified. Swallowing her rage, she turned to him. "Emrys. We cannot fight these brutes. Come, let us save the children."

He looked at her with wild streaming eyes. "But… the others…Bryonia."

"I know. But it was my grandmother who told us what we must do. Now is the time. Come, Emrys, come."

With one agonising last look at the battle, so obviously already lost, she tore herself away. "Come children. We must escape. Run like the deer with me now, through the trees. Their spirits will hide and protect us. Make no sound but follow me wherever I go. Don't try to think, just run." She grabbed the hands of the two children nearest and looked into the eyes of each of them. "Now!"

Some of them were still crying, especially the youngest, who was barely seven years old. "Silence, Beiric! All of you! Be silent. Save your energy for running like the wind. We are going to the west, where the sun sets every night on the sacred burial grounds, and there we will be safe with our ancestors to guard us."

She set off through the trees, her feet swift and silent. Emrys brought up the rear and the children, about a dozen of them, ran between them. Gaine wove in and out of the tree trunks, glancing back every now and then, but no-one followed them.

"Can we rest now, Gaine?" One of the children was gasping for breath.

"No, not for a long time."

Chapter Eighteen, Present Day

I left Percy to her contortions the next morning. She was in no rush to seek Rick as he never surfaced much before midday, so she was going for the full work out. I was late myself having spent more time researching the history of the Roman invasion and getting lost in various virtual labyrinths on the internet.

So, it was past eleven o'clock by the time I walked up to the farmhouse. The door again stood open and this time a stream of relaxed looking people carrying rolled-up yoga mats, mostly women, poured out. I said hello as they passed me and was treated to several beatific smiles and comments about how wonderful the day was. Had Bryony been dishing out magic mushrooms, I wondered?

The slow trickle of spiritual devotees drifted away towards the car park area. Doors slammed and then the small convoy of cars departed up the bumpy track. I took a deep breath, entered the wide hallway, and peered into the front room on the right.

Bryony Howell was there wearing a sky-blue long shirt and jeans, sitting cross-legged on the floor, a remarkable feat for someone old enough to be a grandmother. Her hair was pinned up in a fetching straggly bun and she had her eyes shut with her hands clasped in front of her. She looked incredibly peaceful. I hesitated on the threshold, reluctant to disturb her meditation.

Without opening her eyes, she said, "Come in. I see you have the sight, but your aura is disturbed. Sit down and explain why you are here - where you don't belong."

Startled by the disconcerting truth of her words, my instinct was to do the reverse and run like hell, so I just stood there in a cloud of indecision.

It was Bryony who broke the impasse. She opened her eyes and stared at me with a penetrating look. Again, something in my subconscious pricked my memory. This woman made me feel intimidated and uncertain when *I* had expected to be the one in charge, questioning *her*. It was deeply unsettling. If only Robin was here.

Bryony lifted her hands and turned them, palm outwards, towards me. Then she slowly lowered them in a mirrored shape of my outline as if scanning it.

She nodded sagely. "Yes, it is your heart chakra, I thought so. You are grieving for a lost one. You lost him many years ago, but you cannot let him go."

How dare she! I had not given permission for this intrusion into my private life. It made me feel even more like running away.

Then it occurred to me that she might be able to reach Robin when I couldn't.

Bryony waved a welcome. "Yes, it's time to come in."

I was torn between anger and curiosity. I entered the big room.

"You may sit." The anger started to win. Who did this woman think she was? But the lure of contacting Robin made me accept her offer. There was no way I was flexible enough to squat on the Persian rug, so I grabbed a chair from the stack in the corner and parked my ample behind on its hard surface.

Bryony didn't move an inch. "Lower your defences. I mean you no harm."

"Can I have that in writing?"

"You use sarcasm as another weapon, don't you? And food as your barrier."

I bit my lip rather than answer that.

"Robin is here, and he wants to tell you he will always love and protect you."

I gasped out loud. She had pierced my armour with this disclosure. How could she know his name? I closed my own eyes and willed my mind to empty and focus at the same time, desperate for more direct communication with Robin.

"He does not contact you very often because he wants you to be free."

My voice sounded cracked and dry as I managed to croak, "Free?"

"Free to love again in this life."

"But I don't want to!" Far from a croak, that outburst came out as a shout.

"Do you not understand that possessive love is not true love?" Bryony's voice had changed and deepened, and she spoke with a distinct Northern accent that I instantly recognised as the same as Robin's.

"But Robin, I don't want anyone else. I don't need anyone else but you." I brushed away the tear that tracked down my cheek.

"It's hard to live alone and you are still young, Fay. Loving someone else would not come between us. Let go and love again."

"No! I will not ever do that!"

"You have my blessing to fall in love again."

"I don't want to!" Honestly, I sounded like a spoiled kid to my own ears.

"No one says you *must*, my love, just that you *can*. We'll meet again whatever happens and I will always protect you until then."

The tears flowed freely now, and I knew he had gone. Bryony shut her eyes and swayed slightly in her tailor's posture on the floor. I sucked in some air and slowed down my ragged breathing, forcing it to come back under my control.

"Yes, breathe." Bryony put her palms together in the praying position and nodded her head as if in salutation.

Could she see Robin? Was she saying goodbye to him? I had to know. "Did you see him?"

"I heard his spirit but did not see his earthly body. He has a kind heart and loves you deeply, more than you realise."

"Don't tell me how much I realise about my own boyfriend!"

Bryony shook her head and re-opened her startling blue eyes. "So much anger."

"Do you blame me? I did not give you permission to pry into my innermost thoughts, into my heart!"

She inclined her head in acknowledgement. "That's true. But he so wanted to communicate with you and, really, are you sorry?"

I couldn't deny it. "That's as may be. You should still have asked me first."

"As you should have done before walking through my front door, twice." Bryony stood up in one fluid movement. It was impressive at her age.

I looked up at her tall figure. "You've been talking to George."

"I usually do most days."

"I'm sure. And, as for walking in, the door was open each time and I took that to be a general welcome."

"So it is to those who have positive energy."

"And I don't, I suppose?"

"Not yet."

"Look, I didn't ask for a consultation, or an interrogation. I came here to ask *you* some questions."

"I know."

Really, this woman was infuriating! "Then, do you also know why Rick O'Shea keeps having power cuts?"

At last Bryony looked discomforted and less complacent. "He is disturbing the energy here."

"But that's up to him, isn't it? He owns the place. Presumably he owns this farmhouse and you just rent it?"

A hit. Bryony darted a shrewd look at me, as startling as her piercing perceptive one. "If you know this, why ask me?"

"Bryony, this community you have built around you – it all depends on Rick allowing you to stay here, doesn't it?"

She got up and turned away before filling the kettle from a filter jug of water. "Is that why he sent you? Are you a bailiff?"

I laughed, releasing the tension created by the unexpected exchange with Robin. "Hardly. No, Rick seems to think that his house and studio are haunted by unquiet spirits who want him gone. He's hired me to find out."

"You're hardly qualified to contact the spirit world if you can't even connect with your deceased boyfriend." The scorn in her voice sounded decidedly worldly rather than full of positive vibes.

"That was uncalled for. It's none of your business but it so happens that he's the only one I struggle to see, and he has just told you why. And anyway, I'm not convinced I'm the right person for this assignment. Maybe it's the police who should be involved."

Bryony whirled round. "What do you mean?"

"Are you on the same electrical circuit as the big house?"

"I've no idea."

I snorted my derision. "Oh, come on, Mrs Howell, you're not daft. You've got your finger on the pulse around here and I'm sure you know the real answer. I can always ask Rick or Eddie so there's no point hiding it."

The kettle came to the boil, and she poured water into the mug. "Alright, yes, we're on the same circuit."

"So, pretty easy for you to trip it out, tamper with it?"

"I've no idea because I have never tried."

"Got George to do it for you, did you? He seems like a bright boy, sensitive too. I suppose his family would also be jeopardised if you were chucked off the estate?"

"You are threatening me."

"Not at all. Just asking some questions. Just as you did with me."

"There has been no sabotage if that is what you are implying. The community I have created here *is* important to me, and I have no issue admitting it. I would do nothing to wreck it, there are too many people dependent on its continuation. We are trying to build a different way of life here. Not just self-sufficiency but respect for the planet, for

128

each other, for all forms of life. It matters what we do. The energy spirals out."

"Oh yeah? And Rick's loud music gets in the way?"

Bryony removed her teabag of herbs from her mug and placed it carefully in a little compost bin next to the kettle. "It disturbs the energy we strive to keep pure, yes."

"Right. Well, as Rick is the proprietor and your landlord, you will have to put up with me sticking my nose in from now on until we get to the bottom of things. I hope we understand each other – may I call you - Bryony?"

She shrugged. "I prefer it to Mrs Howell."

"Is there a Mr Howell?"

"There is not and never has been. I don't believe in certificates where love is concerned."

"There we can agree, Bryony. I'll be off, but I'll be back."

"Goodbye."

I left then, glad I had regained my composure so quickly and not wasted my opportunity despite the overwhelming nature of Robin's message. Now, all I wanted was solitude so I could remember every detail of his words – if they were his. Bryony Howell was a clever woman, deluded perhaps, but smart.

Chapter Nineteen, Present Day

I wasn't sorry when I found our shared accommodation deserted on my return. I filled the kettle and flicked on the switch. As I fished in the cupboard for teabags, I caught sight of a note on the counter. Percy's writing was simple and clear, making it easy to read.

"Gone to the studio with Rick. Come on over. Take the path to the oak tree circle but turn left just before. Xx"

I would go but I'd have a cuppa and steady my shot nerves first. I sipped my hot drink and reflected on Robin's message. Actually, now I'd had time to absorb it, it had been very reassuring. Not because I wanted to go on the rampage for a new lover, but because he was determined to get out of my way so I could, and that was the only reason I hadn't been able to reach him properly. Soppy date. Oh, it felt good to be loved so much.

I had another gulp of tea and felt the hot liquid cascade down my gullet, warming me up from the inside out. And it wasn't just the tea making me feel comforted. By the time I left the cottage and took the short walk to the studio, I was smiling like the proverbial Cheshire cat – the one that got all the cream.

A cool wind had sprung up, and grey clouds threatened rain. I found the left hand path on the T-junction in the woods and picked my way over the churned-up mud to the stone barn we'd visited on our first evening. I was glad to open the studio barn door and step inside its warmth, delighted to see that someone had already lit the log burner. Rick and Eddie were deep in discussion over the mixing desk and Percy was once again lounging on the settee against the far wall. She was squinting at her mobile phone and didn't look up until I sat next to her, shoving her legs unceremoniously out of the way in the process.

"Ouch! I'm attached to those feet, you know."

"Well, put them on the ground where they belong then."

"Charming." Percy settled herself into a different position so I could do the same.

"That's better. Have you been researching some history on your mobile?"

"Yes, I was following up about that invasion by the Romans you talked about before you went out this morning." Glancing across at Rick, she surreptitiously rooted around in her bag and drew out her reading spectacles.

"Honestly, Percy. He's not going to care about your glasses." I smiled at her vanity.

"I don't know what you mean. Ah, that's better." She concentrated on the small screen in her hand. "Gosh it's exactly how you described it when we were in Caernarfon."

"Yes, I know, makes me shiver, even now, and I didn't tell you earlier, but last night," I peeked across at the two men, but they were still deep in conversation, "I saw a face in the fire."

"Did you? That's extraordinary. How did it happen? Did the flames change shape?"

I nodded.

"Wow! Whose face was it, someone you knew?"

"No-one I know but I thought it looked like the younger woman I saw amongst the Druids on the shoreline."

"You didn't mention her before."

"Didn't I? Well, she and the older woman were yelling something at each other. You know, now I come to think about it, Bryony bears a resemblance to that chief Druid – would you call her a priestess?"

"Maybe. Goodness, Fay, do you think there's a connection? Could Bryony be descended from that Druid tribe? I thought they were all slaughtered?"

"Perhaps some of them got away, kept the tribe going through the ages."

Percy stabbed at her phone. "Says nothing about it here only that all the Druids were slain en masse. Dreadful. Those Romans might have given us straight roads and baths, but I think they were like the Nazis – you know – just

131

marching into a foreign country and taking it for their own and killing anyone who stood in their way."

"Agreed but conquests have always happened through the ages. Look at the Vikings, for instance. Bryony's resemblance to the Druidess on the shoreline sheds a new light upon her endeavours, though."

"How did you get on with her this morning?"

"It was strange. She contacted Robin, or rather he came through her with a message for me."

"Oh, Fay, how lovely for you!" Percy reached over and gave me a friendly hug.

I blinked a couple of times before continuing. "Thanks. Um, it was just to say he loved me and wanted me to feel free to live my life without him, sort of thing." I stopped and blew my nose in a tissue from my pocket. "It was nice, actually, but I wasn't very nice to her."

"Who? Bryony?"

I nodded. "Yes, at first I was really resentful of the intrusion to my privacy. Bit precious of me, now I look back on it."

"Oh, don't be so hard on yourself. It is a private matter, and it must have been very disconcerting if it was out of the blue, like it sounds."

"Oh, yes, it was. She just launched into it when I walked in through the door."

"Well, then, no wonder you were a bit sharp."

"Hmm, maybe."

Just then, Rick, who had gone back to his guitar and plugged it in, struck a chord, making my ears frazzle with vibration and killing our conversation stone dead. I fished around for the headphones we'd used last time and handed the other pair to Percy, who seized on them and covered her own ears, giving me a thumbs-up as a thank you.

As further chat was impossible, I sat back to listen to the music, now muffled by my earphones but still discernible.

There was much stopping and starting as Rick tuned up his guitar and Eddie experimented with the beat through the synthesiser.

Rick stopped playing suddenly and looked across at Eddie. "Don't lay down a drumbeat yet, Ed."

Eddie frowned. "I haven't."

Rick took off his headphones. "So, where's that drumming coming from?"

We all looked across at the drum kit in the corner. The foot pedal was banging against the skin of the base drum on the floor, not rhythmically but haphazardly and not in the least bit musical.

Eddie, looking very pale, went over to it and pressed it with his booted foot so the pedal could no longer move. Then, behind Rick, an acoustic guitar on a stand rippled its strings in discord.

"What's happening?" Rick looked across at me.

"It's a poltergeist using energy to move the instruments."

"Can't you stop it?" Eddie lifted his boot away from the drum pedal which immediately sprang back into life, thumping again on the big bass drum.

Eddie jumped away from it in horror. "What's going on?"

Rick put down his electric guitar. "I think it's time you girls showed us what you're made of."

I looked at Percy, at a loss as to what we could do.

Percy stood up. "We need to tune in to who is here."

Rick gave a short bark of laughter. "We all want to bloody tune in, girl."

Still the bass drum beat on and the acoustic guitar thrummed, in a chaotic, unpleasant cacophony.

I took my earphones off. "Who is there? What are you trying to tell us?"

Percy shut her eyes. When she started to sway, I gently guided her back to sitting on the old couch.

"Sit there, keep focussing."

133

She nodded, and kept her eyes shut, as if in meditation.

I spoke to the room at large, while Eddie and Rick stood stock still, listening to the erratic noises.

I addressed the room a second time. "We want to help you. Please communicate."

Percy held up one finger. Gradually the drum and guitar quietened. We all waited in the pregnant silence, watching Percy's serene countenance.

She nodded as if listening to someone and spread her palms out as if they were satellite dishes tuning in to radio waves.

After a few minutes, she spoke. "I hear you and I understand." Then she opened her eyes.

I sat down next to her. "Are you alright, Percy?"

She looked drained but gave a little smile. "Yes, I'm fine."

"What just happened?" Eddie came across and loomed over her but Rick, showing more sensitivity, hung back.

"There is a spirit here. I do not know yet whether it is male or female or its name. I saw a picture of trees but then a fuzzy wall or something around them and a sense of irritation from the spirit."

"What do you make of that, girl?" Rick leant against his tall stool.

Percy blinked and gazed back with unfocussed eyes. "I sensed frustration."

Rick raised his eyebrows. "The *spirit* is frustrated? That's rich! How does it think *I* feel?"

Eddie's frown deepened. "Can you get back in touch with it?"

I defended my friend. "It's not like picking up a phone, you know."

Eddie turned to me. "Look, missus, you're here to do a job. You saw those instruments move. How can we work like this? You've got to do better!"

"Have they moved before in this way?"

Rick answered for him. "Oh yeah, that's what spooked me when I sent you my message in the first place. It ain't natural, is it? So, can you contact them again?"

I looked at Percy who shrugged and said, "There are no guarantees, Rick, but I'm encouraged to have made any contact, quite frankly."

"Yeah, but can you do it again?"

"Sorry, Rick, but I have no idea."

Chapter Twenty, Present Day

When we got back to the cottage, I slapped some slices of bread together to make cheese sandwiches and laced them with generous swathes of plum chutney.

I put one on a plate and plonked it down in front of Percy. "Eat that and no arguing."

Percy still looked rather pale and accepted the food without a murmur. She ate the simple meal silently, as did I.

When she had finished, she looked at me with a determined face. "I want to go back to the stones in the circle."

"Why?"

"There was a powerful energy there – you felt it too, didn't you?"

I nodded. "Very much so."

"I think I might be able to channel that spirit who came through me in the studio just now if we went there."

"Okay, but do you feel strong enough? You still look pale."

"Yes, I feel okay."

"Alright. As long as I come with you."

"I wouldn't dare go alone."

We packed a rucksack with drinks and snacks, and took the umbrella, like the last time. Thus armed, we sallied forth in silent cooperation.

There was no sunshine to brighten our path today. Rain threatened, as it had in the morning, and the wind was cool and fresh.

"Glad we brought the umbrella." I climbed over a stile.

Percy didn't answer but walked briskly ahead of me, looking eager and stepping up the pace.

I chugged after her, anxiety spurring me on. At times like these, an accounts spreadsheet held much more appeal than it used to.

It seemed to take less time to reach the oak circle than before. An illusion that always surprises me when journeys are repeated. Perhaps it's because it is no longer a journey into the unknown - except that wasn't true either.

I stood still and watched Percy as she prowled around the circumference of trees that towered over her. Once she had completed the circuit, she went to the centre of the circular space and ran her hands along the carving on the massive capstone that lay flat upon the two which supported it.

I slipped my rucksack off and let it fall to the ground. I didn't want to be encumbered if Percy needed assistance. She was now standing with both her palms flat on the stone, her eyes shut, and her head thrown back a little, as if she was listening to something I couldn't hear.

The next thing she did perplexed me. Percy took off the hair band from her ponytail and let her hair hang free in a shining curtain of auburn glory. She went around to the other side of the stones and again spread her arms wide, putting her palms flat down on the limestone surface. I watched as a shudder visibly shook her slender frame and she opened her eyes.

Percy seemed to be looking at me but not seeing me. Her eyes were unfocussed and staring. I held my breath and braced for whatever came next.

When Percy slumped to the ground, I ran to her. She had fainted clean away. I went back and retrieved my rucksack and took it back to way she lay, inert and unconscious. I took the bottle of water from the bag and then lifted up her head with my other hand.

"Percy, wake up. Drink this." I held the bottle to her pale lips and dribbled some across her mouth.

Percy instinctively licked her moistened lips and her eyelids fluttered open. "Where am I?"

"Drink." I tipped more water into her open mouth.

It worked. Percy sat upright and swallowed the liquid and then opened her eyes fully and looked at me.

"She's Gaine, a young Druid."

"The spirit you channelled?"

Percy nodded. "Yes, I became her during the massacre you saw. The chief priestess was called Bryonia. Fay, Bryony must be her direct descendant! She called her Grandmother, so they must be related. Gaine took the children away from the battle. Oh, it was grotesque. The Roman soldier, he seemed to be their leader, beheaded Bryonia."

Percy put her face in her hands. I remained silent, content to wait for her to regain her composure and carry on.

"He held up her severed head in triumph. There was blood pouring out." Percy gasped out her horror. "He had already speared her body with his sword, and she had fallen on top of him, burning his face with her torch."

Percy stared at me with a shocked face. "But before that, oh, I must remember." Percy frowned in concentration. "Bryonia said something to Gaine, ah it's fading already."

"Focus, Percy, it's important."

She nodded and her brow cleared. "That's it! She told Gaine to take the children away. There was a young man with her. Can't remember his name. They ran with the little ones, away from the dreadful slaughter on the shoreline."

"How many children?"

Percy shook her head. "I can't remember, it's drifting away. I can't recall."

I patted her hand. "You've done well. It's okay. Rest now."

Percy leaned back against the mass of the stone and closed her eyes again. Soon, she was out for the count. I sat back on my heels and tried to piece the story together. The connection between the two women called Bryony was obvious. AD 61 was a huge time lapse with today's date. How amazing that this woman, what was her strange name – Gaine or something - could manifest over such an enormous gap in years. Almost two thousand. It beggared belief but Percy's report of her experience had been utterly convincing and tallied with my own vision from across the Menai Straits in Caernarfon.

138

So, if Bryony was descended from these Druids, was she trying to re-form their cult or tribe here today? Was that why she was so defensive and hostile? And if she rented the farmhouse from Rick, did she fear eviction from him, now he had returned after so many years away? How long had she lived here ruling the roost in his absence? And just how long had Rick, or his family, owned the land? After all, Eddie had told us that he had inherited it.

Maybe he looked like that violent Roman soldier? A passing resemblance perhaps? Or something more? Oh, there were so many questions I longed to ask both him and his tenant.

I took my thermos out of my rucksack and poured a hot cup of tea. I glanced across at my friend, but she was still sleeping, looking as innocent and peaceful as a baby. An image of Percy coming at me with a rose thorn, drawing blood from my arm, flashed across my mind. Percy, once channelling a spirit determined to exact revenge from the past, was no innocent, passive child.

Not at all.

Chapter Twenty-One, Present Day

In some ways I envied Percy her trip back in time. She had told me so little but had obviously seen much deeper into the past than I had on the wharf side at Caernarfon. And yet the two flashbacks did indeed resemble each other. I leant back against one of the stones, wishing I too could connect with its solid, cold mass and be transported.

Any forced or strained attempts to see further back in time always ended in failure and so it was now. The more I tried, the less I could dissolve into the distant past. Only the present pressed in on me with a thousand questions teeming in my brain. We had to go to Bryony's and find out more about the community she was so fiercely defending. Did she know she was descended from those early Druids? Did Druids still practice today? I had no idea. I flicked my mobile on and searched for information, but the signal was completely dead in this enclosed space.

I looked up at the trees, begging them to tell me what they had witnessed over the years, but even though they looked venerable, no tree could survive two thousand years of living on our troubled planet. So, that begged another question. Who had planted this perfect circle? How old were these silent guardians? Were they replacements for trees that had been planted before – maybe at the time these massive stones were laid? And how had these stones been carried here? Were they indigenous and even if they were, how had the horizontal one been lifted high enough to lay upon the upright ones?

The wind picked up its song and the branches on the oak trees swayed in the strong current of salty air coming off the sea. Brown oak leaves floated downwards, and one touched my cheek in an autumnal caress. The sky darkened ominously; it wouldn't be long before the rain came and gave us a soaking. Much as I hated to disturb her, I had to wake Percy before the deluge. She had proven she was the key to unravelling the puzzle and her getting a chill wouldn't help our investigation.

I speculated on the community based around Bryony's farmhouse. That young Russian, George, had looked pretty vulnerable to me. He was obviously a sensitive soul with a tragic history. I'd like to see his sculptures and wondered if they were any good or just a cathartic tool for therapy. Were there other members of Bryony's tribe living there? She had really thrown me when she'd channelled Robin and now, I felt I had wasted the opportunity to ask her more questions.

A spot of rain hit my forehead. The grove had darkened immeasurably, and the wind was now howling through the trees, making more of their leaves spiral down to fall at our feet. Talk about four seasons in one day.

I leaned across to Percy and shook her by her shoulder. "Wake up, Percy. Come on, wake up! It's time to go."

A raindrop hit her eyelashes and she blinked her eyes open. "Whaaa? Oh, I'm cold." She looked around her, a dazed look on her face.

I stood up and held out my hands. "Come on, mate. The heavens are about to open, and we need to find shelter, pronto."

Percy grabbed both my hands and hauled herself up. She still looked confused, so I held on to one of them and lead her back on the path, not to our cottage, but to Bryony's farmhouse. Technically, I told myself, it was Rick's, but Bryony's sense of ownership was stamped emphatically all over it.

The path took us to the cob house first, just as the rain hardened into lumps of ice that stung and bruised our faces. The flimsy brolly was no match for it, and we bumped against each other as we ran towards shelter.

I hammered on the hobbit-like front door with my wet fist. It was opened swiftly, thank goodness, by a fresh-faced young woman with a baby on her hip.

"Can I help you?" Her voice was soft, garlanded with a Welsh accent.

The baby started to whimper at the sight of us and she shushed it with murmuring words.

"Sorry but we need to shelter from the hail!" I gasped out.

"Come in, please."

The baby immediately started to howl in protest at this invasion but then George appeared from the inner shadows of the small house. "Hello again. Not good weather for walking. Come, sit by fire."

The young woman, obviously his wife, faded into the background, still murmuring to her child, who now sobbed quietly into her shoulder.

"I'm so sorry to intrude," I began.

George held up his hand, which I noticed was covered in white dust. "No problem. Come and warm up. I will make tea."

"Thank you, that would be great. This is my friend, Persephone. We're staying in one of the cottages."

"How do you do? I'm sorry," George turned back to me after shaking Percy's hand, "I have forgotten your name?"

"Fay – Fay Armstrong and my friend is Percy Godstock."

He shook our hands and nodded towards his wife and child. "This is my wife, Gwen, and our daughter, Carys."

"Ah yes, I remember." Honestly, I was becoming a seasoned liar.

George indicated the pair of battered-looking armchairs either side of the open fire and we sat down, after divesting ourselves of our dripping fleeces.

"I will take them and put them to dry." George took our flimsy jackets and went into another room, from where we could hear the comforting noises of cups clattering and the filling of a kettle.

I held out my blue hands to the blaze.

Percy looked at her trainers. "I think we should take our shoes off too. We've made a right mess on their rugs."

I stole a guilty look at the jigsaw of colourful squares carpeting the room and undid my laces.

George came in and saw us. "Yes, yes, put shoes next to fire. They will soon dry there."

I smiled my gratitude. "I hope we haven't chased your wife and baby away."

"No, no. It is time for her nap anyway. Gwen takes a rest at the same time, usually. It is very tiring looking after a baby." He went back to the kitchen at the rear of the little building.

"Your house is very cosy, George." Percy said as he came back with three mugs of hot tea.

I took mine and tried not to wrinkle my nose at its herbal aroma.

"Oh, what a divine smell. What herbs did you use?" Percy had obviously regained her aplomb.

"Mint, vervain, and lavender flowers."

"Heavenly." Percy beamed at George.

I took a sip and managed not to wince at the antiseptic, flowery taste. "Have you got any sugar?"

George shook his head. "I have honey, if you would like?"

"Hmm, yes please."

Back he went and brought out a rather lovely stone pot with a little wooden spoon sticking out of a specially made notch in the top.

"Did you make this honeypot?" I took a generous dollop and stirred it into my tea with the ordinary teaspoon he gave me.

George shrugged. "I do some pottery, nothing special."

"It's beautiful." At least I could be honest about that.

"Thank you. I like pottery very much, but sculpting is my passion."

Percy put down her empty mug. "Wow! You are an artist! What stone do you use – or is it wood you carve?"

"I work with both. I have been chipping stone this morning and I'm a bit dusty." George looked out the

143

window. "See, the rain has stopped and there is a rainbow. It is a sign for me to trust you."

"If you say so." I forced myself to finish my tea. The honey helped.

"I do. I will take you to see my sculptures now."

We scrambled our shoes back on. Mine were warm from the fire but still damp. They had developed an unpleasant smell. I crammed them back on my feet over my sodden socks and stood up.

We stepped outside to see the most magnificent rainbow I'd ever seen arcing over the farmhouse garden.

"The angels are pointing the way. You must be very good people, I think." George strode ahead, as if searching for the legendary pot of gold.

We followed in his footsteps through the extensive vegetable plot and out the other side to a wooded glade. At its centre stood an open timber shelter made from rustic poles containing various tools for woodwork and stone.

"Goodness, what a fantastic workspace." Percy looked around her.

"Is very good spot. I can work in peace here."

"I'm not surprised." I traipsed after his eager steps to the far side of the timber shed and gasped at what I saw.

"But these are amazing!" Percy voiced my thoughts exactly.

Grouped around a clearing in the trees were sculptures of both carved wood and stone. Some were unfinished and obviously works in progress, but others stood proudly on wooden plinths, themselves carved in ornate images of natural things – leaves, trees, flowers and ferns.

I gazed at them with interest. "There is so much to see, George. You are a gifted artist."

"I not make them all. We have many workshops and other artists come to work here too." George went up to a stunning wooden carving of a woman bent over picking flowers, a child on her back, held there by an intricately carved shawl. He smiled at us. "Is Gwen. I love her very much."

144

Percy touched his arm. "Oh, I can see that, George. It's really gorgeous and so is she." Percy picked up a wooden bowl. "What a wonderful shape this is."

"Is for Mabon."

"Who is he?"

"Not person, but ceremony for equinox." George flicked off a yellowing leaf from the kerchief carved on to Gwen's wooden head.

"That's quite soon, isn't it?"

"Next full moon." George looked at us quizzically. "We celebrate harvest together."

Percy nodded. "Oh, yes, I know. They did that in our church when I was a kid. Harvest festival."

George smiled his gentle smile. "That's right. We do same but not in a church." His smile widened and he held up a hand in greeting.

I turned around, surprised – but not displeased – to see Bryony approaching, Derwen the collie, trotting as ever by her side. She was wearing a wide-brimmed rain hat over her grey-white hair and her waxed jacket matched its dark green colour, making her seem part of the woodland behind her.

Bryony stopped in her tracks when she saw us and at first her jaw dropped open, but she quickly shut it tight, so her lips became a hard, thin line. "What are you doing here?"

I stepped forward a little. "George is very kindly showing us his wonderful sculptures. We took shelter in his house during the hailstorm."

"I see." Bryony seemed to collect herself. "George is a very talented young man, don't you think?"

Percy smoothed the wooden bowl in her hands. "Oh, I do, Bryony. This bowl is particularly good. George was saying it was for a ceremony for harvest?"

Bryony positively scowled at this and darted a look of remonstrance at the young artist. "Did he? Well, the meeting is nothing special. Just a little thing where we give thanks for what we've grown. Now, was there something else? Only I'd like a word with George – privately, if you don't mind."

"Of course, we were just leaving anyway." I glanced at Percy, and we started to make our way back through the vegetable garden, past Bryony. I could almost feel her raised hackles as we brushed past her. I looked back just once before they were out of sight - and while I could still hear them.

George looked worried. "I'm so sorry, Bryony. I did not know it was a secret about the Mabon ritual."

Bryony darted a shifty look back at us and frowned when she saw we were still within earshot. She shoved George unceremoniously in the back towards the timber shed and he stumbled a bit.

I whispered to Percy. "Think we've hit a nerve with Bryony about the equinox thing."

"Why? Sounded harmless enough to me."

"Yeah, harvest festival? Very innocent if that's *all* it is."

As we walked back to our cottage, we were startled by Rick roaring up on a motorbike, carving up the wet soil in the process. Great clods of mud spewed out behind him in a dark, splattering arc. The loud engine carved up the peace just as ferociously.

"Watcha, ladies!" Rick halted the powerful bike and the engine growled next to us, forcing everyone to shout over its noise.

"Hi, Rick. How's things?" Percy gave him one of those smiles of hers.

Rick's face brightened perceptibly from its earlier dour expression. "Not great. Can't get that riff right. Never found it so difficult before. Had to get out for a spin before I went nuts."

I nodded towards his steed. "Powerful bike that."

"Yeah, Harley Davidson, innit?" Rick looked at Percy. "Fancy a ride?"

Percy looked taken aback at this invitation. "I'm a bit damp from the rain. We were just heading back to the cottage to change our clothes."

Rick grinned. "What's the point of that if you're going on a magical mystery tour with me, luv? Might as well get dirtier, hey?"

Percy hesitated. I could she was tempted though.

"Come on, darlin'. What's to lose?" Rick revved the engine from the handlebar controls.

Trying to help her out, I asked, "Thing is, Rick, have you got another helmet?"

"I don't bovver with one, so I've got a spare in 'ere." He turned around in the saddle, lifted a helmet from the rear storage box and held it out to Percy.

To my surprise, Percy took it from him and shot me a rueful smile. "Alright then."

By the time I had registered what was happening, they both shot off astride the noisy machine and were lost in a spray of mud and grass as they zoomed away down the hill towards the coastline.

"And then there was one," I said to myself as I trudged back to the cottage and my creature comforts.

As I neared the big house, which I had to pass to reach the cottage, I saw a very swanky Porsche departing down the driveway and Eddie watching it leave from the stone steps by the front door.

When he saw me approach, he gave a perfunctory wave and disappeared inside the building, slamming the door with unnecessary force.

"Nice to see you too," I said to the closed front door.

It seemed I was destined to be alone on this odd day of encounters and I was no further forward in working out what was going on.

Chapter Twenty-Two, The Isle of Anglesey, around two thousand years ago

"The children must rest, Gaine. Night is nearly upon us. We are far enough from the battlefield now, surely?" Emrys looked in need of respite himself. He carried one child on his back and held two others by hand, almost dragging them along.

Gaine stopped running and looked at the assortment of children around her. All were exhausted, filthy and no doubt hungry.

"I have a stitch in my side." Morgan, the eldest girl complained.

"Me too!"

"I have so many blisters on my feet, I've lost count." This from Eluned, Morgan's sister.

"I want my mother!" Wailed little Beiric.

Gaine capitulated in the face of these pleas. "Very well. We will find shelter under that big oak."

The children needed no persuading and scrambled across the tussocks of grass to the massive tree. It held out its vast branches in welcome as they sank down under its boughs amongst the mossy roots.

"They need water, Emrys. I think I remember a little stream a short way from here. Can you fetch some while I guard the little ones?"

"I can, but in what? I think we must take the children to their drink rather than the other way around."

"You are right. We have nothing but the clothes we wear." Gaine looked at Emrys. "Water flows. The stream I saw may start further up, near to here. Shush, now everyone. Listen for sounds of water."

The group fell silent.

"There, I hear it!" Morgan pointed to the other side of the oak.

"Come with me, Morgan." Emrys took her hand and, through the gloaming twilight they went in search of the life-saving water.

Beiric began to cry. Gaine was surprised he had enough energy left. "Where is my mother? Why isn't she here? She would give me a drink from a cup and food to eat."

Gaine gathered the little boy to her. "I am your mother now, Beiric. Your mother bade me keep you safe and I will, I promise."

Beiric's crying subsided into pitiful sobs and Gaine was glad when Emrys returned. "The stream is just a few feet away. We will carry the smallest ones. The others must walk. It is just a few steps, then you can drink your fill."

The children slaked their thirst by leaning down into the babbling brook and drinking from cupped hands. Gaine had never tasted anything so sweet. When they had finished, they all drifted back to the welcome sanctuary of the large oak tree and curled up together. The children fell asleep at once, clutching to either Emrys or Gaine for what comfort they could.

When she heard their breathing deepen, Gaine felt secure enough to talk. "What shall we do, Emrys? Bryonia said to take the children to the west to the land where our forefathers are buried but I have only been there once, for my mother's burial when I was seven. I'm not sure I know the way."

"The sun sets west. Look." Emrys pointed to the blaze of red across the sky as the sun slipped down below the horizon. "In the morning, we just keep going in the direction it has set. I have been there a few times and will recognise the burial ground. We cannot go wrong."

"How far do you think it is? The children are already exhausted."

"I think it will take us two days, going at their pace."

"Two days! We shall have to forage for food along the way then. Thank goodness it is summertime. There will be fish in the river and rabbits and berries on the bushes. I wish I had my arrows but at least I have my hunting knife."

"And I mine but I wish we had vessels for water."

Gaine nodded. "I saw him, you know. The soldier from my vision. Then, I thought he would kill me, but it was Bryonia he beheaded. I think she knew all along he would bring her death."

"Once you are safe, I will search for him and kill him."

Gaine looked at Emrys, whose face was set and stony. "No, my love. Our destiny is to protect these children. They are the future of our tribe, and we must ensure they survive to keep our ways. That will be the best way to avenge her death. I am the only Druid left to pass on the knowledge so carefully taught me. I understand my grandmother's plan at last."

"These children will survive a damn sight better if the Romans are killed!" Emrys said savagely.

"It is not for us to do this. We were spared to preserve our bloodline and the ways of the Druid. That is why Bryonia has made me learn so much and why she kept us apart. This is hard enough with young children but imagine if we had a baby to care for as well. No, Emrys. You cannot take on the Roman army singlehanded. They do not know we got away and we must make sure they never find us. Come now, sleep. Tomorrow will be harder still."

Chapter Twenty-Three, Present Day

Percy didn't turn up for supper, so I made myself a bacon and egg fry-up, revelling in a childish pleasure from the lack of censure. But by ten o'clock, any sense of ease had evaporated, and I was getting worried. A steady rain now fulfilled the morning's showery threats, so I slung on a coat, grabbed the battered umbrella, and headed for the studio along the newly made path. When I tried the door, I found it locked and, after peering through the window, saw that the large space was empty and dark.

Alarm bells started murmuring in the back of my head in stealthy whispers. I hunched my collar against the heavy downpour and headed over to the big house, going round the back to the kitchen entrance. Thankful for a porch over my head, I hammered on the door. It was a full five minutes before anyone turned up and it was neither Rick nor Percy who answered.

"Bit late for a social call, isn't it?" Eddie looked less than friendly.

"Can I come in out of the rain?"

"I suppose." Eddie held the door open, and I slipped through, leaving the umbrella outside.

"Yuck, my second soaking of the day."

"It's Wales, what do you expect?"

I decided not to take my coat off at this lack of welcome. "I'm looking for Persephone. She went off with Rick on his motorbike this afternoon and hasn't come home."

"Are you her mother or her keeper?"

I sighed. Eddie was always grumpy, but this was taking it to a new level. "Neither, but I am a good friend. Have you seen her?"

Eddie turned away and lit a cigarette. Through the exhaled smoke, which went all over my face and made me cough, he said, "Yeah, you could say that."

"So, where is she?"

Eddie took another drag and nodded his head upwards. "She's with Rick."

"Upstairs?"

"Yeah, upstairs." Eddie raised his eyes in the same direction.

"Oh. Are they…?"

"For Gawd's sake, what do you think they're doing?"

"Ah. I see."

"Took your time."

"Right, I'll get off then."

"You do that." He opened the door again. The rain had not eased one iota. I put my head down and plunged into the puddles which splashed up inside my trouser legs, adding to my depressed mood and saturation levels in equal measure.

There was no loud music to prevent sleep that night and yet it eluded me. I finally dropped off in the pre-dawn nadir of the night, only to be awakened by the shrill cries of the birds celebrating the return of the sun. I got up and drew the curtains, leant my elbows on the wide stone sill, the way I had on my first morning here, and gazed out at the sea, looking so deceptively blue and benign beyond the oak trees.

I speculated, as I had for many hours last night, what Percy was up to. Had she deliberately sacrificed herself on the altar of our assignment? Or had she succumbed to Rick's aging charms and allowed herself to be seduced because she wanted to? Had he forced her? No, he wasn't the type, and she wouldn't put up with it. I felt lonely without her company. It was a shock to realise that.

I washed and dressed and clomped down the wooden stairs. For once, I wasn't that hungry and made do with a cup of tea and a piece of toast – thickly buttered of course – I hadn't reformed or anything. Without Percy to conspire with I was at a loss as to how to proceed.

I remembered Eddie's hostile reception last night and wondered if it might be connected to the luxury sports car I'd spotted yesterday. That little mystery needed clearing up. Again, I cursed myself for missing an opportunity last night, just as I had with Bryony, and she wasn't being any friendlier than Eddie. The criss-cross of undercurrents between the two households was becoming almost tangible.

I was still pondering my next step when the door opened and Percy marched in. She looked dishevelled and tired, with dark shadows under her lovely eyes. Her long auburn hair was all over the place, and her jeans were splattered with dried mud.

"I'm heading straight for the shower."

"And good morning to you too."

Percy glared at me, her face flushed – but whether from anger or embarrassment, I couldn't tell. "Don't bloody start."

"I'll make more tea."

But she had gone before I could fill the kettle and soon I could hear the swish of the shower above me. I would have to tread very carefully when she returned.

When she reappeared in fresh clothes, a towel turban crowning her wet head, I made her a cup of tea and sat back to wait.

"Thank you, Fay." Percy sipped it delicately. "That's very welcome."

"Great." I ventured nothing more.

"Could you make me some toast, too?"

"Of course. How many slices?"

"Two." Aha. That spoke volumes. I obediently toasted the bread and buttered it. "There you go."

"Thanks." Percy bit into the toast eagerly.

"Hungry?"

"Stop fishing." She swallowed and, before taking the next bite, said, "If you must know, though I'm sure you've guessed, I spent the night with Rick."

I watched as she polished off the first piece and embarked on the second, before braving a reply. "Yes, I thought so. I was worried, so I went looking for you and saw Eddie who said you were with him."

Percy dusted breadcrumbs from her long fingers. "Yes, well, it was the bike ride that did it."

"Powerful machine."

Percy burst into laughter at that. "More tea, please."

I grinned back at her. "Worked up a thirst as well as an appetite?"

She threw a tea towel at me. "Don't be so bloody smug. Actually, it was great. He's a really nice man, underneath..."

"All those wrinkles?"

"Fay!"

"Well, he's no spring chicken."

Percy shrugged. "Didn't matter. I mean, he's never going to be the love of my life, but he has a certain charm. I like him."

"Obviously." I set down two refilled mugs of tea on the table.

"Oh, shut up." Percy smiled again – a very satisfied sort of smile.

"So, did your, um, nocturnal activities shed any light on the ghosts?"

Percy shook her head and her towelling turban wobbled precariously. "We didn't discuss it."

"Ah, I see. Well, when I saw Eddie, he was rather hostile. He had a visitor yesterday who drove a Porsche and he seemed different last night."

Percy visibly relaxed at the turn of subject. "Oh?"

"Yes, it's pure speculation but it seemed significant somehow. Made me wonder what Eddie's game might be."

"What do you mean? He's really supportive of Rick. In fact, Rick was boring on about how loyal he's always been."

I shrugged. "It's probably nothing. Just looking for a lead."

"Yes, we're not getting very far, are we?"

"No, except for you channelling Gaine. Did she surface when you were, um, with him?"

"No. I was very much in the present, if you get my drift."

"Got it. Well, it's pretty obvious that Bryony is descended from the Druids but there isn't really much action, is there? I mean, all that's really happened so far is Rick being preventing from laying down a track. With you around he's going to be more distracted than ever."

"Not necessarily." Percy straightened her spine and uncoiled the towel around her head. "It might help, you never know."

"So, are you going to sleep with him again?"

"How the hell do I answer that?" Percy got up and towelled her hair.

"Do you want to, then?"

"Can't say I'd mind." Percy gave me a smug smile and disappeared back upstairs.

Life is strange. I certainly hadn't anticipated this turn of events and reflected that I didn't actually know Percy that well. There had been many intervening years we had lived our own separate lives between our time at school and the dramas that had played out in Meadowsweet Manor. I decided I'd have to reset the dial on my assessment of my business partner.

She reappeared with blow-dried locks a little later looking much like her normal well-groomed self.

"No yoga workout this morning or perhaps a nap might be more appropriate?"

Percy looked askance at my remark. "Drop it, Fay. You're not as funny as you think."

"Ouch!" I felt ridiculously hurt at this rejoinder and rather deflated. Perhaps my affection for Percy had been misplaced after all.

Percy rushed over to me and hugged me. "I'm sorry, that was uncalled for. I'm a bit tired."

I blinked rapidly before she released me. I didn't want my vulnerability on display. "That's okay, I'm very aware not everyone gets my brand of humour."

155

"I love your jokes. Now, let's make a plan for what we'll do next, shall we?"

I cleared my throat. "Fine, you start."

"I need to go back to the stone circle. That's definitely where I'm more likely to connect with Gaine." Percy seemed surprisingly full of energy now.

"Okay. That's easily managed. At least you don't appear to be an avenging fury when you channel her."

"No, she's no Rose Charlton."

"That's a relief. I think another visit to George might a good idea as well. He's far more open than Bryony and might reveal a bit more about what they're up to."

Percy tucked a strand of shiny hair behind her ear. "Yes, but only Bryony would know anything about her personal history – who she is descended from."

I let out a long sigh. "And she might not even know it herself, but I'm sure she's hiding something. I've never met anyone so defensive."

"Right. I'll pack the rucksack and you fetch the coats and umbrella."

"That umbrella is falling apart."

Percy laughed. "Let's bring it, if only to prevent any rain falling. If we don't, we're bound to have a downpour."

Chapter Twenty-Four, The Isle of Anglesey, around two thousand years ago

Sand burrowed its way between Gaine's toes as she scoured the beach for mussels with, as ever, one eye on the horizon for invaders. It had been ten years now since they had found sanctuary next to the old burial ground on the western coast of Ynys Afallach, but the threat of discovery never left her.

A few times in those years, Emrys, who patrolled the headland every day, spotted Irish boats sailing around the coast, and once, a Roman ship. Each time he had quietly alerted the community and they had put out their fires and retreated into the cave next to the beach. Their small village lay in a deceptive cleft of the hill that sloped down a valley to the sea. From a boat, it would be invisible except for any smoke spiralling up into the sky. Gaine never forgot the ever-present danger. The Romans, even though they had slain the rest of her tribe on Ynys Afallach, had soon retreated back to the mainland. A travelling bard had told them the queen of the Iceni, called Boudica, had drawn them south to fight her. Just as with Bryonia, she had lost the battle and soon after, the Roman soldiers had publicly raped both her daughters in front of her in revenge. Gaine hated them even more as the bard continued his tale.

Boudica's husband, the local king, had died. During his lifetime their lives had changed little except for the added luxury of the Romans providing security from raiding tribes elsewhere. Gaine had listened to the travelling bard with a creeping cold anger when he explained what had happened next. As part of the deal struck with the Romans, Boudica was expected to give up local rule and all the lands that should have been bequeathed to her upon her husband's death. This territory had been signed away when the deal was struck for peace. The bard told them the Romans were doing this everywhere they had conquered and now they owned the majority of land in Britain.

"But not Ynys Afallach." Gaine had almost spat out the words.

Emrys had sighed. "Not yet but they will return."

Gaine made sure there were always supplies in the rear of the cave. It had a natural path curving down the rockface, wide enough for two people to walk to its entrance side by side but invisible from a boat or even the land, as the ground rose up above it, obscuring it from view. The Druids had used it as a mortuary cave before they buried their dead in the nearby cairn. The big cave went deep into the cliffside where it remained dry and above sea level. A spring from the land meandered through a different corner of the cavern, providing a constant source of fresh water. Whenever a ship was sighted, she would help Emrys gather up the youngsters in their care and take refuge in there. The constant supply of drinking water and the dried goods she left on a shelf at the back of the cave meant they would never starve. She would never forget the thirst and hunger they had suffered on the arduous journey to their westerly haven with the frightened children as they escaped from that dreadful massacre. Those children had grown up healthy and strong. Not one had died in the last ten years due to her care. Bryonia would have been proud of her. It gave her great comfort to know that her Celtic line remained unbroken, and she had kept her vow to her grandmother to teach them at least some of the wisdom left behind by her Druid teachers.

When she had gathered enough mussels in her reed basket for supper, Gaine stood a moment, looking out over the ocean. The sun warmed her cheeks, and she lifted her face to the sea breeze, inhaling the salt air. May time again. She must build a Beltaine fire tomorrow for Morgan and Rhys.

Gaine spread her hand over her swelling belly. Their little community was growing. Her daughter, Dryadd, was already seven years old and running with the older children.

She splashed her feet in a rock pool to rid them of the gritty sand and clumsily, because of both her burdens, clambered over the rocks on to the green sward above them.

158

She walked through the burgeoning circular oak grove on her way back home. The young trees stood way above her head now. It always lifted her heart to see the saplings facing each other as if holding hands in a circle dance, pushing their way skywards towards the sun which gave them life. Soon the trees would completely hide their little settlement and she would feel all the safer. Gaine brushed each tree with her spare hand, whispering blessings on each one and feeling their young energy growing stronger, bringing more protection every day. She came here every morning at dawn for her quiet time, willing the energy shield to build and build, calling on her ancestors for protection and healing.

Often, she saw Bryonia in her mind's eye. Always her grandmother's message brought hope and encouragement. She gave her the strength to carry on. Only Bryonia would have understood the weight of the burden she carried every day of her life.

Gaine took one last loving look at the oak trees before passing through the landward exit to the path she had planted with quick setting hawthorn trees and elders. Both these trees bore fruits that healed. Hawthorn for strengthening the heart and elder for easing fevers and rheumatic pain. The leaves of the hawthorn filled an empty belly in springtime and its blossom signalled the season of Beltaine. She hoped she would never have to use the bitter sloe berries in ritual punishment. Neither would she continue with the sacrifice of human blood undertaken by some of the elders. She had never partaken of those ceremonies, having been directed to the healing arts, and she had no desire to preserve this particular legacy of the Druid elders.

She shivered, despite the warmth of the day. She closed her eyes and raised her face once more to the sun to dispel her sombre mood. When she opened them, she saw only the path frothing with fragrant blooms. Gaine inhaled their scent as she walked past these plant friends. The priestesses who had taught her this knowledge often whispered their wisdom through her thoughts and she remembered each one with great fondness, but the anger she felt at their collective murder by the Roman soldiers never left her. It lay, like a smouldering fire within her, just waiting for a spark to set it aflame.

As she entered the circle of stone huts, built with their own hands from stones from the beach and cliff, and now almost hidden by more growing woodland, Emrys descended the hill above and joined her.

He kissed her and stroked her rounded stomach. "All is well above, my love. Here, let me carry that basket of sea harvest."

She kissed him back, grateful for his constant care. "We must build a Beltaine fire, Emrys. Morgan and Rhys are ready, I think."

He chuckled. "Rhys made me very aware of that! There will be more children soon."

"And why not? Is that not why we were spared?"

Emrys nodded. "I have heard more rumours of Romans on the mainland. The Ordovice tribe have risen up against them."

"Good for them! The other tribes have just rolled over and submitted to those conquering bastards. I hate the way their chiefs pay the Romans taxes, then allow these invaders to walk all over them, taking over their territory when they pass into the Underworld."

"I fear it could affect us."

"How so? The straits lie between us and their fields of sheep."

Emrys shrugged. "It makes me uneasy. Maybe the other tribes are right. They have trade through the Romans, don't they? And peace!"

Gaine dropped his hand. "Have you not forgotten what they did to Bryonia and to Boudica? I, for one, shall never forget!"

Gaine snatched back her basket and strode to their hut. She stoked up the fire and poured seawater and seaweed into the black depths of the cauldron hanging above it on a

160

tripod, then she sat down to peel off the mussel beards with her hunting knife, always kept sharp and ready.

"Don't point that blade at me, Gaine." Emrys joined her and picked up a mussel to clean.

"Then don't talk to me of peace with the Romans. Leave me to my woman's work. Go and build a Beltaine fire so we can create more Celts who will fight these cruel, greedy Romans in the future."

Chapter Twenty-Five, Present Day

The oak grove looked different today with sunshine dappling through the trees and no wind to ruffle their branches. Yesterday's storms had stripped away many leaves and under our feet lay a carpet of yellow, amber and gold. The place was quiet, exhausted from the storm and content to rest and heal itself.

Percy surprised me again that day by laying, full length, on the horizontal stone in the centre of the circular space.

"What are you playing at? Inviting sacrifice?" I felt uneasy at her passive posture.

"Kind of. I want to signal I'm ready to play host to Gaine. It was so interesting last time and yet I can recall so little. I confess I'm curious to go back."

"Be careful, Percy. Make sure you return."

But it was I who travelled back in time as I slipped to the ground under an irrepressible pressure. The shafts of sunlight through the canopy of trees fused into each other, obscuring my vision until a different scene enveloped me.

At first, I thought time had not shifted. I was still in a circular grassy space, surrounded by oak trees. I looked up at the leafy canopy and realised these trees were younger, greener, their leaves unfurling in spring, not drying out at the end of summer.

A tall, slim woman, wearing a black tunic against which her mane of pure white hair made a stark contrast, stood in the centre of the circle. Her eyes were closed, and her arms outstretched, as if in supplication. With a shock, I realised the cromlech wasn't there, but a simple standing stone stood upright behind her, covered in a beautiful carving of three interlinking circles, just like the capstone here in the present day. A brazier burned brightly beside her smelling of incense and next to that stood a broad wooden stump, its surface smoothed flat and laid out with rune stones.

With her eyes closed, I felt no immediate connection to the older woman, whose gaunt features looked stern and disciplined, not unlike Bryony's. I sat quietly, unafraid and content to watch anything that might transpire.

I surmised that the woman must have been important. She wore a gold necklace flat against the base of her throat, embossed with the same symbol, and an elaborately carved staff stood propped against the stone.

Fascinated, I gazed in awe as she began to chant and I saw the air around her shimmer, as if she was radiating heat. This must surely be the Druidess leader I had seen being massacred. Well, if so, she looked very much alive. The priestess made gestures with her arms, lifting them high, then drawing them down, as if pulling something towards her heart. Her voice, already strong, grew louder and deeper. I almost felt the sound vibrate in my ribcage, the way you do when the music is too loud at a concert, but this woman had no artificial amplification, just her impressive voice.

She opened her eyes and turned to pick up her heavy staff. Then, she pointed it at me, and I looked into her amazingly blue eyes. I didn't flinch from her direct gaze, I still did not feel fear, but I smiled at her. She planted the staff on the ground, vertically in front of her. Was this acceptance?

She spoke to me in a language I found totally incomprehensible, but I didn't drop my gaze. I shrugged, splaying my arms out to indicate I didn't understand. The priestess dropped her staff once more and used both her hands to beckon me over.

I got up, as if in a trance, and walked towards her. When I stood within touching distance, she lifted her lean, strong arms and placed them on my shoulders. Now, I stood looking directly into those commanding eyes.

She spoke again, more softly now, nodding her head and smiling, pointing to her chest, saying something that sounded like 'Bryonia'. She dropped one hand from my shoulder and pointed to the trees with the other in a broad

163

circular brush stroke. Then she pointed away from the circle, towards the west, nodding gravely.

Oh, if only I could ask her questions in my own language! I could solve the entire mystery of what was happening here, or was it here? I looked around me again, following the direction of her pointing hand, noticing different aspects of the landscape. A boulder here, a hawthorn tree there, and a path in a different position.

The priestess nodded, as if reading my thoughts. She wagged a finger sideways, as if communicating 'not here' and pointed again to the west. She opened both palms towards me and then made the prayer sign by putting them together and bowing her head, as if in acknowledgement of me.

I heard myself saying, "I will do my best, my lady."

She smiled broadly, exposing white teeth against her weathered, lined face and said something that might have been a thank you, I couldn't tell.

She turned then, and disappeared into the trees, as if melting into them.

I opened my eyes, not believing they could have been shut at all, and found myself still sitting, not standing, in the very same spot under the autumnal leaves of a different sacred grove, the familiar one on Rick's estate.

I expected to see a stone pillar, not a cromlech, a sacred space smelling of incense and littered with the tools of ritual, but only the trees whispered around me in the fresh open air. Had these old oaks been listening? It felt like it.

I felt stronger than before, not disorientated like I usually did after seeing into the past. Was Bryonia now a part of me, stiffening my backbone and giving me more clarity of mind? That would be handy. I stood up and brushed down my clothes in an uncharacteristic regard for my appearance. I felt strangely taller and more in command of myself.

I walked over to the stone table to where Percy still lay on top of it in a prone position, her arms outstretched as if in invocation. She appeared to be fast asleep and peaceful. I felt no alarm. Her breath rose and fell in a regular, deep rhythm and the pulse in her neck marked time steadily. I decided to let Percy sleep on. She might be time-travelling for all I knew and wake up full of information that could prove useful, or she could just be sleeping off her hectic night on the tiles. I left her to it and sat down against the sturdy edifice. I needed to digest my own discoveries.

If I could channel the previous Bryonia, I could unlock the whole mystery. That revelation was astounding and infused me with a power I had never before experienced.

I sat, and Percy slept, in perfect peace for the best part of an hour. I drank in the atmosphere of this unique environment. Without needing to merge with the past I let the memories held within the embrace of the oak trees seep into my soul and it comforted me. The sensation wasn't scary; didn't feel dangerous or oppressive but supportive, gentle. I had a strong sense of being healed. My perennial grief for Robin, that sore, bruised spot on my heart, eased. I didn't feel his presence and neither did I long for it. Instead, I merged with old souls in a general sort of way, as if the barriers between this world and others had thinned and become permeable, like a membrane stretched gently to allow osmosis to occur along a willing gradient.

When I had studied Tai Chi for a while, trying to centre myself as Ted the teacher had called it, other students had waxed lyrical about this sort of thing. About being 'At One' with universal energy and it had sailed right over my head. My worldly cynicism, my loneliness, my aching heart had barred this possibility of joy but now, in this sacred place, I just knew it.

I also knew I would never feel quite so alone again, whatever happened.

The peace was shattered in an instant and all my musings and insights dissipated when Bryony marched purposefully into the quiet arena.

"You!" She almost spat the words out.

Derwen, her border collie, did not hesitate as Bryony had done, teetering on the brink of the trees' boundary, but bounded over to me like a long-lost friend and licked my cool cheek with his hot, sticky, and slightly smelly tongue.

"Get down, Derwen!" Bryony bellowed. She looked both shocked and angry to find us here. "I thought I'd warned you off coming here."

Percy, woken from her deep slumber by the disturbance, sat up and I scrambled to my feet like a guilty schoolchild caught truanting.

"How dare you climb onto the stone!" Bryony turned her wrath on to my friend, who was now rubbing sleep from her eyes with balled fists.

"I'm sorry?" Percy dropped her hands and stared at the older woman.

"So you should be." Bryony looked at me and frowned. Could she sense I'd seen her ancestor? Did she even know Bryonia had existed, perhaps in a similar hallowed space such as this one?

I cleared my throat. "We are doing no harm, Bryony. We are simply resting in this lovely spot. We have Rick's permission to go anywhere on his estate, unless…you own this bit?"

Bryony lowered her eyes so that I could no longer read them. Percy slipped off the stone and came to stand near me. Derwen greeted her with a wagging tail and then sat between us.

Faced by this oddly mixed panel, Bryony backed down and parked an insincere smile on her lined, fine-boned face. "No, I don't own any land on the estate. I suppose, if you have Rick's permission, you can go where you like."

I stroked Derwen's head. "That's exactly right, Bryony."

Percy flicked back her hair with a toss of her head. She looked completely awake and refreshed now. "Bryony, can I ask why this place means so much to you?"

Bryony defences rose at this direct question. If she had been a dog, her hackles would have risen to vertical.

Derwen left our sides and went to her mistress, leaning her body into Bryony's legs in loving empathy.

"I...we..." Bryony hesitated. "It's a nice area to hold our classes in sometimes when the weather is fair. We do yoga here and conduct, um, meditations."

Percy walked over to Bryony. "How lovely. Such a perfect spot for it. So peaceful." She laughed softly. "I was out for the count just then - it is so calming here."

Looking mollified, Bryony nodded, but moved away from Percy to stand nearer the stone cromlech. "Yes, well, it does lend itself to that sort of thing."

Percy turned to me as if inviting me to join in the conversation, but I confess I was stumped as to what to say, still cocooned by my internal shift and preoccupied.

"We completely understand why you must feel protective about it. Your students must love coming here. Do you often hold classes amongst the trees?"

Clever girl, Percy. I wished I could charm information out of people like that.

"Every full moon we gather here, if you must know."

"How wonderful, Bryony. Why, that must be beautiful. I would love to join in. Isn't there a full moon coming up soon?"

"Yes, that's right."

"Oh, yes, I remember. George was talking about it being at harvest moon. I used to love that as a child, you know. All those pumpkins and cabbages in our church."

Bryony looked at her sharply. "Church? Are you religious?"

Percy shook her head. "No, I'm afraid I gave that up long ago. I couldn't go along with the rules and regulations once I grew up. How about you?"

How I admired Percy's technique! Nice direct question after bags of flattery.

Bryony shifted from one foot to another. "I don't go to church, if that's what you mean."

"Well, why would you when you have this gorgeous green cathedral!" Percy looked up at the trees surrounding us. "I mean it's more beautiful than any man-made church I've ever been in! Who needs all that fuss and regimentation when you can worship Nature?"

At last, Bryony's face softened almost into a smile, but not quite. "I can see you think the same way as I do."

Percy drew closer to her. "Oh, I do, Bryony, I really do! And I'd love to join your – circle – would you call it? When the moon is full?"

Bryony shrugged. "I'll think about it. The members of our, um, group are quite private, you know. We don't let just anyone in."

Percy nodded. "Oh, I completely understand. I'll wait to hear from you." She turned to me. "Come on, Fay. Let's continue our walk before you succumb to starvation."

I forgave her the sarcastic comment. "Okay. Good idea. I am ravenous." I picked up the rucksack. "Goodbye, Bryony. Nice to see you again."

"Humph." She turned away from me towards the stones. I obviously hadn't made the grade, but Percy was halfway there.

As soon as we were out of earshot, I congratulated my friend. "Good work, Percy."

"Hmm, not good enough. She hasn't agreed to me attending this harvest ritual thingy."

"Not yet perhaps, but I have every confidence you'll persuade her."

Percy climbed over the stile. "Do you know, I'd actually like to go for my own sake. This place is getting its hooks into me."

I put one foot on the stile step. "The sacred grove has cast its spell."

Percy stopped in her tracks. "Let's go to the beach while the sun is still shining."

"I'd love to."

We changed direction and headed down towards the dunes and spontaneously burst into a run as we reached the beach. Big breakers crashed on to the shore making spumes of foam, white against the azure sea. It was intoxicating.

Percy came to another halt. "I just have to paddle." She tore off her shoes and socks, rolled her chinos up to above her knees and headed off towards the surf.

I decided to keep my footwear on and followed at a slower pace, content to let her splash about in the waves. I wandered along the shoreline, hugging my new-found sense of integration to me and happy not to think for a while.

It was Derwen, the collie-dog, who brought me abruptly back into the real world.

"Hello, old girl! You didn't follow us here, did you?"

"No, she's with me and Carys." I looked up and saw Gwen smiling at me. Little Carys was perched on her wide, generous hip and she gurgled her delight as Derwen hopped about me like a young pup.

"Hello, Gwen. What a lovely day for a walk."

"Yes, isn't it?" Her soft Welsh lilting voice invited conversation.

We fell into step at the edge of the water, and I turned back towards Percy, still cavorting in the shallows.

"So, how's life then, Gwen?"

"Oh, alright thanks."

"Only alright?"

"With Mabon approaching, George is very busy helping Bryony to get ready, so I have to manage on my own more."

"But Carys is such a good little girl, aren't you, poppet?"

Gwen squeezed her daughter to her side and kissed her rosy cheek. "She is, but I'm expecting again, and it makes me so tired in the early months."

I was well out of my comfort zone with this news. "Oh, um, congratulations. Could I carry her for you if she's heavy?"

"Thank you, but she is very shy."

169

"Wouldn't that be one way for her to learn not to be?"

"Perhaps you could hold her hand if she walks between us? She's still a little wobbly on her legs."

"I'd be delighted." Cary's tiny hand in mine gave a boost to my earlier sense of connection and I held it firmly, determined not to let her fall.

"There, cariad. Let the lady help you."

We slowed our pace down to that of the toddler's, which was about the same as a snail's. "How old is Carys?"

I could hear the pride in Gwen's voice as she answered. "Fourteen months now. Goodness, how the time has flown."

"I'm sure. Do you like living here? It's quite remote."

"Oh, yes, I'm from these parts, so it's home to me."

"How about George? I gather he's from Russia so he's a very long way from home."

Gwen's eyes lit up at the sound of her husband's name. "He loves it too. He feels safe here, unlike in his home country."

"Did he have a rough time there?"

Gwen simply nodded and looked away, back to where her cob house stood above the treeline.

Subject closed then. "Tell me about Mabon, Gwen. Is it the same as the harvest festival, but with a different name?"

"Oh, no, it means so much more to us at the community."

"The community?"

"Yes, we are a group of pagans who believe in the circle of life, the turn of the seasons and the natural cycle of all living creatures. The equinox is a time of great celebration, and many people will come to the sacred grove next Tuesday."

Pagans, eh? Now we were getting somewhere. "Really? How wonderful. I must admit, I love this time of year."

170

Gwen picked up her child, who was beginning to tire. "Oh, so do I! it's my favourite."

"Tell me about your pagan celebrations."

Infused with enthusiasm, Gwen didn't hold back. "We go to the sacred grove and take wine, and cider and food and we make our pledges and affirmations for the season. We sing and dance and prepare ourselves for the hardships of winter to come. Why don't you join us?"

"It sounds great, but would Bryony want us there, if we are not fully paid-up members of her, um, group?"

Gwen's face fell. "Oh, I hadn't thought of that."

We had caught up with Percy by now and she joined us on the strand. "Hello, Gwen and Carys. Hello, dear Derwen." Percy bent and ruffled the dog's ears, and she barked her appreciation.

Baby Carys wriggled, wanting to join in and Gwen set her back on her feet.

"Percy, Gwen was telling me all about the Mabon festival. It sounds like a great party. Do you think we could wangle an invite?"

Percy took the hint and gave Gwen one of her ravishing smiles. "Oh, I'd love nothing more than to attend, Gwen. It sounds fascinating and I was just telling Bryony how much I'm interested in all you are trying to do here. I honestly feel that if the rest of the world lived like this, there would be no more climate change worries or wars or anything."

Gwen nodded vigorously. "That's what I feel in my heart. Oh, it's so nice to meet another kindred spirit. We are trying to raise the vibration on the earth to counter all the negativity. It's the whole reason we're here! Listen, I'm going to invite you to come to the twmpath, no matter what Bryony says."

"Toompath?"

Gwen laughed. "It means a folk dance in Welsh. It will be tomorrow night, Tuesday. Bring something to share – drink or food – or even songs! We meet at eight o'clock in the evening in the sacred grove. You'll need a lantern – not a

171

torch – we only have real fire. Wear something warm as we stay till after midnight and it can get chilly," she laughed, "unless you are dancing!"

"Thanks, Gwen. We will definitely be there." Percy gave her a quick hug.

I decided to quit while we were ahead. "Right, we're heading back the other way to yours, so we'll see you tomorrow night."

"Okay then." Gwen scooped up her daughter and put her up on her shoulders and turned around to face the way she had come.

At first Derwen came with us, but we shooed her back to Gwen and she went off happily enough.

I winked at Percy. "It's a goal. You scored it. Well done."

"Do you know, Fay, I wasn't scheming. I genuinely want to go. I don't know much about pagans, but they seem harmless enough to me. I think Gaine will be there too."

I told her about my experience with the earlier version of Bryony.

"Do you think it's possible we could travel back in time together, Fay? Maybe being at the ritual will raise the energy enough?"

"Yes, I do but what the present 'priestess' will think about it, I've no idea."

Chapter Twenty-Six, The Isle of Anglesey, around two thousand years ago

Emrys had gone abroad for news of the Romans' whereabouts. Gaine had counselled him not to go but he had insisted and left, ignoring her warning. He'd been gone three weeks and Gaine had known considerable unease, sensing something had gone awry. Now he was returned, not walking on his strong legs, but prostrate on a pallet drawn by the visiting bard's hardy little pony.

She turned to the worried group gathered around her and ordered he be carried into her healing temple. As she followed with her fellow healers, she tried to quell her wifely instincts of anxiety, tried to keep a cool head, to call on her strength as a leader of her people, but her heart pounded in her chest.

Gaine schooled her breath to become steady again and called on the healing spirits to calm her. She laid her hands upon Emrys's inert body. She sensed fear, overwhelming panic. He thought he was going to die. She turned to her assistants.

"Fetch water steeped in lavender and thyme. Bring camomile tea and poppy tincture. Bring also sphagnum moss and clean linen with a washing bowl."

"Yes, my lady." The women disappeared silently.

"Morgan - sterilise a needle and fetch catgut thread."

"Yes, my lady."

Quietly Gaine's apprentices slipped away to their tasks. Emrys's breath was becoming shallow. She must work quickly. She placed each of her palms on either side of his brow. It felt clammy and cold and yet many beads of sweat spread out across his white face and there was a bloody gash along his jawline, just where his short beard began. Gaine stilled her mind and inhaled deeply, as she had been taught in her youth by her grandmother. She attuned her mind to her lover's as he lay under her sensitive hands and saw a vision of who had wounded him and how.

A soldier in a different uniform had slashed at his belly. Emrys had stabbed back but his attacker's torso was impenetrable, covered in the metal breastplate the Romans wore. His arms were bare though and, before Emrys had fallen, he had cut deeply into the other man's forearm. His opponent appeared unfazed and was about to plunge his sword into his throat to kill him, when another native warrior, attacking from behind, stopped the sword from its fatal thrust by making the Roman whirl around to defend himself. A vivid memory flashed across Gaine's mind of the vigil she'd previsioned in the lake - of Emrys as an older man, with a healed scar along his jawline. It gave her hope and strength.

When her women returned to the healing chamber, she opened her eyes and looked down at the man she loved so dearly. Would it have been kinder for Emrys to have died swiftly under the Roman's sword? His skin was now deathly grey, and his breath bubbled in his throat. She tipped his mouth open and dropped in a small amount of the poppy tincture. Not too much or it would slow his breathing but enough to ease some of his pain.

He *must* heal, she'd seen him as an older man in her vision in the lake water. Surely her seeing had not played her false all those years ago?

The young women silently organised her tools. Gaine washed her hands in the wooden bowl infused with the antiseptic herbs and wiped them dry on a perfectly clean cloth. She inhaled again and asked for the Gods to assist her before she carefully examined Emrys's abdomen and checked for internal cuts. Their young daughter, Dryadd, instinctively went to her father's head, as Gaine herself had done, and closed her eyes. Gaine could see their daughter was invoking the Gods to help her. She had done this without any command, and Gaine knew in that moment, Dryadd would replace her as chief priestess when she had left this world.

Gaine found, to her intense relief, no major organs had been damaged. She worked quickly, washing away the stench of the blood and dirt of battle. The liver and heart were untouched. It was his stomach and intestines that had been targeted and that gave her a glimmer of hope. She cleaned the gash, noting that the intestines were intact and that the wound was only skin deep, exposing his gut rather than destroying it. He might just hold on to his life, if the Gods were willing, if her vision had been correct. Then she took up the needle and thread and sewed the cut edges of his skin together over it. He must live for she needed to hear his testimony about the Romans.

Dryadd washed her father's face and tended to the surface wound there, while Gaine dusted powdered herbs of marshmallow root, thyme and camomile over the stitched wound on his belly. When she had finished, Gaine used wet moss to hydrate Emrys's parched lips, and she saw his face relax.

She turned to the other healing women. "We must watch him overnight. We need him to live if only to speak about this attack. We have no other witness. His account could prove crucial to how we prepare our defences."

Dryadd spoke in her soft, low voice. "And we love him, Mother."

Gaine nodded, ignoring the pricking in her eyes. She must stay strong somehow. She addressed the women gathered around her. "Take turns. I will go to my chamber and channel the energy to him from there."

They nodded silently but Dryadd spoke up. "I will take first watch, Mother."

"Very good. Only two hours at a time, mind. I want you all to be alert tomorrow. If he becomes feverish, give him cool elderflower and yarrow tea, and come for me straight away. At any time. Use the poppy tincture sparingly but do not let him suffer."

"Very well, my lady."

Gaine left then for her own room to pray and focus. Emrys must live. She must know if the Romans planned another invasion of Ynys Afallach and, privately, she acknowledged she could not live without him.

Chapter Twenty-Seven, Present Day

That afternoon Percy once again became the domestic goddess, the role she'd assumed as Paul Wade's wife when we'd met again as adults. She donned an apron and pinned up her hair, then set about whisking eggs and butter to make delectable, sweet treats for the pagan festival.

I was packed off to the local village to buy ingredients that couldn't be found at Bryony's wholesome establishment. Items I loved like sugar, more butter, lemons, and chocolate. Whilst there, I took the precaution of buying a few more groceries to tide us over.

As I was leaving the little shop, which reminded me very much of Mr Singh's emporium back at home in Swindon, I saw Eddie in the layby opposite, talking animatedly on his mobile phone. I couldn't wave, I was too laden with my shopping, so I just shouted 'Hi' as I crossed the road to my car, which I'd parked there.

He turned around when he heard me and frowned at my greeting as if I'd insulted him instead.

He finished the call quickly and strode up to me just as I was closing the car boot on my purchases. "Didn't expect to see you here. In fact, we've hardly seen you at all."

"We've been busy sleuthing and even ghostbusters have to eat."

"Don't see you ever catching any ghosts. All you ever seem to do is stuff your faces."

"Charming! I'll have you know we're making progress. Have you had any problems in the studio lately?"

"No power cuts but then Rick's not been working much. Not since he got so chummy with your pal."

I inserted my car key into the door lock. "That has nothing to do with me, Eddie, as well you know. We're trying to help Rick not hinder him."

Eddie ran his hand over his bald pate. "Could have fooled me. We need a result. If Rick doesn't hit his stride soon and record something decent, I'll have to think of another way to get the Inland Revenue off his back."

"Was that them on the phone then?"

"What?" His eyes narrowed. "Were you eavesdropping?"

I hedged my bets, mistrusting his shiftiness. "No, but you were talking quite loudly."

He folded his arms defensively. "The financial side of things is my business."

I opened my car door, ready to climb in. "You know, Eddie, I am a fully qualified accountant. Maybe I could help you prepare your accounts for the tax office? I know all the dodges, believe me."

Eddie looked furious at this suggestion. "Just do what you came here for. I'm perfectly capable of sorting out Rick's finances myself, thank you very much."

I held my hands up. "Just saying."

He turned away back towards his own vehicle. "See you back at the house. Rick's been asking about your friend. I assume she's there?"

"Of course, she is. She's busy in the kitchen, as it happens."

"The kitchen? Cooking, you mean? What's that got to do with the job in hand, for Christ's sake?"

"Plenty. All will be revealed."

"Ye Gods, that's all I need, bloody secrets."

"The Gods do come into it, actually." I laughed and got behind the wheel, shutting my car door to end the pointless conversation.

I did a three-point turn out of the layby, but by the time I'd pulled out, Eddie was long gone.

When I let myself into the cottage, laden with shopping bags, I didn't expect to see Rick in the kitchen too, but there he was, his scrawny arms around Percy's slim waist while she was dusting cake tins with clouds of flour.

They both turned around as I opened the door, looking comically like guilty schoolchildren instead of behaving like the adults they so obviously were.

"Oh, hi, Rick!" I fumbled with the door, trying to kick it shut with my foot as my hands were full. It didn't seem to occur to either of them to give me a hand.

I dumped the groceries on the kitchen table and Percy, looking rather pink with some of her pinned hair tumbling down, gave me one of her devastating smiles signalling contrition.

"Well done, Fay. Good timing. Did you get the lemons?"

"Lemons, butter, eggs, you name it, it's all here."

"Lovely! I'll put the kettle on." Percy busied herself with tea-making while Rick flopped down on one of the wooden kitchen chairs and started to roll a joint.

"It says we're not supposed to smoke in here in the welcome book." I hated the smell of his dope.

"Listen, darlin', I bloody own the place, don't I?" He twirled the end of the Rizla papers into a twist with his stained thumb and forefinger.

I wondered if his breath smelt of stale smoke and how fastidious Percy dealt with that.

"Fair enough." I started putting the shopping away and then sat down opposite him.

Percy placed three mugs of tea down on the table and sat down between us. "I was just telling Rick about the pagan ritual tomorrow night and how we're taking these cakes with us."

Rick lit his reefer. "Never knew the hippies got up to them tricks. Sounds a bit bent to me."

"Haven't you been to the oak grove where the stones are?"

"I used to play on them as a nipper. We used to come here for holidays when I was a kid. Always rained." He gave a throaty laugh.

"Is that why you went to live in California?" I sipped my tea.

"Yeah, at least, after I met Sherry. Brought her here once but she vowed never to return. Said it was a dump and too bloody cold."

"Is she American then?" Percy got up and started adding sugar to her mixture.

"Very, if you know what I mean. Don't get me wrong, she's a looker but a right pain in the arse, as it turned out." Rick turned and patted Percy's bottom. "Not like you, gorgeous."

I cleared my throat. "I saw Eddie in the village. He seemed worried about the, um, business side of things."

Rick waved his hand in a dismissive gesture. "Eddie's always worried about summink. Nothing he likes more than fussing over stuff that don't matter."

"Sounded quite serious to me." I had to raise my voice over the whirr of Percy's electric beaters.

"Yeah, well, perhaps. I leave it to him."

Now I had him cornered, I wasn't about to let it go. "Eddie said you owe the Inland Revenue a fair whack."

"Maybe."

"Divorce is expensive too."

Percy frowned at me over her shoulder at my questioning, but I soldiered on regardless.

"Must add up to quite a bit."

"Listen, lady, I thought you were here to get rid of the spooks, not give me the Spanish inquisition about my private finances."

I spread my hands out in a deprecating gesture. "I'm a fully qualified accountant, Rick. I might be able to help you offset what you have to pay to the taxman."

Rick inhaled from his joint and suppressed his out-breath. When he did speak again, blue curls of pungent smoke carried the words. "I'll talk it over with Eddie. See if he thinks he could use you. In the meantime, what have you found out about the ghosties?"

"We've both had some insights into the past. We think we are getting a handle on who is preventing you working but we're not there yet. Eddie was saying you inherited this estate through your family. Do you know how long they have owned this land?"

"Want a puff?" Rick extended the joint to me.

179

"No, thanks. Don't like it."

"Percy, darlin' – do you want some?"

Percy, now spreading batter into sandwich tins, also declined.

Rick shrugged. "Suit yourselves. I don't know how long it's been in my family. I only came here for holidays. Was a boarder at a school in London, see. Got dyslexia and it never got diagnosed so they just thought I was thick. Didn't do me much good so I left early and lived in a squat in Stockwell and that's where I learned to play the guitar and met Eddie. Was in a few bands before I started the Dreamers. Dad – my Mum died when I was young – he lived here but he got a manager from the village in to set up the holiday lets, but I cancelled them this year. I never asked me old Dad about it before he died, just took this place for granted, like. He turned to drink, you know, after me Mum died. Didn't talk much."

Percy leaned across and kissed his parchment cheek. "Poor you. That must have been hard, losing your Mum."

"How old were you when she died, Rick, if you don't mind me asking?" I really couldn't see what Percy admired in him. Watching her kissing him was deeply unsettling.

"Eight."

Percy kissed his other cheek. "So young!"

Rick stubbed out his exotic cigarette. "Yeah, well. Shit happens."

The way he looked at Percy had me worried they were heading for a proper clinch, so I quickly asked. "What's your real surname, Rick? Can't be O'Shea, surely?"

He laughed. "Nah, it's a good stage name though, innit? Eddie came up with that one. My family name is Ratti."

I tried to suppress a laugh and didn't quite manage it.

"See? That's why I changed it. It really ain't rock 'n' roll, now, is it?"

Percy did laugh. The way their relationship was blossoming, she could get away with it. "Not at all! More 'Toad of Toad Hall!"

"Now listen 'ere, darlin'." Rick got up and put his arms around her.

It was time to beat a retreat. I finished my tea hurriedly and ran up the stairs, two at a time. I shut my bedroom door and used my phone to play some loud music to drown out any unwelcome sounds of intimacy from downstairs. I lay on my bed and before long, had nodded off into an afternoon nap full of sensuous dreams about Robin.

Chapter Twenty-Eight, Isle of Anglesey around two thousand years ago

Gaine lay prone on her mattress of lady's bedstraw. She no longer had the strength to move even one finger. She didn't mind. She had made her peace and knew she would soon be joining the spirits, including her beloved Emrys, who had gone before her. Bryonia was already waiting by her side, shimmering in and out of her fading vision. She did not know if the image was inside her head of out of it anymore, but she did know it didn't matter, that this was her time to hang in the balance between this world and the next.

Bryonia her mentor, grandmother, teacher, healer, smiled at her. "You have done well, my child. You have achieved all I asked of you, and more. Soon, you may rest for a while. Your work in this life is done and done well. The children I placed in your care are all grown with children of their own. Your man, Emrys, survived his war wounds under your care so you could share your burdens for many years more, as I told you all those years ago. Now he is waiting to greet you in the next world. You have succeeded, as I foresaw you would, in keeping our sacred line alive so our people can continue into new lives, new eras. You, Gaine, have managed to keep them safe from these Roman murderers, as I could not."

Gaine looked at Bryonia's neck, where a faint ragged red line could still be seen from her beheading by the Roman General. She looked the age she had been at the hour of her dramatic death. Her hair long and purest white, her fragile skin stretched over her high cheekbones; its lines etching out the dramas she'd lived through during her long life, all those years ago. Gaine supposed her own face bore similar lines from the map of her life, for she was even older at her passing than Bryonia had been at hers.

And her death was peaceful. If she'd still had the strength to open her eyes, she knew she would see her family around her, quietly doing their chores while she slipped away. Her own children, yes, now with grown children of their own who had little ones playing around them, but also the children of this new tribe she and Emrys had created together.

How hard it had been at first. When they had reached this place, the children had been so exhausted from running, thirsty and starving from hunger because she would not stop often enough for Emrys to hunt and fish. They had snatched berries from the trees they'd rushed past and that was all she would allow the children to do until Gaine had found the place of the setting sun where the dead lay buried, looking out to sea, long after its rays had slipped into the west.

Only then, when she had been sure no Romans would find them, had she and Emrys lit a fire and made a shelter under an oak tree. Ah, that first oak tree. How she had loved it. Over the years, they had cleared the land around it and planted other oaks in a circle to protect them. Gaine and Emrys had called on the spirits to cast a ring of protection around those trees, a girdle of loving strength from the gods. Now, those trees were tall, and their branches entangled their neighbours, making a perfect green wall around the sacred space in the centre. They had made other clearings in the wood for the sturdy shelters and huts that housed them and planted many more oaks from the acorns that fell from the old mother oak on the land that sloped gently down to the sea.

Emrys had healed from his wounds and shared many years with her caring for the community that grew around them, sheltered from the outside world by his vigilant guardianship. He had died only the year before and life without him had been lonely for her.

Gaine sighed and her eldest daughter, Dryadd, named after the trees, was immediately at her side. Gaine could feel her living fingers touch her hand while the light-as-air caress of Bryonia held the other. She felt safe, contented, loved. The next sigh took her earthly life with it.

Chapter Twenty-Nine, Present Day

The next morning Percy set about finishing off her culinary confections and I ambled up to George's house to see if I could help with preparations for the evening. There was no-one around so I assumed they must be at the oak circle doing whatever pagans did before such events. I decided not to risk Bryony over-ruling Gwen's warm invitation, but explore my new surroundings to see if I could glean any more clues on a different part of the estate.

I wandered off in the opposite direction to the oak circle to an area I'd not visited before. The land rose and stretched away from the estate house before opening out into grassland, affording an inviting prospect of the more distant sea from the top of the hill. Drawn by its beauty, I walked on and came upon the other stone monument I had spotted from my bedroom window overlooking a cleft of the wide valley below. Not a cromlech this time, but a more rounded affair of smaller stones grouped together to form a large mound about twenty feet across and thirty long. I meandered around it, fascinated to find a sort of door and lintel arrangement at one end. I sat down to contemplate its purpose and decided it had to be a burial mound. If it had not been on private land, surely some zealous archaeologist would have dug up the ancient bones lying beneath it and put them, labelled and organised, in some glass case in a museum far away from this blessed spot. I felt a profound sense of peace here and gratitude that these souls resting under their stone canopy lay unmolested.

I half expected some unworldly communication from the occupants of the cairn, but they seemed to be sleeping contentedly underneath it, so eventually I got up and walked down the valley towards the sea.

I ended up on the cliff tops gazing at the tremendous view across the ocean. Below me I could see a cave, cut deep into the rocks rising up from the beach head. Could this be where the Druids had taken shelter when escaping the Romans two thousand years ago? It was astonishing that spirits could retain their energy over two millennia. Who would have thought dead people could hold a grudge that long?

I followed the coastal path towards the cave and found a rocky path winding steeply down to its open maw. The cave was not at beach level, unusually, but set halfway between the cliff top and the sand. I wondered if the sea level was different then or if the land itself had receded, pounded by the ceaseless tide. An inviting ledge led to the cave opening. Though narrow, it didn't look too scary. I was wearing trainers which provided a good grip, and the drop was only about twenty feet if I did fall. I decided to go for it.

Stony shards displaced by my feet slithered down the rock face as I descended the little winding path. I made the mistake of looking down to see where they landed and felt slightly sick watching them bounce off the rocks before landing in the soft sand below. A twenty-foot drop from a distant perspective looked more like forty from here. When I was halfway along the gravelly ledge it narrowed dramatically. I hadn't been able to see that from afar but now I had to make a choice. Should I return, which would mean turning around to face the other way – a pretty dodgy manoeuvre – or risk carrying on towards the cave with only enough width for one foot at a time? I looked up, which made me feel even more nauseous, to see if there was a hand hold somewhere. I clung on to the side of the cliff with my fingernails, alarmed when yet more tiny bits of shingle crunched under my fingertips before cascading down the crumbly cliff face. There was no way I was going to turn back.

My heart began to thump uncomfortably as I edged along the thin shelf, my toes curling up inside my trainers in an instinctive but futile attempt to cling on to any rock still adhering to the surface.

When I reached the open mouth of the cave, I was aghast to find I would have to jump around a right angle of rock to reach it. The wet and slippery limestone floor, riddled with shallow puddles between little wave-shaped ridges of rock, did not look inviting. I looked back along the shelf I had shimmied along, realising there was no way I could turn around. Retreat was not an option. I would have to jump. I looked down at the beach so far below me. The grains of sand seemed to blur together, and I felt dizzy as well as sick. I viewed the cave's wide opening. Surely the ancient Druids hadn't done this on an everyday basis? The path musts have been broader then. It must have eroded over the years, surely? Weren't sea levels rising because of global warning? I was convinced they had here on this Welsh beach. The seascape had to have been very different to access this cave all those years ago. Now, I was trapped, and I had no desire to go forward or back.

I stood, frozen on the narrow ledge, clinging to the rockface in a whirl of panic and indecision. Why had I embarked on this? Why had I been so reckless? What if Percy was having a trance session on her own and hurt herself – or someone else?

I had to pull myself together. The only person in danger right now was me. Ted's face flashed across my frenzied mind. Remember your balance when you do Tai Chi, he'd said. It had been his mantra as a teacher of the discipline. I focussed on the balls of my feet and let my knees soften so they could unlock and allow my muscles to spring. Then I centred myself using my breath, the way Ted had taught me – except that had been in a nice, safe community hall on a wooden floor. Then there had been no wind to buffet me, and no waves roared and snapped beneath my jelly legs. The strand of sand looked increasingly thin as the tide came inexorably towards the cave.

I took my time. The odds were not in my favour, and I knew it. Only when calm had returned to my solar plexus did I make the leap. I landed on all fours, inches away from the rock edge and its lethal drop to the beach.

"Ouch!" I looked down at my knees. My jeans had ripped open, and blood was already seeping through the cotton. Still trembling with fright, I sat back on my haunches, and scanned the palms of my hands, also both grazed. Gingerly, I moved towards the interior of the cave and slowly, keeping my backside on the bumpy, wet floor, turned around to look outside at the sea.

The seascape was stunning from here and the ocean's rhythm growled in my ears, compounding its noise with an echo from deep within the cave. I had no torch, but I did have the app on my phone. Luckily, I had charged it up overnight and there was plenty of battery left. I switched it on, disappointed to find it had no signal. Not surprising, given my location, but it meant I couldn't call out the rescue service. I turned back towards the hollow carved out from the land and shone the beam of light into the depths of the cavity. It looked extensive and mysterious, and I remembered the old adage that it had been curiosity that had killed the cat. I looked up at the roof and calculated it was high enough for me to stand up, which I did, very cautiously.

My cuts started to sting but I ignored the pain and walked into the depths of the black hole. The acoustics distorted sound even more as I crept further in. I could only see the tiny individual areas that my feeble phone torch illuminated. The interior limestone walls of the cave looked like beaten pewter. I ran my hand over their silky, weather-hewn surfaces. They were wet, presumably from seeping rainwater finding its way down crevices in the rock. The sun would never shine in here and dry it. There was a metallic smell, almost like blood, coming off the angular stone walls and I had no idea if these angles would suddenly project to the middle of the cave and knock me out.

As I delved deeper, the temperature dropped. I heard a drip landing in water and pointed the light down to the floor to see a perfectly round pool surrounded by extraordinary stalagmites towering up around it. I gasped out loud, as I had nearly fallen into it, and I had no idea of its depths. It could be a well for all I knew, penetrating right down to below sea level. I reached out the hand not holding my phone and dipped my index finger in the liquid. I licked it. It was fresh, not salty. This would have been an important resource if you were forced to live here. Across my mind flashed an image of people of an ancient era moving around the cave furtively, as if in fear of discovery, the only light from a flickering torch hanging from the cave wall. I shivered at the prospect of being trapped inside this cold refuge. I had no survival skills, unlike those earlier refugees. What must it have been like to have been in fear of your life trying to escape from your persecutors? You would have to be desperate to hole up in this Godforsaken hideaway.

I looked up at the wall and saw a steady trickle of water cascading down the grey wall. So, it must be coming from above. No wonder it was fresh.

I crept around the circular pool, drawn on by more inadvisable curiosity. Beyond the reservoir of water, I found another slab of stone, just like the one that formed the top of the cromlech in the oak grove. It was exactly the same size – enough to lay a man full length along its flat surface. I shivered again. It was chilly but that wasn't the reason. I smoothed my scratched palm along its horizontal plane, horrified to see a trail of blood from my hand appear red in the torchlight.

I stared at the fluid the cave had extracted from my body. The warm liquid congealed quickly, gleaming in the electric light. Had other blood been shed here? Then to my horror, I felt myself slipping back in time. This was not the place for it! With irresistible force, the scene before me faded and I could do nothing to stop it, however desperately I wanted to.

I heard a crack and knew, with the remnants of my conscious mind, that my phone had fallen from my flaccid hand on to the unforgiving rocks. Then all thoughts of the present left and I was here in the same cave but further back in time, almost two thousand years ago.

The priestess I had seen before, Bryonia, went to the head of the dead body lying so still on the mortuary slab in the cave. Two flaming brands set into braziers on the wall lit the macabre scene.

"My beloved granddaughter, Gaine. You have spent your long life ensuring our tribe and our Druid ways live on, and I honour you for your sacrifice. Brave, honourable fighter; keeper of the old ways; mother to all our children. Come, join with me now in the afterlife, where we must carry on with protecting the energy in the sacred grove you and Emrys created so perfectly. To die peacefully with your children around you is a good death and a generous one, but now is your time to leave and go to the land of spirits in the west. Your kin shall bury your earthly body tomorrow, after you have lain here long enough to allow your spirit to pass over."

She laid her hands upon her granddaughter's chest, where no heart now beat a living rhythm. Although the body under her hands looked solid enough, Bryonia's outline shimmered and faded in and out of my sight.

Bryonia laid her hands along the same nine points of energy Ted had taught me ran in a line along the body. He'd called them chakras. Then she returned to stand with her palms either side of Gaine's brow and closed her eyes for some time before bending to kiss her forehead.

"We shall see each other again, my dearest girl, in the next world, where we shall work together again to keep the energy flowing through the oak grove. Then she drew a very deep breath and withdrew a pace. "Be at peace, Gaine, and I will join you soon."

Her image shimmered even more and then broke into a myriad fragments before disappearing completely.

I was alone. I had been all along, but it hadn't felt like it. I opened my eyes but saw nothing but blackness. It took me a moment to realise the precarious situation I found myself in. I had no flambeaux to guide me, unlike that Druid priestess, and where the hell was my mobile? I would never find it in this pitch darkness.

The panic I had experienced on the cliff ledge was nothing to the fear that overwhelmed me now. I felt the hard stone around me. Surely the phone couldn't be far away?

What if there was another deep pool here and it had been lost in its fathomless depths? I scrabbled around on the floor frantically, hurting my scraped knees and hands all over again, careless of the damage I was inflicting on my poor, bruised body.

Oh God! How was I ever to get out of this predicament with no light to guide me? If only Robin was here. I was always so alone. Then I remembered that feeling of oneness I had experienced at the oak grove. I must retrieve that calm somehow.

I sat back against the icy-cold stone slab and closed my eyes, willing the panic to subside. Breathe. Just breathe. It took a while, but my pulse eventually steadied. I opened my eyes. They felt like they were on stalks under the strain of trying to see. I could actually feel the muscles behind my eyeballs working overtime. I rubbed my hands over them, willing them to see, then I looked up at where the roof must be and, above me, I saw the tiniest pin prick of light. There had to be a way up to the cliff top! Could I climb up and escape that way? It had to be worth a try. The very thought of returning to that crumbling ledge made me want to heave up my guts. Against every instinct, I made myself crawl deeper into the cave.

Every now and then I looked up, searching for that glimmer of daylight, hating the crawling claustrophobia seeping into my bones. My skin prickled with goosebumps from the frigid air, but I kept going. After a few minutes – they felt like hours, but I had no way to gauge the time anymore – I looked up again. A wisp of air brushed my face. Another spirit? My heart banged in my chest. I wasn't sure I could take another trip back in time right now. I just wanted out!

I sniffed, trying to block the tears that threatened to undo me, but instead caught another whiff of fresh air, instead of the dank smell from the innards of the cave. Sure enough, high above me, the patch of daylight had widened a fraction. There must be a fissure in the rock. I crawled further on my hands and knees, egged on by the increasing amount of light helping me to see, if only dimly, the walls and floor of this potential tomb.

I took a sharp inbreath. There was a sort of rugged staircase carved by nature or man, I couldn't tell which, cut into the rock ahead of me, leading up to that precious scrap of sky.

I heard Robin's voice whispering in my ear. "Come on, Fay. You can do this."

"Thank you, oh, thank you." The words came out aloud.

Ignoring my manifold bruises, I inched my way towards the base of the steps on my belly, my breath now ragged with emotion I could no longer control.

I seized on the first one with my hands and pushed myself half-upright. I could smell the oxygen coming from above me. It acted like rocket fuel, and I powered my way up the narrow stairs, my hands scrabbling against the jagged wall running alongside it. The steps were uneven and bumpy, treacherous with damp condensation and covered in an emerald-green slimy weed of some sort. I didn't look down again after that, only up, up, up at that oh-so-welcome patch of grey, cloudy sky. I squeezed my upper body through a tight hole, sliding against the sticky clay around its orifice, to find the surface strewn with shards of rock and little tufts of thrift growing cheerfully between the stones. I drew in great lungfuls of sweet air before scrambling up the last step and clawing my way out of the crevasse. Once free of the clinging mud, I flung myself on to the level ground and inhaled more glorious air.

I lay there on my back, panting with the effort, staring gratefully at the cumulous clouds racing across the sky, which was now where it should be, should *always* be, above me and with solid ground supporting me from beneath. The world was the right way up again and oxygen once more coursed through my veins.

Chapter Thirty, The Isle of Anglesey around two thousand years ago

Gaine looked down on the empty shell of her body. It lay on a large, flat slab of limestone in the cave they used as a mortuary, near the burial chamber. How dry and shrivelled her corpse looked lying there, so cold and so white and yet she, Gaine, had never felt more alive.

She turned to Bryonia, standing so quiet and still by her side. She felt rather than heard her grandmother's words. "Yes, child, you no longer inhabit that tired body, but your spirit will live on forever, as does mine. Some souls go on into another earthly life and maybe you will too, one day in the far future, when all is well again. But for now, like myself, you have powerful work to do in the spirit world."

Gaine gazed at Bryonia's face, looking alive again even after her death. Her hair remained pure white and cascaded down her straight back and Bryonia's eyes, as blue and as intelligent as ever, bore into her. Gaine would do as Bryonia asked; she always had. She would not refuse her command, even though she knew not what it might entail. Gaine respected Bryonia's natural authority because it had never failed her. She stood waiting for her instructions in good faith they would be justified and within her abilities to fulfil.

Bryonia touched Gaine's face with her long fingers. "All that can wait, my dear. Now you must be present and congruent while your loved ones say goodbye to you. They do not know you watch over them still, although they may sense it, but you will gain as much from this ceremony of transition as will they. It is a necessary ritual for the separation of loved ones and will aid you on your way to your spiritual path whilst helping them to live on the good Earth without you."

Bryonia retreated into the soft mist that surrounded them, leaving Gaine alone, but not lonely as the spirit of her beloved Emrys came to keep her vigil in companionable silence. They communed with each other in loving energy without need for words.

Time, as Gaine had known it, dissolved. She watched her daughters wash her body in water blessed by Dryadd and infused with the cleansing herbs of thyme, lavender and camomile. It astonished her that she could smell their comforting aromas as the women worked. Tears welled in her eyes as she witnessed how lovingly they bathed her skin, combed her long, white hair and bedecked her in her best robes. Finally, when the rest of the clan had gathered outside the cave, the women of her tribe returned with baskets heaped with fresh blooms. Four men came too and lifted her onto a bier. Then the women gently placed the flowers on her body and strew them around it until her corpse lay bathed in colourful petals and leaves. The men and women joined hands and chanted her name while the four biggest men lifted the bier onto their shoulders and walked from the cave, up the wide path on the side of the cliff, with the sea frothing so far below in the distance, to join the throng above.

As all the voices she had known and loved in her earthly life joined together in song, a swell of emotion rose in her throat at the beauty and harmony of the vibrational sound. Gaine looked down at all her dear ones as they began the short uphill walk to the burial chamber overlooking the peaceful valley below.

The children went first, skipping and singing, flowers clutched in their sticky little hands. The adults followed behind her body where it rested on the stretcher of wood bound with leather, held aloft in the middle of them all. Although the elders in the group wore solemn faces and some were crying, the younger ones looked uplifted and joyful as they processed to the stone cairn. The burial mound looked as it always had, a huge, rounded heap of limestone boulders piled up on larger blocks to create a cavern underneath. Gaine could see one of the biggest, vertical stones had been moved to one side to reveal a yawning black hole under the lintel. The bier was laid on the ground before it and each person in the tribe, from the smallest infant to the eldest crone, laid a gift on to it. Some gave more flowers, some her favourite things – her curved hunting knife, her 'seeing' crystal, her wooden bowl and spoon, a few clay containers of her dried herbs. Her treasures.

Then, when everyone had had their turn, the bier was gently pushed inside the cairn and two young men, one of them her eldest grandson, crawled inside after it. They laid her body next to that of Emrys, whose spirit had stayed with her through her time of passing. She could not see the outline of his physical remains well in the darkness, but she knew it was him, her lover and best friend and the father of her children. They were reunited again, body and spirit.

The two youths crawled out on their knees a few minutes later and carefully returned the closing stone back into its normal position. Everyone took a displaced stone and replaced it above the lintel. Then they joined hands with the others, and they all raised their arms in a linked chain surrounding the entire cairn, chanting Gaine's name three times. In the following silence, they dropped their hands, and the circle broke up. Chatter broke out, some cried and hugged, and others smiled their memories of her to each other. Gradually they drifted away back to their own lives and left her body laying with her ancestors and theirs under its limestone roof, deep in the earth and safe for eternity.

Now her real work building the energy from this place, communicating with kindred spirits still living, could begin. They must be the ones to keep the energy unsullied and pure in the sacred grove, whatever time they inhabited on Earth, and they would need her support. She knew deep in her cold bones that keeping the flow of power within the circular embrace of the oaks, concentrating it into the triskelion on the capstone, would prove crucial in the long years to come.

This was her destiny and, until she fulfilled it, she would have no peace.

Chapter Thirty-One, Present Day

"For goodness' sake, Fay, where on earth have you been?" Percy opened the front door of the cottage in answer to my pummelling, for I had no strength left to fish for the door key.

I fell into her arms.

"What has happened to you?" She propelled me to one of the sofas and I flopped down into its soft embrace.

"Got stuck in a cave. Saw another priestess. Dead man's cave."

"What are you on about? What cave?"

"Need food. Tea."

Percy put her hands on her hips. "Don't you ever think about anything but your stomach? I've been so worried, and we're supposed to be going to the festival tonight. We're going to be late and look at you! You're plastered in mud!"

My teeth chattered together from my shivering. "Give me a break, will you? I could have died in that bloody black hole."

"Oh, honestly! You shouldn't have gone alone. I thought you were going to help George. I *thought* you'd gone to the oak grove without me."

"Tea, please, for pity's sake!" I grabbed the blanket slung over the back of the sofa and covered my legs.

Percy tutted but she got up and put the kettle on. Soon I was cradling the hot mug in my freezing cold hands. A few sips in, rational thought returned, and my body stopped shivering. I relayed the details of my dangerous escapade and the angry look faded from Percy's lovely face.

"Oh, Fay! Why didn't you wait for me? You shouldn't have tried to go in a cave without someone with you."

"I know that *now*! Your being right doesn't make me feel any better, you know."

Percy patted my hand. "I'm sure. You'd better have a bath to warm yourself up. Will you be able to come to the ritual tonight?"

"What time is it? I lost my phone in that blasted cave."

"Oh no! What a pain." Percy looked at her jewelled watch. "It's almost seven and we're supposed to be there before eight."

I drained my mug. "Make me another tea and a sandwich or something, could you? I'm going to be alright, but I do need to make myself decent."

"Are you sure you're not too shaken up? It must have been hell getting out of there."

"Yes, it was." I was too tired to say more but I was damned if I was going to miss the party. "I'll have a quick shower and change."

I noticed Percy was already dressed for the occasion in a bright red long skirt with a short green jumper on top. Not her normal slick look at all, in fact, quite folksy.

"I'll put a fresh cuppa and a snack in your bedroom. Everything else is ready."

I laid my blanket aside. "Thanks. Give me five minutes."

"I'll give you at least ten. Looks like you need more."

I gave a strangled sort of laugh at the truth of this and climbed wearily up the stairs.

It actually took me half an hour to feel anything like ready to go out again but by eight o'clock that evening I stood at our cottage door, plasters on all the crucial bits, in fresh clothes and with two Paracetamol tablets on board.

Every bone in my bruised body ached as we walked down to the sacred grove in the dark of the equinox evening, but it was worth it. Percy had rigged up a lantern with a candle and its bobbing flame picked out the path, while the full moon hanging low in the sky above us silvered the trees with its monochrome beam. We both gasped in delight as we entered the magic circle and saw the fairy lights twinkling in

196

every oak tree, marking the circumference with more flickering candlelight.

Far from being used for some gory sacrifice, the stone cromlech was covered in all sorts of wonderful food and drink. Around its base stood artfully placed fruits of the earth: traditional pumpkins formed the back row and various vegetables were piled up next to their sisters; fat green cabbages jostled against bunches of orange carrots as bright as the glow of the lanterns; the more mundane hessian sacks of potatoes and beetroots stood to attention in the centre. Wicker baskets of apples and pears overflowed into smaller ones of walnuts, hazelnuts and chestnuts. On top of the stone table, beautiful arrangements of flowers and leaves intermingled with the culinary offerings and Percy was hard pressed to find a space for her lemon drizzle cake and chocolate brownies amongst the plethora of goodies. In pride of place, dominating it all, stood a different wicker basket in the shape of a huge horn, and it was stashed full of various loaves of wondrous designs.

The whole effect was one of surreal enchantment, as if we were stepping back in time. The soft flickering lights spoke of another age and the scene had a timeless quality which I found very soothing to my post-traumatic state.

Percy grinned at me when she returned after making her offering. "Feeling better now you've seen the feast?"

I gave a shaky laugh. "Apart from my tummy rumbling in anticipation."

She gave me a quick hug. "I'm sorry I was so sharp with you earlier. I was genuinely worried about you."

"You're a fine one to talk after disappearing for an entire night so you could frolic with a geriatric."

After a fraction of a minute's hesitation, we burst into laughter together.

"Hey, do you think that frolicking will be the order of the day, or should I say night, after we've filled our bellies? I've heard all sorts of saucy stories about pagans." Percy winked at me.

197

"God, I hope not! I'll be lucky if I stay awake long enough to see the evening through, let alone bounce around with some weird stranger."

George and Gwen came up to us and greeted us with warm smiles and hugs.

"Where's little Carys?" Percy kissed Gwen on the cheek.

"Hello, how lovely to see you. Carys is fast asleep in her pram over there under the trees." Gwen looked relaxed and happy, her arm in her husband's.

How I wished Robin was here too and that I could lean on him in my deep fatigue; that his strong arm supported my exhausted one. "I'll bet she's snug as a bug in there."

Gwen nodded. "Yes, she's wrapped up safe."

George looked at his wife. "And we can have some fun, for a change."

"Tell me, George, what happens at the Mabon ceremony?"

"You'll see." He tapped the side of his noise and smiled before they wandered off to join the throng now gathered around the stones.

"I'm content to watch from the side-lines, aren't you, Percy?"

"Hmm."

I looked at my friend, who's eyes looked a little glazed. I sighed. "Are you slipping away into the past? Couldn't we have some of that gorgeous food first?"

Percy blinked rapidly and straightened her shoulders. "Of course, cariad."

"Cariad? Isn't that Welsh for dearest one?"

"It is."

"But you don't know any Welsh."

Percy didn't answer me but swayed slightly on her feet.

I could see she was only half in the present. I took Percy's arm and marched her off to join the others. She snapped out of her reverie once surrounded by the revellers

198

in the here-and-now. I had just taken my first sip of delicious cider when the group parted, rather reverentially, to allow Bryony to pass.

Dressed in a long black robe with an amber-coloured beaded girdle dangling from her hips, the modern-day Bryony's resemblance to her forebears was uncanny. I did a doubletake when she lifted back her hood and stood on a smaller flat stone in front of the cromlech, just as her namesake had stood in front of the standing stone with the same carved circles. I shivered at the recollection of that earlier sighting, and the more recent memory of her ancestor in the cave this afternoon, talking to Gaine about her future spiritual life. Did that include haunting music studios?

Bryony drew herself up to her full height, tossed back her long, grey hair, and lifted her chin. I heard her deep inhalation before she addressed the crowd in thrilling tones, her strong voice reaching to the furthest listener with ease.

"Fellow worshippers, welcome to the feast of Mabon, the joining of the God and Goddess. Please, form a circle in front of me and hold hands with your nearest neighbour. If you don't know them, all the better; you will after this evening."

Percy met my eyes with raised eyebrows at this invitation, but we dutifully held hands with the nearest person to each of us. I found myself gripping gentle Gwen's hand, so I wasn't too worried, but Percy held the fingers of a tall young man sporting a short beard and dreadlocks. He was looking at her with warm approval.

I turned back to Bryony, who stood above and apart, smiling at her flock. "Good. Let us praise the fruits of the earth we have gathered in such wonderful abundance. Now is the time for gratitude but also fortitude, as we prepare ourselves for the dark months ahead. It is also a moment of release and I want each of you to think of something you can let go of tonight. Something you no longer need. You can shed your burdens together this evening. You may say it aloud to your neighbour or step forward and tell us all." Bryony opened her arms in invocation.

There was a general murmuring around the circle as whispers moved around it like a Mexican wave. Everyone else had obviously prepared for this. I saw the man on Percy's right bend and whisper something in her ear, parting her long auburn locks to do so. An intimate gesture for a new acquaintance. When Gwen gently confessed to letting go her fear of miscarriage, I squeezed her hand in an effort to show I had heard and understood. Gwen looked at me questioningly after she had finished speaking and I was at a loss to identify what I might release. Not Robin, not Robin, not Robin, was the only refrain I could hear in my mind.

"It's okay," Gwen said at last. "It'll come when you are ready."

I mumbled something incoherent. Everyone else had fallen silent and turned back to look at their leader.

Bryony smiled broadly, taking in everyone in front of her. It made her look much younger and quite majestic – and even more like her Druid ancestor. "Good. Now let us bless the food we are about to eat and ask for abundance in the winter to come."

She then said something in Welsh I couldn't comprehend, but everyone else clapped. Bryony held up her hands for silence and an obedient hush descended.

"My friends, today and tonight are of equal length. It is the season of change from light to dark, but masculine and feminine, inner and outer, are in perfect balance tonight. We are on the cusp of transition as the year begins to wane and from tomorrow, darkness begins to defeat the light. The cycle of the natural world is moving towards completion, the sun's power is waning and, as the nights grow longer, the days to come will be shorter and cooler. The sap of trees will return to their roots deep in the earth, changing the green of summer to the fiery flaming reds, oranges and golds of autumn. We are returning to the dark from whence we came. At a time when seasons are mixed up and the weather is more and more unpredictable due to our changing climate, it is even more important that we observe the changing season

200

at its traditional time in the calendar, as Druids and Pagans have always done.

"But tonight, we shall feast on the abundance that came from the sun, the earth, the rain and the stars. We shall celebrate all we have grown and produced together and give our thanks for the safely gathered harvest."

At a nod from her, someone gave Bryony a cup of animal horn and she raised it up to the night sky. "A toast! Thank you, Gaia, for giving us the fruits of our labours with your generous bounty. To Gaia, our mother earth!"

The toast was echoed around the circle, and everyone drank from their more conventional cups, including me. The stirring words had given me quite a thirst. I longed to sit down and give my aching limbs some respite, but the ceremony wasn't over yet. Bryony appeared to be enjoying being the centre of attention far too much to stop now.

She put down her eccentric cup and picked up a lethal-looking knife. Percy shot me a look of alarm at this action, and I shared her apprehension, but I returned my gaze to Bryony, who now held a green apple in her other hand. She lifted the apple and the blade and intoned: "The apple is the symbol for harvest because it represents life and immortality, healing, renewal, regeneration and wholeness. It is associated with beauty, long life and restored youth. It is the epitome of health and vitality."

With a dramatic sweep of her weapon, Bryony sliced the apple clean in half, revealing the seeds inside. "See, the seeds form a pentagram. These five points represent the elements of Earth, Air, Fire, Water with Spirit at the top, and thus also the directions of East, South, West, North and, importantly and not to be forgotten, Within.

"Revere the apple and you will be protected from all evil, so drink, my friends, from its juice and know you will be safe thereby. Do not forget to place apples at the entrances to your homes to ward off negativity. Here is the apple cake Gwen has made. When you eat your piece, make a wish for something positive to come into your life to replace that which you have released."

It seemed she had finished, and everyone smiled and started to clap but Bryony once more held up her hand for silence. I noticed her followers looked surprised as they turned to their spiritual leader again.

"Fellow Pagans, I am hoping that I will have another message for you tonight, one that concerns us all. I am waiting for a sign from a higher source than myself, so please, gather by the stone again if you are called later this evening.

"Now, I shall light the fire that will replace the sun through the darkest time of the year until the sun will shine again."

Bryony stepped down from the stone plinth and entered the circle of people still holding hands around the unlit pyre in the middle. She held a basket of pinecones out to the youngest members of the group, some of them wide-eyed children, and they placed the pinecones carefully around the base of the fire. Then Bryony took a flaming torch from a man dressed all in emerald green and put it to the nearest cone.

The flames caught with a whooshing sound and sent sparks dancing up into the night sky. I looked up and, as I watched their flight towards the stars, I felt a matching glow in my heart.

Everyone piled into the food at that point, but I hung back, still moved and emotionally charged, hoping for a connecting moment with Robin. He had felt so close and my longing for him had been so intense, I was sure it would happen if I just sat quietly alone for a while. I discreetly separated from the happy bunch of people grouped around the cornucopia of food and slipped away to stand underneath the oldest oak. Its bark was ancient and twisted from many years of withstanding the Welsh weather while it stood guard over this sacred grove. I sat down on the grass, not caring about the damp, and leant my weary bruised back against its venerable trunk, willing the tree to serve as a channel between me and my lost love. My eyelids drooped almost instantly and, against my will, closed. Perhaps a nap would refresh me, it had been a hell of a day.

Chapter Thirty-Two, Present Day

When I awoke, I saw that all that was left of the food on the capstone was a pile of delightful debris and everyone was now dancing around the fire, smiling and laughing, lit by the flames in golden flickers of light. A band had struck up some folk tunes and they stood to one side of the littered cromlech, fiddling on their violins, and strumming their guitars to the beat of an Irish drum.

But where was Percy? Had she gone off with the handsome boy with the dreadlocks? No, he was dancing with Gwen. Bryony, too, had relaxed and was cavorting around with George as if she had shed twenty years. No sign of Percy doing a jig, though.

I stretched my stiff limbs and heaved myself up from the dew-laden ground. My muscles felt like they'd been set in concrete, and I yawned, drawing in the night-air for an oxygen fix to wake my tired brain.

I went back to the remains of the feast and found Gwen's celebrated apple cake. I took the very last slice and ate it. I remembered Bryony's instruction to make a wish. Would it work if I hadn't released anything? I swallowed the last delicious crumb and asked for my fears about financial security to disappear and be replaced by abundance from doing this crazy work. If I had been asked to do this exercise twelve months ago, I would have asked for release from this life so I could join Robin. It seemed I had moved on a bit.

I wandered around the periphery in the shadows thrown by the fire, now burning brightly, content to watch the dancers. I didn't feel hungry, I was too tired to eat more. My greatest desire was to return to the cottage and conk out for the night. I needed to find Percy and let her know my plan. Where *was* she?

I'm not sure what it was that made me spin around and look away from the antics of the dancers. They were making so much noise, singing to the music in joyful abandon, I couldn't have heard anything above it. No, my intuition drew me away from the merriment back to the dark depths of the trees beyond the fairy candlelights. I scanned the woodland by the eerie light of the moon and was rewarded by a small movement on the edge of the coppice, towards the sea. Adrenaline began to pump in my veins, dispelling the drowsiness that had so recently threatened to overwhelm me, and I started to walk towards the moving shadows, alert to any sign of life – or death.

Was that a flash of red whisking through the trees?

"Percy? Is that you?" I picked up my pace in pursuit of the phantom, unsure if it was real or if I had imagined it.

No-one replied to my call. I broke into a run, straining my eyes to catch another glimpse of what I hoped was a long red skirt.

As the music faded into the distance, I could hear the swish of the leaves in the wind and some whirled down in a terminal flight to their winter interment. As I crushed those that had already fallen, an earthy smell escaped under my feet. I ran between the tree trunks, brushing my hand on their knobbly bark as if they were friends giving me some much-needed reassurance.

I'll be hugging them next, I thought.

I found Percy standing, entranced, staring up at the full moon. As soon as I approached, deliberately making plenty of noise, I could tell she would have been unaware if an elephant had crashed towards her, trumpeting his arrival.

Wary of what she might do based on grim experience, I circled around her so that I could see her face and maybe try and read her expression. When I had reached a position in front of her, I was struck by how exalted she looked. She stood with her head flung back, so her hair hung down and away from her, with her arms outstretched to the side. Her eyes were closed, and she swayed slightly from time-to-time. Her full lips were half smiling, half murmuring, as if in conversation.

She seemed blissed out, happy even, and obviously in communication with someone I couldn't see.

I stepped forward, quietly this time, trying to catch any words she might utter. As I got close, she nodded as if in acceptance of a command and put her palms together in the prayer position. I would have given anything to know who was coming through to my friend. I fervently hoped it was a benign spirit and not an instruction to murder Rick to avenge Bryonia's gruesome death. You never knew with Percy. So, when she opened her eyes and looked straight at me, I held my breath, braced for whatever might come next, but to my relief, she seemed not to see me, but turned away and headed back to the sacred grove and the dancing Pagans.

I let my breath out again and followed closely behind her. Percy walked as if in a dream, almost gliding along, effortlessly avoiding trees and branches and with a light, different step. She looked as if she belonged in the woods, was a part of it somehow, and knew every twig and leaf within it. I, on the other hand, had a smack in the face from a whip-like branch and nearly fell flat on my face after tripping on a tree root.

We arrived, more or less intact, back amongst the dancers. Bryony was in the centre of it all, jigging away and didn't notice us at first, but the second she looked across and saw Percy, she stood quite still and stared intently at her.

Perhaps it was the intensity of that gaze but everyone around Bryony gradually ceased their gyrations and the band's jaunty music fizzled into silence. All that could be heard was the crackle of the fire, which now blazed with a fierce red core firmly established in its heart.

Percy seemed blissfully unaware of the effect her presence was having on the crowd and walked in that new, graceful dance towards the cromlech stones. Without hesitation, she stepped up on to the plinth in front of it and smiled genially upon the throng now staring openly at her as if under a spell.

I joined them, standing at the front, closest to Percy, whether to protect her or them, I didn't yet know.

Percy spread her hands out and tipped back her head, as she had in the woods. She closed her eyes for a minute, then opened them and cast her gaze around the crowd to encompass everyone in it, in the way accomplished public speakers do, which of course is part of their power, so that everyone feels included and special. Really gifted speakers make each member of the audience feel they alone are being spoken to; they alone can hear the real message. I felt the press of people's bodies as they honed-in on the enchanting woman before them and fell under her spell.

Percy spoke in a strange voice. She used modern English, everyone could understand her, but it was lilting and melodic, almost sing-song in its delivery.

"Lovers of the light and my beloved descendants. It is good to see you here in my sacred grove. I am Gaine, creator of this magic circle and planter of the mothers of these oaks many, many years ago."

Percy flung her arms wider, to their fullest extent, as if to encompass not only the people in front of her but the entire circumference of the oak trees.

"Friends, I have worked tirelessly through time to concentrate the energy in this sacred place. The Earth is composed of a fine balance of dark and light energy and this portal is an important source of light and positivity which spreads powerful energy out all over your world. Can you feel it, my dear ones?"

Murmurs and nods acknowledged her words, but everyone looked pretty stunned even as they answered her.

Percy smiled at them. "My children, I have seen much trouble in this world but always good has triumphed over evil, even at the darkest of times. The time that approaches now is the greatest challenge the Earth has ever faced. I see huge wildfires, invasive floods, drought and famine breaking out in so many areas on our beautiful planet. This grove, this very sacred circle, will soon be under threat. I have a message to the world, and you are the ones who must deliver it. My energy is fading now but come back at Samhain, gather everyone you can to hear this message. It is the most important one I shall ever give. You must make sure no modern sound interferes with the vibration of this place. It has been hard lately to communicate with your priestess, and I must have a clear channel."

Towards the end of her speech, Percy's voice grew weaker and faint. I'm sure I wasn't alone in straining to hear the last few sentences. Then I forgot everything she said as Percy crumpled up and fell in a heap on to the trampled grass in front of me.

I ran to her side, and unceremoniously put my hand over her heart, to check it still thumped with life.

Within seconds, Bryony was at my side, feeling for a pulse in Percy's neck. We looked up at each other.

"She's alive," Bryony whispered. "Put her in the recovery position."

We manhandled Percy into a comfortable posture, and I made sure her airways were clear. Percy looked as white as a sheet and completely exhausted.

Bryony looked at me across Percy's inert body. "I think she'll be fine."

I nodded back. "Yes, this has happened before. She just needs to sleep it off."

Bryony stood up and turned to her followers, who stood, mouths agape and their eyes no less wide open. "Our friend will be well. She is exhausted and must sleep. Please, move away to the other side of the stones."

Everyone shuffled off, muttering quietly.

Once they had reassembled, George asked the question that must have been on everyone's lips. "But what does it mean?"

Having checked Percy really was alright, I joined them on the other side of the cromlech and listened to Bryony's response.

"It means, George, everyone, we have an important task to do, one that effects every living soul in the world."

Someone else asked, "But who was she, this, Gaine, was it?"

Bryony gave a ragged smile. "Yes, her name is Gaine, and she created our sacred grove around two thousand years ago."

A collective gasp responded to this astounding statement but, other than that, the only noise was the slight rustle of the dying autumnal oak leaves that encircled them.

"So, is she a ghost?" This from the young man with the dreadlocks.

"Yes, I suppose she is."

Another outbreath rippled through the crowd.

Bryony nodded acknowledgement. "I know, it seems very strange."

"Too right!" I heard the man next to me mutter.

Bryony continued, "Yes, it's strange but it's true. I have had the privilege of communicating with Gaine myself on several occasions. I was hoping she would come through tonight with her message about climate change."

I had the intuitive insight that Bryony wished that message had come through her, not Percy.

George, his eyes shining, said, "But, Bryony, what can we do that we don't do already?"

"Hear, hear."

"Yeah, what can we do?"

"Gaine told us to gather at Samhain. That is six weeks from now and she will come again with another message that we must get the world to hear."

"How can we do that?" Gwen said in her quiet way.

Someone excitedly answered for Bryony. "We must get the media here for Samhain! The BBC and journalists from all the papers. Get them to record it, bring cameras, see it for themselves!"

The crowd burst into debate, no more mutterings in subdued tones now.

"In our sacred place?"

"But they would ruin what we have!"

"How could we let the world in here? What would happen to the energy then?"

"They would trample all over it!"

Bryony held up her hands for silence and got it. "Friends, we have much to discuss but perhaps this is not the moment. Let us go home now and reflect on what we have heard and meet again."

"But when?"

"In two weeks, it will be the dark of the moon and a new beginning. Let us meet here on the nearest Saturday - in the afternoon?"

Heads nodded and voices concurred. I watched as the group split up, chattering in hushed, awed tones at what they had witnessed.

I went up to George. "You know, just a mobile phone could record Gaine's message? Things can go viral from a phone."

He turned to me his eyes still alight with a worrying fervour. "Is true, Fay. No one had time to think of recording it tonight. Did you see anyone taking a photo?"

I shook my head. "Definitely not. It was all so quick and unexpected I don't think it occurred to a single soul."

"This is good." He turned to his wife. "Let us go home, Gwen. We shall see you soon?"

"I hope so, goodnight both." I hugged each of them with sincere affection.

Soon, only Percy and I were left in the sacred circle amongst the littered debris of the feast. No one bothered to stop and clear it up before leaving. Even Bryony had gone along with the others, fending off questions fired at her from all sides.

I slid down against the solid limestone rock and leant my weight against its comforting support. Percy's breathing was deep and even, but I must wake her soon or she would catch a chill.

I just needed to sit for a moment. There was a lot to take in.

Chapter Thirty-Three, Present Day

The exhausting day took its toll, and I was asleep within seconds, slumped against the hefty stone. How long we both slept for I have no idea, but we were rudely awakened by a terrific roaring noise wrecking the peace.

"What's that?" I looked across at Percy, curled up in a foetal position beside me.

Startled, she roused up from her deep sleep, looking disorientated as well as unusually dishevelled.

The roaring stopped suddenly, and a blinding light shone directly into my eyes. I put my arm across my face to shield it from the powerful beam. This was no visit from the past illuminating us but an altogether twenty-first century blast of electric light. Just as abruptly it was switched off, leaving both of us blinking and bedazzled.

Before my sight returned, a man walked towards us, and I only vaguely recognised him as Rick. Before I could stop her, Percy sprang to her feet, teeth bared, and yelling something at him that sounded like abuse to me.

As my eyes adjusted back to the dim light of the moon, I saw that Rick held his hands up in the air, as if surrendering, and his face wore a terrified look.

I turned around to see what had spooked him. "Percy! Percy, it's me, Fay!"

She turned around in a semi-circle at the sound of my voice. As soon as I saw her face, I knew Percy was in a trance. Her eyes showed no recognition of me, and she pointed a vicious-looking knife, the one Bryony had used for her dramatic apple-slicing trick, straight at my heart.

"Percy! No! Don't do that! I'm your friend!"

I dodged the blade as it descended, and it only missed me by a couple of inches. Much too close for comfort.

"Hey, man. Stop that." Rick appeared behind Percy his hands once more held out in supplication.

Caught between us, Percy looked from one to the other, then lunged at Rick with a primeval scream.

"Murderer!" This time, the knife found its mark in Rick's thigh, and he yelled out in pain.

He tried to block it with his arm. "Argh! You bitch!"

Percy's eyes blazed at him. I grabbed her arm before she struck again, as Rick fell back against the stones, providing her with an altogether too vulnerable, trapped target.

I shook her hand fiercely, using all my strength, gripping her by the wrist in a painful hold. To my relief, her fingers opened, and the weapon fell from her hand. She reached out with her other arm to hit me, but I blocked it with mine and put some force behind it. We fell to the ground together and I pinned her arms to her side, straddling her body with my spread legs.

"No, Percy. Come out of your trance. This is dangerous."

"Let me finish off that Roman brute, once and for all."

Rick, who was clutching his leg and wincing with pain, looked on with a horrified expression. "Can't you stop her? Who does she think she is?"

"Gaine."

As I spoke the name, Percy's eyes narrowed. "Who are you? I do not know you. Are you Celt or Roman?"

"I am neither and nor are you. Wake up, Percy. It's time." I slapped her face, dreading she might respond with her freed hand but instead she held it to her red cheek and blinked rapidly.

"Fay? Is that you?"

I let out my breath. "Yes, it's me. Come on, sit up."

Rick rubbed his hand across his eyes. "Bloody hell. Thank God she's snapped out of it. If you hadn't come along, I'd be a gonner. She is one strong lady."

I nodded my head towards him. "Believe me, Rick, I'm very aware of that."

Percy sat up and brushed some dead leaves from her face. "What's happened?"

"You tell us, babe." Rick slithered down to the ground, still clutching his leg.

I turned back to Percy, who still lay pinned by my legs. "You were Gaine and trying to kill this feller in revenge for Bryonia's death by the Roman soldier."

"I did what?" Percy looked at Rick, who was holding on to his thigh and groaning. "He looks exactly like him."

I heaved myself upright and went over to look at Rick's wound. "Oh dear, the knife must have gone through your trousers, Rick. Thank God they're made of leather. Hopefully it hasn't got deep but we'd better get some help. Can you walk?"

"Dunno, it's hurting like hell."

"Oh, what have I done?" Percy got up and joined us.

More blood seeped through Rick's trousers. "Listen, we've got to bandage that tightly before he can walk. Percy, take the bandana off Rick's head and tie it around his thigh."

Percy, now fully present, obeyed with deft, quick movements. "Come on, Rick. Let's get you upright."

We pulled Rick up to a standing position and put our arms around his waist on either side.

"Right, let's get back to the farmhouse. Someone will have a first aid kit there." I wasn't actually sure about that, but it would be a start.

"Should we use the bike?" Percy nodded towards the Harley Davidson by the trees.

"We couldn't all three get on and Rick could be injured even more if he passes out and falls off at speed."

Percy looked back at me. "You're right. Okay, here we go. Hold on tight, Rick."

We hobbled forward, Rick groaning under his breath. "This is bewildering. First you come at me with a flipping knife and now you're helping me to get mended. I don't know which way is up with you."

I gave Rick what I hoped was a reassuring smile. "You've got to realise that Percy can channel dead people. She has an affinity for Gaine."

"Who?"

Percy answered his question. "I'm so sorry, Rick. It's really not me trying to kill you, but this young druidess seeking revenge for the death of her grandmother. You look so like the Roman soldier who murdered her, you see."

"Bloody hell, it's all beyond me." Rick was looking pale, and I insisted we went faster.

I didn't give much for our chances if he passed out. He might be skinny, but it felt like he weighed a ton. We walked on, with Rick supported between us, towards the farmhouse.

"Not far now." Percy hitched her arm around his waist a little higher.

To my immense relief, the big stone house loomed into view, its lights blooming out into the garden from every window. It looked like the meeting had already begun as all the cars were still parked, higgledy-piggledy, in the spare ground in front of the house.

The front door stood, as ever, open in welcome and we stumbled through it.

"Hello there! We need help!"

George greeted us in the hall, looking shocked at Rick's state. "Come in, come in."

Grateful for his strong arms, we manhandled Rick into the big yoga room.

There were quite a few people in there, all looking animated and deep in discussion but as soon as Bryony saw Rick, she took charge and asked them to leave. As one, they obediently shuffled out.

"Put him down on the floor." Bryony bent over him. "How did this happen?"

Percy seemed to have disappeared with the others, so I volunteered. "Knife wound to the thigh."

To do Bryony credit, she didn't even blink at this news.

George alone stayed to help.

Feeling out of my depth, I said, "Surely, he should go to A&E?"

Bryony shook her head. "It's too far. The nearest one is Bangor, over the Menai Straits. We must arrest the bleeding before he goes any further."

"But can't you just ring 999?" I was appalled at this development. It seemed very high-handed to me. I reached in my pocket for my mobile then remembered it was still in the depths of that dangerous cave.

Bryony frowned. "Let me look at him first and make an assessment. The hospital really is miles away." She placed pillows under Rick's head and feet and took off his leather jeans, with George supporting his bottom as she pulled them down to expose the wound.

A nasty gash, about four inches long, oozed bright red blood from Rick's thigh.

Bryony looked up at me. "I think he'll be alright, it's only skin deep and it's nowhere near the femoral artery. It just looks alarming because of the blood loss but it's not pumping. We must elevate his foot."

She got up and grabbed some yoga blocks and put them under Rick's foot, so it was higher than his uninjured leg. Then she turned to me. "Fay, put your hand over the wound and press hard. George, fetch as much clean linen as you can."

Swallowing my revulsion at this order, I knelt down next to Rick's leg and placed my hand on the exposed red tissue. I don't know why, but somehow, I hadn't expected it to feel warm under my palm. The blood ran through my fingers in sticky rivulets. Far too much of it for my liking and I still felt uneasy about the lack of trained paramedics at the scene.

George returned with a bundle of white cloth. Bryony gave him a brisk nod. "Good, now fetch ice from the freezer and put it in a clean plastic bag. Hurry!"

George disappeared in an instant and came back only minutes later by which time Bryony had manufactured a tighter tourniquet above the wound and already, with my hand pressed against it, I could feel the blood flow lessen.

"It's easing, Bryony."

"That's good but keep up the pressure after I put this wad of cotton on the wound. Ready?"

I whipped my hand away and replaced it quickly once the pad had been put in place.

Bryony held out her hand to George. "Give me the bag of ice and bring strong camomile and yarrow tea in a china bowl with six drops of tea tree oil."

She packed the ice around the wound, and I could see the flow slow down remarkably quickly.

"It's working!"

Bryony's expression looked grim. "Yes, I think it'll be okay."

Percy came back into the room, looking extremely pale. "Oh God, what have I done?"

Bryony stared at Percy. "What do you mean? *You* did this? You stabbed Rick?"

Tears welled up in Percy's eyes. I could barely hear her whisper, "Yes."

"For God's sake, why?"

Percy looked unable to answer, overcome with emotion, she put her hand across her mouth, which had creased up.

I hated to tell tales, but Bryony deserved the truth. "Gaine took her over a second time and made her do this."

Bryony's hands halted their work for a moment, and she shut her eyes. Then she looked directly into mine. "I see it now. We shall talk more of this but now is not the time."

Percy had recovered her sangfroid and crouched down to Rick, who visibly recoiled at her nearness. "How are you feeling, Rick?"

"If you back off, I'd feel a lot more relaxed, luv."

Percy stood up, her face slightly flushed. "Of course. Listen, I'm ringing 999. We've got to get the paramedics out. I can't live with my conscience if I don't." She had tapped the numbers in as she spoke, before anyone else could countermand her.

"Hello, yes, it's an emergency." We all listened as Percy told the emergency service about Rick's injury, but

216

she quickly turned, surprisingly, to Rick. "They want to speak to you."

Percy handed Rick her phone. "Yeah, that's correct, yeah." Rick's answers stayed monosyllabic until he raised his eyebrows. "What? Nah, did it to meself, didn't I? How? Um, I was doing some DIY, you know, like you do, and the knife slipped in me hand, like."

Percy and I exchanged astonished glances. I hadn't expected Rick to be so generous, or quite frankly, so quick-witted.

"Yes, I'm fine. No, I don't need any more help. No, I'm not dizzy or anything. It's been bandaged by a, um, a friend and has stopped bleeding. Yeah, I had a tetanus last year. Yeah, I'll check it out at my local surgery in the morning for antibiotics. Okay, then. Bye."

Rick addressed us all in his cockney voice. "No need for the flipping Air Ambulance. Got to go to the doc's if it goes red or more painful but I reckon I'm in good hands already." He grinned at Bryony, but she didn't smile back.

Instead, Bryony took off the ice pack and applied Steristrips to the edges of the wound, bringing the sides together neatly. Then she dusted it with some sort of powder and bandaged it up with fresh white cotton, designed for the purpose. She gave Rick some hot tea and dropped some brown liquid from a bottle with a pipette into the brew. Despite my anxiety about what this might contain, his colour returned. Looking satisfied, she asked him how he felt.

"Alright, I think. It don't hurt so much. That tea was good. Spicy and sweet."

Bryony put her face closer to his. "And do you feel dizzy or lightheaded?"

"Nah, bit wobbly perhaps but I reckon I could stand now."

"You're sure?" Bryony held his wrist and I realised she was taking his pulse. "Stay still for a moment, Rick."

Rick obediently went quiet. We all did.

After a minute, Bryony nodded briskly. "You'll do. I suggest George takes you home in the Landrover and you go straight to bed. You know my mobile number. Ring me if you feel unwell, but I think you're going to be fine."

Then she did something less conventional. Bryony knelt behind Rick's head and held his head between her palms. It spooked me a bit because the last time I had seen someone do this it was her namesake performing the same trick on Gaine's dead body in the cave. She shut her eyes and went very still. Rick didn't resist but lay there quietly. Gradually his own eyes closed, and a peaceful look stole across his lived-in face. There was something about the quality of the silence that ensued for the next ten minutes that we all respected, without being bidden. The atmosphere in the room changed too from fraught crisis mode into one of reflection and tranquillity.

In the calm aftermath George quietly brought the Landrover round and we all climbed in, even Rick, who needed lots of help as he had become extremely sleepy after his tea. George drove us back to the big house, where Ed, who I had decided never slept, immediately came to the door and took charge. George quickly explained what had happened.

Eddie didn't bat an eye. "I'll handle this. You go off to your accommodation, girls. George? Help me get him upstairs."

Within a minute, no more, we had been dismissed.

Chapter Thirty-Four, Present Day

Over our morning cup of tea, Percy spoke little but I could see she was troubled.

"Do you want to talk about what happened last night, Percy?"

She still looked tired and sighed. "I don't understand it. When I've channelled Gaine before she seemed benign, almost saintly in her desire to help the world, so I'm puzzled – and mortified – as to why she attacked Rick."

I cast my mind back to the dramatic events of last night. "I've been wondering about it too and my theory is that she was startled into it. She obviously loved her grandmother, Bryonia, very deeply and remained justifiably angry about her violent death. You said last night that Rick looked just like the Roman soldier who killed Bryonia. I can see a resemblance myself, but I didn't get as good a look at him when I had my vision at Caernarfon. If there is a strong likeness, it's not such a surprise that she sought revenge."

Percy sipped her herbal brew. "Maybe, but it's such a contrast to her message to the group. I guess, when it comes to our loved ones, we none of us know what we are capable of."

I put my empty mug back on the table. "Love and hate often go together."

Percy nodded. "But why is it always me that ends up being a vehicle for violence?"

I shrugged my broad shoulders. "You can't blame yourself for being the host to another spirit, Percy. It's not your fault."

"Poor Rick. I was getting quite fond of him. Lord knows what he must think of me now."

Very gently, I said, "We're here on an assignment, remember. Maybe it's better to keep things professional?"

Percy got up and took the mugs to the dishwasher. With her head averted, she mumbled, "You could be right."

"Let's go and see him and I'm sure you will be reassured. He looks like a born survivor to me."

We donned our coats and shoes and walked over to the big estate house that afternoon. We found Rick in the big sitting room, ensconced in a comfortable armchair next to a blazing fire, his wounded leg propped up on a footstool and a glass of whisky nearby.

"Yeah, man. I'm good, thanks."

I'd been thinking hard since the previous night's drama. "Rick, Percy is adamant you resemble the Roman who invaded the Druid village two thousand years ago. Ed has told me that you inherited this estate. Can I ask when?"

Rick shrugged his shoulders. "It's just always been in my family. Never questioned it."

"Do you think your family claimed this land when the Romans conquered Britain?"

"How should I know?"

"But your family is Italian, isn't it?"

"Yeah, there are Ratti's all over bella Italia, but my lot always lived here."

"Have you any documents – house deeds – that sort of thing?"

"Gawd, I dunno. Maybe."

I leaned forward. "It's important, Rick You see, if you inherited it from a Roman ancestor, it would explain one of the reasons why Gaine is angry with you. I don't think it's just about disturbing the energy with your loud music. Would Ed know?"

Rick took a sip of whisky. "I suppose so. He keeps all my paperwork under lock and key and I'm happy for him to get on with it." He smacked his lips and put the glass down. "But listen, I've had an idea, actually. Dunno where it came from. It was after Mrs Hippy-Dippy held my head. That was really weird. Don't remember nothing about it but I felt different after, you know? I slept like a baby last night and then, ping, this morning, it came to me."

Percy sat quietly. I could see she was dying to ask him to explain himself but was still feeling too awkward to dare opening her mouth.

220

Having no guilt to shut me up, I asked for her. "What's this idea then, Rick?"

"Well, see, I dreamt about that place with the trees, you know, in a circle? It was like I was really there, just standing quiet. Didn't have my bike and the trees seemed smaller, younger, and so was I! I was all alone, and I felt this amazing sort of energy, you know?"

Rick had a faraway look in his eyes. "That place has a great vibe, don't you think?"

"I suppose so."

"Oh, yeah. Deffo. Used to go there as a kid but got spooked and never went back until now." Rick rolled a cigarette. "I only went there last night because I heard music, but it seemed to stop all-of-a-sudden. After I had that dream, I thought, you know, I keep getting problems in the studio, so why not record in the circle of trees, by that weird stone arrangement. Then I could use the sounds of the birds and that as the backdrop? It would be so cool, so different. No one's done that before in rock music, as far as I know. It would give it the edge I need. What do you reckon?"

"I think Pink Floyd did something similar in a meadow years ago."

"The kids will have forgotten that by now."

I shrugged. "And, I see a bit of a flaw, Rick."

He lit his roll-up. "Ah, you don't, do you?"

I shrugged my too-broad shoulders. "How's anyone going to hear birdsong over the top of your noise, I mean, music?"

"Yeah, I know, but like, I can tune in to the birds' singing and build on it, see? I mean, they're amazing, right? I can have quiet bits and then record them and sort of, you know, pick up on their tunes, kind of thing. Then I can play around with it and amplify the bird song and weave it into my guitar sound."

"Oh, okay. I suppose that could work."

"Of course, it will, man. It's going to be terrific and it's not just about the birds singing their guts out. I reckon it's the vibe. There's something extra there, I could feel it in my dream, like someone was telling me to do it. It'll give me a whole new take on my work and I'm going to make a video to go with it. It's going to be ace."

Percy spoke at last. "Um, how's your leg, Rick?"

Rick waved a nonchalant hand in the air, making ash fall from the tip of his cigarette. "It's fine. Don't know why everyone made such a fuss. It's nothing." He picked up his whisky glass. "This anaesthetic helps."

"I'm so glad. I feel terrible about it." Percy gave one of her devastating smiles.

Rick didn't respond like he used to. "Yeah, well. I think you should steer clear of me from now on, darlin'. No offence, but you are just too weird. See if you can sort the whole ghost thing out far away from me, yeah?"

Percy's face fell back into seriousness. "Understood."

I got up to go. "Right, well, we'll leave you to it then. By the way, Rick, how will you power the recording away from the studio?"

"Oh, Ed will sort somefink out. Run a cable or summat from the studio, it's not far. I dunno. He's a genius at that sort of thing."

"Right. Have you asked Bryony about this project?"

"Who? Oh, hippy-lady. Nah, she looked after me good and proper last night, fair play, but at the end of the day, it's my land, innit? I can do what the hell I like."

He got his mobile phone out of his jeans pocket and started tapping on its screen. We were once more dismissed.

As we walked back to our cottage, Percy voiced her misgivings. "Don't you think someone should warn Bryony about Rick's idea of playing in the oak grove?"

"Definitely. Rick's not going to, that's for sure."

Both George's cob cottage and the farmhouse looked quiet and dormant after the previous night's hectic activity. Bryony's front door was shut, unusually, but not locked. I gave a brief warning knock and turned the handle.

The house was silent and seemed deserted inside.

"Everyone must be asleep." Percy peered down the hall.

"Maybe." I poked my head through the doorway of the yoga room, surprised to find Bryony sitting cross-legged, forefingers and thumbs connected and resting on her knees in a classic yoga pose.

I put my finger to my lips and Percy nodded. She jerked her thumb in the direction of the hall and we started to turn around and make out way back outside when Bryony spoke.

"Come in, now you're here."

Percy, polite as ever, hesitated. "No, no. So sorry to disturb you. We'll leave you in peace. We shouldn't have just walked in when the door was shut."

"That's very true but you are here now, and my meditation has already been ruined. There is much I wish to ask of you."

I felt trapped and would rather have left, despite the austere invitation, but Percy had already entered the hallowed space and sat down on one of the chairs around the periphery of the room. There was no way I was going to leave Percy's side with Gaine so eager to channel her into violence, so I felt I had no choice but to join her on the chair beside hers.

Bryony took a deep breath and exhaled it incredibly slowly before she opened her eyes and looked at us with piercing blue clarity.

"I think you were meant to come here today, at this moment. I sense Gaine organised it. She drew you to this room this morning and maybe she drew you here to Anglesey in the first place. You are part of her plan."

Bryony gaze focussed on Percy. "And you can channel her, it seems."

Percy gave a confident, calm smile. "Yes."

Some of Bryony's meditational tranquillity deserted her at that point and there was a bitter edge to her words. "*I've* been channelling her for years, so I confess I'm surprised she's chosen *you* for her message."

Percy shook her head. "I don't know that she will. It could just as easily come through you, Bryony."

Before the competition for Gaine's chats got too animated, I chipped in. "Frankly, does it matter who it comes through? Isn't the message what's important?"

Bryony blinked rapidly. "Forgive me, that was my ego speaking. You are right, of course, and we need to formulate a plan to enable her to say what she so desperately wants to convey."

It was my turn to smile. "I do love a plan."

Chapter Thirty-Five, Present Day

"Oh, hell, Rick's got there before us." Percy looked despairingly at me as we walked along the path to the sacred circle and heard him yelling at Ed through the trees.

Bryony had given her blessing for Percy to try and connect with Gaine again and had had the grace to let us get on with it without her.

"There's no way Gaine will come through if he's there when she's still so angry with him, and frankly, Percy, if she did, it might get ugly again."

The wail of his electric guitar hit us like a howling dog as we approached.

"I don't think there's much point even trying to connect with her in the grove with that racket going on and I promise I won't try." Percy stopped walking and tucked a strand of hair behind her ear, making the long earring hanging from it dance.

Its unusual pattern caught my attention, and I also came to a halt. "Are those earrings new? They look Celtic, in fact, I've seen that pattern somewhere before – I know! On the capstone and I saw it on Bryonia's necklace and the upright stone she stood next to one time."

Percy fingered the one dangling on side of her head nearest me. "I couldn't resist them. They were for sale in George's workshop and such good value because they look like real gold, but I don't think they can be for that price. I blew all the remaining cash I have on them. Bit mad really but something just compelled me to get them."

"They must be real gold, or they'd rust in that set-up."

Percy laughed. "Yes, I suppose so but if so, they were ridiculously cheap. It's quite strange because I'd not noticed them before, but they sort of called to me. Like I said, it sounds a bit crazy, but I felt they belonged to me."

"I should have looked it up before now but what does the symbol mean?"

"It's called a triskelion and the three spirals represent connection to the Sun, the source of all life."

"It's lovely how the line of spirals is unbroken."

"Funny you should mention that because that's what drew me to them. It means the continuity of life. You know, how life goes on and on, no matter what?"

"They suit you, Percy."

"Thank you. I love them. You know, being here has changed me. I'm learning so much and I feel connected to the Earth in a way I never have before."

"Hmm, I hate to admit it, being a heathen, but I feel it too. That session with Bryony, when Robin came through telling me how much he loved me, well, it got to me."

Percy gave me a quick hug. "I'm glad we came."

"Me too, come on, let's see what Rick is up to and if I see you going into a trance, forgive me if I shake you up a bit!"

Percy laughed. "Deal!"

There were electric cables everywhere, looking as out of place as spaghetti in a crystal wine glass instead of on a plate.

"That's it, Ed!" Rick pressed his wah-wah pedal with the toe of his cowboy boot. "Crank her up a bit, mate."

We entered the circle of oaks just as Rick hit his stride and Eddie turned up the volume. We both clamped our hands over our ears as the music pounded out.

When I felt my ribcage vibrate, I went over to Eddie. "Can't you turn it down a bit?"

He yelled back at me. "Rick wants to check it out at concert volume, see how it sounds."

"If he wants birdsong, he's going the wrong way about it! They'll all fly away!" I shouted.

Rick stopped playing when he looked up and saw us, and like a child needing attention, put down his guitar and strolled over. "What do you think, girls? Neat, eh?"

Percy stood with her hands on her hips, her cheeks flushed with anger. "No, it's not the least bit neat, Rick. I thought you were going to record the birds singing and the natural sounds of the grove?"

"Well, I will, but just wanted to check it out first, like, you know, as if it was a concert."

"And why do you think this will give it the 'new' sound you're looking for?" Rarely had I seen Percy so furious. "You're just doing what you always do – blasting out at such a volume you can barely survive it!"

Rick stroked the stubble on his chin. "Hey, man, calm down. Maybe you've got a point."

"Yeah, maybe I have!" Percy was obviously not about to back down, but I wondered if she might want some backup and fervently hoped it wasn't Gaine prompting her anger again.

"She's right, Rick. You could do this anywhere. You need something different, like you said. Something new and fresh and surprising."

Eddie raised his eyebrows at our bold suggestions. "I hate to say it, Rick, but they have a point. I mean, you're a great guitarist, one of the best, but it's old hat. Let's have a listen to the birds, hey mate?"

Rick shrugged his thin shoulders and slumped down against the stones in the centre of the grove. "If you like."

Percy went and sat next to him. "I should give it a few minutes for the birds to return, they've probably flown as far away as they can."

Rick immediately stood up. "Yeah, I get it, okay? Just don't come so close to me, girl. I don't want a knife in the other leg."

"How is your leg, Rick?" I sauntered over and stood between the ex-lovers on the alert for any change in Percy.

"It's alright, as a matter of fact, and I want to keep it that way. Nuff said. Listen, I'm going to muck about with my acoustic guitar. Don't worry, I won't plug it in."

He sloped off to where his equipment lay on a tarpaulin by a couple of camping chairs, picked up his guitar and sat down with it. I was pleasantly surprised at the

227

soothing strumming that emanated from it and, I have to say, impressed at his diversity and skill.

I wandered back to Eddie, who was fiddling with his tablet.

"I see you've managed to run a cable from the studio to here. Do you get an internet signal as well, Eddie?"

"Got a mobile Wifi router, haven't I? Why do you ask?"

"Oh, just wondered. How's things? Any more trouble in the studio?"

"Nah, as it happens, it's been alright."

"Oh, great. I think the spirits are busy elsewhere."

Eddie snorted. "Yeah, right."

I was longing to ask him about the history of the estate and was quite curious about that visit by the driver of the slinky Porsche, but, at that moment, Bryony and Derwen burst through the trees from the direction of the farmhouse. The dog was barking its head off and Bryony joined in as soon as she reached Ed.

"What the hell do you think you're playing at with that totally inappropriate level of noise?"

"That ain't noise, lady, it's music." Ed didn't bat an eyelid at her intrusion.

"Music? You don't know the meaning of the term. How dare you pollute this sacred space!"

Rick heaved a sigh and put down his wooden guitar. "The one making all the noise is your bloody dog, missus. Can't you shut him up?"

"It's a her, and why should I, after the racket you've been making?" Bryony did however shush Derwen who stood, hackles raised and ears down.

"Enough to wake the dead perhaps?" Ed smiled unpleasantly.

"That's just it!" Bryony shouted. "The dead will never wake up with that deafening noise and we must reach them, we must!"

"What are you on about, woman?" Rick looked perplexed. "Is it you that's been interfering in the studio all along?"

Bryony ran her hand through her long grey hair, making it stick out in chaotic strands. "No, I'm not interested in your bloody music." She gave a shuddering sigh and reined herself in. In a more moderate tone, she said, "Look, Rick, I know you are the owner of this land, but I have been here for many years while you've been God knows where. There is a community here who depend on me. We are trying – no - we have *created* something really special here. You wouldn't understand, but the energy is what is important and for that we must have peace. The trees need silence."

"The trees need silence? What planet are you on?" Ed guffawed.

Rick however was more thoughtful. "There is a vibe here, I admit. Look, I'm sorry if I ruined the atmosphere of this place. It's not something I've felt before. I came here as a kid and the vibe then was really spooky, you know, kinda scary?" Rick nodded, "Yeah, it's different now."

"Yes, it's different. It's taken years and years of meditation and chanting to achieve this."

Ed rolled his eyes and drew out his cigarette packet. "I've heard it all now."

Rick waved a finger at his colleague. "Nah, mate. She's on to summink."

Ed blew smoke into the air. "If you say so, Rick. I'm just the sound engineer."

Rick looked around the circle of trees. A blackbird broke into song. "That's it! Ah, man! That is beautiful." He turned to Ed. "Record it, quick, can you?"

Rick looked back at Bryony. "Listen lady, I get what you saying, well, sort of. But I've got to make some dosh double quick, and I got to follow through with my idea. You do your stuff, no problem, I'm not going to throw you off the land, but it is *my* land, get it? Now, if you don't mind, I gotta get back to work."

229

"Oh, you are such fool!" Bryony spoke through gritted teeth.

Ed laughed. "Hey, don't put a witchy spell on us, will you?"

Incensed, Bryony squared her shoulders and almost growled, "I am not a witch! I am a Pagan priestess, descended from a long line of Druids, but don't think I can't influence the energy here, sonny, because I can, and I will!"

Ed stubbed out his cigarette on the grass with the heel of his trainer. "Now listen, love, I think you need reminding that Rick is the owner of this precious circle of yours. He's too nice to send you an eviction order, but I'm not and I'm in charge of his affairs, see?"

I heard Bryony's sharp intake of breath and saw her face blanch. "I understand you perfectly." She put her hand on Derwen's furry head. "Come on, Derwen. Let's go home." She looked at me and Percy, standing dumbly by through the exchange. "Thanks for all your help, I don't think."

With that parting shot, she and her collie dog trotted off back towards her farmhouse and the community who revolved around it.

Chapter Thirty-Six, Present Day

We were out of supplies. I couldn't operate without food in my belly and although Bryony's veg box was great and her organic sausages even better, I needed more sustenance.

"I'm off to the shops for food. Want anything?" I shouted up the stairs to Percy, who was deep in some cosmetic ritual in the bathroom.

"Oh, great. There's a list on the fridge."

"Okay, got it. See you in a bit."

I grabbed the car keys and headed for my little hatchback in the communal yard at the back of the house. That Porsche was there again. I bet it cost as much as my small flat. More probably. At least it wasn't Paul Wade's grotesquely huge 4x4 but still, a very expensive motor.

I put the key in the lock of my car, which was so old it didn't have central locking. The kitchen door of the estate house opened and Ed and another man, young, suited, wearing sunglasses on a cloudy day, walked down the couple of steps into the old stable yard.

They shook hands as they stood next to the shiny silver bonnet of the modern car. Then the younger man looked across at me with a smug smile.

"Morning. That your car?"

My driver's door squeaked open. "It doesn't belong to anyone else."

Ed laughed and his friend joined in. "Not surprised. I wouldn't be seen dead in it."

"Could be arranged," I muttered under my breath.

"What was that?"

"Nothing. I'm just off to the shops, Ed. Do you want anything?"

The young man in the too-tight suit looked quizzically at Ed. "You know her?"

"Yeah, Alan. She works here."

"Cleaner?"

I wasn't having that. I marched over to the two men. "Not a cleaner, exactly. More of a detective, you might say."

Alan screwed his face up in disdain. "Really? Work for the police, do you?"

"No, for myself."

This seemed to discomfort them both. Alan turned to Ed. "What's going on?"

Ed waved a hand in dismissal. "It's nothing, Alan. Honest. Some daft idea of Rick's."

Alan lowered his voice, but not quite enough. "But Rick doesn't know about – you know – does he?"

Ed positively squirmed as he darted a look at me. "No, no, don't worry, mate."

Alan bleeped his remote key at his low-slung sports car. "I hope you're right, Ed, because if word does get out, I'm off."

Alan unbuttoned his straining jacket and got in his car. The engine purred into life. The electric window slid gracefully down, and Alan stuck his thick neck out. "I meant what I said, Ed. No deal if you blow it."

Ed simply held his hand up in acknowledgement and turned it into a wave goodbye as the Porsche slunk around in a three-point-turn and sped off down the driveway.

Ed turned to go back into the house. I hurried to catch up with him. I knew I must try and talk to him about the deeds of the estate as well as what this slick Alan was up to.

"Hey, Ed. Not so fast."

"Oh, for pity's sake, what now?" But he stopped, one foot on the step.

"What's this deal?"

"None of your bloody business." The front door slammed behind him.

I turned back to the driveway, climbed inside my hatchback and turned the ignition key. "Well, Edward, I'll just have to make it my business, won't I?"

When I got back and dumped the shopping on the kitchen table at our cottage, Percy was less interested in my encounter with Ed and his stout friend than the contents of the carrier bags.

"Oh, Fay, you're making too much of it. Ed must know loads of dodgy, rich people. He probably does deals all the time."

"Maybe, but he looked pretty shifty when I turned up."

"You flatter yourself, my dear. Ed looks shifty all the time, if you ask me, and as far as he's concerned, we are small fry."

Only a plate of beans on toast slathered in Worcestershire sauce could mollify me after that.

Percy returned to the bathroom after lunch. On the shopping list had been some sort of hair solution that took hours to process. I just managed to catch her before she disappeared upstairs, laden with bags and boxes of cosmetic chemicals and perfumes.

"I'm going for a walk while you make yourself even more beautiful. Promise me you'll stay in the cottage and not go out to attack Rick or anyone else?"

Percy tutted. "Oh, for goodness' sake, Fay! I'm having a thorough MOT today and I shall be fully occupied restoring my tatty nails and having a soak in the bath."

I raised my hands in surrender. "I have your word on that?"

"Fay! Honestly! Okay, okay, you have my word I will not leave this house. Lock the door behind you if you want."

Though tempted to do just that, fear of Percy being trapped by a natural disaster like a fire or a supernatural one caused by some ancient Druid, stopped my hand on the key as I set off for my walk. I needed to clear my head, think for a while, or maybe not think at all.

I decided to walk along the clifftops to maximise the breeziness of this fresh-feeling autumn day and get a wider perspective from a view of the sea. It wouldn't do me any harm to take a break from the tensions around the estate and the grove, either.

My jaunty mood dissipated in an instant when I saw Ed, jabbering away on his mobile phone, as I crossed the yard. He had a lit cigarette in one hand and the phone in the other and stood with his back to me. I had decided to risk a rain shower and wore rubber-soled trainers rather than my hiking boots and they made no sound on the cobbled yard where we parked our cars alongside the old stable block. I could have turned and walked the long way around the front of the house, but even though I wasn't a cat, curiosity hadn't killed me yet. I walked softly and slowly towards Ed's broad back, my ears alert to his side of the conversation.

"Yeah, Alan, that's brilliant about the planning permission. How much do you think it'll cost you to pay him to shut up?"

I stopped walking. Planning permission for what?

"Phew, that's a lot for a backhander!"

Were they bribing some planning officer?

"No, it's okay, I can raise it. I understand he would be taking a massive risk. When will you know?"

Don't turn around Ed, please don't turn around.

"Friday? You mean tomorrow? Oh, cool. Didn't think it would be that quick. And you have explained about the holiday village? Good, good. Does he realise the trees will have to be felled as well, you know, to access the beach?"

Holiday village? Surely not the oaks in the grove? My mind whirred. The best path to the beach lay on the seaward side of the sacred circle of trees.

"Yeah, that's what I thought. Make those stones a feature. Trippers will love that. Bit of history, you know, mysterious and all that. Yeah, we could leave a few trees and you know, put up a big sign bigging up the Druids and all that shit."

It had to be the grove! A holiday village next to the sacred cromlech? Surely, he couldn't do that without Rick's permission? And Rick was just waking up to everything Bryony was trying to do, wasn't he?

"Okay, mate. Keep me posted, yeah?"

I had to get out of sight before Ed saw me! I cast my eyes around and saw nothing but the cars to shield me. I darted back to mine on silent feet and crouched behind its familiar hulk just as Ed finished his call and stubbed out his cigarette on the ground. Through the rear windscreen I saw his smug smile and air punch before he went back inside the house.

I sat back on my haunches, walk forgotten, as this revelation sunk in. My mind reeled with the implications. It was obvious Ed was doing all of this in secret, but how to snitch on him to Rick? I didn't want our relationship with Rick threatened at this delicate stage. No, I'd sit on it, and I wouldn't even tell Percy. Everything hung in the balance. It would soon be the dark of the moon. Anything could happen then.

Chapter Thirty-Seven, Present Day

By the time the moon had waned, we had made no progress in our investigation. Not a single spirit came calling and Eddie was also away for a few days. So I was eager to attend the pagan meeting in hopes of some enlightenment. I took the precaution of having my own lantern as we walked along the wooded path to the sacred grove on the appointed evening, there being no moon to light the way. We found the others huddled around the stones in the centre of the grove, talking in low voices.

Bryony wasn't there, surprisingly.

Percy looked at me, eyebrows raised. "No Bryony?"

I gave a little laugh. "Don't forget how she loves to make a dramatic entrance."

Sure enough, five minutes later, in she swept in her long black gown, girdled with her amber belt and her hair hanging freely down her back. Again, I was struck at her resemblance to Bryonia.

A spontaneous clap broke through the crowd as she appeared, and I smiled at her gratified face. Maybe all leaders need applause to fuel the extra load on them.

The tight cluster of pagan followers parted, and Bryony stepped on to the shallow plinth in front of the cromlech to address them. Light from the lanterns hanging from the trees and on the stone altar illuminated her face.

"Friends, we are gathered together in the dark of the moon to share our thoughts about Gaine's message from the Mabon feast. Let us raise the energy by chanting and holding hands in a circle to encourage this wise spirit to come through to us again."

Everyone shuffled round to form a circle around the stones.

Bryony waited till everyone had settled and started to hum. Percy and I held hands with each other and a stranger on our other side. The expectant atmosphere was almost tangible as people joined in with the humming when they each felt ready. I felt a tingling in both hands after a few minutes and my own hopes of seeing Gaine were raised.

Bryony signalled when to start the chanting by softly hitting a small gong. Unaccustomed tears pricked my eyes at its melodious beauty. Male and female voices rose and fell in unison, bass notes with tenors, contraltos with sopranos; all worked together to make a chorus of ethereal music. The pleasurable tingling sensation spread throughout my body, and I shut my eyes to better absorb the mellifluous sound of many human voices chiming in harmony. Soon we were swaying in time to the beat, and I had the heady sense of Robin's presence joining us.

Oh please, come through to me, Robin. Share this enchantment with me!

Although my hands were engaged with other living ones, I felt two big palms resting on my shoulders in a warm hug. He was here! He had come! Joy welled up from my inner core and I sang out with the rest of these kind-hearted people with a full heart.

The music reached a crescendo that almost overwhelmed me before Bryony sounded her little gong again. She stopped humming and instead sang out her instructions to lower the volume and subside into silence. Gracefully, slowly, the chanting quietened back into a collective hum before dwindling into companiable silence - a silence rudely interrupted by someone emerging from the black depths of the trees, clapping loudly.

"Amazing, guys. Simply amazing! Wow, that was beautiful, man."

My eyes snapped open. Rick stood there, palms banging together in an insensitive staccato of applause.

I looked up at Bryony, standing in the centre, slightly higher than the rest of us. "You! How dare you come here during a ceremony!"

Rick spread out his hands. "Hey, man, don't be uptight. I was out for a stroll, and I heard this fabulous music. Really cool. It's just what I'm looking for with my new sound. You know, with the birdsong I've already laid down, this would be fantastic. I can lay my guitar riffs over it, yeah? Or maybe I'll use my acoustic one to accompany it instead. Yeah, get back to you on that one."

Bryony retorted, "I wish you would get back, you idiot. You have completely halted the build-up of energy that we were so carefully cultivating. You are a prize fool!"

I was so preoccupied with the withdrawal of Robin's arms around me, I barely noticed Percy drop my hand and step forward. Bereft of his comfort, I was momentarily distracted and didn't see what she was up to until I saw her standing next to Bryony on the stone dais.

She had all my attention as soon as she spoke, or should I say, Gaine spoke through her.

She ignored Bryony completely, who stood, fuming, and glaring at her.

Percy looked unearthly and was obviously in a trance. A little smile played at the corner of her mouth. Maybe it was all the cosmetic chicanery she'd embellished herself with, but she had never looked more beautiful than in this moment, as she addressed the crowd in that sing-song voice she had used last time she channelled Gaine.

"My beloveds. Do not mock this man of music. He is also here for a reason."

I heard an audible hiss from Bryony at this point. So much for meditation purifying the soul.

Percy spread her arms wide and smiled on Rick, who looked as if he might melt in front of her. She pointed her finger directly at him.

"You will spread my message far and wide through your music. Let these singers chant their vibration at Samhain and then I will come through to speak to you all. You must replicate this and send it around the world. You have to do this to compensate for killing my grandmother and stealing my land, or I shall continue to interrupt your work."

The air surrounding Percy's svelte form shimmered. "I can stay no longer. Gather at Samhain. Make music together then."

238

Percy lost her balance and her foot slipped on the edge of the plinth, making her fall forward, straight into Rick's open arms.

Chapter Thirty-Eight, Present Day

The next morning, Percy was tired and out of sorts.

"I need to get out in the fresh air, Fay. Blow the cobwebs away."

"Yes, I know what you mean. I want to know more about Gaine's plans too. She came through you so briefly last night."

"Did she? I can't remember." Percy yawned and stretched. "My head feels like cotton wool."

"Ah, so you don't recall swooning in Rick's arms then?"

Percy looked taken aback. "Absolutely not. I don't remember anything except waking up in my own bed this morning feeling tired, as if it was only three o'clock in the morning. I'd love to reconnect with Gaine and find out what I've missed."

"Yes, and I'd love to connect with dear Ed but he's proving a slippery customer. I really want to understand if Rick is directly descended from that Roman who killed Bryonia."

"Why do you say that?"

I scratched my head. "Of course, you don't remember, but that is what Gaine said last night. She said Rick will have a role to play with his music as his penance for his ancestor killing her grandmother and stealing her land."

"Ah, now I understand the link. And that is why Gaine made me stab the poor man!" Percy rubbed her hands across her eyes.

"Yes, but hopefully that won't happen again if he obeys her command to use music at Halloween, although I'm not quite sure how it's all going to work."

Percy yawned. "No, but he's so different since I attacked him and Bryony gave him healing. If anyone can do it, I think he can."

"I hope you're right and it will be interesting to see what he comes up with. At least it's something I don't have to worry about, although it will affect you, of course, if you've got to channel Gaine at the same time. I've been thinking along more material lines. If Rick is descended from him and the Romans got the land from the Druids, or maybe the Celts, all those years ago, who holds the deeds of the estate now? I don't suppose the ancients had conveyances where it was all written down, but I bet Eddie knows more than he's letting on. I'm going to tackle Ed as soon as he returns from wherever he's gone."

Percy rubbed her eyes. "I'm so tired but I wish I knew more about what Gaine expects of me. It's so difficult that I'm the one who can't remember what she said. I have to admit, I feel pretty daunted about doing it again and so publicly."

I ran my hand through my hair. "Oh, my head keeps going around in endless circles without getting anywhere. I tell you what, how about I show you that cave I told you about? I saw Bryonia and Gaine there, well, her dead body anyway. If there is anywhere else apart from the oak grove where we can connect with them, I'm sure it's there."

"Alright, Fay. You're on. Show me the way. I'd like to see it actually."

"It's really hard to get to but there must be another way in. Let's go down to the beach and look up from there, see if we can find another entrance."

We gathered our things and set off into breezy morning. We skirted around the sacred oak circle and took a path veering away from the estate buildings, as I had done before. We climbed up the hillside until we came to the open grassland I had discovered on my previous excursion.

"Oh, this is just what I needed, Fay. I'm feeling better already."

"Great. Look, the burial cairn is over there."

Percy looked briefly over to where I had pointed. "Oh yes, it's quite big, isn't it? But let's concentrate on the cave for today."

I gazed across the panoramic coastline. "Alright. We need to find a better path down to the beach, I think. I wouldn't take my worst enemy on that other one I used. Never been so scared in all my life!" I marched swiftly on, galvanised by my quest and the brisk wind rippling through the grass, making it resemble a dry, green sea.

Percy laughed and I turned to look back at her. She stood with arms outstretched to each side of her slender body, with her unbound auburn hair flailing behind and her long red skirt clinging to her legs, pushed on by the wind. She didn't look like a fashionable, well-groomed model anymore, but she certainly looked happier and more vibrant than at any time I'd known her. Sort of free and elemental.

"Oh, this wind is so strong it's forcing air down my throat!" Percy laughed again and span round in a circle, so her hair whipped around her face in a spiral, not unlike those carved into her new earrings.

I smiled at her antics.

She jubilantly shouted her reply, "Doesn't being this high up above the sea make you feel wonderfully alive?"

"Not really," I hated to dampen her spirits, but the same gale was finding every gap in my clothing, which I now realised was totally inadequate for windswept seascapes, and I was feeling distinctly chilly.

"Oh, don't be a spoilsport, Fay!" Percy grabbed my cold hand. "Let's run!"

And run we did, like children on holiday. I even laughed myself at one point, till I got so out of breath I had to stop and catch it.

"Hey, look! I see a break in the rocks over there. Looks an easy enough way down." Percy pointed to a gap in the limestone cliffs a little way off.

"Oh, yes, I think it must be just beyond the cave. Pity I didn't notice it last time." Panting, I slowed down and walked in the direction of her pointing finger.

We scrambled down a narrow path that looked downright perilous to me, as it was flimsily underpinned by some loose shingle, and squeezed between crumbling earth escarpments scantily clad in tufts of marram grass and spent thrift flowers. The only robust scaffolding I could see were some bent hawthorn trees clinging to its side, sculpted into fantastic shapes by the constant westerly wind.

As my foot slipped a second time, I voiced my doubts. "I thought you said this would be easy?"

Percy shouted back over the wind. "It's not too bad, look, I'm on the beach already!"

I slid the last bit, catching my bottom on a jutting rock. "Ouch! Good job I'm well padded."

Percy chuckled at my misfortune. "You're alright. Don't make such a fuss. Which way is the cave?"

I pointed back towards the estate land with one hand and dusted off my backside with the other. Now I was on solid ground - well, soft sand - and with both feet on the same level, I found Percy's confidence contagious. "Come on, then! We have to double back on ourselves towards the way we came."

We walked side by side, barely able to hear each other over the sound of the crashing waves. The tide was about halfway out. With a jolt, I realised I didn't know if it was coming in or ebbing out, or, crucially, whether this unknown part of the beach would be underwater at high tide.

"Percy, have you got your phone with you?"

"Yes, why?"

"Can you look up the tide times, please?"

Percy's eyes widened in alarm. "Does the sea come right in here?"

I shrugged, making my rucksack bang uncomfortably against the small of my back. "I don't know, that's why we need to find out which way the tide is heading."

Percy stabbed her index finger on the face of her phone. "Oh no! No signal. It must be all those rocks above us."

I looked at the edge of the white foamy waves, noting exactly where they lined up against a distinctive rock island in the centre of the cove, undecided whether to go or stay.

Percy didn't seem to share my doubts. "Come on, we should have a couple of hours to explore even if it is coming in."

Percy and I picked up our paces just as a sudden shower of rain stung our faces on the seaward side.

"Oh hell, now it's raining. Do you think we should just turn around and head back?" I felt suddenly weary.

"No way! We've got this far and as I said, we've got time to reach the cave before the sea does." Percy broke into a run, and I reluctantly jogged behind her.

We rounded a jutting piece of cliff and the bay widened. "There's the cave, look!" I pointed upwards to the open maw of the giant hole in the cliffs.

"Wow! It's huge! I hadn't realised how impressive it would be. And isn't that a path winding back upwards to the cliff top?" Percy shielded her eyes as she gazed up the cliff face.

"Yeah, it's impressive alright but that path is deceptively narrow. Doesn't look it from here and I don't think it used to be in Gaine's time. Must have been eroded by the waves."

"Well, it has been two thousand years since she used it."

I looked back at the tide, worried to see confirmation that it was incoming. "We haven't much time, Percy. The little rock island is disappearing fast under the water. I don't want to follow it."

"Just a little look?" She had already run towards the cave and was now directly beneath it, staring up at its circular entrance.

I followed her in a lumpy trot. "If the beach is lower now, wouldn't that mean that the cave would have flooded years ago, if it was at sea level?"

Percy scanned the beach. "I guess so, unless the sea was much further away then, or maybe the path was not only wider but extended down to beach level, with the cave above it and more rocks below than there are now. Seascapes have a habit of changing."

I tried to visualise how it might have been. "Ah, yes, I hadn't thought of that, but you'd think, with sea levels rising because of climate change, it would actually be lower than the sea now."

I was thinking of little else than where the sea was, as the towering surf encroached further up the sand towards us.

Percy turned back to look at the cliff face. "Yeah, it doesn't make sense but let's not waste time chatting about it now."

Salty sea spray mingled with the rain and a sudden gust of wind spiralled the drops of water into a mini tornado directly in front of me and a few grains of flying sand scratched my eye, making it water.

I turned up the collar of my jacket. "I don't think this rain is going to let-up."

But Percy wasn't listening. She'd already started clambering up the rock face towards the beckoning cave.

"Don't Percy! It's not safe! We should turn back now, while we can." Either she was ignoring me or couldn't hear me. Either way, she wasn't taking any notice of my earnest counsel.

Percy scrambled up the rock face like a lithe monkey. I couldn't believe how fast she ascended. With the sea pounding and snapping at my back as I watched, open-mouthed, Percy reached the cave's wide mouth in a few minutes. She stood, panting slightly, in her flapping long red skirt, her hair whipping around her lovely face, now rosy from her climb, and smiled boastfully at me where I still stood on the wet sand below.

In that get-up, with her hair unbound and her eyes shining in triumph, she could have been Gaine standing in that very spot two thousand years ago. She said something to me, but I couldn't catch it against the roar of the incoming tide. Then I gasped out loud with a warning. There was someone behind her. I screwed up my eyes, forcing them to focus but the figure was shadowy and faint. Hang on, it was another woman. Was it Bryony? It looked like her, but the figure was so indistinct I wouldn't have been surprised to find it was her ancestor, Bryonia, back from the dead – and with what intention?

"I'm coming up too," I yelled, though my stomach lurched in fear at the prospect. I was no sprightly rock climber.

I hitched my rucksack to a more comfortable position, wishing I could abandon it altogether but another glance back at the crashing waves convinced me that neither my rucksack nor myself would be wise to linger any longer on the rapidly disappearing beach. Shaking my head in disbelief that I was again mounting this slippery, almost vertical, wall of rock, I looked up at where Percy had been standing, shocked to find that she had already disappeared inside the enormous cave.

I could hear the faint trace of voices but could not make sense of any of the words. I had, once more, no choice but to visit that claustrophobic black hole.

Chapter Thirty-Nine, Present Day

By the time I reached the cave entrance, which took me a lot longer than it had Percy, the rain was bucketing down in torrents. In a way it did me a favour by incentivising my lumbering ascent, rock to rock, ledge to tiny ledge with trembling, bruised fingers and wet, slippery trainers. Many times, I bumped my knees against a sharp edge and cursed roundly. Now that was something I was very skilled in. I could swear with the coarsest of sailors, if pressed.

I heaved myself over the last slithery ledge in an ungraceful lunge, ending up on my abused knees with a sigh of relief. Once inside and upright, I turned back to look at the sea through a curtain of rain hammering chaotically down as if the raindrops were dancing a whirling dervish. The cacophony of sound from the combination of the gale force wind, pounding surf and thundering rain deafened me. This was no ordinary weather but a storm of some magnitude that had suddenly whipped up. If I hadn't lost my phone, I would have checked the forecast before setting out, but it was too late now. I fished a tissue out of the pocket of my jacket and wiped my streaming face with it. Percy had been lucky to have gained access to this rocky shelter before the rain had become so heavy. And where was she now?

I turned my back on the maelstrom outside and focussed my eyes on the gaping cavern before me. Fear once more gripped my insides but going back was no longer an option with the waves now licking against the rocks immediately below. I gulped the fear down and steadied my breathing. I must locate Percy, find out who was with her. I stepped away from the precipitous edge of the cliff face and walked forwards, straining my ears above the raging storm outside to catch any sound of conversation within.

With no sunshine to illuminate it, the cave was darker than I remembered and far more menacing. I scolded myself for my hesitation, after all, I knew now that there was a way back up to the cliff top from inside. I just had to find it – and my friend - who seemed to have entirely disappeared.

The deeper into the cave I ventured, the darker it became. Where was Percy? She had a phone with a torch app so why wasn't she using it? And why the hell hadn't I had the wit to bring an ordinary torch on this jaunt?

I decided to keep the wall on my left within touching distance, having remembered the freshwater pool was located on the righthand side of the cave. The cold stone was wet from the rain hurling itself against the rock face, but it was reassuringly solid and immovable. I flattened my palm against its bulk and edged forwards. The bumpy wall curved slightly after a while, bearing even further left, but I kept my hand flat against it, more for comfort than anything else, as I didn't know if it would take me away from the exit I knew lay behind the pool on the right.

As I rounded the bend and was on the point of abandoning my strategy in fear of veering off in the wrong direction, I stopped in my tracks.

At last, there was a light, in fact there were two, and they were facing each other in white beams not unlike lasers. Shadowy faces flickered behind each one and I screwed up my eyes to see who was there, to see if it was the living or the dead.

Suddenly one of the beams blinded me by shining right in my face. I put up my hand to shield my eyes from the glare. No ghost could have done that, surely?

"Fay! You're here at last. What took you so long?"

"Is that you, Percy? Shine the light away from my eyes, I can't see a bloody thing!"

The beam deflected to my bruised knees, and I could see Percy standing there, looking calm and collected, not a hair out of place. If there was such a thing as magic, it was in all those mysterious chemicals she inflicted on her long mane.

"I'm glad I found you." I meant it too.

"Bryony's here, Fay."

"Oh, hello, Bryony. This is a strange place to meet."

I could barely see Bryony's face, but her voice was strong. "Both you and that wretched man have ruined all my attempts to reach Gaine at the sacred grove. It's imperative I speak with her before Samhain."

I walked towards the two women, still facing each other as if in combat. "And you thought she'd be here?"

Bryony nodded. I could see her more clearly now as she was barely two feet away. She looked grumpier than ever, and I could see she was as bedraggled as I was.

Percy turned her torch back to the older woman. "And have you seen her?"

"No, no, I haven't. I'm sure she was about to come through when you two showed up."

Percy reached out to touch Bryony, but the Druidess recoiled. "I'm so sorry if we interrupted you but we had the same idea and for the same reason."

Bryony scowled. "Why would you need to contact her? You're not leading the group! You already took it over last night and made me look like a charlatan!"

Percy shook her head. "No, I'm sure you didn't. Your followers have complete faith in you. I just wanted to reach out and see if she had another message."

Bryony shouted her reply. "She doesn't need you. *I* don't need you! We were managing fine without your butting in and taking over! Why should she give the message to you anyway? I've never had a problem connecting with her before you turned up with your pseudo-sleuthing and creeping about the place!"

"Hey, now, Bryony. Gaine won't come through an angry person, you know." My attempt to mollify her had the opposite effect.

"How dare you! I'm not angry with *her*, but *you*! And that blasted Rick – and now he's actually playing his infernal racket – I will not call it music – in the oak grove itself! How will I ever prepare for Gaine's message with him in the way?"

I could see Bryony was more stressed than angry. She ran her hands through her long hair, leaving it looking even wilder. She looked on the point of tears.

"It must be so frustrating, I'm sorry."

Bryony heaved a sob. "I've worked all my life for this moment, can't you see? I've built up the energy for years so that Gaine could come through me and now you've snatched it away from me. If we have cameras and film crews and I don't know what careering through the grove and Rick with his confounded screaming guitar and amplifiers, how the hell can she connect with all that going on? And everyone is expecting me to sort it out! Expecting *me* to make it happen! I can't, I can't." And Bryony sank to her knees on the hard rock, her body wracked with suppressed tears.

Percy went straight to her, putting her phone down on the ground next to them. Having lost mine in just such a spot, I picked it up and trained its light on to the two women, now held in a comforting embrace.

"There, there, it will be alright, you'll see." Percy murmured into Bryony's shoulder. A flash of lightning brought a blaze of light into the chamber, followed by an almighty crack of thunder from the storm outside. I turned my back on the women to peer outside. Through the distant opening, I could just make out the white surf, luminous against the broiling, dark sea, before another fork of lightning rent the sky. Another rumble followed but this one sounded different, much nearer, and I could feel vibration under my feet.

Bryony stopped snivelling and stood up. "Was that thunder?"

I shook my head. "I'm not sure. I'm going to look."

Percy shouted, "Don't go, Fay! It's not safe."

"Too late for that." Using the wall again and with the benefit of Fay's phone torch, I crept forwards toward the mouth of the cave. The rumbling grew louder and louder until I could hear nothing else, not even the crashing rhythm of the waves. More lightning flashed, a sheet of it rather than a fork, and it lit up the scene outside of the cave.

Horrified, my flesh crawling with goosebumps, I stared out at the land, or where it had been. A massive rockfall had cascaded down the path that we had used barely

250

an hour since. It looked like it had never been there at all. Even with the rain lashing down, huge clouds of dust rose up from the landslide, merging with the salt spray and then spiralling up to the lowering, bulging grey storm clouds above. And to my increasing terror, the land continued to slip down in an avalanche of rocks - shingle and pebbles, tufts of marram grass, clumps of thrift and spiky hawthorn - all ripped out of their crevices and hurling down in a deafening race to the bottom.

"Argh!" I jumped in shock as Percy crept up behind me and touched my shoulder. "I thought you were rocks falling on me!"

"Oh, my God! What is happening?"

Bryony joined us and spoke in a deadened voice. "It is happening. Gaine forewarned me of this. I had hoped to ask her specifically when it would come. Now I know."

Irritated with her dramatic doom-laden pronouncement, I turned to Percy. "Question is, is this cave going to go the same way?"

Percy gripped my arm. "We have to get out, Fay! How did you do it last time? Show me that staircase you found."

I nodded, only too eager to comply. "Come on Bryony, we've got to go."

But Bryony stood there transfixed by the catastrophe. "It is the end."

"Oh, for God's sake, woman!" I had no patience for this melodrama. "This is real! Don't you realise? It's got nothing to do with ghosts but everything to do with soil erosion from climate change. The bloody cliff face is collapsing." I grabbed her arm and yanked her inside the cave. "Come on, I'm sure you know the way out better than I do."

"Get off me, you idiot! Can't you see this is what Gaine *wanted* us to see?"

"Whatever Gaine wants will have to bloody wait. We won't be much good to her if we're dead too!"

I frogmarched her towards the interior of the cave trying, but not succeeding, to ignore the small pebbles dribbling out of crevices in the rock and the sensation of movement within its walls.

"Quickly - before the roof collapses!"

Chapter Forty, Present Day

More stones tumbled around us, picked out by the thin beam of the two electric torches. Some fell into the freshwater pool, making splashes against the stalagmites surrounding it.

"Bryony, come *on!*" I pulled at her arm. The woman appeared to be transfixed and stood as static as the stalagmites themselves, her mouth hanging open in horror, as if screaming silently.

"Show us the way, Fay. Bryony can't do it. *You* must find the staircase." Percy tugged at my wet fleece.

"Yes, of course. Argh!" A wide crevice split open to our left and bigger rocks, some the size of footballs, cascaded down its newly opened crack.

"Quickly, for heaven's sake!" Percy tugged harder.

"I'm coming."

"Go in front, Fay. Here, take Bryony's torch and I'll bring her and follow close behind."

I nodded. My mouth had gone dry in this wet place. I took the torch and tried to hold it steady, flicking its light up and down so I could get a level for my feet on the trembling floor of the cave. The walls were slick with water and slimy with mud.

"Percy, keep hold of my fleece or my rucksack and don't bloody let go!"

"Got it."

I felt the tug on my back. "Have you got Bryony too?"

"I can't hold you both and the torch."

"Get her to hold my rucksack strap then." I felt a stronger pull as both women grabbed a strap from the bag on my back. Their combined weight unsettled my equilibrium and I stumbled on the uneven rocks beneath my feet.

"Go, Fay. Just go! Soon, it will be too late, and the cave will fall in on us!" Percy joggled my rucksack strap as if I was a pit pony.

"I'm going! I'm going! Just stop pulling on me or I'll fall over!" I felt the drag on my back ease and concentrated on what was ahead of me instead. It was so hard to see. Everything was moving all at once and I couldn't get my bearings.

I scanned the rocks on my right, making the beam travel past the water pool and on up to where I remembered the staircase cut into the rock. I crept forward gingerly, feeling with my toes and craning my neck to see further into the blackness of the cave with my feeble light.

I used my left arm to feel the void immediately in front of me. "Ouch!"

Percy stopped too. "What is it? Oh, please hurry!"

"Stubbed my toe." I looked down, dismayed to see a pile of rubble across my path. I climbed up it as another flash of lightning penetrated through the mouth of the cave. "There it is! I see it!"

The roughly hewn staircase rose up to my right. I hadn't turned enough. "Step over this pile of stones and follow me over there. I can see the stairs."

A crunch of displaced rocks and pebbles accompanied me as I walked, more quickly now, to the first step that would lead us to sweet fresh air and daylight. I turned around to the others, still clutching me from behind, and pointed Bryony's torch up the flight of steps. "Look. See the staircase? That's where we are heading."

I almost fell as Bryony let go of my rucksack and pushed past me. "I know the way! I have been up and down those stairs all my life! I don't need you to show me."

"Fine! I don't care. Lead the bloody way, then." I held Percy's hand, grateful to be steadied by her holding on, helping me keep my balance while Bryony broke free.

I shone the torch on Bryony's patchwork skirt as she scrambled up the stairs like a woman half her age. We swiftly followed and this time, I went last, shining the torch ahead to light the way.

When I was halfway up there was another huge crash as a gigantic piece of rock gave way behind us, spraying us with small shards as it thumped down, swallowing up the lowest part of the steps. I pushed at Percy's back. "Hurry, hurry, for God's sake!"

I looked up at the opening to see Bryony's hand extended down to Percy who gripped it tightly and disappeared. Another massive crash sounded so near I felt I was within a thunderclap and a piece of the roof above the lowest rise of the stairs stoved in completely, exposing a larger expanse of sky and allowing me to clearly see the exit. I mounted the last few steps two at a time, despite their irregular shapes and, as I reached the narrow opening, the earth around it started to crumble.

Two different arms yanked me out on to the earth.

"Run! Run like hell!" Percy yelled.

Winded, and on jelly legs, I obeyed. Gasping for breath, we all ran up the bracken-covered hillside with the rain slashing down, washing off the mud and debris that covered each of us.

"Keep going higher." Bryony gasped out, after glancing behind me.

Another roar and the very cliff we had just climbed onto broke away and fell into the cave, forming a new ledge of earth on the rock we had so recently stood upon.

We all stopped and watched in horror as the ground disappeared. Some of it slipped off the rocky shelf and fell into the sea, now swirling angrily directly below the cave.

Bryony took both our hands. "We must go higher. We don't know how much more land will return to the sea."

I had a stitch in my side, my heart thumped so much it was painful, I could barely breathe, and my knees screamed in agony, but I had no hesitation in complying. We jogged uphill for a full ten minutes before anyone dared stop. When we did, we all collapsed onto the soggy grass and, through the driving rain, watched as the earth beneath us surrendered to the tumultuous sea below.

I lay back on the grass, unable to watch any more destruction. My chest heaved with the effort of clambering up the hill and I could barely catch my breath. I felt dizzy and my throat felt scratched and sore from inhaling dust and stony debris. With my mouth open to snatch at the fresh air, I felt the fat, cold dollops of rain drum against my hot face, and when some dripped onto my tongue I thought I had never tasted anything so good in all my life.

The three of us lay there for quite a while in the rain, buffeted by the whirling savage wind and soaked by the cleansing rain. Percy was the first to recover. She sat up and wiped her face with her sleeve.

Even now, her breath was ragged, but she managed to croak, "That was as close as I have ever come to losing my life."

I heaved myself up into a sitting position, propped up by my aching arms. "I've never seen anything like it. The sheer power of nature. I feel very insignificant."

Bryony tried to sit up but couldn't until I leant her a hand. "Thank you. Thank you both for everything. I would have died in that cave if it wasn't for you."

We murmured breathless denials.

Bryony shook her head. "No, it's true, but now I wonder if that was my true destiny."

I started to protest but she held up her hand.

"I'm not being melodramatic but practical. If Gaine can come through Percy here, what use am I? Maybe I should have died and gone to help her in the afterlife."

I took a deep breath in and coughed out some mud. "Look, Bryony. Whatever you might think, your destiny is not to snuff it, obviously, or it would have happened, if you want to think in that fatalistic way. We're going to need you to lead your merry band of followers. They are going to need you more than ever after this, don't you think?"

Percy nodded. "Of course, they are. They couldn't manage without you, and neither could we. You said the other day we needed a plan, and we do. This is the best message Gaine could have sent. We weren't meant to die in there but experience the force of nature so we can explain it to the world about the need to change. Don't you see? And we must do this together, Bryony. You are needed in this world, my dear."

Bryony broke into sobs then. Too tired to comfort her and with only enough energy to keep myself from doing the same, we both let her cry out her shock. I lay back against the sodden turf and shut my eyes. The wind and the rain howled and spat at me, but I was too exhausted to care.

Chapter Forty-One, Present Day

It took us a whole week to recover from our narrow escape. A precious loss of time when there was so much to do but we were all so traumatised, bruised and cut, even super-fit Percy took a while to heal.

George came round on the second day with an enormous box of vegetables, organic meat and a bunch of flowers from Bryony.

He delivered the goodies with a sweet smile. "Bryony hopes this will keep you going while you get over your adventure in the cave."

Percy smiled back. "Oh, thank you, George. That is so kind of her. Could you put it on the table, please? I couldn't lift a thing!"

"No problem."

I staggered over to help. "How is Bryony?"

George put down the heavy box. "Not so good, actually. She's been in bed since it happened."

"Really?" That news made me feel less of a wimp.

George nodded. "She was pretty beaten up, you know." He cleared his throat. "Um, I must say, you don't look too clever, either."

Percy grimaced. "I am bruised all over. Everything hurts."

George turned to the front door. "I almost forgot, there is something else for you."

He came back with a smaller box of bottles and tubes that smelled more fragrant than medicinal to me. "Bryony got Gwen to make up box of medicines for you. She said something about arnica for shock and bruises?"

Percy delved right in. "Oh, lovely! Flower essences!"

I frowned. "What are they?"

George shrugged. "I think they heal you vibrationally."

I raised my eyebrows. "Of course they do."

258

Percy turned and kissed George's cheek. "Thank you. Please pass that on to Bryony and say we hope she's better soon. I would hug you, but my ribs ache too much! Tell her this massage oil smells heavenly."

George grinned. "I pass on your message. Bye, now, ladies. Heal quickly, won't you? Those cuts and bruises look nasty."

We stood at the door and waved him off.

Percy shut it after he drove away. "So kind of Bryony."

"Yeah, she's not such a bad old stick, I suppose."

"Come on, let's put this lot away."

I winced as I reached up to a cupboard. "Only if we do it slowly."

Quite a few days later, when the contents of the vegbox had dwindled to a few wrinkly carrots, we were feeling a lot better and over breakfast, I decided the moment had arrived to venture forth. "I think it's time we visited the grove, Percy."

She sipped green goo from her liquidiser goblet. "I was thinking the same. I wonder what on earth Rick is up to?"

"I dread to think."

We walked, more-or-less without limping, down the leafy path to the oak grove later that morning.

"What's that?" I looked up at the sky at the whining noise above us.

"Too small for a plane, isn't it?" Percy squinted against the pale autumn sunlight.

"It's one of those drone things, heading for the coast."

Percy gasped. "I bet it's someone photographing the landslide! Could be the local press!"

"Or the national one. It's just the sort of story the BBC love to cover."

"But it's private land, isn't it? Surely they would need Rick's permission?"

"Good point." I suddenly remembered Ed's so-called deal with that slimy looking Alan. "But Ed could do it for him. He might be surveying the land for that bloke I saw him with."

Percy lowered her eyes back to mine. "I'd forgotten all about that."

"I haven't. Come on, it's high time we caught up with things."

We found Rick in the grove, not with his manager, but the handsome boy with the dreadlocks we'd seen at the pagan rituals.

"Hey man! How are you?" Rick looked up from a monitor screen set up on a table covered with a jumble of techno junk.

Percy seemed a little tongue-tied again, so I answered for us both. "We're okay but we had a close shave in the landslide."

"Yeah, I heard about that. Meant to come over and see how you were but I've been pretty tied up here with Winston. We're laying down some tracks, you know, for the song at Halloween? This guy knows his stuff, he's well cool."

Winston gave us a shy smile and I noticed Percy replied with one of her showstoppers.

"How's it going then?" I kept my own facial expressions low key.

"Man, it's taking a while, you know? I mean, I kind of know what I want to do but it's tricky, really tricky. If it wasn't for this guy, I'd have given up. He's a techie wizard, works in the music and film industry all the time."

I nodded to Winston in acknowledgment of his apparently remarkable skills. "I see. So, where's Ed, then?"

Rick shook his head. "Dunno, he's always busy with something at the moment. Don't think he's keen on the whole druid/pagan thing, you know."

I could easily believe that. Too busy selling the land from under Rick's feet. "Well, good luck with the recording, Rick."

I turned to Percy. "I think I'll go and find Ed, have a chat."

"Oh, don't you want to know more about the music?"

I shook my head. "Not my thing, either. You can stay, if you promise to behave yourself."

Percy chuckled. "I don't think there's much chance of Gaine coming through me with all this technology around. It's bound to mix up the energies."

"If you say so." I turned to Rick. "I'm going to see Ed but Percy's going to stay here. Winston? Will you get between them if Percy turns a bit crazy?"

Winston raised his eyebrows. "Yeah, but why?"

"Oh, come on, you've seen Percy channel Gaine at the Mabon feast and the meeting at the dark of the moon. Gaine isn't keen on Rick, remember?"

Winston gave a broad smile, showing incredibly white teeth against his dark skin. "Understood. I shall be sound engineer and bodyguard in one."

"Brilliant. I'll be off then. Percy? Be good!"

I waved them all goodbye and turned back along the tree-lined path towards the estate house. I wasn't worried about Percy. She was right, it was highly unlikely any spirit could communicate across all those wires, Bryony had said as much herself. I liked Winston. He had a very calm demeanour and looked both tall and strong. If it came to it, I had every confidence he could protect Rick from anything Gaine might attempt.

My brow cleared with that thought. Playing bodyguard to Percy could be a heavy responsibility at times and I was very curious about what Ed had been getting up to in our absence and whether that drone had anything to do with it.

My step became downright jaunty once my muscles loosened up. I loved a mystery, and I could smell one brewing in the Ed department. The cool wind refreshed me after a week of convalescing indoors and I inhaled the salt-laden air with relish. A long-lost sense of wellbeing stole over me, and I made a mental note to go shopping for my kind of food later that day. A welcome sense of normality, in what was in anyone's estimation a fairly abnormal situation, energised my body and cleared the fog from my mind.

My smug self-satisfaction received its first dent when the drone reappeared and almost sliced my head off as I reached the courtyard by the old stables.

"What the…?" I swore out loud at the whizzing contraption as I felt its draught ruffle my short hair.

Laughter behind me made me turn around. Ed stood on the backdoor step, a remote-control widget in his tattooed hands and a rare grin cracking his face.

"Nearly had you then!"

"Thanks a bunch!" Anger rose up in me, born of fear. I still hadn't got over the cave trauma and I didn't need any more shocks.

Ed ignored my indignation, keeping his eyes on the mini-plane and guiding it remotely down to the cobblestones between us. "How about that for skill, hey?"

I marched up to him. "So, nearly slicing my head off was deliberate, was it?"

"Oh, give me a break, lady. It was just a bit of fun." He fiddled with a control knob and the little engine ceased its irritating whine.

"Not funny, Eddie."

He shrugged his big shoulders. "Made me laugh. Haven't seen you around for a while?"

"Hoped we'd left, did you?"

Eddie picked up the annoying drone and walked over to me. "See how small it is? Ingenious little thing."

"Good for spying, I should think."

"Takes excellent videos, if that's what you mean."

I looked at the gadget. It really wasn't very big. Sneaky-sized. "Remote videos are very helpful when you want to find out things you shouldn't."

"Are you naturally suspicious or does it go with the job?"

"Both, so you'll understand my questioning."

262

"Doesn't mean I'll give you any answers."

"Let's give it a go, shall we?" I nodded at the little plane. "What were you filming?"

Eddie's eyes narrowed slightly but he answered me, which was more than I expected. "The estate. Like I said, useful tool for scanning an area."

"Did you see the landslide by the cave?"

"Yeah, impressive. You were lucky to get out alive."

I tipped my head to one side in acknowledgement. "You heard about it then?"

"Everyone did. I mean, the storm was wild, but you could hear the avalanche above even that. Pretty big event."

Memories of the terror I'd felt flooded back. "It was the most frightening thing I've ever experienced."

Lowering my defences had a surprising effect. Eddie's face softened and he nodded towards the house. "Yeah, must have been. Do you fancy a coffee?"

I leapt at the chance of more interrogation. "I'd love one, thanks, Ed."

We walked into the house while he told me, in boring detail, how the drone worked. I let him ramble on, hoping it might lower his guard.

The kitchen smelled of coffee already drunk, and cigarettes already smoked. It was no tidier than when I'd first seen it. Eddie cleared the sagging sofa of dirty plates and invited me to sit down.

"Thanks." I sank into its fusty depths, tired from my walk.

Eddie fussed about with a complicated-looking coffee machine, the only twenty-first century object in the old-fashioned kitchen. "Milk?"

"Yes, please, and two sugars."

"You're a girl after my own heart."

I laughed and it broke the strained atmosphere. "Nice to drink coffee with a kindred spirit. Percy only ever has vegetable juice."

"I can imagine. It pays off though, she's stunning."

I sighed. "Oh, I know, believe me."

"Looks aren't everything, babe." Eddie passed me a stained mug of steaming coffee and sat at the other end of the sofa. "Tell me how you got out of that cave before it collapsed."

It was my turn to witter on and I did, watching him carefully as he listened to my thrilling anecdote. I felt rewarded for my volubility when he visibly relaxed.

"Wow! Another five minutes and you might not be sitting here."

I nodded. "That's absolutely right, Eddie. It's taken a week to get over it."

"Not surprised, but you're alright now?"

I smiled as warmly as I dared. "Yes, pretty much. So, what have you been up to?" Time to go for the jugular. "Done any deals lately?" I laughed to take the sting out of the question.

Eddie had bushy eyebrows in a farcical contrast to his shiny bald head and they came together in a frown. "Don't know what you mean."

I drank the last dregs of my coffee. "Yum, that was delicious. Thanks."

The frown stayed. "There's always lots to do around Rick."

"I'm sure. I suppose that tax situation must weigh heavily on your shoulders."

Eddie looked animated at my statement. "God yes!" He got up and took the dirty mugs to the sink. "If only Rick would listen to me! He's got no bloody idea how deep is the shit he's in. I've been trying to get a postponement from the tax office, but they haven't agreed to it yet. He's going to be ruined if I can't come up with a solution."

"That's tough, Eddie. I know just how much because of my old job."

He swung around and rubbed his eyes. "Rick just doesn't get it! He wafts about with these bloody hippies talking about dead spirits and all that crap but ignoring the real world. He thinks I can just magic it away but it's not so easy."

264

"Have you got any ideas on how to raise the cash?"

"I've met this bloke."

"Oh, the guy I saw you with? The one who drives that swish Porsche?"

Eddie raised his eyes to the ceiling. "God, yes, it's beautiful, isn't it? Yeah, Alan. He's had a pretty good idea, actually."

"Oh?"

Eddie came and sat down on the sofa next to me, much closer this time. I forced what I hoped was a friendly smile on my face.

"Do you know, it's so good to talk about it with someone with one foot in the real world. Someone who actually gets the gravity of the situation." He shuffled closer so our hips touched.

I longed to get up and run but I didn't. "Talk away. Believe me, I've heard all the tax dodges in the world. I worked in the corporate sector, you know, Eddie. You wouldn't believe what these really big companies get up to when it comes to tax returns."

Eddie lifted his arm, so it rested behind my shoulders along the back of the sofa. "Is that right? You know, you're not half bad-looking for a big girl."

I tried not to squirm, but it was becoming a massive struggle. "Thanks. So, tell me about this scheme of Alan's then."

Eddie shrugged, and to my relief, withdrew his arm to scratch his shiny pate. I noticed his tattoos extended right up the back of his neck to where his hair must once have been.

"I'm not sure I should disclose it, even to you, babe."

I leaned into his shoulder. "Doesn't mean anything to me. What can I do about it? Not my business but you looked like you could do with offloading. Problems like that are hard to bear alone."

He put a meaty hand on my thigh. "You know, I'm getting to like you."

265

I swallowed. "That's nice."

"The thing is, Alan's got this idea of making the estate into a holiday complex."

"Oh, wow, amazing!"

"It is, isn't it? I knew you'd see it my way!"

I wasn't sure I could keep up the pretence much longer. "Of course, it would be ideal. What would it be like? What kind of tourist market would you aim for? Wouldn't it take time to build and make a profit?"

Eddie's frown returned. "That's just it but I could take out a massive bank loan, see, on the potential and Alan said he would cough up a fair bit, up front, so I could start paying off the taxman in instalments. Then we could crack on with the development work."

"Have you got a design then?"

To my intense relief, Eddie got up off the sofa and fetched something from the next room. I let out my breath while he was gone.

He came back quickly with a roll of large paper, about A3 size. He opened it up on the kitchen table. "Look, here's a rough drawing. Firstly, you need access to the beach so we'll need to make a clearing and put a tarmac path down so people can use cars – you know, for jet-skis, trailers with canoes and paddleboards, that sort of thing. See, we can fell some of those stupid big oak trees near the sea, where those daft hippies congregate but we can keep the stones, make them a feature – you know maybe for a dance floor outside with floodlighting on the stones? Then we can create better access to the beach. Maybe have tree houses in the remaining oaks. The farmhouse would be perfect for a restaurant and that little cob house – honestly – that would be fab for an office, don't you think?"

"Wouldn't tree houses be a bit rustic, I mean, romantic, yes but not that comfy?"

Eddie smiled at me. "You really get it, don't you? Yeah, between here and the stones we'd have lots of holiday bungalows – you know - really high spec with plenty of bathrooms and a pool complex in the middle. Got to have a pool, haven't you? It would have to be covered in this climate – I thought clear Perspex with loads of night lighting and a bar with surround sound."

He put his arm around my bulky waist – I was surprised he could find it – and squeezed.

I didn't know what to say. The plans were worse than I ever dreamed they'd be. In the vacuum Eddie leaned in and kissed my mouth. He tasted horrible. Bitter coffee and smoke. Yuck.

I stepped back. "Hey, I never said you could do that."

Eddie grinned. "Sorry, babe. Got carried away. It's exciting, isn't it?"

"It's certainly radical. Wouldn't it be easier to sell the land to Alan?"

He shrugged, looking disappointed at my reaction. "Don't think Rick would do that."

"You mean, you haven't told him about this scheme?"

Eddie backed away and rolled up the paper. He stretched a rubber band over the cylinder, making my teeth twinge, and shook his head. "I'm not going to tell him till it's a done deal."

"What? You can't do that!"

"Who says?"

"But surely, Eddie, you can't just go over Rick's head?"

"He'll love it when the tax man is off his back."

"But what about Bryony's community?"

"Who cares about that bunch of losers?"

I realised I did. I stood up. "I won't let you get away with this! Rick has to know!"

Things turned ugly after that, and I made a quick and very awkward exit, scrambling for the back door, with Eddie threatening all sorts of hell if I told Rick about it.

From the safety of the yard, I turned back to him and almost shouted my response. "I am damn well going to tell Rick about your plans! How could you *do* this behind his back? This place doesn't belong to you! You're nothing but a manager – an employee! You bet I'm going to tell him."

When Eddie started to follow me, I broke into a run. I only just reached the cottage door and slammed it in his face in the nick of time. I leant against its wooden rampart within the refuge of the cottage and felt the blows hammering on its outside surface rebound on my sweaty back.

"Open this bloody door, you devious cow!"

Instead of answering him, I turned the key in the lock, and slid down into a squat against the stout door. The cottage didn't have a rear entrance and I knew I was safe - until I left it.

Chapter Forty-Two, Present Day

If only I still had a phone, I could ring Percy and tell her what had happened. I got up and stood by the window at an angle where I was confident Eddie couldn't see me.

Eventually, after prowling around for a bit, he gave up and stomped back to the big house. As soon as he was out of sight, I opened the door and legged it to the grove.

Sure enough, Percy, Rick and Winston were still standing there, engrossed in Rick's latest creation, in a hastily erected gazebo.

Puffed out and needing to catch my breath, I grabbed Percy by the arm and separated her from the others.

"Just seen Eddie."

"Have you? Why are you so out of breath?"

I took a gulp of fresh air. "Ran here. Must tell Rick what he's up to. It's important."

"What have you found out?"

"Ghastly plan for here. Holiday village."

"What? He can't! Does Rick know?" Percy looked even more shocked than I expected.

I shook my head. "No, that's the point. We need to get them together so Eddie can tell him himself."

She nodded. "Agreed. Never a good idea to be the go-between."

"Exactly. Now, can you persuade him to come up to the big house? Eddie's still there, I think."

"I'll try."

She went back to the two men. "Time for lunch, guys."

Rick gave her a perfunctory smile. "Oh, man, this is going so well. I don't care about lunch."

Percy said firmly, "I think not, Rick. You need to get back to your house and see Eddie about something very important."

Rick finally drew his eyes away from the computer screen on the camping table and looked at Percy. "What's up?"

269

I joined them. "It's better you hear it from Eddie."

"Tax issues again? Surely they can wait?"

I shook my head. "Not this time."

My serious demeanour must have convinced him. Rick sighed and turned to Winston. "Sorry, man. Looks like I'll have to split. Catch you later, yeah?"

Winston smiled. "It's okay. I'll close things up and take the equipment to the farmhouse. Looks like rain, anyway."

We walked back to the farmhouse with Rick between us. "So, what's this about then, girls?"

"Wait till we see Eddie."

"If you say so, but it's all bit weird."

We went through the back door and found Eddie in the kitchen, still looking furious and with his mobile clamped to his ear. The back of his neck was red under the tattoos. As soon as he saw us, he switched off his call and put his mobile in his jeans pocket where it bulged in a rectangle against the strained denim.

"Thought you were busy recording, Rick?"

To my mind, Eddie's guilty face had already betrayed him but, having dragged Rick here, I was determined to go through with his confession. "I've brought Rick here so you can tell him about your plans, Eddie."

"What the…? What have you told him?"

I pulled out a dining chair and sat down. "Nothing. I've left that to you."

"You've done what? I've nothing to tell him."

"We both know that isn't true, Eddie." I indicated the chair opposite. "Sit down."

"Don't come in here and boss me around!" But he sat down.

Percy turned to Rick. "Let's join them round the table, shall we?"

Rick and Percy took the other chairs and quietly sat down. Rick turned to Eddie. "I think you'd better spill, man."

Eddie squirmed on his chair like a rabbit in a trap. He glared at me, sitting opposite him, with pure hatred. "It's just an idea." He sounded like a sulky teenager.

Rick fished in his pocket for his tobacco. "What is? Come on, open up, Eddie."

Eddie heaved a huge sigh. "It's just that, with all your debts, I was trying to find a way out. This estate is really valuable and if it was me, I'd sell it outright, but you won't do that, will you, Rick?"

"Never." Rick sprinkled tobacco along the line of his Rizla paper.

"So, I thought outside the box, and I've got, well almost got, planning permission to turn it into a holiday village."

"A what?" Rick's fingers paused in mid-air.

"It could be really cool. You know, with the access to the beach cleared and a pool complex, this place could be stunning."

Percy jumped in. "How would you make the access to the beach easier?"

"There's too many trees in the way. Would be easy enough to get rid of them."

Percy gasped. "You mean, cut down the trees in the oak circle?"

Eddie shrugged. "Why not?"

Percy looked deeply shocked. "But it's sacred! It's a holy place of worship for Bryony's Pagans!"

Eddie made a noise of derision. "That bunch of hippies? They'll have to leave, I'm afraid. They're never going to make any money. Rick's better off without them. That farmhouse alone would sell for hundreds of thousands with that view it's got. Make a perfect hotel or restaurant. But I see it being much bigger with holiday bungalows between this house and that old pile of stones. They could be a mysterious feature, you know, all lit up at night…"

Eddie trailed off as Rick held up a flat palm. For once he spoke without his affected drawl. "Enough. None of

271

this will happen. How far have you got with this plan, Eddie? Have you committed any cash to it?"

Eddie looked unsure. "Not much so far, but I've arranged a bank loan and the planning permission is pretty much in the bag. That cost a bit."

Rick put down his unlit cigarette. "You have bribed a local planning officer?"

Eddie gave a rueful grin. "It's the way the world works, Rick, you know that."

Rick laid both his palms flat on the table. "I do not, and I will not have my name sullied around this area. You have done all this behind my back, Eddie. You have betrayed me."

Eddie looked appalled. "But…"

Rick stood up and squared his narrow shoulders. "Consider yourself dismissed from my service."

Eddie stood up too, scraping his chair on the dirty floor tiles. "What? You don't mean it? After all these years together?"

"Not only do I mean it, Eddie, but I want you to leave immediately. Take nothing with you except your personal items. All the accounts and files are out of bounds to you from this moment. And you can give me your phone too. I don't want you making any more calls on my behalf."

I could hear Eddie's intake of breath rasping his throat. "No, no, no! Come on, Rick! I was only thinking of you."

Rick folded his arms. "You were thinking of yourself. No doubt you would cut yourself a big fat wodge of profit on this deal and any income from this horrible holiday village."

Eddie went silent but his face flushed an ugly shade of red to match his bull-neck. "I, I, I've never seen you like this, Rick. I can't believe you mean what you say."

I looked at Rick. He did seem different.

"Never been more serious. You've got fifteen minutes to collect your stuff. You can give me your phone right now. Come on, I know the account is in my name anyway. There's no way you would pay the bill."

"You can't take my phone off me!"

"I think you'll find I can. Now go."

I actually felt quite sorry for Eddie in that moment. He opened his mouth and shut it, twice. He pulled his phone out of his pocket and slid it across the sticky table to Rick, who picked it up and calmly started scrolling through the contact list.

I think it was his calm that convinced Eddie. He turned to me. "You are a scheming, lying bitch! I told you all this in good faith and you ran with it straight to Rick, didn't you?"

I held up my hands in denial. "I didn't tell him anything, Eddie, except that he needed to speak with you."

"Yeah, right." Eddie shoved his dining chair roughly under the table, so its legs hit mine.

"Ouch!"

Eddie shoved his face into mine. "That's the least of what I'd like to do to you, witch!"

Percy made to get up, but I pushed her gently back down to her seat. "Leave it."

Rick looked up from Eddie's phone. "Yes, leave it, Eddie. Get out."

A quarter of an hour later the three of us stood on the steps of the big house and watched Eddie drive away.

When he had gone, Percy turned to Rick. "You were very harsh on your manager, Rick."

Rick put his unused cigarette to his lips and lit it with his lighter. "Yeah, I know. I dunno what's happening to me, man, but I feel kind of different about things, you know?"

"In what way?" Percy inclined her head to one side.

"I swear it's that hippy woman. Ever since you stabbed me and she sorted me out, I kind of see things in a new way and that time when her mates were singing, something changed inside." He patted his chest and smiled at

Percy. "You didn't help, with your spooky ghosty stuff, neither."

I let out a relieved sigh. "I think this place has changed us all."

Percy nodded. "And for the better."

Chapter Forty-Three, Present Day

With Eddie gone, everything seemed to flow more easily. Rick remained different – quieter and even more focussed on his work. Nothing went awry in the studio and Winston became a fixture inside it, hunched over the computer. If Rick wasn't in there, he was at the grove nearby, wandering around with a microphone or a guitar in a dreamy bubble of creativity. He even got the local pagan community to join in on a few evenings and at weekends and sing some chorus he'd written, but I declined the invitation.

Percy was with either him or Winston most of the time looking equally absorbed and happy. I felt at a bit of a loose end and anxious to communicate with Gaine through someone, anyone, to make quite certain she would come through at Samhain. Nobody else seemed to realise that everything depended on that. No matter how great Rick's music turned out to be, without Gaine or even Bryonia coming through with this much-heralded message for the world, it would all be for nothing, and we'd all look like fools. If the media got wind of it, it would gobble up this innocent pagan community and enjoy spitting out the pips in public. I could just imagine the splashed headlines across the tabloids.

'Crazy hippies in failed spiritual communion with ghosts!'

'Rick O'Shea loses it at last.'

'Fake ghostbusters rip off Pagans in desperate bid to be famous.'

We'd be mincemeat.

Full of apprehensive anxiety, I went to visit Bryony.

The door of the farmhouse stood open in welcome as usual, so I went straight in. The door to the classroom was shut however, so I wandered into the dining room but found it equally empty. I was just about to leave when the classroom door opened, and a stream of serene yoga enthusiasts filed out. I waited a few minutes, so Bryony had some personal space after her class, then knocked and went into the teaching room.

She was making herself a cup of herbal tea and turned around at my knock.

"Oh, hello."

"Hi, Bryony. Thought I'd find you here. How are you?"

"I'm well, thanks, though it took a while to recover from the cave episode. Would you like a cup of tea?"

I hated herbal tea with a vengeance, but this wasn't the occasion to admit it. "Lovely. Peppermint, please."

She brought the brews over to the peripheral chairs and we sat down together.

I took my mug. "Thanks. I'm glad of a hot drink, it's so cold outside."

She nodded. "The winter is nearly here. I hope it will be dry at Samhain."

"About that?"

"Hmm?" Bryony sipped her tea.

"Have you had any contact with Gaine?"

"No, sadly."

I took a tentative sip of my own brew. "Neither has Percy, not a glimpse."

"Are you concerned she won't come through for the ceremony?"

"Aren't you?"

Bryony put her mug down on the adjacent chair. "I was but then I thought, she's waited two thousand years for this, she won't let us down."

Horrified at her complacent attitude but aware accusing her of it wouldn't help, I tried to tone down my reply from the shrieking voice in my head and simply said, "I admire your faith and wish I shared it."

"I was worried Rick's music would get in the way but after what she said at the dark of the moon, I've stopped."

I couldn't believe how sanguine she was being compared to her earlier stress before the cave collapsed. Was she suffering from concussion or from some spiritual inner conviction? I decided to play along. "And he isn't playing that hard rock anymore."

Bryony smiled. "No, in fact he's got the group singing along to his music."

"Have you heard the whole thing?"

"No-one has. He's keeping everything separate – the birdsong, the chorus and his own accompaniment."

"I hope he can bring it together on the night." I finished my tea. It hadn't been too bad. "Has the group decided how to film the occasion?"

"Winston has taken that on. He's pretty media savvy, by all accounts."

"And he's genuine? I mean, he seems like a nice guy but after what happened with Eddie…"

"What did happen with Eddie?"

I explained about the holiday village and Bryony blenched. "Gracious! I can't think of anything worse!"

I laughed. "Sorry, it's no joke really, but what a nightmare that would have been."

Bryony nodded sagely. "Gaine and Bryonia are working their magic behind the scenes."

Again, such unquestioning faith in our essential spiritual aides! Incredible. I had to press her, but I would do it gently. I had already learned how brittle she was underneath that Buddha pose.

"You could be right, but I still would like an exchange with either of them."

Finally, it seemed I had got through because Bryony nodded.

"Why not now? We could do it together, here in this very room. I've not tried to connect in here before, but everything is different now. I used to think it could only happen in the sacred grove or the cave. It would be interesting to find out if it can happen elsewhere, now things have changed."

"Perfect, I'm game."

277

We got up from our chairs and sat on some yoga mats in the middle of the room. I tried to get comfortable and couldn't.

Without any complaint voiced by me, Bryony sensed my discomfort. I suppose she'd had years of experience with students. "Use a chair if it helps you concentrate. Your posture doesn't matter for this purpose."

"Thanks." I unwound my legs from their excruciating lotus position and pulled a chair into the centre of the large room. "That's better." I parked my behind on its steady surface and looked at Bryony. She seemed to already be under a meditational spell.

I closed my eyes. A vague waft of spent incense helped me to get in the mood before birdsong from the front garden floated through the slightly open window. I recognised it immediately as the song of the robin. Not *my* Robin, obviously, but it was a comforting thought that he might be here with me, if only symbolically. My muscles relaxed, all-at-once, and I let go of all conscious thought.

How long we sat there in silence together I shall never know as I lost all sense of time. Even the robin piping and trilling outside faded away until all I could see was a white light between my eyes. My heart beat slower, my breathing deepened and yet I wasn't sleepy.

Two hands slipped into both of mine and held them lightly in a dry, comforting grasp. I felt a current of electricity pass between them. The sensation crept up my arm and, when it reached my mind, an image softly stole in, and I saw the Bryonia of old.

She told me to open my eyes. When I did, I saw the living Bryony, now close to me, holding my hands. I saw nothing around her but a blur of pastel shades.

When Bryony spoke, I knew at once it was through the voice of her ancestor.

"At last, you are together as one in cooperation. This is good and what we need. Be not alarmed. This was meant to happen. You will separate afterwards. For now, trust in each other, for you both have a role to play. My granddaughter, Gaine, will give her message at your gathering at Samhain but not through either of you. She will speak through the younger woman with the tawny hair. Her beauty will ensure the world listens. This woman must be rested and tranquil before the event and you will ensure she is. The communication will be much longer this time, Gaine has much to say. Be sure her words are spread around your world. The music man will help you with this. I do not understand your modern ways, but he does. Go now, trust all will be well."

I sat in the ensuing silence, content to wait for Bryony to return to being in the present. Eventually she opened her eyes and blinked before they focussed.

"Oh, we are sitting so close!" She dropped her hands and looked embarrassed.

For once, I didn't feel awkward being near someone else. "Don't worry, Bryony. We had to hear that together. You do remember what Bryonia said, don't you?"

Bryony sat back on her yoga mat. "Yes, I do. It confirms my sense of peace and confidence that everything will happen at the right time, in the right way."

"I am reassured, I admit, but I don't share your level of confidence. Seems we had better look after Percy over the next couple of weeks. Let's hope Gaine doesn't go all violent on Rick in the meantime."

Bryony actually smiled at my words. "She won't, I know she won't. That was a one-off and, I believe, a mistake on Gaine's part she will not be willing to repeat. And anyway, Rick is helping her now. His Roman ancestor has been forgiven."

Unconvinced but unwilling to spoil her tranquillity, I thanked her for the tea and took my leave. A bracing walk was what I needed. I strolled out along the headland to look at the sea. The wind blew from the west, as usual, bringing a hint of rain and a very cool breeze. I looked out at the infinite horizon and implored whatever Gods there were to come to our aid at Halloween. And Robin. I always wanted Robin. I hoped he might reach me now, in this private moment but the strong wind blew any hopes away, and I turned back towards the cottage feeling a strange conflicting sense of loneliness mixed with connection.

I took good care of Percy over the next few days, but it turned out to be Rick who really needed my help. He knocked on the cottage door one morning and I opened it.

"Rick! Well, this is a surprise. You're not usually up so early."

"I'm getting to like this time of day. It's fresh, innit? Gives me energy, like."

"Come in and make yourself comfortable. I'll put the kettle on."

"Ta very much." Rick folded his long legs under the kitchen table.

We both looked up as Percy descended the stairs in her beautiful green silk kimono wafting fragrant aromas with every movement.

"Bloody hell, babe, you look good enough to eat." Rick winked at her.

Unabashed, Percy glided to the table like a swan.

I turned to practical matters. "Who wants tea?"

"Coffee please, darlin'." Rick got his cigarette paraphernalia out.

Percy stayed his arm with her own. "Please don't, not here."

Rick shrugged. "Fair enough."

I plugged a coffee pod into the little machine on the counter. "Percy? Tea?"

"Lovely, could I have Redbush, please?"

I clattered about getting the drinks together. "So, Rick, to what do we owe the honour of a visit from our noble landlord?"

Rick laughed. He seemed to be doing that a lot lately. "Got a letter from the effing taxman, haven't I?"

I put the drinks on the table. "Oh, dear, and no Eddie to sort it out for you."

"Yeah, but I remembered you said you were a trained accountant?"

280

"That's right, I am." I took a sip of tea. "Got the letter on you?"

"As a matter of fact, I have." Rick passed me a letter folded into three.

I opened it up and whistled. "Wow! That is a tidy sum."

Rick looked at Percy. "You sure I can't smoke in here, darlin'?"

Percy's reply was emphatic. "No, however much debt you're in."

Rick shrugged. "Harsh."

I looked again at the tax demand. "So's this. You'd better give me all the correspondence Eddie has had with them and I'll chase them up."

The lines on Rick's forehead slackened. "You would? You're not fazed by the amount?"

I shook my head. "No, I'm not. I'm not saying it will be easy, but I can try for an extension."

"What do you mean?"

"A stay of execution. You could pay by instalments. Eddie was talking about doing that and may have opened negotiations already."

Rick leaned forward and kissed my brow. "You, girl, are a star."

Sorting out Eddie's filing system and getting acquainted with the complicated records of Rick's up-and-down fortunes over the last couple of years kept me busy for quite a few days and I worried about Percy wandering around without escort, but she seemed fine, a bit spaced out and dreamy but that was probably a good thing. We both made sure we had early nights and regular meals. When I had formulated a plan for the tax return, I phoned the relevant office and managed to negotiate an instalment plan with the helpful guy who answered.

Rick was genuinely chuffed when I told him. "Amazing, girl. I mean, really amazing. That's a weight off my mind and no Eddie dramas like usual."

"Wasn't that hard, to be honest, but you must make the first payment before the deadline. You've got till the end of January."

"Really? That's plenty of time. I'll have this album cracked out by then."

"Can it be done that quickly?" I was surprised.

"These days, girl, everything happens fast." Rick clapped me on the shoulder. "Thanks. I really appreciate what you've done. You must give me an invoice for your accounts work, yeah?"

"We've been living here rent free for weeks. Consider that my payment."

Rick tapped the side of his bony nose. "We'll see about that."

Chapter Forty-Four, Present Day

Samhain dawned, not in a fiery blaze of light, but stealthily and shrouded in grey drizzle, as befitted Halloween, when the veil between the living and the dead is at its thinnest.

I hadn't set the alarm on my new phone. The important gathering wouldn't be until it was dark and, it being my job to keep Percy rested, I wanted to sleep as late as possible. I looked at the time, pleased to find it had already reached nine o'clock, due to the clocks going back an hour the night before as British summer time had ended at midnight. Mornings and evenings enclosed short days at this time of year.

I rolled over onto my back and contemplated the beamed ceiling with my hands behind my head. I had the day carefully planned out for my friend. Shower, breakfast, stroll, lunch, afternoon nap and a light supper before we got ready for the grand event.

Even lying there thinking about what was ahead made my empty stomach flip over, keeping my normally ravenous morning appetite suppressed. I stretched my legs to their fullest extent and lay under the bedcovers in the shape of a star, hoping to relax but the knots in my belly refused to release their hold on my churning solar plexus.

I wondered how Rick was feeling with such a momentous task resting solely on his shoulders. If anything, he'd seemed more confident as the date approached. Bryony had been less so yesterday when I'd called round. A proper case of the jitters. I speculated on how she would be if she didn't meditate every day and, for the first time, tried to imagine her as a younger woman but the image eluded me, which was probably just as well.

I heard movement from the bathroom that divided the two bedrooms in the cottage. Percy must be up and doing. That meant it was time I got up too. Bodyguards must stay close.

We met on the landing, me in my chunky towelling bathrobe, Percy in her floaty green kimono.

"Morning. How's the star of the show?"

Percy raised perfectly arched eyebrows. "Oh, don't Fay, you'll make me nervous!"

"Far be it from me to bring on a bout of nerves, especially as I'm commanded to keep you relaxed!"

"Exactly! I'm going to do some yoga in my room before I come down to breakfast so don't come bothering me."

"I hear you, oh goddess." I bowed my tousled head in mock salute.

"Enough!" Percy laughed and disappeared into her bedroom.

I took my time in the shower, willing the hot water to drum some clarity into my brain. Unconvinced it had worked, I got dressed and went downstairs to see if food might help.

When Percy didn't appear for a whole hour, I abandoned all attempts not to worry and pounded up the stairs, two at a time.

I knocked on her door, but no answer came. I banged louder but still there was no reply. I opened the door and found the room horribly empty. Where the hell *was* she? There was only one staircase in the house, I would have seen her descend it, wouldn't I? Then I remembered I'd emptied the bins half an hour ago and got wrapped up in listening to a robin singing on the bare branches of the apple tree in the back garden. She must have left in those few minutes when I'd shirked my care of duty to her.

A ridiculous level of panic set in. She couldn't have gone far, after all. Probably went for a jog or something equally healthy. That must be it.

I pulled on my trainers and almost flew down the stairs and out of the front door. The soft silent drizzle hadn't let up, making it hard to see through the resulting mist.

"Percy! Percy! Where are you?"

The robin chirruped hello but he was alone in responding. I tried to think where she would have gone. The grove. It must be. She would be trying to get in the mood, surely? I ran down the wooded path towards the oak trees and arrived, panting, into the big circular space.

And there she was, alone with Rick. I stopped in my tracks to stare at them.

Rick was kneeling in front of her, while Percy towered over him, looking tall and majestic. He bent his head and she placed both her hands upon his greying dark hair and murmured some words I couldn't catch.

What were they up to? I screwed up my eyes to try and focus on her beautiful features, to search for signs of anger, impending violence, or any stress, but there was only peace written across those high cheek bones.

She smiled and lifted her hands away, so they hung at her sides. Rick raised his head and stood up. I didn't know whether to approach or stay put; neither did I know what on earth they would do next.

I watched, primed for action with every muscle twitching, but nothing much happened after all. They each reached out a hand and held it, before turning towards the gazebo Winston had erected for all the musical gear and walked towards it, hand-in-hand, serene and calm.

They both appeared to be blissfully unaware of me, so I took a moment to allow my breath to flow more evenly and for the adrenaline pumping around my system to dissipate.

Feeling like an intruder on a private encounter, I approached softly and, when they still didn't take any notice, cleared my throat loudly.

"Good morning, you two."

Unperturbed, they turned to me as one and smiled their greetings.

"Um, everything alright?"

Percy nodded and let go of Rick's hand. "Lovely, thanks. We just had a wonderful message from Bryonia. I haven't seen her before – she's so like Bryony!"

285

"Yes, yes, she is." I waited for more.

Rick joined in. "Never seen nuffink like it, girl. Gives me a funny turn just to think about it but it was real alright."

"What did Bryonia say?"

Percy beamed at me. "Just said everything would be fine later. I must say, I feel much more relaxed now."

Rick nodded. "Yeah, it was weird alright, but sort of calmed me down too." He turned to all the gadgetry on the makeshift table.

"I'm just going to go through everything real methodical-like."

He looked at Percy, his eyes soft and gentle. "You'd better get some rest, babe. And eat something, yeah?"

"Alright, Rick, I will." Percy leaned over and kissed his wrinkled cheek. "See you later."

Rick touched his face where her kiss had landed. "Yeah, see you later."

I linked arms with her on the way back to the cottage, just to be sure.

The rest of the day passed according to my ultra-safe plan. Boring and quiet and that was fine by me. I would have stood guard at Percy's bedroom door when she was despatched for her compulsory afternoon nap if she hadn't shooed me away.

The last day of October is never very long and, with the hour change, it was surprisingly dark when we ate the light supper I had prepared.

Whilst I was loading the dishwasher Bryony appeared. She was already wearing her long black tunic with the amber girdle and carrying a large linen bag. "This is for Percy to wear. It is a very fine tunic of white linen that has been handed down through generations of my family. I have been guided to give it to her this evening."

Percy looked slightly flummoxed by this gift. "Oh, I was just going to wear my long red skirt with the green jumper."

Bryony shook her head firmly. "Oh, no. That wouldn't be good enough. Come, I will help you dress."

I took my role of bodyguard very seriously. "Who was your guide about this, Bryony?"

Bryony gave me one of her flinty blue-eyed stares. "Gaine."

Percy smiled at her. "Then there is no more to be said. Let's go upstairs."

I was determined not to be left behind. I shut the dishwasher door and set the programme before following them. Percy's room was tidy, unlike mine, with her bed neatly made and all her cosmetics lined up like soldiers in formation on her chest of drawers.

Bryony took no notice of any of this. Her focus was strictly on the contents of her bag. She drew out the tunic and hung it on its hangar on the wardrobe door. "It's good there is a long mirror on this door."

"Yes, I find it very useful." Percy, fragrant from her second shower that day, her make up already delicately applied, drew off her outer clothes obediently and submitted to Bryony throwing the white tunic over her head. It transformed her in an instant.

I shivered in an irrational reaction. "Wow, you look as if you lived in an earlier age."

Bryony pulled out Percy's long auburn hair from under the collar of the tunic and let it cascade down her back. "I have a girdle for you. It is plaited leather, dyed blue with woad."

I sat back on the bed, feeling entirely redundant and content to watch the makeover develop.

Around Percy's shining head Bryony placed a circlet of ivy leaves and tied bracelets of the same plant around her wrists. Then she took a slim box from the capacious linen bag and withdrew a necklace made of pure gold.

"It's Welsh gold, that's why it's so yellow." Bryony put it over Percy's head and let it fall around her neck where it gleamed and shone in a wide circlet.

It reminded me of something I'd seen somewhere. "It's like the torc I saw on Bryonia."

Bryony looked over at me. "Yes, torcs are too solid to get on and off easily but this necklace, though it looks similar in shape, has a clasp at the back."

"It still looks quite old."

Bryony nodded. "I have no idea how old it is; it's been passed down in my family since time immemorial."

"Have you never had it valued? You should, if only for insurance purposes."

She shook her head. "Never, and I never will. It is sacred. The gods protect it."

Percy put a hand to the symbol embossed on the front. "Oh, it's a triskelion! Like my earrings!"

"You know what it means?" Bryony looked surprised.

Percy went to her dressing table and took her new earrings out of their little cotton pouch. "Yes, look! I bought these in George's workshop. He said Gwen had made them and told me the three circles represent the continuation of life on and on through the ages powered by the energy of the sun."

"That's right, that's exactly right! They also stand for body, mind and spirit." Bryony picked one up. "They look like they are made of Welsh gold too."

"I must wear them tonight." Percy looked in the mirror to hook them into her pierced ears.

Being of a more practical nature, I volunteered, "How about shoes? Very wet out there. I mean the rain has cleared up, but the ground is sodden."

Bryony was stumped for once. "I haven't thought about footwear."

"I have." Percy opened the wardrobe door and took out her smart leather knee-boots. "These will keep me warm and dry."

I got up and went to my bedroom where I rootled about in the top drawer of my dressing table and went back to the others. "Especially with these underneath." I handed over a thick pair of long woollen socks.

Bryony laughed. "Very sensible!"

Percy kissed my cheek. "You can always rely on Fay."

I felt myself blushing. Ridiculous! "Well, put them on then."

At last, she was ready. Percy stood in front of the mirror looking like a medieval queen.

Bryony clasped her hands together and looked positively sentimental. "You look perfect, cariad."

"Yes, I think you'll do Gaine proud. Let's just hope she comes through!" I grabbed her overcoat. "Cover yourself up until the moment arrives, Percy. You don't want a chill."

Percy laughed as she put her arms through the sleeves. "Alright, Mummy."

"You may mock but you know I'm right. Just let me grab my things and we'll go."

We each picked up a candlelit lantern from the kitchen and ventured forth. None of us spoke on the way but I'm sure the others had minds as preoccupied and tense as mine.

The usual crowd had already gathered within the embrace of the oak circle. They spoke in hushed tones, huddled together in groups. Rick and Winston were in the gazebo that housed all their kit but as soon as Percy entered the sacred space, Rick broke free and came up to her and kissed her softly on the mouth.

"You look beautiful, babe."

I looked sideways at Percy who seemed entirely unconcerned at this greeting, but Bryony frowned.

"You must put your lanterns on the capstone, so she's illuminated." She pointed at the cromlech. "Actually, I must speak to Winston about the lighting."

Bryony bustled off and her followers drifted towards her as if they were one amoeba clutching to their nucleus.

Rick put his hands lightly on Percy's shoulders. "Feeling alright, luv?"

Percy nodded. "A bit nervous but okay, thanks."

"You'll be great. I've given enough concerts in my time to know that you need some nerves to give a good performance. Just relax and let Gaine do the talking."

Percy leant into his arms, and he held her for a moment. Then she quietly withdrew. "Thanks, Rick. Hadn't you better get ready too?"

He kissed her brow under its ivy crown. "Yeah, I'm off. Break a leg."

We stood alone then, Percy and I. Considering I was supposed to be her guardian, I suddenly realised I hadn't attended any rehearsals, having been preoccupied with the more worldly matter of Rick's tax duties.

"Is there a sequence to follow? I mean do the others know what to do?"

Percy squeezed my arm. "Don't worry. Everyone's been practising and Rick knows what he's doing. Just stay close to me, please? I always feel safer when you're around."

I chortled at that. "Then that's more than I do with you, going on previous experience!"

We laughed, then hugged each other, and my tension eased by the tiniest fraction.

Bryony went to stand on the plinth in front of the stone table and clapped her hands. "Gather round, everyone! Now, I know you have all rehearsed with Rick but this time we are filming our Samhain meeting and we want our ancestors to speak to us." She crooked her finger to Percy, who went to her side.

"I'm sure you all know our friend, Persephone, here and hope, as I do, that Gaine will speak through her tonight with the message she wants us to relay around the world. Winston?" Bryony waved a vague hand towards the musical headquarters and Winston bowed his dreadlocks in recognition. "Winston is in charge of filming and recording and it's imperative that nothing goes wrong. George is also going to film it on his camera as a back-up, so there is no need for you to do the same. We do not want to send it anywhere, not even to our dearest friends, until the final version is prepared properly. Then, you can share it on as many social media platforms you like. I'm sure you are all too aware of how negative the press can be about our pagan celebrations however innocent we all know them to be."

There were murmurings of assent around her. Bryony continued. "I am trusting you to obey me on this so can I hear your agreement out loud before we begin? All those in favour, say 'aye!'"

A rousing chorus of affirmations rippled through the small crowd. Bryony nodded in acknowledgement. "And because we are always democratic as Pagans, are there any who do not agree to abide by this secrecy?"

Not a single voice spoke in answer.

Bryony smiled. "My dear friends, thank you. If all goes well, this story will spread far and wide, never fear."

I looked round at Rick and Winston and felt a thrill of anticipation as I saw Winston manning a proper film camera on a wheeled tripod. A wooden floor had been rigged up just outside the gazebo to give it a level platform. That boy was a professional. Rick looked incredibly calm and sat on a garden chair, hugging his acoustic guitar nearby.

I turned back when Bryony addressed the group again. "We shall light the fire now but only feast after we have heard from our ancestors."

Bryony nodded at George, who lit the bonfire which had been piled high on the other side of the stones, well away from the expensive modern recording equipment and the overhanging bare branches of the guardian oaks. The wood caught quickly and formed a flaming backdrop to Bryony and Percy standing together on the plinth.

Bryony nodded at George as he re-joined the group. "Thank you, George. Let us remember the loved ones we have lost, as we always do at this time of year." She bowed her head, and everyone followed suit in front of her.

In the respectful silence that followed, Robin immediately sprang into my mind. I could see his face clearly for once and he was smiling. He didn't say anything, but a warm glow began in my chest and spread to the rest of

291

my body in a comforting fuzzy sensation, and I don't think it was coming from the bonfire, however brightly it was now burning.

In a quiet voice that yet could be heard easily by all, Bryony invited everyone to begin to hum the 'Awen' chant when they were ready and sounded her gentle gong to signal the start. As the single note began to fade, Bryony hummed gently and carried it on before it died away.

People joined hands with whoever was next to them and broke into a low musical note that never ended, not even when one person took a breath, because the others were still humming. The glow I'd got from Robin grew. I felt it pass to me from each of the hands I held, and I knew I was smiling.

Bryony broke into a chant praising their ancestors and inviting them to join us.

"Oh, ancestors all, may you be blessed, may you be blessed
Oh, Grandmothers all, may you be blessed, may you be blessed
Oh, Grandfathers all, may you be blessed may you be blessed
Oh, ancestors all, may you be blessed, may you be blessed."

A prickle of excitement accompanied my warm glow, and a few butterflies took flight in my stomach.

The communal singing continued for some time with different songs, but always with the theme of honouring and inviting their ancestors and the loved ones who had gone before, as well as celebrating life on earth. I could feel Robin behind me, his hands on my waist, his chest against my back, moving in time to the music as if we were one person.

My usual shyness about joining in with anything, but particularly in song, evaporated and I sang as loud as the best of them, my throat open and vibrating with sound within the enchanted space. Everything seemed dreamlike, timeless and safe.

After the next song, Bryony once again tapped her soft gong as a signal to silence which was filled by the most beautiful birdsong. Not a robin this time, but a blackbird chirruping into the night. Then, almost imperceptibly accompanying it, was an acoustic guitar, picking out the notes with consummate skill and sensitivity. I did not need to look around to know that it was Rick strumming his guitar with perfect ease.

Gradually the music faded away and all eyes turned to Percy. She stood tall in front of the cromlech, her arms outstretched as if in welcome and her hazel eyes alight with love.

"My beloved descendants, thank you for your beautiful welcome. You have given me the strength I needed to come here tonight, for I passed away over two thousand years ago, here in this sacred place and I can only manifest through universal energy. You do not know how much your gathering of loving energy helps those who have gone before, and your honouring of your dead is very beneficial to those who have passed, and also to all of you gathered here tonight who have yet to pass, when it will return to you tenfold.

"Since my passing, I have worked hard connecting with like-minded souls living in this sacred spot to continue building the energy between us. Although this oak grove with the triskelion symbol carved into the stone is a special portal, these connections happen all over the world. These centres of communication are vital to strengthen the force for good and to lend power to those who work towards peace and healing on Earth.

"I am here tonight with an urgent message about our beloved planet Earth. Not only can I see the past, I can also see the present. We are at an unprecedented moment in time when this earthly home of ours is in great peril. The vast numbers of humans consuming energy and resources today are draining our earth and upsetting the natural balance by heating up our planet. You are at a crossroads and the actions you take now will decide if you perish or survive. Indeed,

293

you must move to a new way of living in harmony with nature, as did the people of my time, or perish you certainly will.

"As Pagans, you continue to honour the seasons and the world around you, but it is not so elsewhere. I see huge floods in some places and wildfires out of control in others; pollution obscuring the mountains; glaciers melting, and seas rising, whilst industry keeps gushing out its toxins.

"Even here, in this blessed spot, the soil has been washed away by a severe storm. You will all have seen our sacred cave for the laying out of the dead crash into the ocean. More will follow, my dears, much more. The soil is dying and all the millions of tiny creatures within it are poisoned by forcing it to yield a harvest beyond natural levels. The earth can no longer provide this. She is spent.

"The insects, especially the bees who so generously give us their healing honey, the fish and the animals can no longer thrive as their habitats are destroyed around them and they are farmed unnaturally. The forests which guard the air you breathe are being cut down and burnt in such numbers it is polluting the clean air necessary for life.

"You may think you know all this already, that what I am saying is not new, but I forewarn you that the very moon above us will stand still and make the earth realign its angle with the sun, as it does every eighteen years, but the next one will amplify the tides still further as they are already swollen. Many more cliffs will fall into the sea, and big storms will wash away huge areas of coastal land all over the world.

"My dear ones, our sacred oak grove itself will soon be under threat. The majestic trees that surround and shelter you this Samhain will themselves wash into the sea. These stones standing behind me, huge as they are, will be like tiny pebbles when the sea sweeps in and carries them away, together with the bones of your ancestors which lie under the cairn nearby. All will be gone unless the planet is stabilised. Your scientists know this already, but they are not being heard.

"You must tell all the rulers in the world this message and make them listen. Every person who wields power over others must hear about this. The time has come. It is the moment of decision, of truth, of action.

"However, do not despair. There is no going back but there could be a way forward. A way to live differently in harmony with nature, not in conflict with it. New ways for mankind to light up and power his world. If action is taken now, the future could yet be beautiful, my beloveds, but hurry towards it, reach out to others, learn these new ways. The lives of your children and grandchildren depend upon it. Your modern world needs much energy to power its tools but there will be new ways to do this which will provide unlimited power without harm. You must share your food and your resources with everyone and then there will be no more wars such as I have witnessed over the millennia. Unite, cooperate, learn and experiment. There are exciting times ahead, but you must ensure it happens.

"Your leaders will meet soon, for I have seen this. They must hear my words and your music. Go now and spread the word. Do all you can to inspire positive change and create the political will amongst those who make the decisions. Your future, indeed that of the entire world, lies in the balance."

Percy clasped her hands together. "My beloveds, the future need not be hell on earth, but a paradise of peace and plenty for all.

"I am fading now and cannot last longer. You are much loved, as is every man, woman and child on our beleaguered planet. Go in peace *but take action*."

Percy smiled on every person gathered around here before sliding down into a slumped sitting position with her back supported by the big chunk of limestone Gaine's descendants had placed there nearly two thousand years ago.

Rick began to play again, softly at first but then building into an exquisite crescendo that gently dwindled away even as the blackbird began his swansong in a smooth segue.

When even that cadence ceased, I looked around at the gentle people surrounding me and saw that not one person had dry eyes.

"Excuse me, sorry, got to get past." I elbowed my way to the stone plinth where Percy now sat with eyes closed, dark shadows beneath them, and her face pale.

I felt the pulse on her wrist before laying it back down, satisfied with its steady beat.

I stood up. "She's alright. She will be fine. She just needs to sleep now."

Quietly, the crowd dispersed and gravitated to the bonfire on the other side of the stones where they spoke to each other in respectful low tones.

I slithered down next to Percy against the massive stones, content to savour the moment, the knowledge that Robin had been with me, and remember the divine music surrounding her dramatic message. Whatever spell or enchantment had happened here, I never wanted this feeling to end.

Chapter Forty-five, Present Day

The month of November declared its presence with a brighter dawn than had greeted the end of October. I woke earlier than yesterday due to the sun streaming through the bedroom window. I had been too tired the night before to even draw the curtains but had fallen into bed and slept as one dead. Except now I knew they didn't. Knowing that life was a continuing circle of renewal, as portrayed in the triskelion symbol, gave me immense comfort.

I got up and went to the bathroom and peeped in on Percy, but she was fast asleep, her hands in a prayer position under her cheek, looking like an innocent, carefree child.

I decided to make a cup of tea and bring it back to bed as a treat. Once ensconced under the bedcovers again, I switched on the new mobile phone I had purchased while working on Rick's accounts.

Winston must have worked through the night, loading the short film of last night's events on to YouTube and TikTok. Somehow, he'd found a video of the collapsed cave and fronted it with that catastrophe. He had edited it skilfully and kept the most important chant, the one about the beauty of the earth, for the soundtrack, sung by his fellow pagans. Then came Percy in all her splendour as the centrepiece, with Gaine's singsong voice giving her plea to the world and the warning about the so-called moon wobble. The film ended with the blackbird and Rick's acoustic guitar accompanied everything in a seamless stream of music underpinning the singing and speaking.

I have to say I was impressed and played the sequence over and over again. Then I looked down at the comments and realised I was not the only one. Hundreds of people had watched it and been wowed by it. Of course, most thought it was fake and that it was no ghost speaking but Percy rigged up to look like one. I had no idea how we could prove it otherwise, but the powerful strength of the music spoke for itself and somehow the enchantment also came through, and I didn't think it was based on my memories of the occasion.

I turned to the news, and it was all about the climate change conference which began today. All the world leaders were gathering together to discuss the fate of our planet.

Good timing, Gaine.

I sipped my tea, content to know that we had done our job. Rick would not be haunted any longer, except perhaps by Percy's beauty. They had seemed so tender together yesterday. Not my business, I decided.

I had seen my Robin too. Yes, actually seen his face properly for a long time, and he had been smiling. I felt again that hug he'd given me during the chanting. Oh, to feel it again!

I drained my mug and yawned. Feeling sleepy, I snuggled back under the duvet and dozed. It was Percy who woke me with another cup of tea sometime later. I opened my eyes to find her standing by my bed, fully dressed and looking delightfully normal in a pair of smart walking trousers and a warm jumper.

"I thought you'd never wake up, Fay!" She put the mug down on the bedside table and picked up the empty one. "Have you been up in the night?"

I struggled to sit upright, and she put the pillow behind me. Sinking back against its comfy support I picked up my second cup of tea. "No, I woke at dawn and made a cuppa then. You were out for the count."

Percy sat on the end of my bed. "I had the deepest sleep of my life, I think."

"Me too." I took a sip. "Yesterday was quite a day."

"But it went well, didn't it?" Percy frowned.

"You don't remember?"

"Not much."

I picked up my mobile. "Look at YouTube. You're a star on there."

"What do you mean?" Percy picked up my phone and opened the screen.

"Check it out."

298

Percy tapped into the screen. "Oh, my word! That's so effective with the fire and the lantern lights. Oh, everyone sang so wonderfully well."

"Wait for the best bit – you."

Percy stared at herself on the screen. "I don't look like me, do I? I wonder if I look like Gaine? And my voice is completely different. Oh, it's so strange seeing myself being someone else!"

"Yes, it must be. Rick played his guitar well, didn't he?"

Percy nodded, still listening to the track. "He's very gifted and the chanting is superb. That birdsong fits perfectly at the end. Makes it so emotional."

"Proper poignant. It's a blackbird. I wish he'd chosen a robin."

Percy smiled at me. "Did you see him at all?"

I put my mug down and smiled back. "I did, I really did. I saw his face and he looked so happy. Being here has brought us closer. It was worth coming just for that, but I guess our work for Rick is over."

The music pouring out of my phone finished and Percy switched it off. "I suppose so, though I'm not sure I want to leave just yet."

"Are you and Rick...?"

Just then, there was a knock on the front door downstairs.

Percy got up. "I'll get it as I'm dressed."

"Good, because I'm sure I'm not fit to be seen. I think I'll have a shower - unless it turns out to be another crisis!"

I heard Percy clatter down the wooden stairs and answer the door. It sounded like Rick's drawl, so I was certain I wouldn't be needed. I grabbed some clothes and headed for the bathroom.

When I came downstairs, I found Winston, Bryony, George, and Rick all sitting around the table.

"Hi, Fay!"

"Hello everyone. Looks like you're having a meeting." I sat down amongst them.

Bryony smiled from ear to ear. "You could say that. Seems we've hit the zeitgeist on social media, thanks to Winston."

Winston nodded his head. "It's going viral. It's everywhere – Twitter, Facebook, Instagram – and it's starting to trend."

I smiled at him. "That's great Winston but where did you get the video of the collapsed cave?"

Rick chipped in. "It was on Eddie's phone, you know. He took it with that stupid drone thing. Turned out to be really useful."

I nodded. "Hoisted by his own petard, you might say. It certainly adds impact."

Winston looked up from his phone. "Has anyone looked on TikTok yet?"

There was a general murmur in the negative and we all browsed our phones to take a look.

"Man, how can they do that?" Rick stared at his small screen.

Winston explained. "It's a TikTok thing. People can add their own videos to yours, so it looks like tiles stacked up together. Wow! There's even more than last time I looked. It's amazing! There's films of the wildfires in California, drought in Africa, flooding in China and failed crops all over the place."

I gazed at my phone in wonder. A seamless stream depicting other horrific consequences of climate change happening all over the world was mounting up. I looked up at the others. "The whole world is joining in! It's going crazy!"

George spoke in an awed voice. "Do you think the ghost knew the climate conference was beginning today?"

"Can they see that sort of thing?" Rick took a rollie from behind his ear and stuck it in his mouth without lighting it. He looked excited and his chair was very close to Percy's.

Everyone was looking at me for an answer. "Honestly? I have no idea but it's brilliant synchronicity."

"Isn't it just?"

Bryony's phone rang and she answered it. "Yes, that's me. No, I'm not sure I can disclose our address. An interview? With me? When? You don't mean today?"

Rick's phone then went off. "Yeah, I'm Rick O'Shea, who wants to know?"

Then it was my turn. The voice at the other end was female. "Are you the owner of the Spirit Level website?"

How did they connect us so quickly to our website? "I might be."

"So, you were at this pagan thing last night?"

I remembered Gaine's request to spread the word. "Yes, that's right."

"Look, we're sending a team to come and film that location. Can you tell me exactly where you are?"

"Who is calling?"

"I'm from The Guardian. We're very interested in your story and want to run an article, but we'd rather do it face-to-face."

"What's your take on it? Do you believe us?"

"Well…it's pretty far-fetched, I must say but the music was fantastic. Who is the person pretending to be the ghost?"

"My colleague, Persephone."

"She's very beautiful. So, she works with you at Spirit Level?"

"That's right and she wasn't pretending. Look, give me your number and I'll get back to you. I need to think about this."

The journalist laughed. "Don't take too long! This is massive and we want to be the first to run a story before it hits the tabloids. The message about climate change is important and I hadn't heard about the tilting of the moon before. We want to help spread the word, whether your friend is genuine or not doesn't really matter. What she said is true and we would like to help you reach people, especially while the conference is on. Did you time your stunt deliberately to coincide with the COP26 Summit?"

"I didn't, but Gaine did."

"Who is Gaine?"

"The spirit who talked through Persephone."

"Look, can't you drop all that ghost stuff? It really doesn't help your message."

"I'm only telling the truth. Gaine waited two thousand years for this. Listen. I'll ring you back when I've decided."

I truncated the call and put my phone back down on the table when it immediately rang again. Like every other phone on the table. We all looked at each other.

Winston grinned. "I had a feeling this would happen when I saw those videos piling up on TikTok!"

Rick took the unlit cigarette out of his mouth. "Man, it's insane! I never seen anything like it, not even on tour."

Percy picked up her phone. "Let's put all of these on silent for a minute, shall we?"

We eagerly complied.

"Phew! That's better."

Bryony looked thoughtful. "It seems the world has come to Gorphwhysfa."

Percy looked at her compassionately. "How do you feel about that, Bryony? You've always kept the grove and your followers so private. If we invite any of these journalists here, they will totally invade your space."

Rick put his phone on the table. "And mine, don't forget."

Percy laid her hand on his arm. "Of course, sorry, Rick. The land belongs to you."

Rick put his hand over hers. "Through my Roman forebears who stole it from the Druids. I know that now, thanks to Bryonia. Gaine forgave my ancestor for murdering her and that changes things."

Bryony nodded. "Everything has changed. So, what shall we do? Let the world in, or not?"

Chapter Forty-six, Present Day

We all trooped off to the big house to watch Bryony's interview on the television the next evening. George had driven her to the BBC studios in Glasgow straight after we had all agreed Gorphwhysfa should be allowed to remain incognito, and Bryony should be interviewed elsewhere. Everyone also agreed that the most important thing was to maintain the pure energy in the sacred grove in case Gaine had further messages to convey. We were fast learning how the world these days was all too easily reached via the media. It was only a useful tool if it could be tamed.

Just before she got in the Landrover that morning, Bryony had voiced what we all felt. "Let's keep it ours for as long as we can."

We settled down on the L-shaped settee together. I sat at one end, next to Gwen, whose baby lay asleep in her pram in the corner. Winston occupied the middle section and Rick and Percy sat, hip to hip, at the other end. This being Rick's house, no-one complained when he lit a cigarette and blue smoke spiralled up to the ceiling. The woodburning stove was also alight and gave a comforting warmth to the proceedings.

"Oh, my goodness, there she is!" Percy sat bolt upright on her seat.

"She's wearing her black robe." Gwen looked a bit doubtful about that.

"And very dignified she looks too." I stood up for my erstwhile enemy.

Rick frowned. "Shush, let's hear what questions she has to face."

We all focussed on the TV screen. Despite my anxiety that she might crumble under stress, as I had seen her do before, Bryony didn't look the least bit nervous but instead rather regal and self-possessed. Then I remembered how she always thrived during a performance.

303

The interviewer seemed sincere about global warming, at least in her initial questions. Then she pumped Bryony on Paganism. When Bryony told the simple truth about the way they celebrated and respected the earth, and that they had no witches casting evil spells, rather the reverse, the well-groomed but hard-faced woman turned to the camera.

"Thanks, Bryony, for filling us in on your pagan beliefs. They certainly seem benign and well intentioned. And now, viewers, let's watch the video that is causing such a stir. I believe it was filmed at Halloween?"

"That's right." Bryony's voice sounded good, low and confident. "We call it Samhain, which is pronounced Sarwen."

"And it's to call up the dead, is that right?"

"To celebrate our ancestors, yes."

"Hmm. Let's watch, shall we?" The interviewer nodded her smooth blond head at someone to her right.

The camera panned out and played the short film of our Samhain celebration right the way through, beginning with the cave collapse video.

Watching it, I felt emotional all over again. It was the sheer beauty of it. The lanterns and fire, the chanting, Rick's guitar and Percy's impassioned speech and finally, the blackbird's plaintive song. I confess, I had tears in my eyes by the end.

The camera returned to the studio where Bryony sat composed and smiling in front of the seasoned journalist, who was now dabbing her eyes with a tissue.

"Forgive me, that was incredibly moving!" She cleared her throat. "Sorry, not sure what happened there. Now then, Bryony. Tell me, who is this so-called spirit who gave us this important message? Is it really true that the lovely young woman in the white dress was, how would you describe it - channelling a ghost?"

Bryony explained what had happened and the journalist regained her cynical aplomb.

"Well, I'm not sure about all of that, but the words she spoke certainly rang true. I had no idea about the tilt of the moon – is that really true?"

Bryony assured her it was and that the matter was urgent.

"Then let's hope people at the conference listened to her message about climate change! I gather it's gone wild on TikTok with people all around the world adding their own videos of climatic disasters."

Bryony nodded vigorously. "Everyone is under threat, and I want the world leaders here in Glasgow to sit up and listen."

The announcer nodded back. "I'm sure they will." She went on to thank Bryony for coming and the programme switched to an article about coal power plants in China.

Rick flicked the television off with his remote-control device. "Well, what do you make of that?"

Percy poured everyone a glass of wine from the bottle on the coffee table. "I say, let's drink to Bryony!"

"To Bryony!"

The red wine slipped down my throat like an oyster, smooth and easy. "Yes, she held her own really well. Now we'll just have to wait and see what people make of it."

Bryony returned a couple of days later looking shattered. She told us that every journalist in Glasgow wanted to speak with her either about ghostly apparitions, the coming tilt of the moon, the landslip, or coastal erosion. She proudly reported that she always turned the conversation to a sustainable lifestyle and respect for the earth.

"I tell you, I'm worn out, and sadly I don't think it will take long for them to put two and two together and work out where we are. I predict a fleet of drones overhead."

"I'm afraid you are right," Rick said. "Our phones haven't stopped pinging. We all turned them off in the end. We've put the message out. Now it's up to the powers that be to act on it."

Percy squeezed his arm affectionately. "Let's hope to goodness we're not too late."

Bryony was right about the drones, of course, but although she was interviewed again at the farmhouse by the BBC, Bryony refused to take any stranger to the sacred grove, insisting that it be kept private for future ceremonies and to protect its energy field. Astonishingly, this was respected, especially when Rick waded in and employed some hard-nosed security guards to keep the place secure.

Punters inevitably turned up, but most were respectful, a little awed if anything, and wanting to learn as much as they could. Bryony was kept busy teaching them about the community lifestyle they needed to adopt, and the farmhouse filled up with willing guests, eager to listen. Bryony, prompted by the ever-resourceful tech wizard, Winston, started up a podcast and soon had thousands of followers on the internet.

I couldn't feel smug about it, the whole concept of the climate changing was far too scary for complacency. I would never forget our frantic escape from the cave when it collapsed, but I did feel part of something important, that we had done our best by Gaine and brought her some peace. I was confident she wouldn't prevent Rick playing his music ever again. And maybe, just maybe, the politicians would listen. All I could do now was hope they would take Gaine's message on board, and soon, for all our sakes.

Percy spent the following week with Rick. I hardly saw her. Not being one to enjoy the limelight or having played any public part in the film, I was left alone. I took to wandering the headlands, far away from the cairn, the landslide and the grove. I didn't want to talk to anyone about it. We had done our part.

I saw Robin every day after that. I'd walk until my legs were tired and my head clear and sit on a tuft of grass or a rock, looking out at the ocean, and he would come to me. I felt he was sitting by my side, just as we used to do as kids, dreaming of our future life together. That wasn't going to happen in this lifetime, I realised and accepted that now, but it could well do in the next.

A strange and unexpected thing did happen though. I lost my ever-present craving for comfort food. I ate well and heartily but I didn't stuff my face like I used to. That gnawing, hollow hunger that used to reside in the pit of my stomach had gone and I no longer had the urge to constantly fill it. Instead of feeling I needed to eat incessantly to fuel my day, I had more energy if anything, through eating less. Now I slept serenely through each night, something that had eluded me since Robin had died all those years ago.

At the end of the week, Percy sat me down at the kitchen table in the cottage.

"I'm ready to leave, Fay."

I was surprised, I admit. "Are you? I thought you might stay here indefinitely with Rick?"

She shook her head. "We've decided we're not for forever."

I reached for her hand. "I'm sorry."

"No, it's fine, actually. We're both really happy about it. It's been lovely but it's enough."

"Oh, I'm a bit taken aback. You did seem happy enough to stay together."

"No, it was a special time and I think we needed to connect to make it all happen, but Gaine has what she wants now and it's time to go."

I ran my hand through my hair. "I see. So, what do you want to do next?"

Percy spread her arms wide. "Rick is insisting on paying us a small fortune for our services."

"Is he? I had no idea. I told him living rent-free was enough for the tax work."

Percy laughed. "Oh, no, he's not having that. You'll get a separate sum for your accountancy skills. You see, he's been quietly working on his album all this time and he published it a week ago. It's already selling masses worldwide and Rick reckons it's because the video with me in it has gone viral, so he's determined to give me a share of the profits."

"Well, you were the star of the show."

Percy gave me one of her ravishing smiles. "Thanks, but I'm insisting that he gives a portion to Bryony's project too."

"And did Rick agree?"

"Oh definitely. He's setting up a concert tour with his old band and that alone will raise enough for his debts. Rick wants us both to share in the bounty and said to tell you he can pay off the Inland Revenue well before the deadline you agreed with them."

"Wow! That's just great!"

She nodded. "Isn't it? I think I'll have enough to rent somewhere of my own."

"Do you want to go back to Wiltshire and live there again?"

"I think so, I'm not sure. I've still got to sort things out with Paul and that's bound to be messy."

I leant back in my chair. "Hmm, I think you're right about that. And what about work? Shall we carry on with Spirit Level?"

Percy's eyes lit up. "Oh, yes, Fay, I'm loving it! It's so interesting, isn't it? I mean, Rose Charlton was scary, but this assignment has been so enlightening, so informative and life-affirming. I feel I'm a different person! And I'm no longer scared about death, either."

I gave a big sigh. "I know what you mean. There is so much fear about death but it's just a continuation of energy, really, but in a different form - like the triskelion symbol."

"Exactly!" Percy fingered her new earrings. She'd worn them every day since she bought them. "I feel we can do more important work, don't you?"

I switched on my phone. "It's funny you should say that because another message has come up on our website. It looks very intriguing, and I think someone really needs our help."

The End

<u>The Rose Trail, Book One of the Spirit Level Series,</u> is a time slip story set in both the English Civil War and the present day woven together by a supernatural thread.

Is it chance that brings Fay and Persephone together?
Or is it the restless and malevolent spirit who stalks them both?
Once rivals, they must now unite if they are to survive the mysterious trail of roses they are forced to follow into a dangerous, war torn past.

"The past has been well researched although I don't know a lot about this period in history it all rings so true – the characters are fantastic with traits that you like and dislike which also applies to the 'present' characters who have their own issues to contend with as well as being able to connect with the past."

"A combination of love, tragedies, friendships, past and present, lashings of historical aspects, religious bias, controlling natures all combined with the supernatural give this novel a wonderful page-turning quality."

"The modern day was funny and very clever and had everything right and the historical story came alive in way that set it apart."
Winner of 'Chill with a Book Award' Winner of 'B.R.A.G. Medallion Award'

The Katherine Wheel Series

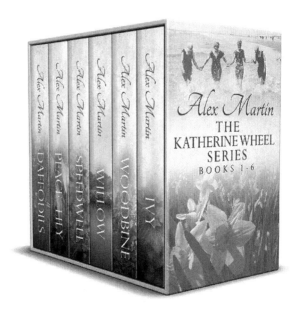

"*Excellent novels with a well-rounded and strong central female character. You do need to read all the books, but they are all good so go for it and enjoy.*"

"*Family and friends are what keeps many of us brave, strong and determined. Absolutely loved all six books. Didn't want to stop reading them. Just such lovely stories with some insight on how people may have coped in the past and through the Wars. Nothing too complex. Cannot Thank Alex Martin enough for this series.*"

"*5 stars this series always kept my rapt attention -- the characters were well developed complete with their own brand of sweetness or not, successes, quirks, and flaws -- includes an education in the harsh truth of the world wars*"

**Daffodils is also available as an *AUDIOBOOK*
Narrated by the author**

You might also like Alex Martin's first book,

<u>THE TWISTED VINE</u>

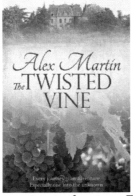

Every journey is an adventure. Especially one into the unknown.

The shocking discovery of her lover with someone else propels Roxanne into escaping to France and seeking work as a grape-picker. She's never been abroad before and certainly never travelled alone.

Opportunistic loner, Armand, exploits her vulnerability when they meet by chance. She didn't think she would see him again or be the one who exposes his terrible crime.

Join Roxanne on her journey of self-discovery, love and tragedy in rural France. Taste the wine, feel the sun, drive through the Provencal mountains with her, as her courage and resourcefulness are tested to the limit.

"This is a wonderful tale told with compassion, emotion, thrills and excitement and some unexpected turns along the way. Oh, and there may be the smattering of a romance in there as well! Absolutely superb."

Developments about stories as yet unborn will be posted at: http://www.intheplottingshed.com/ Constructive reviews are always welcomed and oil a writer's wheels more than anything else.

Goodreads Author Page
Alex Martin's Author Page on Amazon
Twitter: alex_martin@8586
Facebook: https://www.facebook.com/TheKatherineWheel/
Email: alexxx8586@gmail.com

A FREE copy of Alex Martin's short story collection is available by going to www.intheplottingshed.com and clicking on the shed

FREE

A COLLECTION OF 3
SHORT STORIES
BY ALEX MARTIN

The Pond
A Tidy Wife
The Wedding Cake

Alex Martin
TRIO
A COLLECTION OF 3 SHORT STORIES

Printed in Great Britain
by Amazon